Maggie

M. E. BERRY

Orla Rae Publishing UK
MANCHESTER, UK

M. E. Berry/Orla Rae Publishing UK
Greater Manchester, UK

Publisher's Note: This is a work of fiction. Names, characters, places, and incidents are a product of the author's imagination. Locales and public names are sometimes used for atmospheric purposes. Any resemblance to actual people, living or dead, or to businesses, companies, events, institutions, or locales is completely coincidental.

***MAGGIE'S BOOK*/M. E. BERRY.** -- 1st ed.
ISBN 978-1-7399805-0-4

Photographs by author.

For my wonderful family

"Family is the most important thing in the world"

—PRINCESS DIANA

ACKNOWLEDGEMENTS

I would like to thank all my friends at Tyldesley Creative Writers for their interest, encouragement and support that has enabled me to complete this novel. A special thanks to my wonderful family and also to Phil Tomkins, Diana Brooks and Rudrani Kadiyala for their help by reading and advising. Thank you to my husband Joe, whose love inspired and sowed the seed of an idea for the story.

CHAPTER ONE

RETURN OF THE SEAFARER

Ireland 1999

Peter sits slightly unsteady on the high stool at the mahogany bar. His suitcase is at his side. 'The Ship Inn' is quiet at this time of day – Peter is the only customer. Through the mirror opposite, behind all the bottles and optics, he notices how disheveled he looks and finger combs his steel grey hair. Amid the quietness, in the background, the juke box gently plays – Foster and Allen sing, "...my face is a well written page, Maggie, and time all alone was the pen..." and he thinks *never a truer word.*

'Hello, Sir,' the landlord says, 'what can I get you?'

'A pint o' the black stuff please.'

The landlord reaches to the shelf above him and brings down a handled pint glass, 'It's not very often that song gets to be played on the old juke-box there.'

'No – probably not. It's a favourite of mine that I haven't heard in ages.'

They both listen to the song as they watch the black stout slowly and reverently pour into the glass and eventually, the landlord expertly presents the exquisite, creamy-topped beverage to his customer. He watches Peter lick his lips in anticipation of the unique taste. 'A stranger to these parts, are you Sir?'

'No – not exactly,' says Peter, wiping away the froth from his bearded lips. 'I was born here, just down the street there, near the playing field. My cottage still stands – only just. I've been told that the cracked windows need replacing, paint won't cover the rot in the wood, slates are missing and the birds are making themselves at home in the eaves.'

'Oh, I know the one you mean – the one they call old, O'Malley's place. He's been dead a while now – some people have been interested in who owns that. It's yours then is it?'

'Yes, that's mine. The old family home; old and a little neglected and in need of some tender loving care.' Peter laughs. 'Tis a bit like me, I suppose.' He holds out his weathered hand and greets the landlord. 'Peter's the name – Peter O'Malley.' He wobbles a little on the stool as he struggles to retrieve his wallet from his back pocket.

'Well, welcome home, Peter. I'm Terry.' He holds up a hand in a gesture to halt Peter from paying. 'This one's on the house'.

'Thanks. That's very kind of you.'

'I've been the landlord here for the past twenty years, so it must have been quite a while since you were last here in Athgarvan!'

'Over forty years in fact – a lifetime! I was seventeen when I left and nothing seems to have changed.'

'Apart from the size of the tourists' coaches, very little changes here in the village – I think that's why I like it.' Terry helps himself to a shot of whiskey then leans on the bar, 'Anyway, what brings you back now then, Peter, after all this time, if you don't mind me asking?'

Peter moves uncomfortably on the high, swivelling stool. 'Seafaring days are over for me now, Terry. It's the eyes you see – losing their sight and the old sea legs have no more balance in them. I've been beached like a whale, so I'll have to get used to life on dry land.'

'Well it'll be good to have your company here at 'The Ship' – I hope it makes you feel at home.'

'Thanks. I was hoping to meet up with some old friends but many of them, I've found out, have either moved away or are long dead and buried.'

'Sorry to hear that. Is there no one still here that you know?'

'There's one very special friend I'm meeting up with today. Her name's Maggie. Margaret Ryan.'

'Oh, I know her. In fact, nearly everyone here knows Miss Ryan. A good-hearted woman. She taught my kids – brilliant teacher – retired now – an author as well.'

'A schoolteacher was she now! Was that what she became? And an author as well! I'm not surprised at that – her father was the English teacher at our school.' A wave of inferiority panics him. 'Oh be Jasus! – do you think I should have worn a suit? You know, I did try one on but it felt so uncomfortable. She's bound to make some remark about my appearance.' He combs his fingers through his hair again and straightens the ribbing on his thick, faded blue sweater. "You scruffy old sea dog" she'll say. That's if she recognises me at all!'

'You look what you are Peter, if you don't mind me saying; as if life hasn't been too generous.'

'Ah – but that's where you're wrong, Terry. Never go by appearances. Apart from horses, that is. Life and lady luck has been more than generous; made me quite prosperous in fact. An empire – that's what *I* have – a *property* empire. It's not a girl in every port that I have, but a house. Well, perhaps not a house or in every port but…'

'Well I never. Tell me more.'

'To begin with, I must tell you that I would have wanted to marry Maggie, if she'd have had me, but for the call of the sea and some other stuff.'

'Did you ever ask her?'

'No. I'd just turned seventeen when we parted. You don't think of marriage at that age. I couldn't have made her happy anyway because, you see, *I* wouldn't have been happy. But, as I grew older, there was many a time that I nearly attempted to ask her, and then thought better of it…' He pauses for a second and reflects on how tormented he felt at those times when he thought of Maggie. '…I wanted her to have a good life with some lucky man who claimed her, not a numbskull like me, and I didn't want to interfere. I just sent her the odd postcard.'

'Wasn't she upset when you went away?'

'If she was, she didn't show it. I think she understood. She seemed happy for me. She knew my dream – a young man's dream; a way of life I dearly wanted, and needed, at the time. I never craved anything other than to be a sailor. So you see, I couldn't have married. It wouldn't have been fair. I had a yearning for freedom and adventure. None of that indoor reading and writing stuff for me – oh no.'

'And you haven't seen her for over forty years?'

Peter is thoughtful, 'No. Do you think she'll have changed much?'

Terry laughed, 'I'm sure she will have, but does it matter?'

'No – no. Not at all. She's always been special to me has Maggie, and I'm sure, even after all this time, she knows that. But, as she's the nearest and dearest to me, I need to tell her, and I want her to share the rewards of my life with me now. Do you think she'll be impressed when she learns about my property empire?'

'How big an empire?'

'Three if you count the old cottage here. One in Mahon port. That one is high up in Miranda Square, a one bedroom apartment, overlooking the harbour. You can watch the liners coming and going. It's a beautiful place.'

'And the other?' asks Terry.

'Cyprus. Poseidonos Avenue. I can say the address but I can't spell the bloody thing! Anyway, that apartment is near the harbour in Paphos.'

'Well, *I'm* impressed, Peter. I'm sure *she* will be. You've obviously never regretted going away, have you?'

'No regrets at all. It's been a great life; I've loved every minute of it. I just hope that Maggie's been happy too. Do you know Terry, every time I saw a place I liked, I thought of her – I wanted to buy it, thinking that I would get in touch with her to ask her to join me, and then the sea would call and I'd be off again. So it was just a postcard I'd send. It's all a bit late now, I think. Anyway, "home is where the heart is", so the saying goes.'

'What time is she meeting you?'

'She's promised to meet me here at four.' Both Peter and Terry look at the mirrored reflection of the reversed time clock.

'That'll be any time now then,' says Terry. 'How about moving over to the comfortable seats over by the fireplace there.' He looks through the window. 'Speak o' the devil; I can see her coming down the street now, as bright as a button, looking like spring itself in a canary yellow dress. Go on; get yourself comfortable over there, Peter and I'll bring some drinks over to you – on the house!'

Flustered, Peter nearly falls trying to get off the stool, as, through the window, he catches sight of his very dear old friend. He manoeuvres his way to the chairs near the fireplace.

Maggie carries an overlarge handbag and yet, in her other hand, holds a book to her breast. She enters the familiar pub and is greeted with a welcoming smile on Terry's face. She notices a knowing twinkle in his eyes. 'Hello, Miss Ryan,' sings Terry as he presses the buttons on the juke-box.

'Afternoon, Terry,' she replies with some suspiciousness in her voice and expression.

Terry nods his head in Peter's direction, 'He's over there.' The music begins to re-play Peter's favourite song and Maggie momentarily pauses and takes a deep breath as if to compose herself before walking over to greet her old friend, Peter – the love of her life.

Peter stands with open arms. 'Maggie!'

'Pete O'Malley! Well, look at you! You look like the sea's washed you to shore several times over. Give us a kiss then, if you can find your lips under all that grey, hairy mop of a beard!' They embrace and Peter gives Maggie a kiss on her cheek.

'Maggie. Oh, Maggie!' laughs Peter. He holds her shoulders, takes a good look at her and gives her another kiss. 'Still the same. Sit yourself down. You look wonderful – and still as pretty as the last time I saw you,' he grins. 'What are you now – sixty five?'

'Would you ask any other woman her age, Pete? Your manners are atrocious – only *you* could get away with it mind. And you were never too bad at numbers! Anyway, you know how old I am but I'll always be younger than you!'

They sit down at the table and enjoy their drinks; Peter buys two more rounds including whiskey for Terry. For an hour they keep the conversation light and they talk about their old school friends; those that Peter had tried and failed to contact on his return, Maggie bringing him up to date with all the details that she knew.

Peter points to the book at the side of Maggie's bag. 'Is that the book *you've* written?'

'It is. How did you know I've written it? I used a pen name – my mother's maiden name, Jenny O'Hagan.'

'The landlord has just been telling me that you're an author and it's lovely that you've used your mother's name. Clever Maggie! What's it about?'

'In short, it's just a love story…' Maggie looks straight into Peter's eyes as she continues, '…of a young couple's escapade.'

Peter stares straight back. 'Am *I* in it anywhere Maggie?'

'Yes. All the way through it – a character named Brendan is based on you – with a few changes.'

'That's a good name – I like that.'

'Would you like to read it?' She looks closely at his eyes and wonders if Peter senses that she sees a weariness within him and if he can sense her heart weeping.

Peter's voice is fainter and a little croaky, 'My eyes are not good, and you know I'm not good at reading, but I'd like you to read it to me, if you would?'

'Course I will,' she pauses and sighs. 'You know it's so good to have you home again. I couldn't believe it when you phoned to arrange to meet me – it's been so long. Where are you staying while you're here?'

'I'm home for good, Maggie. I thought I'd get the old cottage comfortable and ...'

'*That* place will be in no fit state to live in – not yet anyway!'

'I know. So I've been told. I thought I'd ask the landlord if he knows ...'

'Look – I've got a spare room. You can stay with me till you get your house sorted.'

'Oh, Maggie, I don't want to impose...'

'Pete – don't say another word. 'Now get your coat and let's get you home.' Maggie hands her book to Peter to carry as she links his arm and takes charge of his battered, wheeled suitcase, securely anchoring her handbag on top of it. She calls out as they make their way to leave, 'Bye Terry, see you soon.' Peter holds up his hand in a farewell gesture.

Maggie slows down her usual walking pace to match Peter's unsteady gait as, arm in arm, they slowly stroll home.

Peter normally avoids books like the plague but, seemingly unafraid, he holds Maggie's book to his chest and for the first time in his life, knowing that Maggie's words won't hurt him, is looking forward to hearing it and experiencing the literary adventure that the words will unfold.

CHAPTER TWO

THE BEGINNING

'Here we are,' says Maggie, standing the suitcase upright on the step and rooting in her handbag. 'Why do keys always go to the bottom of…? …Oh, here they are!' She unlocks the door and enters. Peter, follows, struggling to climb the two steps up to the entrance and he holds the side of the doorframe to elevate himself over the threshold. *Be Jasus! How much worse am I going to get!* He sighs. 'Still living at your old home then? Nice houses these.'

'Yes, still here,' says Maggie, leading Peter into the front room. 'Mother died a couple of years ago. She needed me after her stroke.' Maggie plumps up the cushions on the sofa. 'Sit yourself down and I'll put the kettle on – we'll have a nice cup of tea.' As she makes her way to the kitchen she continues the conversation. 'But, she was in her late eighties, you know – a good innings, as they say!'

Peter breathes in the familiar smell of polished, wooden, wall panels. It brings childhood memories flooding back; to a time when he would call for Maggie and her mother would ask him to wait in the front room – he learned that girls were never ready on time. He remembers how he studied the drawings and paintings that decorated some of the panels. How real he had thought the exotic fruit looked; so real he wanted to reach out and take some to eat. He remembers how his mouth used to water at the thought.

Because of his many voyages to France, Italy and Spain over the years, he is more knowledgeable now and feels some smug satisfaction that he recognises the prints of the work of Jean-Baptiste-Siméon, Chardin, Giorgio Morandi and Juan Sánchez Cotán. He can distinguish Anna's mother's own, excellent, still life paintings that hang alongside the renowned artists and wishes that he could have had a discussion with her about them. *Too late.*

From his comfortable position, Peter observes the room and with his sharp sense of hearing, hears the domestic activities in the kitchen – the running water, the water filling the kettle and the clinking of cups and saucers.

The large bay window opposite from where he sits, is framed with weighty, champagne drapes anchored back by cream, silky, tasseled ropes – ropes that are weak and miniscule compared with a ship's ropes he'd hauled so many times. His strength now, he thinks, is only capable of securing a curtain!

His attention moves to the strong, oak fireplace with a generous mantelpiece, like Atlas, supporting two heavy, brass horses doubled in number by the reflection in the massive, expertly carved, leaf edged mirror. He hears the rattling of spoons being taken out of a drawer. He hears the whistle of the kettle.

The antique sideboard is littered with smiling photographs in an assortment of elegant frames. He imagines from the noise, that Maggie is setting out a tray with sugar pot and milk jug. The multi-coloured cushions on the cream armchairs give the room a homely touch. He hears the rattling spoons again. His gaze moves to the floor to ceiling wall shelves, built into the recesses that bow slightly with the weight of books and a wave of nostalgic fear sweeps over him. *So many words*! Some of the books, through lack of space, lie as outcasts on the floor in small, stepping heaps. *How embarrassing it would have been to have a son-in-law that couldn't read or write properly.* He calls out to Maggie, 'What happened to your Daddy? Is he…?'

'My Daddy? Oh yes. He was eighty three… and…' There's a pause – a short silence, then the sound of the boiled water being poured into the teapot.

A few moments later, Maggie carries the tray into the lounge and places it on the coffee table, '…My Daddy died on his eighty third birthday.' She sits down on the sofa alongside Peter and sees that he seems surprisingly interested in the book collection. 'If you remember, he used to read a lot, did Daddy. Most teachers of English do, I suppose. It's where I get *my* love of books from; through his inspiration.'

'I remember. You were lucky to have such wonderful parents. They were always good and pleasant to me. Your Daddy tried his best to help me to read and write. I'm sorry for your loss, Maggie.'

'I know. They always worried about you and were sorry when you left.'

'I had to leave. The time was right. My Daddy was the worst...'

'You told me at the time. I understood.' She sighs and begins to pour the tea. 'Here, drink your tea and let's not dwell on what's past and gone.'

'They must have been so proud of you. You were always so clever at reading and writing and such.'

'Did you ever improve on *your* reading?' She gestures towards the wooden treasure chest box on one of the book shelves. 'I know from the postcards that your writing skills improved *slightly…*'

'You saved the postcards then, did you?'

'Oh, yes – every one of them. Could you not have improved a bit more? Or at least enough to put a letter together, eh?'

'No. Dyslexia! That was the problem, and it wasn't even mentioned to me until about twenty five years ago. My Mammy wouldn't have known about it. And my Daddy wouldn't have even bothered about me anyway. My Mammy would. She would have done something about it if she'd known – if she'd lived.'

'Thirty six was far too young.'

'Brain haemorrhages just don't happen to people so young. I told the doctor at the time that I thought it was because my Daddy used to hit her but he just ignored me. Who listened to me? I'll never forgive – never.'

'I know.' Maggie taps his hand. 'So you were diagnosed as being dyslexic?'

'Yes. When I first heard about dyslexia, and realized that that was a condition I suffered from, it did make me feel better, you know, knowing why I never could grasp the reading like everyone else and *I knew* it wasn't because I wasn't very bright. *I knew* I was much smarter than most in that class…'

'You were.'

'…but I…, well, it was just too late then to do much about it. I could never be in your league though, Maggie, with the learning. But I've not done badly for myself. Anyway, water under the bridge now.' Peter picks up the cup and tries to disguise the shakiness in his hands by holding it steady with both. 'I hope the postcards were meaningful.'

Maggie pats the book that Peter had placed on the coffee table. 'They were Pete. More than you know.'

Through that gesture, Peter is intrigued to think that the postcards have some relevance to Maggie's story. 'All will be revealed, eh?'

'It will.'

Peter leans back into the sofa and looks around the room. 'It's so warm and comfortable here Maggie; tis a lovely home, you have. I'll make a start on sorting out my old cottage tomorrow. I'll get some people in to do the jobs that are necessary and move in as soon as I can. I'll find a…'

'Look Pete, stop worrying. You're welcome to stay here until the cottage is fit to be lived in. Do you know there's a tree growing out of the chimney pot! I bet it'll take a lot longer to sort out than you think.'

'That bad eh?'

'That bad! But I'll help you to fix it up, if you like. But for now, I'll make up the spare room for you and you can make yourself comfortable for as long as you need to. Okay?'

'Okay. That'd be great. Thanks, Maggie.'

There's a comfortable silence as they drink their tea and ponder for a short while. Peter feels such relief to be made so very welcome in his friend's home, knowing that she is capable and strong enough to cope with a burden of organising his short future. He will explain to her the purpose of his homecoming in due time. When he feels less tired. It's been a long day. A pleasant day. He then mentions the book. 'You promised to read your book to me.'

'Yes, I did. I'm always happy for my book to be read. I'll tell you what – I'll read the first chapter and then we'll have some dinner. How does that sound?'

'Sounds good to me.' Peter lifts up the book and hands it to Maggie but before she begins, she roots in her handbag, finds her reading glasses and places them on the end of her nose.

Peter sits back into the sofa and grins, 'I'm not the only one with failing eyesight, I see.'

Maggie giggles, opens the book and begins to read.

* * *

A Different Life by Jenny O'Hagan

Chapter 1 – The Runaways (**Ireland, Wednesday 1st April 1953)**

The leather belt snaked from around his trousers and with his large fist gripping it, he wielded it like a cowboy's whip; the buckle end of it swishing through the air. 'I'll show you – you little…'

'No!' shouted Brendan, dashing around the table. 'You can't keep doing this! You're drunk! Go to bed! Sleep it off!'

Tom O'Connor clumsily chased his son around the table in an attempt to vent his drunken anger upon his innocent victim. 'GO TO BED! – YOU TELL ME TO GO TO BED! Come here you little piece of…'

'Oh no you don't! Not any more you don't! I'm not my Mammy and I'm not so little…' They dashed around the central dining table several times; a ritual war dance, side to side, side to side, back and forth, side to side. Brendan picked up the bread knife. 'You're not going to belt me or beat my head in!' He gestured feigned bravado, 'So come on *Big Man* – try it! Try and catch me, you big drunken, murdering fool…' Brendan caught hold of the buckle end of the swirling leather and they tussled; tug-of-war. Brendan had the advantage of sober steadiness but Tom's bullish power pulled Brendan across the table. He dealt a knuckled punch to Brendan's head that sent him crashing to the floor.

Tom wobbled and wavered above, spitting shouts that rained down on his son. 'You think you can take me on, do you? Think you're all grown into a man now, do you? No Mammy to protect little sonny boy! You little, no good…' He raised the torturous weapon and crashed it down with such a mighty blow that hit its target; it ripped into Brendan's cotton shirt – through to the skin and drew fresh young blood from the wounded youth. Again, Tom raised the belt to strike yet another powerful blow but Brendan reached out and with as much strength as he could muster, grabbed his father's ankles and managed to unbalance him. The intended blow failed to land upon Brendan's bleeding back as Tom staggered and fell. A boney CRACK! Tom's head hit the corner of the table and then CRACK! CRACK! His head crashed onto the stone floor. Brendan watched the blood as it pooled red on the grey, stone flags.

* * *

'Be Jasus, Maggie!' Peter sits upright on the sofa and stares into Maggie's eyes. 'You sure recall *and exaggerate* some reality there! I know you said *I* was in it but it's quite a good account of how I explained things to you all those years ago.'

'It's just the beginning of the story, Pete, and I changed all the names – to protect the innocent, so to speak.'

'Okay, so what happens next then?'

'If you'll let me read it, I'll tell you! Are you going to interrupt all the time?'

'No, no. Carry on,' he says and wriggles back into his comfortable position, closes his eyes and listens.

Maggie continues to read:

* * *

In blind panic, Brendan hastily grabbed the old hold-all from behind the door. In three strides, he flew upstairs, opened drawers and cupboards and threw in a few clothes and his passport. He jumped down the stairs and threw in a half-loaf he found in the kitchen, a lump of cheese and a bottle of lemonade. He grabbed his coat from the back of the chair and without a glance back, he left the cottage. He ran over the playing field. *I never want to see that bastard again.* He ran past *The Ship Inn*; down the steps to the alley. *He must be dead – he must be! Oh God! But he deserves it!* He stopped running when he reached the school gates and held onto the railings, bending over to catch his breath; he winced from the pain in his back. His eyes stung and uncontrolled, involuntary tears washed over his bruised face. He shook his head in an attempt to destroy the volcanic emotion that was erupting. He shook and punched the railings. 'Aagh!' *Why? Concentrate! I have to get away! I have to tell Anna! I have to tell her I'm leaving. God – where will I go?* He picked up his pace again and ran down the street to Anna's house. *She'll understand. She knows what I've had to put up with – with that – that..., drunken, pathetic..., monster... bloody pig. Some Father he's been – he's never deserved the title! It must be great to have a proper Daddy? Anna's Father is a proper Daddy to her. A good, honest, clever man who helps people and loves his family. He might be strict but he's kind. Not like that bastard...not like...* He muttered all these thoughts and arrived at Anna's house. Out of breath, he knocked hard on her door hoping it would be she who answered it. It was.

'Hi Brendan, whatever's the matter?'

'I'm leaving, Anna, I...'

'You look white as a sheet. And... oh, no, not again! Come in and let me look at that bruise...'

'Anna. I haven't time. I have to leave now!'

'Why? Oh, heck! Where to?'

'Anywhere I can get a lift to. Hopefully Dublin and then on to Liverpool. Don't tell anyone you've seen me. Or where I'm going.'

'Well, wait. I'll get some things and come with you.'

'Anna – you can't. I don't know where…'

'Just you come in and wait a few minutes while I get some things together. I'm coming with you!'

'But you can't! Your parents – they'll worry!'

'They're away for a week at Aunt Florrie's, over the Easter holiday. They won't be back till next Tuesday. They'll be furious but I'm coming with you. I'll think about what to tell them later.' She rushed upstairs and there were sounds of banging cupboards and drawers. She shouted down to him, 'Will I need my passport?'

'Not sure,' he shouted up to her. 'I've got mine, the one we got for the school trip to France.'

'Yeah, that's the one I've got,'

'We should be okay with them'.

Brendan paced nervously up and down the hallway. He wasn't sure about taking Anna along; how to tell her the full story or how she was going to feel about it but he decided to tell her exactly what happened as soon as they got on their way and then, he thought she would surely change her mind and come back home. *We won't get too far away in two days. I'll leave her somewhere safe and her Daddy will pick her up. I mustn't drag her into my problems.* He winced again at the pain in his back. *That's something else Anna will heal.'*

* * *

'If we could turn back the clock, Maggie, would you have run away with *me*?'

'No – not to sail away on a boat – no! And you never asked me anyway!'

'No. I know. But I had to go, didn't I?'

Maggie didn't answer his question. 'You look tired, Pete. We can read some more tomorrow if you like. Why don't you go to your room and get yourself settled in while I make something special for dinner and then I think you should have an early night. I'll take your case up to your room – my old room. You know where it is. I have the big bedroom now. Mammy and Daddy's old room. Can you manage the stairs?'

'Yes. I think you're right, Maggie.' Peter struggles to raise himself from the comfort of the sofa and follows Maggie, using the bannister to slowly pull himself up the stairs.

CHAPTER THREE'

DECISION TIME

'So how have you used the postcards in the book then?' asks Peter, as he tucks into his hearty breakfast, dipping his toast into one of the fried eggs on the plate.

'You'll see as we read on. I used a few but it was the first one that gave me the inspiration for the book when I was looking through them. It was when my mother was really poorly and she began to reminisce and asked about you and if I knew how you were. She enjoyed looking at the cards.'

'I'm glad about that.'

'If you like, I'll read some more, when you've finished your breakfast. Would you like some more coffee?'

'Oh, please.' Peter holds up his cup and Maggie fills it. 'It's a lovely breakfast, Maggie. Thanks. I'll do the washing up.'

'No need. I have a dish washer!'

'Well, how can I repay you?'

'I'll think of something.'

Breakfast is over and the used pots and plates are being merrily swished in the dish washer.

Peter goes in the lounge and resumes the same comfortable position that he had the previous afternoon. Maggie follows him and brings down the wooden box of postcards from off the book shelf and places it on the coffee table in front of Peter. She opens it and picks out one of the cards. 'This is the first one you sent me.' She hands him the card. It's a photograph of Bella and Bertie, Carl Bernard Bartel's mythical liver birds, set high upon The Royal Liver building, on Liverpool's water front.

He looks closely at the picture. 'That was the first time I'd seen anything like a big English city.'

'Look at what you wrote.'

Peter turns over the card and reads slowly. '*"From me. X."*' He laughs, 'I remember writing that. I got the ship's doctor to write your address on it for me. I told him I had something in my eye and couldn't see properly. I think he guessed I couldn't write very well.'

'Was he the one that diagnosed you?'

'Oh, no, that was years later, on a long distance voyage to America. A big liner – that was an exciting time. America – what a country! Everything is big, and I mean big! Do you have the postcard I sent from New York?'

'They're in order, so we'll find it as we go through them. My Mammy used to laugh at some of the cards you sent, especially the cat one. "He goes all the way to Spain and sends a postcard of a cat!" she said, "Why not one with some scenery?"'

'That's because I just used to buy a bunch of cards and not always in the same country.'

'I understood that – we looked at the postmark and the stamps to see where you'd posted it. It was nice to receive them.'

'Good. That's okay then.' Peter settles back into his comfortable position. 'Read some more please.'

Maggie picks up her book and finds the embroidered book mark at the required page and reads.

* * *

Chapter 2 – Thank God for George

Anna sat down on one of the large boulders that stood regimental along the roadside. 'Okay then, so we hitch our way to Dublin and then the ferry to Liverpool.'

'Yes. Oh, here comes another lorry – quick – get up – put up your thumb!' Brendan waved his arms to attract the driver's attention. 'HEY – ANY CHANCE OF A LIFT!' The lorry sped by, either oblivious or uncaring of their plight. 'Oh damnation!'

'Stop swearing – there'll be another one along in a minute. I'm sure someone will stop for us...eventually.' Anna secretly crossed her fingers on both hands. 'Have we got enough money for the ferry?'

'I've got six pounds. I think we'll need about five. What did you bring with you?'

'Ten.'

'We should manage then. I'll get a job as soon as we land in Liverpool. There's lots of building work going on.'

Anna decided to resume her seat on the boulder. 'Do you think our passports will be enough or do you think we should have brought our birth certificates?'

Brendan sat on the boulder next in line. 'No – I don't think we'll need them. I know they pay cash daily for casual labourers.'

'How do you know?'

'I overheard Uncle Kevin telling a mate of his about it. He goes over on the ferry regularly to get some work.'

'And what will *I* do?'

'I'll phone your parents when we get to Liverpool and explain everything to them. They'll tell me what to do – probably never speak to me again – ever! But they'll tell me what to do about you.'

'You'll do no such thing! *I'll* ring my Daddy and tell him I'm staying with you, no matter what! *I'll* get a job too. In an office or something.'

Brendan was exasperated and stroked is fingers through his hair, 'Well let's get to Liverpool first and on that flaming ferry!'

Both Anna and Brendan saw the horse box approaching, travelling more slowly than the previous vehicles going in their direction. They jumped up from their seats and waved their hands to attract the driver's attention. They shouted, 'HEY – A LIFT? ANY CHANCE OF A LIFT?' It pulled over towards them.

The driver had a friendly smile on his moon face. He leaned over towards the passenger window. 'Where're you two going then?'

'Dublin' said Brendan.

'Hop in,' he said and the two travellers climbed up and filled the empty spaces on the long seat alongside the driver. 'Whereabouts in Dublin?'

Brendan didn't get the chance to answer.

'The nearest to Dublin Port please' said Anna. 'We want to get to Liverpool.'

'I'm going to the Freight Ferry port if that's any good.'

'That's great. Thanks,' said Brendan.

The driver set off on the road again relatively slower than the other traffic and from the vibration of movement in the rear of the vehicle, Brendan realized that he was carrying livestock. 'Have you got some horses in the back?'

'Well, you could say *some*, I suppose. There's only one really but she's in foal.'

'Awe,' cried Anna, 'is she alright?'

'She'll be fine. She's used to the road. The only trouble is, she's never been on a ferry before. I hope it's going to be a calm crossing for her.'

'Can we see her when you stop?' asked Anna. 'What kind of horse is she?'

'A Palomino Gypsy Horse.'

Brendan blurted 'Roy Roger's horse is a Palomino – is she like Trigger?'

The driver laughed. 'Quite a lot heavier! A good breed though; a two year old filly with a lovely rich golden colouring. Expected to mature to 14.2 hands. She's been running with a son of a famous stepping stallion.' He looked at his passengers and they looked confused. He coughed. 'Anyway, enough shop talk. Tell me whereabouts in Liverpool are you two heading?'

Again, Anna answered before Brendan had a chance, 'We're hoping to visit an Uncle. So we need to book tickets for the ferry.'

'Do you know how much they cost?' asked Brendan.

'I've only used the freight. 'Not sure about the passenger ferry.'

'Oh, I see.'

'How much will it cost us to go on the freight ferry? Can we use the freight ferry?'

'Not sure, but we can ask when we get there. If you like, I can say that you're my assistants and looking after Amber – that's the horse's name, by the way. You can stay in the box with her; reassure her like, and that'll be a good help to me. It'll give me a chance to go and get something to eat and have a bit of a rest.'

'That should make the tickets cheaper eh?'

'Tell you what,' said the driver. 'If you do that job for me, I'll pay for your tickets. How about that?'

'Awe thanks,' said Anna. 'We'll look after her, won't we, Brendan?'

'I'll say. Thank you… er…'

'I'm Djordji – it's a Romani spelling, D-J-O-R-D-J-I… but never mind, I get called George all the time – so call me George.'

'I'm Brendan, and this is Anna.'

For the rest of the journey, the teenagers learned a great deal about George's expert knowledge of horses; how he learned everything he needed to know from his mother as her large family travelled around the British Isles and eventually settled in different parts. They learned about how he settled with his own family on his farm in Ireland; all about the horses he breeds and the work he does for the Dublin Horse Fair that happens every August; how he loves his work and why he was taking Amber across to Liverpool. Anna could see that, like her, Brendan was taking in all of what George had to say and seemed in awe of the man's business knowledge and ability and she was very surprised to learn that he never went to a conventional school. *What a wonderful mother he must have and she certainly made him kiss the blarney stone!*

'My mother will be waiting with her caravan all ready. She likes to take it out and up to the Lake District every summer to visit an old family friend.'

'Where does your mother live?'

'In the family home, with my sister, on the outskirts of Liverpool,' said George. 'She's quite, or should I say, very independent and capable of managing but, she's getting old now and I think she would appreciate some help with Amber and settling her in so to speak. Amber can't pull the caravan until after she's foaled. Old Topaz will last a while yet.'

'Is that your mother's name – Topaz?'

George laughed, 'No, that's the name of the old mare who pulls my mother's caravan at the moment.'

'Oh sorry. I didn't mean to be…'

George laughed again, 'I know. We've had Topaz a long time and she's ready to rest now and be put out to pasture.

But tell me, are you and your sister staying with your Uncle for long?'

Anna could tell that this question threw Brendan a little because he stammered his reply. 'Oh... oh... er... hopefully... over the summer while we both look for work.'

'There are more opportunities for us in Liverpool,' said Anna. She hadn't lied and said that she and Brendan were brother and sister, George had jumped to conclusions because they just happened to look very much alike with their fair skin, red hair and slightly freckled complexions and was quite happy to go along with what George thought. She wasn't sure about Brendan, but glad that he kept quiet and didn't put George straight on the matter. She thought that, to a stranger, a brother and sister would seem to be more trustworthy and not present as much of a problem as that of two unrelated runaway teenagers.

Dublin Port was as busy as always. The loud metallic sounds of heavy ramps being aligned; the shouts of stewards instructing other stewards; the rattling of security chains and the quick rolling off of transport vehicles onto Dublin turf. There was a strong smell of diesel fumes mixed with the salty sea air as queues of lorries were lined up in their respective lanes, waiting to be given permission to be driven on to the last ferry of the day heading for Liverpool docks. George went to the booking booth to show his contract papers and have them amended to cover the tickets for his two new assistants. Anna secretly crossed her fingers as she and Brendan waited in silence and she nervously hoped that there were no notices of "missing teenagers".

Brendan broke the silence, 'Do you realise this is our *first* job?'

'Oh, yes. Feels good, doesn't it?'

'Hmm. We've been paid with the cost of ticket fare. That's some wage!'

'We've been paid then, *before* we've done the work! I can't wait to see Amber. I hope she's alright.'

'Well, I'm glad you know a bit about horses because I sure as hell don't have a clue!'

'Don't tell George that. Just go along with what he wants us to do.'

'It can't be that hard, can it? Just keeping an eye on a horse – in a horse box. I mean it's not going to go anywhere – we won't have to catch it – or anything.'

George returned, climbed into the cab and gave a thumbs up gesture. 'We're all clear to go. The paperwork is sorted. You might need to show them some identification if they ask. Have you got some?'

'Yes,' they both said and glanced at one another, a look that said how glad they were they had brought their passports.

George handed over some folded papers to Anna. 'Here are your tickets and make sure you keep hold of this certificate, it's important and has to be kept with Amber *at all times*.' Anna took the forms and felt pleased to be given some responsibility. She looked at Brendan who smiled back as if knowing how she felt.

The ferry stewards began to gesture to the drivers in the first lane to stand by to begin loading the liner. George's vehicle was in lane three but once the vehicles began to move, the stewards worked quickly and efficiently – expertly choreographing the manoeuvre of traffic onto the ferry.

The sound of seagulls mixed with engines, whistles and melodic, metallic banging of the ramp and the rattling of chains, attached to cranes, created a cacophony of sound that only belongs to busy ports. The sound changed to the echoing sounds of bumping vehicles moving over the rubbery ramps as they entered the hold and then the wait for the remainder of the vehicles to be loaded. Once the loading was complete, it didn't take long before the sailing commenced.

'Right,' George said, 'come with me and I'll let you in the back. Only approach Amber when I tell you, okay?'

Anna was in her element. Brendan kept his distance, three feet behind her as they made their way to the side of the vehicle. George opened a small, red door and pulled down some wooden steps. George went in first, followed slowly by Anna who waited just outside the door. She peeped in.

'Hello Amber, my beauty,' said George as he approached the most radiant of horses that Anna had ever seen. Amber was big and majestic. Her coat shone like golden thread and her mane, feet and swishing tail were as white as silver speckled snow. Anna fell in love with her as soon as she saw her. 'Meet your new friends. This is Anna,' said George as he affectionately stroked Amber's nose. George gestured to Anna to approach and took hold of her hand and placed it on the side of Amber's face. 'Let her get used to you and your voice.'

'Hello Amber. You are so lovely.' Anna felt the warm, silky softness of the golden coat. She looked into the large, dark eyes that reflected an instant love and admiration.

'Brendan,' said George, 'you can come to her now and stroke her – let her get used to *you*. She seems fine with Anna.'

Brendan approached, looking nervous and cautious. Anna was aware that he had probably never been so near to a horse before. He copied Anna's example of gentle approach.

'That's right. Slowly does it' said George, and took Brendan's hand and placed it on Amber's nose. 'There we are girl. Your two new friends.' George stepped back and left the two of them to get acquainted with their new charge. Amber seemed to enjoy all the loving attention she was getting and George seemed pleased with that. Anna was enthusiastic to do the job well and hoped it would give George the impression that she had a natural ability to understand and care for horses. She had always wanted a horse of her own but her parents would only agree to her having riding lessons – not to own one.

'Right, then,' said George, 'I want you both to stay here with Amber. Anna, you've got the paperwork if any officials come along. Brendan, before I go, will you take those two lidded buckets and fill them up with fresh water. You'll find a tap at the back of the hold – over there.' George pointed to his right. 'Ask a steward if you get lost. Don't forget, we are on level three deck.' Brendan went out with the buckets, eager to do as he was instructed.

'Can I ask if you've got a first aid kit in the cab,' asked Anna.

'Yes. What do you need? Are you okay?'

'Just some cotton wool and perhaps some plasters please.'

'Oh, shoe trouble eh?' he surmised. 'You girls and your fancy shoes! Yes, you'll find it under the passenger seat. Make sure you put it back.'

'Yes, I will. Thanks.' That was the second time George had jumped to his own conclusions which made it easier for Anna not to tell a lie.

'Right, I'm off. I'll be in the restaurant and then I may sleep in the lounge for a while. Any problems, or if you need me, you can ask the steward to put out a message. Tell them to ask for George Grey. Or one of you can come and find me in either of those two places. *Do not* leave Amber alone – *at any time*! Okay? Are you okay with that?'

'Yes. Thank you, I understand,' said Anna.

George stepped out of the horse box. 'I'll bring some food back for you.' he said, then left.

Anna was left alone with Amber. 'What a lovely creature you are,' she said. She couldn't stop stroking her new friend. 'I'm sure we're going to get along fine. I'll really look after you and your new baby. How exciting!' Amber nuzzled towards Anna. The bond was strong already.

Brendan returned with the water buckets and Anna took one from him and placed it in front of Amber who drank thirstily.

'Brendan, can you go and get the first aid kit from under the passenger seat. While we have the chance and some fresh water, I'll bathe that wound of yours and put some antiseptic dressing on it.'

'Okay. I'll bring some of that bread and cheese. I don't know about you but I'm starving.'

'George is bringing us some food when he comes back.'

'Awe that's good. Proper food. The bread and cheese will keep for later then.' Brendan made his way out and around to the cab and found the first aid box. He took off his coat and removed the bloodied shirt carefully, as it had stuck to the congealed wound. He fished out a clean tee shirt from the hold-all, stuffing the old one to the bottom of the bag.

Shirtless, with his clean tee shirt thrown over his shoulder, Brendan returned to Anna who he could see was really doing a great job making friends with Amber. 'Got it,' he said and opened the box. 'What do you want?'

'A few pieces of cotton wool first. Sit here on this stool and lean over. Let's have a look.' Anna scooped some water in her hand and wet the cotton wool pieces. She leaned in to get a close look at the wound. She thought it may be quite a deep cut but the blood had congealed and hid the depth. The surrounding skin was beginning to change colour to patchy yellow, brown and blue. Brendan winced a few times as she bathed the cut and wiped the stale blood away until fresh blood began to flow. She bathed the wound with some antiseptic and to stem the blood flow, she applied some thick lint dressing, anchoring it down with a few plasters. 'We'll have to keep an eye on it and do it every day. We're going to have to buy some dressings as soon as we can. Fingers crossed it won't go septic.'

'It feels better already. Thanks.' He scooped up some of the water and washed his hands and face before putting on his clean tee shirt. 'I'll go and get some more fresh water.'

Amber was no trouble at all and seemed to observe with some understanding as to the predicament of her guardians.

They talked to her and stroked her as they kept her company for the time George had rested.

George returned, sometime later, with some welcome food. Sandwiches, crisps and best of all, some hot, hot chocolate in a flask! What a treat. 'Off you go you two,' he said. 'Have a little wander around the ship before we dock, if you like. We should be docking shortly. Be back well in time. You've been a great help. Thanks.'

Brendan seemed to be in his element exploring the vessel. Anna wasn't impressed with any of it. She didn't like the drunken motion; she didn't like the feel of the sea spray on her face; she didn't like the oily smell or the humming, droning sound of the ship's engine. In fact she now knew she hated sailing and was beginning to feel quite queasy and wishing she hadn't eaten the sandwiches. She could see that Brendan loved all of it, 'Look at the vastness of the open water – the space,' he said, flinging his arms open wide.

'Hmm.'

* * *

'If Brendan's based on me, why is he not confident around horses? I am!'

'It was just to fit the character with the story – and to be *different*!'

Peter laughs. 'I see – but Anna is certainly *you* and I can see you now, on that top deck with all your beautiful, dark auburn curls being blown about your face. What a lovely image you make, Maggie.'

'Well, I tried to imagine what you, as my character Brendan, would have felt like the first time you went on a ship or boat or whatever – sailing. Was it the vastness of the ocean that you liked?'

'It was just the freedom of it all. The freedom away from that bastard. The freedom of independence really. And yeah, Maggie, the vastness of the ocean; with the spectacular sunrises and sunsets. And the quiet beauty of the moon and sparkling stars at night. It's quite something.'

'I think I can understand that,' said Maggie.

'It was the not knowing what would happen in the future and the adventure of life – can you understand that?'

'Oh yes. For you it was important, I know. For me, I wanted the home life – the countryside and my horse.'

'So you got one then? One of your own?'

'I did. She was exactly like Amber.'

'How long did you have her?'

'I'll tell you all about her later.' Maggie gets up and goes to get her coat from the hall stand. She brings in Peter's coat. 'Come on. Let's go to the pub for our lunch. It's *Pensioner's Specials* today!'

'Good idea. My treat!' says Peter, struggling once more to get up from the sofa.

'I told you I'd think of something!'

CHAPTER FOUR

LIVERPOOL

Maggie and Peter get back to Maggie's house not realizing how late in the afternoon it is. Maggie struggles to find her keys again.

'Are you tipsy?' asks Peter.

'A bit. I don't usually have more than a couple at lunchtime.' She finds the keys and goes into the hallway, puts down her oversized bag and hangs up her coat. 'Give me yours.'

Peter hands his coat to her. 'He's a nice landlord, that Terry. It's the second time in as many days, that he's given us a drink on the house.' Peter makes his way into the front room and takes his usual seat.

Maggie follows Peter and sits down beside him. 'He's a bit nosey but knows how to keep his customers happy – and the food is good.'

'I can't drink as much as I used to. Especially with the tablets I have to take.'

'Well, we won't be going in again for a while.'

Peter picks up Maggie's book. 'Are you in the mood for reading to me?'

'Glasses!' Maggie gets up and goes to get her glasses out of her bag and returns to find Peter dozing. She sits down beside him and closes her eyes.

An hour later, they both rouse. 'I feel better for that' says Maggie and she stretches. 'I don't think I would have been able to read much if I hadn't had a power nap.'

'Me too.' Peter eases himself more upright. 'These days I seem to need them more and more.'

'Right,' Maggie fixes her glasses and sighs. 'Let's relax and I'll read a bit more.'

* * *

Chapter 3 – Liverpool

Anna and Brendan's first view of Liverpool was through the vehicle's window. Because of its precious cargo, it moved at a relatively slow speed away from the docks and the water front, through the busy city streets; past massive, impressive and important looking buildings. Past the building work on bright new shops and offices amid areas of brown desolation and mounds of rubble.

Leaving the city behind, George drove for half an hour before turning to enter a wide driveway and up towards a large old house surrounded by lots of what Anna could only think was scrap-yard junk; fairground ride parts, wooden wheels and other large stuff hidden beneath tarpaulin covers.

'My sister Rosa and her family still live here in the family home, with my Mother.' George beckoned. 'Come and meet my mother?'

It was getting late and Brendan was concerned about where they were going to spend the night. 'Yes, but would you be able to drop us off at a hostel after?'

'I thought you were going to visit your uncle? I was going to take you later.'

'We haven't told him. We were going to surprise him,' said Brendan. 'But it's getting a bit late now.'

'I see,' said George. 'Well, there's the cab in the wagon. I'll be sleeping in the house. I have to catch the early ferry back home tomorrow. Or, if you want to be more comfortable, you can sleep in mother's caravan – there's plenty of room.'

'That's great George. Thanks,' said Anna. She looked towards Brendan and nodded her approval.

'Come on, meet my mother and then we can get Amber unloaded and into the field.'

They followed George around the side of the house and he pointed out a large barnlike building. 'That's where we overwinter the caravan.'

They walked further around to the back of the house and Anna's jaw dropped in awe as they came across the most beautiful, colourful Gypsy caravan, with its large, painted wheels. The panels were painted green, red and gold with elaborate woodwork designs. Brendan raised his eyebrows in amazement.

'It's a Reading Vardo,' said George. 'Beautiful, isn't it?'

'What do you mean by Vardo?' asked Anna.

'Romani Wagon,' said George.

'Oh, I see. It really is absolutely beautiful. And can *I* sleep in this tonight?'

'Yes. It's actually all packed and ready to go on the road tomorrow. Mother takes it up to Cumbria every summer and what she doesn't know about vanning and horses isn't worth knowing. She can talk all day about them. But I'm a bit worried about her. She's getting on a bit now but won't admit it. She still thinks she can do what she used to but I know she can't. Speak o' the devil, here she is. Hi Mother.' He gave her a kiss on her cheek. 'Meet my young travelling companions, Anna and Brendan.'

'Hello,' said George's mother. Her warm smile was instantly noted by Anna. 'I'm Mrs. Vadoma Lee Grey,' she said proudly, 'but you can call me Mother V, if you like; that's what my grandchildren call me.'

'That's lovely, thank you,' said Anna. Brendan nodded.

'They're looking for work, mother. What do you think about them travelling with you?'

'What do you mean?' Mother V seemed confused.

'I was just thinking they would be company for you and on hand to help you.'

'Would you like that?' Mother V directed the question to both Anna and Brendan, who both looked taken aback and surprised at George's impromptu idea. 'I don't think George wants me to travel alone, although I've been doing the same journey for years.'

'What would we have to do?' asked Brendan.

'Would it be an actual job?' asked Anna.

Mother V looked at George and nodded to him to give them an answer.

'There would be no actual money as wages,' he said. 'You would have the luxury of travelling and living in the caravan with food and necessities that my mother will provide you with. I would expect you to look after her, helping with washing, cooking and cleaning; taking care of the horses and keeping the caravan in good shape. How does that sound?'

'That sounds good to me,' said Brendan.

'It will be like a travelling holiday,' said Anna. 'Thank you.'

'Yes. Thank you,' said Brendan.

'We'll be travelling slowly because of Topaz's age and Amber's condition. She'll be walking but Topaz will be pulling the wagon. I know all the places to rest along the way.'

'Where is Topaz?' asked Anna.

'The old girl's in the field at the moment. I'll show you how to hitch her up to the caravan tomorrow.'

'So that's settled then, is it?' asked George. 'Are you happy with the arrangements?'

'We are,' said Brendan. Anna nodded.

'I'm so glad we met up with you, George,' said Anna.

All the employment details were arranged, agreed and finalized. Amber was happy to be in the fresh air in the company of Topaz. George and his mother retreated inside the house to discuss some other private business. Mother V had insisted that they both came back to the house for something to eat once they'd put their belongings in the caravan. She told them that her daughter's Irish stew and Colcannon was not something they would want to miss. Anna heard Brendan's stomach rumble at the thought of food, but she suggested that she and Brendan should first go and look for the nearest public telephone to ring home and tell her parents of their plans.

They didn't have to look far, there was a post office with a red telephone box in front of it straight across the main road from the exit of the driveway. Anna bought a couple of postcards and two stamps. One of the cards showed a picture of the Liver Bird building with written details about it on the back, the other one was a picture of a lovely cat, sleeping in a basket beside a fireplace.

They closed themselves inside the telephone booth and Anna put an assortment of coins on the top of the ledge at the side of the phone, ready to be used when necessary. To always be prepared was a lesson she learned from her Girl Guide days. Brendan was eager to listen in to what she would tell her parents.

She dialled a number and waited. *'5462 McKinley speaking.'* It was her aunt's lovely, familiar voice that spoke. Anna pressed the A button and the money could be heard dropping into the empty belly of the box.

'Hello, Auntie Flo. It's Anna. Can I speak to Daddy, please?'

There was a short silence. *'Anna?'* Her father's familiar voice sounded worried. *'Are you alright? Where are you?'*

'Okay, Daddy. I'm okay. I'm just ringing to tell you the good news.'

'*Good news!*'

'Yes. I've got a job!'

'*A job! What do you mean a job! You've only just left school! What about college? I thought...*'

'I knew you'd be pleased. You said you'd be happy if I was happy doing whatever I decided to do. You said that!'

'*And what is it you're doing exactly? And where are you?*' His voice was getting louder.

'A friend told me about this vacancy, so I'd no time to lose, I've had an interview and I've got the job.'

'*Doing what?*'

'I'm a companion to a really lovely, elderly business lady who travels the country giving advice on a number of subjects but, listen to this – her speciality is horses! And Daddy you know how I just *love* horses! It's the perfect job for me. And she'll speak to you if you like. If you want to speak to her, I'll get her to call you.' She looks at Brendan and his mouth is open in surprise as to the way it sounds. She mouthed to him *I'm not lying!*

'*Where are you travelling to?*' Anna's father asked.

'All over the England.'

'*Engl... Where are you now?*'

'Liverpool but we'll be leaving soon for a place in the Lake District.'

'*LIVERPOOL! How did you get there? How are you getting to the Lake District?*'

'Oh, my boss has *her own* transport!'

As if on cue, the pips sounded to indicate more money was required to be fed into the slot and she had the best excuse for not being able to go into too much detail.

'But listen, Daddy, I'm running out of change for this phone. I'll keep in touch with you and phone you regularly. Don't worry. I'll send some postcards and let you know where I am and what I'm doing. So don't worry. I'll ring soon. Love to Mammy. Bye, Daddy. Bye.'

She just heard her father say a faint "*Bye*" and she put the phone down. Brendan just shook his head in disbelief as to what she had just told them.

'"Oh, she has *her own* transport!"' What was that? It sounded as though she had a Rolls Royce or something?' He shook his head again. 'You are unbelievable.'

'But clever – go on, say it! And I think Vadoma's caravan is much better than a Rolls Royce.'

'Yes. Clever, Anna Walsh.'

'Well, it will keep them off our backs for a while and stop them from worrying, so I'm happier now knowing they're okay but what are we going to do about *your* problem?'

'I don't want to think about it. Your Daddy didn't mention anything then – about me? He doesn't know I'm with you?'

'No. When it all comes to light, *if* it comes to light, I'll just tell them that you were the friend who knew about the vacancy and you were going to the same place for an interview for a position in... er ...what shall we say? Transport? Transport maintenance! And you got a job with the same company – Mrs. Vadoma Lee Grey via Djordji Grey – Irish businessman and a horse breeder of repute! It's no lie! We've got jobs and somewhere to live. What more do we need? It feels just great.' She looked upwards as if to heaven. 'Thank you God for sending George to us!'

'We don't want the police to be searching for us. I can't sleep for worrying.'

Anna could see the effect of the worry on Brendan's face. Now that he has had time to reflect on his recent experience she could see that he was beginning to realise the enormity of the implications that would surround his sudden disappearance. 'I've got an idea', she said, 'why don't you ring the pub landlord tomorrow and ask him to pass a message onto your Daddy and then he's bound to tell you about him. Pretend you don't know anything. You've been away – looking for work – which you have; although you left later than they may think, and say you want to let him know you've got a job which entails travelling and that you won't be coming home. He'll buy that, I'm sure. And you're not lying.'

'You can't stand direct lies, can you?'

'No.'

'So yeah, okay. He already knows I've been looking for work, so it's... okay, yes, I'll ring him.' He looked as though he was pondering. 'Or do we just try and forget all about it and just disappear forever?' Anna saw his eyes light up and an excited expression crossed his face. 'Did you see that big liner in the port? I overheard someone say it was set for America. It crossed my mind that we could find work on that ship and sail across the Atlantic. That would be some adventure, wouldn't it?'

* * *

Maggie puts the book down on her lap and lifts her glasses to the top of her head. 'I was just wondering what you really thought when you sailed away from Liverpool for the first time.'

Peter opens his eyes. 'It was an adventure, like you mention. I remember having butterflies at all the excitement. That's what I wanted. It was an exciting time for me, learning all about the ship's rules and regulations and the duties I was expected to carry out.'

'Was it hard work?'

'Yes, but the rewards were worth it. I've seen some beautiful countries.'

A quietness descends as Maggie tries unsuccessfully to understand the magnetic draw that the sea has for Peter. 'So you never tired of it?'

'No. But I did think of you, Maggie, often, very often; whenever I was on shore leave in a tropical climate and wondered if you were happy. Were you happy?'

'I was. A tropical climate sounds good though.' She picks up the book and draws her glasses on to the end of her nose. 'I'll just finish this chapter and then we'll eat?'

'Yes Maggie. Sounds good to me.'

Maggie continues to read.

* * *

Anna felt disappointed and not a bit excited about the prospect of sailing. 'Not for me. I like this idea of countryside travelling. All summer in a gypsy caravan. It'll be heaven and it beats all that studying at college that I know my Daddy had hoped I'd choose. And, I bet, he already had planned for me.'

She looked at Brendan and saw the worry on his face. She instinctively knew the torment of the choices before him. She had to help him make his decision easy and without guilt. 'But *you* do whatever makes *you* happy. Make up your *own* mind as to what *you* want to do.'

Surprisingly, there was no hesitation. 'If *you* don't want to sail to America with me,' he said, 'then I'll stay here with *you* and face whatever happens. I'm never, ever going to go anywhere without *you* Anna – ever. You've always stood by me.'

'Okay then' she said, trying to be cheerful and swallowing hard to force back the emotional tears that were rising to the surface. 'We're a team then are we?'

'A team.'

'So let's go and eat some of that Irish stew and find out from Mother V what time we're leaving tomorrow. We need to know what we have to do to get that caravan on the road to the Lake District.'

* * *

Maggie stops reading. 'That's the end of chapter three.' She puts the book mark at the page and closes the book. 'Have you ever been to the Lake District Pete?'

'No. Is it nice?'

'I went with a few other teachers with some of the children on a school holiday there one year. I loved it. We stayed in a lovely hotel near Lake Windermere and went to research some information about Beatrix Potter – that was interesting. And there's some lovely walks.'

'Perhaps we can have a trip there sometime.'

'I don't think you would manage some of the walks. But you'd like the lakes probably.'

'Probably, but I do like the idea of a lovely hotel. We'll go sometime shall we?'

'Okay. That's a date!' Maggie puts the book down on the coffee table. 'I think I've done enough reading for today.' She yawns, 'Let's watch a bit of television, shall we?' She switches on the television and sits back down on the sofa.

Peter takes hold of Maggie's hand. 'I'm happy to do whatever you want to do.' He leans towards her and kisses her cheek.

Maggie feels such a warmth of familiar love wrap around her like a blanket and she snuggles up to Peter as they watch the chosen programme.

CHAPTER FIVE

GARDENING

Maggie and Peter finish their tour of the garden. She shows him the vegetable patch and picks some lettuce. They decide that the day is just too nice to sit inside. Maggie hands the lettuce to Peter. 'We'll have a cheese salad for lunch tomorrow,' she says.

As they make their way back towards the house, Maggie names all the flowers and shrubs in the borders.

'I don't know how you remember all their names,' says Peter. 'I only know daffodils, tulips and snowdrops. Oh, and crocuses and gardenias. Not much more.'

'You would if you did some gardening. You'd get to know more.'

'Gardening has never been an interest for me,' says Peter. He sits down and makes himself comfortable in one of a pair of wicker chairs as Maggie sits beside him on the other and they both admire the colourful view. 'But I must say, I love being here with you. It's a lovely place to be, so it is.'

'Yes, it's very relaxing.'

‘I bet your book has some sort of gardening in it. Does it?’

‘Is that a hint? Are you hooked?’ Maggie laughs.

‘Yes,’ says Peter. ‘I’ll just take this lettuce into the kitchen and I’ll go and get your glasses and your book.’ He shows an eagerness to continue to listen. ‘I want to find out how the characters are doing.’

Glasses on; book in hand and opened at the continuing page, Maggie reads.

* * *

Chapter 4 – Appletree Farm

‘Would you like to take the reins?’ asked Mother V.

Anna was only too pleased to be asked and loved being in the driving seat. Anna noticed several signs: “Appletree Farm. Fresh Eggs, Farm Shop and Café.” There was a large arrow pointing to the left and Mother V instructed her to turn left off the tarmacked road and they travelled slowly along a dry, dusty, dirt track. A cockerel crowed noisily. The spring sunshine was warm and beneath the hedgerows were a multitude of bright dandelions; the seeds from the one o’clocks floated on the gentle breeze like summer snowflakes with a hope of finding fertile ground. The road was very straight and deeply rutted.

There was another arrow pointing to the right and Anna felt the elevation of the caravan as the wheels lifted over the ruts as it turned right into the farm lane. Topaz seemed to know her surroundings. She needed no guiding to the front of that farm. ‘You like coming home, don’t you my girl?’ said

Mother V. 'Topaz was born and raised on this farm,' she explained, 'I bought her as a two year old.'

'Aww, I just love the way you know how she feels. I just *guess* at their feelings, but you *know*!' said Anna.

'Believe me Anna, you'll *know* when you work with horses for any length of time.'

Topaz stopped directly in front of a rambling, stone, two storey farm house. An extension building at the side of it was a farm shop and café. All kinds of foodstuff: fresh eggs, potatoes, fruit and vegetables were on a large table in the cobbled yard.

The farm shop was busy with customers and some children came running out to see the Gypsy caravan. 'Can we go in it?' they shouted. 'Can we ride in it? Can we feed the horses?'

Anna's instinct was to protect the caravan and the horses, especially Amber from this hysterical invasion but Mother V soon controlled the situation. 'One at a time children,' she said. 'Anna and Brendan will take you round the caravan and show you.' Brendan was beside Anna by this time, and she guessed he had the same instincts. 'You can feed the horses with an apple each, not too many! Said Mother V. 'Talk quietly and kindly to them.' Mother V's wisdom was once again shown. "Suffer little children" they had often heard her say, "remember that they learn by example."

A lady came out of the farm shop and greeted Mother V with a warm, welcoming smile and a friendly hug. They disappeared into the shop, leaving Anna and Brendan learning how to supervise three giddy children, overseen by their concerned mother.

Eventually, the children were taken away by their mother who gave them each a paper bag, filled with fruit, to carry home.

Anna and Brendan weren't waiting long before the lady and Mother V, carrying a basket, came out of the shop.

'Katie, meet my young travel companions, Anna and Brendan,' said Mother V and turning to Anna and Brendan, 'this is Mrs. Patrick. She owns Appletree Farm.'

'It's so lovely to meet you both,' said Katie.

'Thank you', said Anna. Brendan nodded.

'V has told me all about you. I hope you enjoy your work with her. George, I'm sure, will feel better knowing his mother has company on the road. I know I do.'

Anna noticed the smile on Mother V's face, as if she agreed.

'Look,' said Katie, 'why don't you come up to the farm later? It's our John's birthday – he's nineteen today! I can't believe my son is growing up so fast. He says he's too old to have a party as such, but he's having some friends round this evening. It'll be good for you to meet him and some of his friends your own age.'

'Thank you,' said Brendan, 'are you sure he'll want us there?'

'I'm sure. He loves meeting new people.'

'What time do you want us to be here?' asked Anna.

'Let's say about seven thirty. That will give you plenty of time to get the caravan parked, see to the horses and get settled.'

Katie turned to Mother V. 'There are a couple of touring caravans in the west field.' She looked towards Anna and

Brendan. 'One of the tourers belongs to John's cousin, Mark; he'll be at the party tonight.' She then spoke to Mother V, 'I've put them on the north side, well away from your usual place; I'd never let anyone take your space near the stream, knowing how much you love that spot.'

'Thank you,' said Mother V, 'Topaz will no doubt take us straight to it. It's lovely to be back here, if only for a short visit.'

'It's so lovely to have you, and stay as long as you like.' The friends hugged.

'Okay,' said Mother V, 'let's get going then. 'Thanks Katie, I'll see you early tomorrow then.'

'Not too early! Bill and I are disappearing to the pub later while the party's on. We'll be home before midnight though. I'm hoping to have a bit of a lie in, although there's never much chance with that damn bird cock-a- doodling.

Anna climbed into the seat alongside Mother V and waved goodbye to Mrs. Patrick. Brendan rode at the rear of the caravan to keep an eye on Amber. His affection for the beautiful mare was clearly growing day by day.

The farm track to the west field looked as if it was well used. Perhaps a public footpath. The hawthorn was in full bloom and the scent was heavy on the warm air. Anna breathed deeply.

Mother V smiled at her. 'You love the open countryside don't you?'

'This is perfect.'

'Good.'

As they drove slowly along the track Mother V explained that Katie, although unrelated, was like a daughter to her. A very good friend of Mother V's daughter, Rosa. When Katie's mother had died when Katie was only in her early teens, she spent most of her time at Mother V's home. 'I always thought she would marry my George but she fell in love with his friend Bill,' she said with a sigh, 'but she's done so well.'

When they came to the bridge, Topaz stopped. 'Brendan,' Mother V called out, 'can you unhitch Amber? Then watch and guide the wheels as there isn't much width to manoeuvre.'

'Did Topaz know?' asked Anna as she climbed down.

'She does. She senses the danger even though she's been across this bridge a hundred times. You go and watch the wheels from the front.'

'Okay.' Anna walked backwards a few yards to get a good view of the wheels. As she did so, she bumped into a young man who was watching the scene. Anna turned to face him. 'I'm so sorry. I was concentrating on…'

'Yes, that's okay. I know what you were doing. Can I help?'

'Oh – okay – right.' Anna was taken aback by the young man's appearance. She thought he was so good looking. He reminded her of James Dean in a film she had seen recently.

'There's not much on either side of the bridge,' he shouted, 'so keep it straight as it is. The body of the caravan is only just clearing the bridge railings and well overhanging them.'

'Careful,' called Anna, 'the wheels look straight to me.'

Brendan shouted, 'I've got Amber. The wheels look straight from here. You have about three inches clearance on each side.'

Topaz did not move until Mother V calmly instructed by a click, click sound and, 'walk on.' The horse pulled the caravan slowly across the creaking, wooden bridge then without instruction began to turn right.

'Thank you, young man,' said Mother V as she drove past.

'That's okay,' he said. He gave Anna a wink then carried on his journey across the bridge.

Anna and Brendan, leading Amber, followed the caravan, making their way towards an open horseshoe clearing bordered by large hawthorns. Topaz manoeuvred the caravan into a perfect position. Anna was in awe of the working relationship and understanding between Topaz and Mother V.

Hidden from view, was a small sloping pathway down to the stony bank of a sparkling stream. 'Brendan, will you unhitch Topaz please, then take the horses down to drink. You can let Topaz roam but tether Amber in the shade, she needs some food and rest.'

Topaz didn't need to be led to the water. She clearly knew the way and the routine, which allowed Brendan more freedom to concentrate on Amber who was in unfamiliar territory but seemed to be trusting and complying with Brendan's commands.

Anna had to make several trips in and out of the caravan as she set about setting up the outdoor kitchen equipment and preparing some potatoes for cooking. She kept glancing over to watch Brendan caring for Amber.

Anna also watched Mother V who, as was her usual routine, brought out a chair from the caravan and placed it on the grass; then brought out some heavily embroidered cushions to make it look really comfortable. Mother V stretched, then sat down. She then produced a small knife and a white, long stemmed pipe from a deep pocket of her skirt and then from another pocket took out a small tin which she opened and took out a stub of tobacco and began to scrape and fill the pipe. She used a lighter to light a spill which she then used to light the tobacco then puffed away at the pipe. What a ritual, thought Anna; not exactly feminine but nevertheless, always fascinating. The sweet aroma of the tobacco wafted on the air and Anna thought it was quite a pleasant smell.

Brendan brought some water then set about making a fire to cook the food. 'What are we having?'

'Boiled potatoes with onions, carrots and…'

'Stew?'

'Chicken and vegetables!' said Mother V.

'Chicken?' asked Anna, 'where did we get that from?'

'Katie cooked a chicken for us. There's all kinds of food in one of the baskets hanging at the back.'

'Oh, how kind!' said Anna.

'Chicken!' said Brendan. 'Great! I'm starving! My mouth's watering. Hurry up Anna with the potatoes!'

'And that's not all. She's made an apple pie for us!

'Ooh! I love apple pie,' said Brendan.

* * *

Maggie notices Peter licking his lips. His eyes are closed as they usually are when he listens to the story. 'Pete, are you hungry?'

Peter opens his eyes when he realizes that Maggie has stopped reading and is speaking to him. 'Oh, I am. It's all that food you're reading about. Roast chicken with apple pie for pudding. I'm like Brendan now – I'm starving!'

'The next chapter's only very short, so shall I read on and then I'll make us something to eat?'

'Please tell me you have some chicken!'

'No. It's a pork chop but I can put a fried egg with it and a few chips.'

'That sounds nice.'

'But surprise, surprise! I have some apple pie!'

'Ooh! I love apple pie!'

'I know. But anyway; let's read on with chapter five and then I'll read some more later on.' She fixes her glasses into the usual comfortable reading position and continues with the story.

* * *

Chapter 5 – Anna and Brendan Get Ready for the Party

After such a lovely meal, Mother V was sound asleep in her chair and Anna placed a patchwork quilt over the old woman's knees.

Anna became very excited about the prospect of going to a party. Her mind was on what to wear. She was so glad that, when she had left the house, she had thrown into her bag the green, satin dress that her mother had made for her last Christmas and her best black patent shoes. It will have to do, she thought. It'll be creased.

She had been allocated a cupboard in the caravan for her personal use and the dress had been folded neatly and placed on a shelf. When she unfolded it, it wasn't as bad as she thought. She boiled a pot of water and wafted the dress over the steam for a few minutes then hung it up while she tried to do something with her hair. There was a matching ribbon with the dress and she decided to tie it like an Alice band and wear her hair loose.

'You do look nice,' said Brendan, 'kind of… well… more grown up like, than usual.'

'You look okay yourself,' said Anna. She realized that Brendan had no choice but to wear his one and only shirt with his best jeans. They were washed and clean and she thought he looked respectable enough.

Mother V was awake and listening to their conversation. 'You both look fine.' she said, 'now have a good time. Keep to the track to the farm and take the torch for when you're coming home. Don't be too late.'

'Okay,' said Anna. 'Thanks.'

'Anna, I have the perfect shawl to go with your dress, if you want to wear it.'

Anna wasn't sure about wearing a shawl but didn't want to offend Mother V. She was surprised with what the old woman brought out of the caravan and handed to her. It was the most beautiful beaded shawl Anna had ever seen. It was a spider-web pattern of the most intricate detail, encrusted with emerald green and midnight blue beads. It complemented Anna's dress beautifully.

'That's nice,' said Brendan, 'have you got one for me?'

They all laughed.

'Come on,' said Anna, giggling with excitement.

* * *

'I like Brendan,' says Peter. 'He's got a cheeky sense of humour.'

'I like *all* my characters. They've become friends.'

'Is that what happens to a writer; do your characters become real to you?'

'Mine do. And I hope they feel real to the readers.'

'Well, I'm enjoying listening to your story Maggie. I think it's great! And they feel real to me. And I think I recognize which post card you secretly inserted into this bit. It's the one with party balloons flying over the Eiffel Tower, isn't it?'

Maggie laughs. 'Yes. The balloons. Party in Paris!'

'I'm glad that chapter was a short one. I'm hungry and looking forward to that pork chop. Do you want me to make the chips?'

CHAPTER SIX

IN THE GARDEN

Maggie and Peter return to their seats in the garden. There's a sense of peace and calm and the twittering birds are perched on the highest branches of the trees.

'You're not going to fall asleep, are you?' asks Maggie. After all that lunch you've eaten, it wouldn't surprise me!'

'That meal was lovely, thanks.'

'I don't want to be reading to myself. And it's quite a long chapter.'

'No. I'm looking forward to it. I might just close my eyes because I want to see the pictures you make with the words. I won't be going to sleep.'

'Okay. Are you comfortable?'

'Yes. Read on.'

* * *

Chapter 6 – The Party on Saturday 16th May 1953

'Do I look okay?' asked Brendan. 'I feel a bit… you know… awkward, going to a party where we don't know anyone.'

'You look *okay*. Let's enjoy it. It's not often we get a chance to do this sort of thing. What do *I* look like?'

'You already know. You look lovely. *Older,* but lovely.'

'Is it the shawl thing that makes me look old? It's beautiful and I like it.'

'No. Not *old*! I didn't say *old,* I meant older. More mature like. Grown up like. Nice.'

'Okay.' She sighs and pats her hair. Have you got the torch?'

'Yes, but I don't think we'll need it, do you? It's a straight road from the farm to the bridge.'

'It'll be dark though, when we're coming back.'

'Well. I've got it if we need it.'

'Okay.'

They followed the track towards the farm, past the stables and the little barn. Two sheep dogs were tied up and barked fiercely on their approach. They looked around in case Roger made an appearance and decided to attack them. They made their way across the cobbled farm yard to the back door of the farmhouse. There was no need to knock.

'Hello, said Katie, opening the door. 'I thought it must be you when I heard the dogs. Have you all settled in okay?'

'Yes,' said Anna, 'thank you. And thank you so much for the chicken. The apple pie was lovely too. Mother V sends her thanks.'

'It was really nice,' said Brendan.

'Good,' said Katie, 'come on in and let me introduce you to our son, John. Some of his friends are already here.'

The porch was cluttered with wellington boots, coats, hats, baskets, walking sticks and bulging sacks. The homely smell of freshly baked bread wafted on the air as the door to the kitchen opened. There was a stone step that led down to a stone floored kitchen with a centralized, enormous, wooden table that had several odd chairs around it.

A man, was sitting in one of the chairs. He lowered the newspaper he was reading and nodded. 'How do?' he said.

'Hello,' said Anna. Brendan nodded.

'My husband Bill,' said Katie. She led them across the kitchen. The floor-to-ceiling, yew wood cupboards with glass doors were on two of the walls and probably stored enough equipment, utensils and produce that anyone could possibly need. A massive, black, ancient fireplace dominated. A traditional cat basket was at the side. It would have been a complete post card scene but it was – minus the cat. It was too warm an evening to expect a fire to be lit but Anna could imagine how cosy it would be in the depths of winter; coming in from the cold to a large log fire in such a room. She could almost taste the hot broth that would be served at the table with delicious crusty bread.

The farmhouse was a maze of rooms. Brendan and Anna followed Katie in single file, up another stone step to the next room; a small room, full of more cosy comforts: two large armchairs with floral covers and plain, red, silk cushions.

There were some still-life paintings on the wall that reminded her of home and she thought about how she must telephone her mother soon. And the books – lots of books. A reminder of her father. She began to feel quite homesick and saw Brendan looking at her. She knew, he knew, what she was thinking. He squeezed her hand.

They could hear music and chatter as Katie opened the door to the next room which was a very spacious lounge with a low, beamed ceiling. The daylight through four, square windows, two on each of two walls, was sufficient to add enough brightness. The large, Yorkshire stone fireplace had a floral display of red and russet flowers instead of flames. It was grand. Two Oxblood-red Chesterfield sofas and a matching armchair surrounded the largest, oak coffee table that Anna had ever seen. The people sitting there smiled as they walked in.

'John! Your guests are here. I'll leave you to it. Bye everyone, we're going now. See you later. Enjoy yourselves.' Katie left, closing the door.

'Hello, hello,' said John, 'so glad you could make it. Come and sit down. Brendan and Anna, isn't it?'

'Yes,' said Anna.

John introduced the other guests to them. 'This is my girlfriend, Jean.'

'Hello,' said Jean.

'Hello,' said Anna. Brendan nodded.

'And my cousin, Mark.'

'Hello,' said Mark, who got up from his seat, gestured a wave of greeting then sat down again.

'Hello,' said Anna. Again Brendan nodded.

'Make yourselves at home. There are some drinks on the sideboard and lots of things to eat... well... everywhere. Just help yourselves to what you fancy.'

'Come and sit here,' Jean said, gesturing to the space on one of the Chesterfields, 'we were going to watch the television until the others arrive.'

'Television?' asked Brendan.

'Yes. Do you like television?'

'Well… er… yes. But I haven't watched much of it.'

'*We* don't have one yet,' said Jean, 'so, when John comes home, I come with him. They bought it to be ready for the Coronation – I can't wait. John thinks I'm only pretending to be his girlfriend so that I have an excuse to be here.'

'*We* don't have one yet,' said Brendan who glanced at Anna.

Anna was listening and thought to herself, *what does he mean by 'yet'*? 'Where is it?' she asked.

'Here,' said John who was standing near the recess at the side of the fireplace. He was opening up the doors of a highly polished cabinet, the front of which opened up to reveal a twelve inch, glass screen and underneath were a range of shiny, black knobs and underneath those, a brown, woven fabric inlay, patterned into the wood. John turned one of the knobs and then sat down in the armchair, turning it slightly so that he faced the television. It was a few seconds before a black and white picture came on the screen. A posh, elegant, lady was speaking: "*At 8:30 we have, Looking at Animals, presented by George Cansdale…*"

There was a knock at the front door and John got up, 'better let them in' he said.

Anna saw Brendan's eyes, glued to the new experience of the latest, greatest, piece of technology that seemingly had taken over the world. He was quite oblivious to what was going on in the living room. 'Brendan,' she said, 'John's friends are here.'

More than a dozen chattering people traipsed into the living room and John gave up trying to be mature and introduce everyone. 'Oh, just make yourselves at home, everyone.'

'Ah, my little gypsy girl,' said the boy who had earlier helped them to get the caravan across the bridge. He was moving towards Anna. Her heart skipped a beat.

'Excuse me? I am not a…'

'Not expecting to see you here,' interrupted Brendan.' He subtly nudged Anna in the back.

'You must be her brother?' the boy said.

'Brendan. And this is Anna. Thanks for helping us today.'

'Oh, that's okay. A great caravan – so colourful.'

'Yes, thanks. So much nicer than a Rolls eh?' said Anna.

'Well, I don't know about that. I'm Tim, a friend of Mark.'

'Are you in one of the caravans?' asked Brendan.

'Yes, I drove up from Manchester a couple of days ago. Four of us from University. We share accommodation with Mark. John's dad said we could sleep over in one of the empty caravans on the site.'

'*You drove?*' asked Brendan, clearly impressed.

'I've been driving for three years.'

'So how old are you?'

'Twenty one at Christmas. That's going to be some party! You'll both have to come to that one.' He looked at Anna. 'Meet the others. Hey Sam,' he called out, 'bring the girls over here!'

Sam ambled over; two giggling young women came with him.

'Meet Brendan and Anna, the gypsy family I told you about that I met today.'

'Oh, hello,' said Sam. 'This is Tina and Sophie.'

The girls smiled and offered a tray towards them. 'Would you like some vol-au-vents?' asked Sophie.

'Some what?' asked Brendan.

'Chicken and mushroom vol-au-vents; little filled pastry cases,' said Tina. The girls giggled. 'Try them, we've made them ourselves.'

'No thanks,' said Brendan. I don't like mushrooms.'

'You'll love these. A special country recipe. They're sooo delicious! Go on – try one!'

Brendan pushed the tray away. 'No thanks.' This was the first time Anna had seen Brendan refuse food. *He must hate mushrooms!*

'You'll have one, won't you Timothy dear?' one of the girls said, pushing the tray right under his nose.

'Okay. I'm sure you two wouldn't poison me – how would you get home?'

The girls laughed a little hysterically.

The joke wasn't *that* good, thought Anna; how ridiculously childish these young women were behaving. Their clothes were smart and their hair and make-up so nice and yet their manner was not that of someone she could admire or what she expected from academics. Her father was her role-model when it came to education. He wouldn't think much of these two. Her mind wandered. Her father had really wanted her to study at University. No thanks, she thought, if these were the girls she would have to share accommodation with. Sharing with Tim, though – now that would be interesting. She was beginning to feel very much more like a sister to Brendan, just like everyone thought she was, rather than his best friend.

She was brought out of her day dreaming thoughts when Tim nudged her. 'They're quite good,' he said, munching, 'try some.'

The girls pushed the tray in front of her. 'Come on, Anna, try a couple. We've slaved over these, all afternoon.'

She took one. The girls watched her eat it. 'Mmm. They taste nice.'

'Have another,' said Sophie, 'you too Tim.'

'Take a couple,' said Tina, 'they'll be gone soon, once we've been round to everyone.'

Anna took a couple and so did Tim. She liked sharing something with Tim. She thought Brendan looked a bit uncomfortable. 'Go and watch the television if you want to,' she said to Brendan.

Brendan didn't need telling twice. He was drawn back to the television that was showing some sort of game show. He took a seat next to Jean. Even though there were lots of seating spaces, there were three other guests sat on the floor, eating, drinking and watching the programme. They all seemed to be fascinated. 'What time did the lady say that series was starting?' asked Brendan.

'Half-eight, I think,' said Jean. 'Are you going to watch it?'

'If I can. If nobody minds. Do you think John would mind? Seeing that it's his party?'

'John won't mind. Knowing John, he'll be watching it with us. He'll leave his guests to party or talk or do whatever – he's so laid back he'd fall over. It's his Mother who wanted him to have a party. She dotes on him and wants to give him the world.'

Anna was enjoying the experience of being a guest at, what she considered, was her first sophisticated party. She knew she was probably the youngest of all who were there and was flattered that Tim, at *twenty one*, was paying her a lot of attention. More attention than he was giving to Tina or Sophie.

'You look so cute,' he said, 'in your emerald green dress.'

'Thank you,' she said, a little shyly.

'With your little green hair band.' He touched her hair. 'You remind me of Alice in Wonderland.'

'Alice in Wond….'

'My little Irish Alice.'

'Come on, let's get something to drink. I'm feeling a little thirsty. I think those volley things were a little salty.'

'Yes, I know what you mean. I feel thirsty.'

They made their way through the throng of guests to the drinks sideboard. 'What would you like? Ginger beer? Or something stronger?'

'What is there?'

'What about a shandy? Nice and refreshing?'

'Yes please.'

Tim began to search the table for large glasses, beer and lemonade. While he was doing this, Anna's eyes searched for Brendan. He looked quite happy next to Jean, watching the television. It made her feel more comfortable to enjoy Tim's company.

The drinks were made and Anna was so thirsty that she drank it down in one go. So did Tim. 'Another?'

'Yes please,' she said.

They took their time with the second. Anna was beginning to feel so relaxed in Tim's company, she felt she knew him but wanted to know more. 'What are you studying at University?' she asked.

'Accountancy,'

'Oh my!' said Anna. 'All those wonderful figures! It's a subject I would choose.'

'It's probably the only thing I'm good at – except sports. I like running. I'm quite good at running actually.'

'What about reading? You referred to me as Alice in…'

'Oh, yes. I like a good book. Alice is one of my childhood favourites. I liked the thought of a Mad Hatter and a Queen of Hearts who wants to chop off everyone's head. So funny, I thought, at the time, when I was young.'

'And what do you read now?'

'Dennis Wheatley.'

'Ah – Satanic stuff?'

'Good writing. What about you?'

Anna's head was beginning to feel a bit fuzzy. 'I like, err… I like mythical, mystical stuff. Tolkien. I like romantic novels too. I like Pride and Pre….

Anna thought that Tim's face seemed to be glowing as if there was a halo around it.

'I thought you might. You are so, so lovely. Your lovely hair, so bright and…' he didn't finish what he was saying.

Tim shook his head, as if to wake himself up. 'Shall we have another drink? I'm still thirsty, are you?'

Anna felt as though she could understand how he was feeling, she too, felt as though she was in a dream world. Perhaps the excitement was getting to her. Was it Tim – was she in love? Was this what writers write about? Is this how you feel when you fall head over heels in love with someone? Dizzy? She didn't feel like this with Brendan. She had read about it but never felt so alive and so in love with the world and everything in it.

Tim passed her the drink. 'Here.'

'Thanks.'

She drank thirstily. Every sense in her body was so much more alert. The taste of the drink was delicious; the scent of Tim's body that was so close and the touch of his hand as he stroked her arm was sensuous and sent shockwaves through her nerves; the scintillating brightness of his sapphire eyes as he gazed at her, was mesmerizing. She could feel herself blinking rapidly. She felt as if there was only the two of them in the room. The other guests were fading into the distance and their voices were joining together and making terrible, squeaky noises that hurt her ears.

Tim took the glass away from her and put their empty glasses on the sideboard.

'Come on,' he said, 'let's go in search of the mystical unicorn!'

'What?' Anna giggled but she didn't resist the hand that gripped her wrist. She didn't resist this mad hatter who made her laugh. He playfully dragged her through the throng of extremely loud, chattering, partying people.

'Come on, my little Irish Alice – where oh where can he be?'

Anna thought he was singing; he was swaying and turning as he pulled her along through the familiar rooms and then out into the fresh air that hit her lungs. The summer, sunset sky was redder than she'd ever seen it before and, like Dorothy, when she first entered the glorious, colourful world of Oz, she felt as if she was dreaming. James Dean was kissing her; he was touching her breasts and she loved the exciting feeling. James Dean's voice said 'Here we are, my lovely, lovely Alice,' but the head that spoke was now bright and colourful, like a clown wearing his mad hatter hat. She laughed hysterically at his painted face. He had his arm around her waist and was leading her. She put her head on his chest and enjoyed snuggling into him. There was a noise of a very loud creaking door. Then she covered her ears when dogs barked, then a horse neighed, screamingly loud, and when she looked towards where the sound came from, it wasn't a horse; it looked like a horse but it had the head of a rabbit – a very large white rabbit! The horse's hooves stomped the ground and then she could see the hooves had changed to rabbits' feet and the sound of thumping, thumping, and thumping! She felt warm and tired as the mad hatter pulled her to his side on the straw that was strewn about. He then lay on top of her and kissed her very hard on the lips. He wasn't gentle any more. The high beams moved and swirled in a kaleidoscope and she felt like a Catherine wheel – pinned. She felt sick and then an excruciating pain of torture. The rabbit was thumping, thumping, thumping! The laughing, mad hatter was eating her. 'Don't eat me,' she whispered. She fell down a very deep hole. Blackness.

* * *

'Please don't tell me anything like that ever happened to you!' said Peter. 'You're not writing from any bad experience, are you? I'd have knocked him out…'

'It's fictional drama Pete! You weren't there – what I mean is, you weren't there as Pete – but you were there as Brendan – in fiction, not real life – I think that's what I mean.'

'Well, I hope Brendan lops him one for me! Go on. What does he do?

Maggie, finds the place in her book and continues to read.

* * *

'Anna! Anna!'

Her name was being called and Anna opened her eyes. The dogs were barking. She felt the sharpness of straw on her cheek and it took a few seconds to adjust her mind as to where she was. The moonlight shone a path into the barn through the small open door set into the large barn gates. She raised herself on her elbows and saw her dress above her hips and her knickers tangled around her ankle. A smattering of blood had stained the straw between her legs. *Oh no, no, please God. no!* She gulped back a sob and wanted to scream. A little blood was on her dress and on her legs. She drew them together, dragged up her knickers, drew up her knees and wrapped her arms around them and rocked herself. She wept with shame. It had not been a dream. She scattered the straw to disperse the bloodied strands in an attempt to destroy all evidence of her lost innocence.

'Anna! Anna, where are you? We have to go!'

Brendan's voice echoed in the yard and the dogs began to bark. She couldn't let him see her like this. She crept to the open door and peeped around it. She saw Brendan at the back door of the farmhouse and then saw him go back inside.

The moon was very bright and she could see the path clearly. When she began to run, she felt dizzy and her legs ached. She slowed down to a walking pace. She tried to fathom out what she would say to Brendan but failed to come up with anything that wasn't a lie.

Feeling dizzy and weak, Anna took hold of the railings on the bridge; grateful for the support it gave her. She gazed at the glistening water below and saw a basin shaped area that was about a foot deep. The thought of washing away the whole episode was foremost on her mind but she would start with washing the blood from her dress and legs. She walked carefully down the sloping banking, took off her shoes, and stepped into the shallow brook, making her way towards the deeper section under the bridge. She sat in the water and the coolness soothed her. All she could think about was what her parents would think of her – how disappointed they would be with her behaviour. Her father's voice was in her head. As she looked at the stream that reflected the bright moonlight onto the sparkling water that rippled over the mottled stones, for some strange reason, she could hear him reciting lines from one of de la Mare's poems, *"And moveless fish in the water gleam, By silver reeds in a silver stream."*

'Anna!' shouted Brendan, 'how on earth did you manage to fall in the water?'

Anna, shaken from her dazed state, looked up to see Brendan shaking his head in bewilderment. 'Well I…'

'Come on…' he was now in the water and holding out a hand towards her. '…let's get you out of there. Have you had too much of that shandy, or what?'

'I had some shandy, yes…'

'Good job I found you. I looked everywhere. Why didn't you tell me you were going back?'

'I didn't…'

'It was my fault. I know. I was watching that programme – the whole first episode. It was brilliant. But I didn't know where you'd gone. Thank goodness I've found you before we get back. Mother V would be mad knowing you've walked back on your own.'

Anna's hand covered her brow, 'Mother V's shawl! – I've left it back at the house!'

'I've got it.' Brendan picked it up from where he had laid it on the banking before wading into the stream. 'Here you are.' He wrapped it around Anna's shivering shoulder. It wasn't the shawl that comforted her, it was the tender way that Brendan was looking after her that made tears flow down her cheeks and she bowed her head low so he wouldn't see her crying; moonlight was sure to enhance and silver the teardrops if she could only catch them. Stifling the sobbing was easy – she pretended to be cold.

Anna just listened to Brendan as he recounted the eventful evening.

'Television Anna! What a wonderful invention. I'll have one of them – one day.' He paused for a while in thoughtfulness and then asked her, 'Did you see Tim on your way home? When I was looking for you in the yard, I saw him running like a bat out of hell across the field!

Anna scoffed, 'He did tell me he was good at running.'

'Well it was as if his pants were on fire! And I think it was him driving that car that just went across the bridge. I wonder where he's going at this time of night.'

The last of the embers still glowed red in the campfire when they approached the caravan and Mother V was fast asleep in her easy chair. A blanket was over her knees and her long-stemmed, unlit pipe still in her hand. Brendan sat down at her feet.

'Anna, you go and take off those wet clothes and hang them somewhere to dry before Mother V notices.'

'Okay.' Anna was glad to do as Brendan bid her.

She felt more comfortable now in her pyjamas and gathered together the wet clothes. As she came out of the caravan she saw Brendan wake Mother V.

'Night, Anna,' he said as he guided Mother V into the caravan. He glanced at the dress she was hanging carefully on a tree branch.

'Night', she said quietly. Her head hurt thinking whether to tell him about what had happened to her or perhaps tell Mother V – or keep it all a big guilty secret and bottle up the shame and guilt and worry. She wanted to go home and confess her sin. Her Mother's voice came into her head now – *Go to bed Anna; things always seem better in the morning.*

* * *

'Poor Anna!' says Peter. 'What the devil is she going to do?'

'You'll have to wait till tomorrow to find out. I've read enough for today.' Maggie sighs, takes off her glasses and rubs her eyes.

'I'll get you some wine, shall I?' Peter gets up from the chair.

'That'll be nice.'

Peter returns with two glasses of white wine. He hands one of them to Maggie. 'Cheers!' he says clinking the glasses.

'I'd like to hear some more of *your* real life adventures Pete. What part of the world did you like best?'

Peter begins to tell her a story about his voyage to the exotic continent of Asia and then he hears a soft snoring sound. He looks at Maggie and chuckles when he realises she is fast asleep.

CHAPTER SEVEN

A RAINY DAY

Maggie looks through the kitchen window. The black clouds are moving nearer to overhead and the sky is darkening. 'It's going to pour down any minute,' she says. 'A big difference from yesterday!'

'It'll be good for your garden,' says Peter. 'Did you have anything planned for today?'

'I thought we could go and look at your cottage and see what needs to be done but the weather...'

'Let's be leaving that for another day. Can we have a marathon reading day?'

'Okay. You're beginning to love my book, aren't you?'

'It's better than watching a serial.'

'Okay. Have you finished your breakfast?'

'Yes. I'll make some coffee. Go and find your glasses and I'll bring the coffee in.'

Peter brings in two mugs of coffee and places them on the mats on the table. Maggie waits for Peter to get settled.

'Are you sitting comfortably?'

'Yes Ma'am.'

'Then I'll begin.' Maggie reads.

* * *

Chapter 7 – The Water Mark

The dawn breeze wafted the delicious smell of fried sausages into the caravan and Anna could hear Brendan and Mother V outside, chatting about televisions. Their voices mingled with the noisy, happy songbirds perched in the overhanging tree branches. She looked through the window and the sunrise was so gloriously blinding that she had to put her hand across her forehead to shield her eyes. The familiar magpies were scavenging for food in the distance and she counted them in her head – *one for sorrow, two for joy, three for a girl, four for a boy, five for silver, six for gold, seven for a story never to be told, eight...* One flew away, so it was still seven this morning. How appropriate, she thought as a heavy, grey cloud darkened her world even though the summer sun was shining.

She washed and dressed quickly and went out to retrieve the dry clothes from the tree branch. She noticed the obvious water mark stain on the rich green material.

Mother V came up behind her, 'I doubt if you'll ever be able to remove that stain, my dear.'

Anna turned to her. She was surprised at Mother V's tone of voice, as if she was saying something else. 'It's ruined, isn't it?'

'Afraid so. But I think you may have outgrown it soon anyway.'

'Yes. You're right. I'll throw it away.' Anna thought she would be glad to be able to throw away any reminder of last night.

'No – don't be too sad about it. Something your mother made for you is too precious to throw away – keep it in your memories box.'

'Mm,' she murmured, but in her head were the words, *Oh, Mother V, I don't want to keep a memory of last night.* She responded with a quiet, 'Okay,' folded the dress with her underwear and returned to the caravan.

'Breakfast is ready!' shouted Brendan.

Later in the day, Brendan was busy painting the wheels on the caravan. He seemed to take his responsibility of maintenance very seriously, and took pride in his work. Mother V always praised his efforts.

Anna noticed that Mother V didn't eat much at breakfast and could see how much of a strain it was for her to move in and out of her chair – a big difference from her usual agility.

'Anna, would you come with me to look at one of Katie's horses?' asked Mother V. 'I'd like you to look him over and tell me what you think is wrong.'

'You want *my* opinion?'

'Yes. You have a good, natural way with horses and I think it would be good for you to develop your skills in their psychology.'

'Okay, yes. Thank you.'

They walked slowly down the lane towards the farm. Mother V was much slower today than usual. 'Are you okay?' asked Anna.

'A bit of pain in my old legs today but I'll walk it off.' And she did; gaining a little more speed as they drew nearer to the farm.

Katie was waiting outside the small barn in the farmyard. 'Hello,' she said, 'How are you?'

'Good, thanks,' said Mother V, 'or should I say as good as anyone my age can be!'

'Did you enjoy the party last night, Anna?'

Anna didn't want to lie. 'Brendan loved watching the television.'

Katie laughed, 'I believe so.' She opened the door. 'Well, let's get on, shall we?' She ushered Mother V into the barn. 'In you go.'

Anna began to tremble at the thought of having to go back inside the surreal place where her recent nightmare was, in fact, reality. She took a long intake of breath and closed her eyes briefly as she entered. When she opened them it felt as though the barn had returned to a normal, peaceful place. The smell of the straw was something that she used to love, now she related it to self-hate. She wondered if that would change over time. Her stomach lurched. The group assembled near to the lone horse, whose eyes were familiar to Anna. She looked at them and saw in them a knowing acknowledgement of a secret they shared. 'What's his name?' she asked quietly.

Katie was stroking him. 'This is Danny.' Danny lowered his head as if bowing in greeting.

'What do you think of Danny?' asked Mother V.

'He's handsome, isn't he?' said Anna. 'He seems like a dark, handsome, gentle soul.'

Katie moved aside to allow Anna to get nearer to Danny.

Stroking him, Anna examined him. 'He's strong and healthy as far as I can see. But there seems to be a sadness about him – a loneliness that is showing in his stance, like his head down and cowering.'

Mother V smiled. 'I think you're right. He's not afraid of us but he's been afraid of something that bothers him.' Mother V posed a question to Katie. 'Have you taken in any new horses recently, say, just before Danny showed any problems?'

Katie thought for a moment. 'Yes, about three, I think.'

'And are they stabled or out in the field near to Danny?'

'Yes, in the same block but they seem fine. No problems.'

'Is one of them livelier than the others? '

'Yes, I would say that two of them are quiet but seem happy and content. Tornado is the livelier one and likes a lot of attention.'

'What do you think Anna?'

'Perhaps Danny is being bullied but is trying to stand up for himself and not happy with the stress.'

'Yes, I think the other two are quite happy to let Tornado be boss but Danny isn't – so, yes, stress is something that can make him physically ill eventually. It's good that you thought of isolating him.'

'To be honest, I didn't know why he was becoming difficult and I thought he might be suffering from a virus or something – that's why I moved him then the others wouldn't catch it.'

'Put him with Topaz, She'll be a calming influence and let's see how he is in a couple of days.'

'*I'll* take him to the field to Topaz if you like,' said Anna.

'Okay,' said Katie, 'thanks. And then come back to the café and have some tea?'

'Do you mind if we have tea another time, perhaps tomorrow?' said Mother V, 'I'm feeling a little tired and I'm going to have a lie down this afternoon. But Anna, you stay if you like.'

'Thank you, but after I've seen to Danny, I'll walk back to the caravan and give Brendan a hand with the painting. Can we have tea another time Mrs. Patrick?'

'Okay, see you both tomorrow…' She nodded towards Mother V, '…and you have a good rest!'

Anna and Mother V ambled slowly with Danny, discussing causes and cures of equine stress. They separated ways as Anna took the turning to the enclosure where she would leave Danny with Topaz to enjoy the rest and peace of the pasture.

'See you back at the caravan,' said Mother V as she wearily took the rough, uneven lane leading in the opposite direction.

* * *

'So Anna doesn't tell anyone. Poor wee girl – bottling up all that guilt and worry.'

Maggie loves Peter's reaction to Anna's dilemma. She loves the way he gets involved with her characters and feels for them. 'What do you think she should do, Pete?'

'I think Mother V knows something is wrong. I think Anna should tell her. Does she tell her?'

'You'll find out in time. We'll carry on with the book later. I think I'll get some housework done while the weather is too bad to go anywhere.'

'Can I help? What do you want me to do?'

'If you can manage to run round with the vacuum cleaner, while I do the kitchen floor – that'll help.'

'Okay.'

'We'll read some more after lunch. Okay?'

'Good.'

CHAPTER EIGHT

RAIN AND READING CONTINUE

When Maggie looks through the kitchen window, she sees that the sky is still overcast. 'Not much chance of any sunshine at all today,' she says.

'Well, it's not been a wasted day. We've got the housework done, so tomorrow we can relax and perhaps have a day out somewhere.'

'Yes. Okay.' Maggie uses the lettuce from the garden and makes cheese salad sandwiches for lunch. After eating them, they settle down to the reading of the next chapter of Maggie's novel.

* * *

Chapter 8 – Amber's foal.

Anna thought it was most unusual for Mother V to sleep so long. It was well into the afternoon and the sun was beginning to lower. She began to worry about her. She felt responsible for looking out for her and thought about ringing George to ask if she should consult a doctor. Brendan had thought that was the best thing to do but Anna knew Mother V would be angry if she did. She would wait and see how Mother V was later and, if she still felt worried about her, she would ask Mrs. Patrick what she thought would be the best thing to do.

When, at last, Mother V did come out of the caravan, she wasn't her usual agile self. She was struggling to eat some chicken soup that Mrs. Patrick had sent over. There was also some homemade pies. Mother V was quite happy to let Brendan have her pie, saying she was quite full with the soup. Brendan, as well as his share of food, was always willing to eat whatever was going! There was never any food wasted where Brendan was concerned, as his developing physique proved. Anna was satisfied with the one delicious pie and a crusty bread roll. Mrs. P always sent some fruit from her farm shop which was so appreciated, but Mother V couldn't be tempted.

Anna had never seen such kindness and friendship from anyone like Mrs. P and her husband. She wished she could stay here forever; a life in the beautiful countryside and among horses. She also knew Mother V was looking forward to going to Appleby – wherever that was. The way she had excitedly described the gypsy horse fair; it was something not to be missed.

Mother V looked across to where Amber was tethered. 'Anna – look at Amber, she's stamping a lot. I think we need to get her into the barn tonight. Will you go and ask Katie if that's okay?'

'Yes. I'll go now. Is she ready? How do you know?'

'I can tell with the way she's restless. She's shown a lot of signs in the past few days and I checked her earlier – she's milk dripping.

'Milk-dripping? Is that a sign?'

'I think it will be in a matter of hours.' Mother V struggled to get up from her chair and Brendan went to help her. As he did so, he glanced at Anna, enough to say, *we need to do something.*

'*I'll* take Amber, so don't you worry. I'm sure Mrs. P will make her comfortable in the barn.'

'Okay,' Mother V said, her voice trembled slightly, 'I'll see you there.'

Anna walked at a slow pace with Amber towards the farmhouse. The dogs were busy eating their food and Roger, the farm cockerel, in his magnificent plumage of brilliant russet browns, reds and dark blue and who could often be as menacing as any guard dog, was perched on top of the tractor observing her like a detective, as she entered the farm yard.

Anna knocked on the back door and Bill came out to greet her.

'Hello, young lady,' he said, 'what…?' He looked at Amber. 'Oh, I see.'

'Would you let us use the barn, Mr. P?'

'Yes, come on, let's get her comfortable.'

Amber was swaying, restlessly as Bill opened one side of the large barn doors. 'Here let me help.' Bill stroked Amber at the side of her face and spoke to her gently. 'Come on girl, you'll be quiet and cosy in here.' Once Amber was settled in the large stall, he took off the rope reins. 'There's new straw in here so she'll be okay, but she'll need some fresh water,' he said to Anna. 'There's a bucket at the side of the water tap just outside the back door. She may not want to eat but I'll get some hay.'

'Right, okay. Thank you.' Anna was getting quite excited and also nervous at the prospect of being with Amber when she gave birth.

As she was getting the water, Katie came out to see what was happening. She was wiping her hands on her apron.

'Hello, Anna, is everything okay?'

'I've brought Amber to the barn. I hope you don't mind. Mother V thinks she's ready to foal. I'm just going to take her this water.'

'Oh, I see. That's fine. It's always quite an event to have a new foal on the farm.' She looked around. 'Is V with you?'

'No. She's not been her usual self in the last few days. I'd like to talk to you about that when you have a moment.'

'Oh. Right. Well, let's get Amber sorted first and then we'll have a chat.'

'Will I be able to stay with Amber tonight – until she's had her baby?'

'Of course, no problem, I understand. I'm surprised V isn't here. She's never missed any of her foals being born.' No sooner had she finished her sentence, she looked up and saw V entering the farm yard and making her way towards them. 'Here she is – told you.'

Not long after Mother V had gone into the barn, Brendan arrived, carrying Mother V's chair. It was obvious he hadn't noticed that the curious Roger was trotting along behind him. Brendan acknowledged Katie and Anna with a nod as he followed Mother V.

Anna, with the water filled bucket, followed Brendan and Katie shooed away the colourful bird before going into the barn.

Brendan was helping Mother V to sit into the low armchair. 'How's that? Are you comfortable?'

'Yes. Thank you.' Mother V sighed. 'It may take all night, so you and Anna can go back to the caravan. Come back in the morning.'

Anna's expression of disappointment that she wouldn't be allowed to stay was evident to Katie.

'I think Anna should stay with you V.'

'Would you like to, Anna? It may be a long wait.'

'Oh, I don't want to miss it. Please. I want to be here for Amber… and to keep you company too.'

'That's good. Okay. Get yourself comfortable then. But we need to keep a distance and quiet – foaling mares don't usually like to have an audience.'

'And what about me, then?' said Brendan. 'If you're staying, so am I.'

Bill was already bringing over a couple of bales of straw for Anna to make a chair. 'Okay, lad, grab yourself a couple of bales, then.

'Thanks Mr. P.' said Anna who was now stroking and comforting Amber as best she knew how.

V and Katie watched them and could clearly see the love and bonding between them.

'Okay, it looks as though you're all comfy,' said Katie, 'I'll bring you some tea and toast later.'

'Thank you, Katie,' said V. 'What do you think she'll have?'

'Oh, V, I can only guess. I know you always seem to know, so, tell us. What will it be?

'Not telling Katie – not telling!'

Amber kept lying down, and then she'd get up, stamping and kicking and very restless. Anna soothed her by stroking and talking to her. Anna had never heard a horse groan and her heart went out to her equine friend whom she loved. Amber's lips were curling and she was clearly well into labour.

Brendan was fast asleep and Mother V was watching how Anna was doing her best to comfort Amber.

'I wish I felt strong enough to do the comforting,' she said. 'Thank you Anna – you're being such a benefit to her.'

'I want to do more. Is she okay?'

'Yes, she's doing fine. I can see her belly, she won't be long now.'

Brendan roused and stretched. 'Has she had it yet? Have I missed it?'

'No,' said Anna. 'Come and give her a comforting stroke – she needs it.'

Brendan had come to have an affection for Amber but was unsure if he would be of any help to her in this situation, but he did as he was asked and moved over to her and stroked her nose gently, holding his head at the side of her face, whispering something to her. He then left her and went to sit quietly next to Mother V. 'How much longer will she be, do you think?'

'Not long now,' whispered Mother V.

Anna joined them, leaving Amber to foal privately.

Amber lay down and then got up again, her legs quivered a little and there was a gush of water that splashed over towards Brendan. Anna was quite frightened by this. 'Is she okay, Mother V – is she okay?'

'Quite normal for her waters to break. She's doing fine. Keep calm – anytime soon.'

Brendan is quite shaken. 'What happens now?' Has she started?'

'Shh. Watch her – she's doing fine.'

Amber lay down on her side. Her legs quivered and the foal's forelimbs were being expelled. Brendan gasped. 'Oh look – aww look!'

An extended head followed the forelegs and then with a gush, a whole new foal, covered in the white sac of new birth, slid onto to the softness of the straw. Amber's ears tilted back as she stood and turned to lick and nuzzle her newborn.

Mother V suggested that they just leave Amber and her beautiful, snow white foal alone for a few minutes and they just watched in silence at the miracle of reproduction.

Anna's eyes filled with tears of so much joy and love for the animals. Brendan blew a sigh of relief and wonder at the experience.

It was Mother V who broke the silence. 'Isn't nature wonderful?'

'Are they both okay?' Anna asked Mother V.

'Yes. We just have to wait for the placenta and check all is well with that. I'm sure it will be.'

'What's the placenta?' asked Brendan.

'The simplest way to explain it is that it is the membranes sac that feed the foal during the term of the pregnancy and it has to be expelled. It may take a little while.'

'Have you got a name for the foal? Is it a boy or a girl?' asked Anna.

'Why don't you go and have a look. I'm sure Amber will let you near – just take your time.'

Brendan held his breath while he watched Anna softly and slowly approach Amber, whose head was down towards her baby. Anna stroked Amber softly and followed the line of her head downwards and then stroked the beautiful, radiant foal who, encouraged by its mother, began to struggle to stand.

'A boy!' said Anna.

'Yeah!' cheered Brendan, a little too loudly.

'Shush,' admonished Anna.

'Sorry.'

'What name do you think will suit him?' asked Mother V.

'What? Aww – can *I* name him?'

'Yes.'

'Well, he's so very precious. And he's sparkling white – so… I'd like to call him Diamond.'

'Diamond he is then, good choice,' said Mother V.'

Anna and Brendan, although they were tired, felt it was their duty to stay with Amber and Diamond for as long as Mother V wanted or needed them. Anna was so drained from all the excitement and experience of the birth and so full of love for the animals, she couldn't do enough for them; she followed Mother V's instructions as to what to do to clean up the birthing area, she changed the straw, filled up the water, topped up the hay, soothed Amber and practically cuddled the foal – her Diamond! Mother V was then quite happy to leave mother and foal. 'Come on,' she said, 'let's get back to the caravan. We've done all we can now. They're both fine and healthy.' She struggled to get up from the chair and groaned when Brendan tried to lift her. 'Give me a minute,' she said, then took a deep breath. 'Right,' she took hold of Brendan's arm and he gently lifted her out of the chair.

Anna was worried and looked to Brendan for a glance of support, but he was now lifting the chair to carry it back to the caravan. 'What about Mrs. Patrick? Do we let her know Amber's foaled?'

'It's a bit too early to wake them. They'll be in here as soon as they're up and they'll find them well looked after. Let's get back now and have some rest. Give me your arm Anna, I feel a little unsteady.'

The dawn light was just breaking quite red and a few birds were twittering. Mother V looked up at the sky, 'I think we're in for a thunderstorm today.'

'Better get everything in then – see you back there.' Brendan walked quickly with the chair and was soon out of their sight.

Anna walked slowly with Mother V. 'What a night!' she said.

Too tired, none of them noticed Roger was on the fence observing their retreat. He was fluffing up his magnificent feathers and getting ready to welcome the dawn with his loud, familiar crowing.

* * *

'I've never seen a foal being born,' says Peter.

'They don't usually like anyone being near them when it's their time.

'Like Mother V says, "Isn't nature wonderful?"

Maggie smiles. 'It is.'

'Do you want to put your book away till tomorrow?'

'Yes. I want you to tell me some more about your life at sea.'

'So that you can fall asleep again?

Maggie laughs. 'I'm sorry, I didn't mean to. Go on. I won't fall asleep.'

They spend some time telling each other stories of their own life experiences and realise one important fact – that their love for each other was always embedded in their souls.

'When did you first fall in love with me Maggie?' asks Peter.

'A long time ago. Do you remember when we were studying poetry in our last year at school?' she asked. 'And it was your turn to read out a verse?'

'And your dad saved me from embarrassment by saying it was a girl's voice that the verse needed, so he moved it on to you. I remember that well. Yes.'

'You winked at me!'

'I did. And I remember the verse you read out. You looked at me each time you mentioned Porphyro.'

'I've loved you ever since that day.'

'That wordless wink was to say I love you.'

CHAPTER NINE

THE COTTAGE

'I'm going down to the cottage this morning to clear out some stuff,' says Peter. 'Do you want to come with me?'

Maggie picks up the used plates from the table. 'Yes, okay,' she says, loading the dishwasher. She wipes her hands on her apron. 'What sort of stuff needs clearing?'

'I want to keep some reminders of my Mammy and get rid of the rest – there's quite a bit of rubbish.'

'Okay.'

'Let's just do a bit at a time,' says Peter, 'then be back home for lunchtime.'

They arrive at the cottage and Maggie is a little apprehensive of going inside. 'I bet there's a load of spiders – no one's lived in here for ages.'

'We'll just look around and pick out the items I want to keep and put them to one side – the rest can be tipped.'

They look around the front room where a sideboard dominates; demanding space. 'That's quite nice – I remember that! You're Mammy used to keep lovely ornaments on that top shelf. Where did those go?'

'I've no idea. They were probably sold.'

'Is there anything in the cupboards?' Maggie opens the doors slowly, as if there might be a bomb inside, stepping back quickly in case any alien species jumps out to attack her.'

Peter laughs at the way she attempts to look inside. 'Here let me have a look.' He peers inside each of the two cupboards and finds two old leather handbags. 'These belonged to Mammy. She used them to store photographs and papers she needed to keep.' He opens one of them.

'Is there anything still in there?'

'Just photographs. I've seen them before.'

'Are you keeping those then?'

'Yes. I'll take these.' He puts them near the front door. 'We'll keep the sideboard then, shall we?'

'I would. It'll be nice with a bit of attention.' Maggie looks around the rest of the room. 'I'd get rid of those old armchairs but keep that nice little corner table.'

They move past the stairs and into the kitchen. 'That table is too nice to throw out. It needs some renovation, like the sideboard, but keep that and the chairs.'

'I'm glad you said that. I can see my Mammy now, setting out all her baking things on that table. Me trying to help. I can see her smiling at me when I got flour everywhere. She was happy then.' Peter pauses for a moment deep in thought.

'So the table and chairs then?' Maggie purposely brings Peter out of his nostalgic moment. 'Anything else in here?' she asks, looking around. 'What about those wall cupboards

– anything interesting in there you want to keep?' Maggie does not even attempt to open any of them, and keeps well away.

One by one, Peter opens them, revealing old crockery items, pans and cooking utensils. 'Anything you think could be useful?' he asks.

'No. I'd bin them with the cupboards,' says Maggie.

'So just the table and chairs then, to keep.'

'Yes. What about upstairs? Is there anything up there?'

'I think the old wardrobes might be worth saving but let's do upstairs another day. I don't think my legs will manage to get up there today. Unless you want to go up on your own and have a look!'

'No thanks, we'll leave it for another day.'

They return home to spend a pleasant afternoon looking through the old photographs and papers that Peter's Mammy kept in the two leather bags.

After dinner Maggie continues reading her book to Peter.

* * *

Chapter 9 – Mother V

Mother V's wellington boots were a size too big for Anna but she needed them today to walk down to the farm.

'Wear some of my socks,' said Brendan. 'What if you put something soft into the toes?'

'I'm sure they'll be okay,' said Anna, stamping her feet into the wellies.

'The rain isn't going to stop today,' said Brendan, 'Just look at that dark cloud. I thought we were going to be washed away down the stream earlier with all that thunder and lightning – what a downpour!'

'Mother V warned us. Good job she knew what to expect. Did you bring everything in?'

'Yes. Everything fits exactly in its place and seems to disappear – this caravan amazes me.'

They both looked around 'Beautiful, yes,' Anna sighed, 'but I have to go. When Mother V wakes up, tell her I've gone to see Mrs. Patrick and I'll be back soon. Don't leave her – she isn't well… and make her some of her herbal tea.'

'I know what to do Anna.' Brendan pulled a face which told Anna she was being bossy. 'And don't forget to ask Mrs. Patrick about the…'

'…the jobs, I know.'

The rain made everything look grey and misty but it wasn't cold. Anna actually enjoyed walking along the farm lane in the rain. She breathed in the fresh aroma of the washed hawthorn as it perfumed the damp air with the smell of spring. She thought of Amber and her foal; warm and comfortable – *I bet they're sleeping*. She was still amazed at the experience and dreaded the thought of ever having to leave them. She could share with no one the thoughts that had gone through her mind when Amber was giving birth. It had dawned on her that she too could be pregnant – a thought that terrified her. What on earth will I do? She so wanted to talk to her mother, but how would her mother react? She was starting to panic and talking to herself. Wait and see. Don't say anything – wait and see! I think I need to go home! Tears burned her eyes.

The rain was cooling as it dripped from the hood of Mother V's mac and she squelched her way on the muddy path to the farm. She made her way to the farm café entrance. The lights were on inside and it looked cosy and inviting. Anna entered, removing the dripping mac and muddy wellingtons, leaving them behind the door. There were no customers. Katie was behind the counter cleaning a shelf and looked round. Her smile was so welcoming.

'Oh, hello. What a day eh?' said Katie. 'Would you like a hot chocolate? I've just made some.'

'Ooh, yes please…' then Anna realized she had no money with her, 'but I haven't…'

'On the house dear. A thank-you for yesterday with Danny and a celebration! What a night you must have had!' Katie said, passing a large mug to Anna and gesturing to a small table in the corner, 'Let's sit down over here and you can tell me all about it.'

Anna put the mug on the table and sat down. She recounted to Katie the recent experience of Amber's foaling. 'Mother V said *I* could name him.'

'Oh, that's lovely Anna – what have you called him?'

'Diamond. Mother V said the birth was a lot quicker than she expected it to be but she says they're both fine and healthy.'

'That's a perfect name for him. I went in to see how everything was as soon as I got up but you'd gone and everything was quiet, so I just crept in and took a peek. He's so beautiful and they looked so peaceful. Shall we look in on them later? We'll check the food and water.'

'Yes, I need to make sure they're okay and let Mother V know. 'How is Danny?' asked Anna, 'When I put him in the enclosure with Topaz, he seemed a little nervous at first but Topaz just looked at him and then carried on grazing. He went to the opposite side of the field though. Have you been up to see him?' She wrapped her fingers around the mug and sipped the delicious chocolate.

'I bet they had a right good natter – in horse language.'

'Yes – Danny telling old Topaz about his trouble.'

'And Topaz a shoulder to cry on.' As she said it, Anna wished for one.

'They're just like us and we all need one of those at some point in our lives. I think he'll be okay. None of the horses seem too bothered by the storms but I'll check on them later.'

'Can I go with you?' asked Anna.

'Yes, of course.' They paused their conversation for a moment as they drank their chocolate. It was Katie who changed the subject. 'And how is V today? Feeling better, I hope.'

'She doesn't seem to be herself. She seems to be tired, which isn't like her – I don't think she sleeps very well. Before she went to bed, she was holding her hip as if she had some pain.'

'That's not like V. I've never known her to complain about any ailment. I've never known her to see any doctor for anything to be honest.'

'She does have her own herbal tea. She says it cures anything. Do you think we should call a doctor? I don't like to do anything that would upset her.'

'Unfortunately, no herbal tea or any medicine will turn back time – she's old.'

'What do you think I should do? Do I need to contact George?'

'Not yet, I think I may have a solution but I need to talk to Bill first. I'll call up at the caravan around five o'clock when the farm shop closes and we can discuss it with V. Then we'll go and see how Danny is getting on. I'll come in my car and keep to the track then we don't have to walk across all the muddy fields.'

'That'll be good – thank you. Will Bill be with you? Brendan wanted to talk to him. When he has time, that is – he's always so busy, Brendan says.'

'Brendan's right. Do you know what he wants to talk to him about?'

'It's about doing some work on the farm, if we can, that is. You see, we're employed by George to look after his mother and the caravan and horses while we're on the road and where Mother V wants to go. But you've been so kind to us while we've camped here, we feel we could work for you as pay back for allowing us to stay; especially while Mother V is sick. Brendan doesn't think we should go on the road with her like this and we won't get to Appleby in time for the fair and… well, he thinks we should let George know how she is. We're worried.'

'Say no more – I understand. I'll speak to Bill when he gets in and we'll see you later. We'll ring George.' Katie glanced through the window. I doubt if we're going to have any customers today. It's still overcast, but the rain's stopped.'

'I'll get back now then and see you later.' Anna went to get her wellingtons and mac. She put them on.

'Well, you're certainly dressed for the weather. A bit big though. Are they V's?'

'Yes.' Anna grinned.

'I have loads of wellies, boots and macs in the back vestibule – all different sizes for when the farm hands need them. What shoe size are you?'

'Five.'

'And Brendan?'

'Eight's. I think.'

'Okay. I'll see what I can find. See you later then.' Katie opened the door and Anna left.

'Bye,' said Anna and as she looked back, Katie was changing the sign in the door window to "Closed".

Mother V refused to eat the soup that Anna had made, 'I'm sorry,' she said, 'I've no appetite.'

'You need to eat something. You've had nothing all day!' said Anna.

'Stop fussing,' said Brendan. 'You'll eat when you feel like it, won't you Mother V?'

'Yes – I'll have some toast a little later. It won't go to waste though, will it Brendan.' Mother V passed the bowl to him.

'Certainly not,' said Brendan, taking the bowl and lining it up at the side of his own. He glanced up at Anna. 'It's good,' he said, dunking a big chunk of bread into the steaming bowl.

Anna sat down to eat and noticed Mother V struggled to get up from her seat at the table and she didn't pick up her pipe when she went to sit at the front of the caravan. She definitely wasn't her usual self. Katie would see the difference in her.

Katie and Bill finally arrived, laden with boxes; wellingtons sticking out of the top. 'Sorry to be a bit late,' said Katie, 'Bill was late getting home. Oh, and these are for you and Brendan – just a few things you might find useful,' she said to Anna, who put them under the table.

'And...,' she directed her gaze to Mother V, '…Bill's been on the phone to George.'

Mother V sat up straight, 'George? Is he alright?'

'Yes, he's fine,' said Bill, 'it's *you* we've been a little worried about, so I told him and asked him what he would like us to do.'

Mother V sank back into the chair, 'I'll be fine – just a bit under the weather.'

'V – You've never been "under the weather" in your life! I think you need to see a doctor,' said Katie.

'And what will a doctor say? "Old age – rest …"'

'That's what George said,' Bill interrupted,' but what George added was that he doesn't want you on the road in the caravan anymore – he thinks the time has come for you to retire – like Topaz, and that you've got to be sensible.'

Anna looked at Brendan. His eyes met hers with the same question behind them. *What will we do?*

There was a pause as everyone could see the tears of Mother V's sensibleness emerge, shimmering her dark grey eyes. 'I know. He's right. And I did think it would probably be my last time at Appleby. I just… I just wanted to get there to see all my family gathering around the fire and catching up on how they're all doing and seeing the new children. It's the only time that the family meet up – they all come to Appleby if they can make it.'

'I understand,' said Katie. 'I know George never misses – he just loves all the bartering and tradition.'

'They all do, and I so wanted to bathe Amber's new foal – Diamond…' she glanced at Anna, '… in the river waters; do you know, there's been a new foal in the family group every year since I've travelled. We were just waiting for Amber to foal and then we could be on our way to get to Appleby in time for the fair. Amber can't pull the wagon for a few months and now I don't think I want to take Topaz away from the pasture. Have you seen how content she is? No, it probably wouldn't be right.' She sighed.

'I really don't think we would feel… well, you know, I think I'd be a bit nervous about travelling with you if you're not well,' said Brendan. 'We promised George to look after you. And… well….'

'I think we should see how you are in a few days,' said Anna, who could see that Mother V was getting distressed, which wasn't like her at all. Anna was worried, like Brendan. She guessed he felt responsible if anything horrible happened and he wouldn't want to let George down.

There was a subdued silence for a moment or two.

'Katie and I have been talking and we think we have a solution,' said Bill, breaking the worried silence that had descended. 'The flat, above the new offices is ready for the new campsite manager to occupy once the holiday caravan business takes off which, won't be till next Easter, so V, you could move in there for a while?'

'You'll be comfortable there,' assured Katie, 'there's a double bed and there's a phone extension connected to the house and reception. And we'll get the doctor to look you over. If he says you're okay to travel, *we'll* take all of you, Amber and her foal and anything else you want to take, to Appleby in our new transport van. How's that? And George will see you at Appleby and you can sort everything out with him then. Your home is here for now.'

'But what about my caravan?'

'It can stay here for as long as you like,' said Bill, 'forever, if you like, it can be our first campsite holiday home. Come to think of it, it will look so good on the advertising brochure. By the way, you've done a brilliant job with the painting you two.' Brendan beamed.

'I hope they won't think all our caravans are as glamourous as that – my goodness!' said Katie, 'trust you Bill – always the businessman.'

'Did you say a double bed?' asked Mother V, rubbing her hip, 'I think it might just help. Thanks Katie.'

'It's a bit late to get you over there tonight, but get all your things together, and tomorrow we'll get you settled in. Are you okay with that?'

'Okay,' said V. She looked over to Anna and Brendan and saw the worried look on their faces.

'I'll be alright in a couple of days,' she told them. They nodded.

'We'll get the doctor in tomorrow to check you over. Okay?' said Katie

'Okay.

* * *

'I know exactly how Mother V feels,' says Peter. 'Knackered!'

'Come on, bed-time,' says Maggie, putting the book down on the coffee table.

CHAPTER TEN

ANOTHER TRIP TO THE COTTAGE

'Is there anything you want to do today?' asks Peter.

'I was going to meet up with Brenda for coffee and a chat this afternoon. But if there's anything you want to do, I can re-arrange…'

'No, don't change your plans. I'll go to the cottage and make a start on restoring the furniture. I'll check out the stuff upstairs and put the rubbish to one side. I think we should keep the wardrobes and perhaps the dressing table.'

'Yes. Okay. I should be back around four and we'll have an early dinner at six.'

Peter calls at the hardware store and purchases the materials needed to renovate the old furniture.

When he arrives at the cottage, he goes up the stairs to check out what has been left to him and finds what he expects – the wardrobes and dressing table that are too good to throw away. When he opens the larger of the two wardrobes he is surprised to find among the old clothes, his father's old military uniform and, next to it, a cream satin dress embellished with an artificial, pink gardenia flower on the shoulder. He knew it was a gardenia because it was his Mammy's favourite flower. He never knew his dad had kept their wedding outfits. *Perhaps he did love her – once!* He tries not to get too sad when he thinks of the past but finds it hard not to; his condition seems to make him more emotional than he used to be. *Or it may just be because I'm getting old!*

There isn't much to salvage from the second bedroom and Peter manages to sort out what he wants to keep – a familiar ornament of a racehorse and a framed photograph of him and his mother. Everything else he intends to get rid of. *We're going to need a pretty big skip!*

After spending some time refurbishing the kitchen table, Peter realises how tired he is and decides to go home. He looks at his watch – *four thirty. Maggie should be back now.* He downs tools, leaves the cottage and slowly makes his way home.

A delicious smell of roast pork greets Peter as he walks in the house. 'No need to ask what's for dinner,' he says. 'It smells delicious.'

After their meal, they relax and Maggie reads some more of her book.

* * *

Chapter 10 – The flat

The private road on the farm continued well past the farmhouse, over the bridge and past the stables and pasture, continuing towards a large field where building work was being carried out. There were several touring caravans already on the site. Katie pulled up in front of a new, brick, two-storey building to show V the new holiday campsite which was being situated well away from the farm house. 'Those are the workmen's caravans and that's what they're working on; where the showers and laundry rooms will be,' said Katie, pointing to the far edge of the field. 'These,' she said, pointing to the new building on her left, 'are what they have finished – the reception and office.'

'Is the flat above that?' asked Brendan, 'it looks big.'

'Yes, Bill's quite excited about the project. There will be a signage over the main entrance – our name: "Appletree Holiday Camp" and "Reception". The private flat above has its own entrance at the back.'

'I'm very impressed,' said V.'

'It's Bill's idea and George is happy to invest – he says it's the future and will give us more income than farming.'

'Will you still have the horses?' asked Anna.

'Oh yes. There'll be more! We hope to make it the main attraction of the holiday experience – horse riding lessons, grooming experience, competitions – all sorts of equestrian activities. We're going to have some small animals too for the younger children – a little bit of everything and see how it goes.'

'And the café and shop should do well,' said Anna, 'you may have to extend.'

'I know, but it's quite a way to walk to the café.'

'Perhaps hire out bikes!' said Brendan.

'That's a good idea – but perhaps we need to have something a bit nearer the campsite. But we haven't got that far with the project yet. We'll see. Anyway, let's get into the flat and I'll show you where everything is. The doctor will be at the farmhouse at eleven, so I'm going to have to go back in a few minutes and bring him here to examine you V.' She retrieved the keys to the flat from the glove compartment and they all got out of the vehicle.

'Lean on me,' said Brendan to Mother V as he helped her descend from the high vehicle, 'I've got your bag. Are you having more pain when you're walking?'

Mother V just nodded.

Katie put the key in the lock and opened the door, 'Leave your shoes in the vestibule here. There's a new carpet in the flat,' she said. 'There's some slippers you can have V.' Katie handed them to V. 'I've kept them here when I've been up to check the work.' I'll get some more.'

Anna helped Mother V to change her shoes for the fur lined slippers.

Following Katie, they climbed the staircase and they noticed what a struggle it was for V who had to stop halfway up. She was clearly in some pain. 'Nearly there,' said Katie.

At the top of the stairs, on the landing were four doors. 'The one on the left, there,' Katie pointed, 'is the living area and kitchen. This one here on the right,' she said as she opened the door, 'is the bathroom.' They all just peeped their head in to see a white, gleaming, bathroom suite. 'You can all use this but all I ask is that you please keep it clean.'

'Thank you,' said Anna, 'we will.' Anna, understanding what boys can be like, gave Brendan a look to say *that means you too!*

Katie opened the door opposite the stairs, next to the living room. 'This is the second bedroom.' They all crowded into the small space that seemed to be used as office storage with several large cardboard boxes, tidily stacked against the wall.

'We'll move these boxes and Bill is going to put a single camp-bed in here for you Anna, so that you can be on hand for V.' They all shuffled out of the room and followed Katie who opened the other door facing the stairs which was next to the bathroom.

'This is the main bedroom,' she said, 'all fitted out. You'll be comfortable in here V.'

Katie ushered them into the more spacious bedroom. There was a pale wood, double bed with a headboard that had two little side tables attached; a matching large wardrobe and dressing table complete with stool.

'Oh, this is lovely,' said Anna, 'you've made it so modern. And I like the way you've matched the curtains with the frill around the bed.'

'I was going to go for a flowery pattern but Bill reminded me that it shouldn't be too feminine – so I went for plain, sage green; but I managed to get a bit of a pattern in the rug.' It was a large rug between the bed and the dressing table, giving a bit of warmth to the linoleum flooring.

'I like sage green,' said V, a little quietly, 'does this room overlook the campsite?'

'Come and have a look,' said Katie. They both went over to the window. 'See,' said Katie, 'from here if you look left you can see the pasture and the enclosure with the stables there at the back – and see – there's Topaz and Danny.' V was smiling now. 'And, of course, all you can see in front and to the right will be the first campsite area; touring caravans for now, but Bill and George are expanding and investing in more static ones. All that area…,' Katie pointed, '…over the two fields, will be allocated to the campsite.'

Brendan and Anna came over to view the scene Katie was describing. 'Any campsite manager that gets this job will be so lucky,' said Brendan.

'Bill's going to start advertising for the Managerial position in the papers soon,' said Katie. 'The person that gets the job will have to be here from about February when the brochures will be out and before the bookings for next Easter start rolling in – hopefully.'

'It really is a lovely place here – good luck with everything Katie,' said V.

'Aww, thanks V.' Katie looked at her watch. 'Hey, look at the time. I'd better get back to the house. The doctor will be here in a few minutes.' Katie put V's bag on the bed. 'Anna can you put these things away for V and get her settled in and Brendan, would you put the kettle on please and make V a cup of tea? There's everything you need in the kitchen. I'll be back soon.'

'Okay,' said Brendan.

Katie left them and hurried down the stairs – the door closed behind her.

Brendan left the bedroom and opened the door on the left of the landing. This opened into the living room area. Everything smelled so brand new. The brown and cream speckled carpet felt softer and warmer to his stockinged feet than the beige, linoleum flooring in the rest of the flat and there was a small beige couch and two matching chairs facing a fireplace, a wooden surround and an imitation coal effect electric fire. Nothing adorned the cream coloured walls. Opposite the fireplace, at the windows, there were half-open blinds – the same colour as the furniture.

To his left, there was a wall halfway across. The opening led into a kitchen area. A long workbench on one side with cupboards above and the same linoleum flooring as in the bedrooms. On the window side of the room that overlooked the front of the building, was a sink with a cupboard beneath it. On the side opposite was a cooker and a small worktop where he found the kettle. There was a drop leaf table on the separating wall, with a chair on either side. He filled the kettle with water from what he thought were fancy taps.

Brendan found some cups in the cupboard above the worktop. He found a teapot and some sugar in a tin and was looking for some milk when Anna walked in. 'Have you found everything?' She was followed by Mother V.

'This is lovely and so new and modern,' said Anna.

'You can use this whenever you want to,' said Mother V, 'all I ask is, like the bathroom and the rest of the flat that you keep it clean for Katie.'

'Oh we will.'

'I'm sure you will. I know you've done a good job with the caravan. Brendan, will you be okay looking after the caravan and everything until we know what George wants us to do? I'm thinking that I may have to go back home.'

'I'll be fine – no problem.'

Brendan and Anna's eyes met. Both knowing what was in each of their minds. *What do we do then*?

Within minutes, Katie arrived with the doctor. Brendan, Anna and Mother V were in the living room drinking their tea when Katie introduced the very smartly dressed, Doctor Unsworth. The doctor smiled at them, 'Hello,' he said, in a friendly manner, then looked towards Mother V. 'Katie tells me that you're not your usual self.' He spoke with a hint of a Scottish accent.

'No… no, I'm not, but… I think… Oh, I'm sure I'll be okay in a couple of days.'

'Well, let's hope so. But shall we have a little chat about exactly how you're feeling?'

'Would you like to use the other room Doctor?' said Katie, gesturing to V to move to the bedroom, 'to give V some privacy?'

'Yes, certainly. Lead the way.'

Katie led the way, followed by V and the doctor. 'You've got a lovely place here, Mrs. Patrick – nice and comfortable.'

'Thank you,' said Katie, leading them into the bedroom. 'Will this be okay here, doctor?'

'This is fine, thank you.' He gestured to V to sit down on the bed and Katie sat next to her. He then saw the stool and drew it near to the bed and sat down, putting his bag on the dressing table. 'Right then, Mrs. Grey, tell me about this pain. When did it start?' He took hold of her wrist and checked her pulse as V related to him all the details of the pain in her hip and her tiredness and the doctor listened carefully to what she told him.

'I did take notice of the way you were walking and if you say you haven't had a fall or anything to cause it, it sounds very much like arthritis. I'll give you something to ease the pain. Now let's check you over for this tiredness.' He took out his stethoscope from his bag and examined V's chest and then he listened carefully to the sounds he was hearing when he checked her back. 'Right,' he said, as he put away his stethoscope in his bag. 'The treatment for tiredness is obviously plenty of rest, so I suggest that you make sure you do that for the next few days and I'll come and see you again next Tuesday.'

'What about Appleby? I must to go to Appleby?'

'Appleby?'

Katie explained. 'The Gypsy Horse Fair. We are going to take V and her horses.'

'I'm going to see my family,' said V, 'we meet up there.'

'Well then, okay. I'll give you something to ease the pain. But make sure you take it easy and don't exert yourself. And I'll see you again next week.' He took some pills from his bag and gave them to V. 'One, three times a day.'

'Thank you,' said V and put the pills in her pocket.

Doctor Unsworth picked up his bag and made his way to the door. 'Goodbye, Mrs. Grey.'

'Thanks for coming, doctor. I'll take you back for your car,' said Katie.

On the way back to the farmhouse, Doctor Unsworth told Katie what he *thought* was wrong with V. Something he didn't want to tell the patient until he was sure, or if he needed to tell her at all.

* * *

'Oh my,' says Peter, 'it looks like Anna and Brendan may lose their jobs if V goes!'

'Did you recognize the hidden postcard in this one?'

'No! Which one was it?'

Maggie gets up and goes over to the sideboard. She brings the box of postcards over to the coffee table and begins to search. 'Here it is – this one!' She hands it to Peter.

'I don't remember that one!'

'It's horses swimming in the river Eden. Appleby!' Maggie looks at the back. 'I can't make out the postmark but it's from abroad somewhere!'

'Well, like I said, I just picked up a bunch of cards and I didn't know it was Appleby! What did I write?'

'Not a lot, it says, "Maggie. Hot here. Pete X."'

'Cyprus. I remember now. We were stuck there for a lot longer than expected. It's a lovely place but it was very hot then.'

'Anyway, the card inspired the visit to Appleby.'

'Good. Read on.'

ANOTHER CHAPTER

After a short break and a glass of red that Maggie insists upon as a reward, she continues to read another chapter of her book.

* * *

Chapter 11 – The New Horse Box

'Is that coming with us?' asked Bill, 'we've already got some deck chairs loaded.'

'Mother V said I had to make sure she had it, "if I can't take my caravan, at least let me have my chair," she said to me; so here it is,' said Brendan, placing Mother V's scruffy old chair in front of Bill, 'she's the boss! So where do you want me to put it?'

'Well, I'll find a space, once we have Amber and Diamond loaded. Put your rucksack in the cab. Anything else *the boss* wants to take?'

'I don't think so, she's not mentioned anything else.'

'Okay – let's not ask then!' Bill chuckled.

Brendan touched the side of the vehicle. 'It's a lovely horse box – a lot bigger than George's and you've got your name on it too. We won't mistake it! Mrs. Patrick's taking the land rover isn't she?'

'Yes, so V and Anna can travel with her; we'll go in this little beauty.' Bill tapped the side of the vehicle and looked it over with pride. 'We won't be staying though, we can't leave the farm for long; so after we get everyone there, me and Katie will drive back in the land rover and come and pick you all up again on Monday.'

'What's it like – at Appleby?'

'Oh, you'll enjoy it – lots of young people – music, horse events. The horses and riders swimming in the river. There's a lot of noise and bartering going on with horses exchanging owners. There can be a few rogues on the site but George knows the ropes – he won't be done! That's if he buys any. He's more into thoroughbreds than gypsy vanning now. There's so many horses and carriages and such a lot of riding up and down the main streets – very busy. A very entertaining few days of gypsy gatherings.'

Brendan followed Bill to the barn at the back of the farmhouse, 'Will George be there before us?'

'Yes, I bet he's there now, setting up camp. He only goes for the main event days over the week-end although the fair's on for a week until next Wednesday – he's a busy man, like me! I can't wait to show off my new horse wagon! If there's anything you or V needs, or any problems, let George know – he'll get in touch with me. And don't worry. V will be with many of her family, so you and Anna can have a little holiday – make the most of it. The weather forecast is good.'

Brendan pulled back one of the barn doors to allow Bill to enter. He followed and watched Bill rope the horse to lead her into the vehicle. 'Hello Amber,' Brendan said. Less nervous of her now, he went over to pat the side of her face and stroke her nose. Diamond was close to his mother and Brendan tickled his nose. 'How is this little man today?' There was a quality of gentleness within Brendan.

'Right,' Bill said, giving the ropes to Brendan, 'let's load them up and we can be on our way.' Brendan led Amber and Diamond to the vehicle and Bill closed the barn door.

Amber was no problem loading into the horse box and Diamond kept very close to his protective mother. They seemed quite happy as Brendan tethered them – the ride to Appleby wouldn't take very long.

V's squishy chair was squashed into a corner, so everything was loaded.

Katie came to the back door, wiping her hands on her apron, 'Are you off now then?'

'Yes, we'll see you there,' said Bill, giving his wife a peck on the cheek.

'Enjoy yourself, Brendan.'

'Thank you, Mrs. P – and thanks for the clothes and stuff you sent up – they fit.'

'That's good. Glad you can get some use out of them. See you there.'

Brendan climbed into the passenger side of the vehicle and closed the door. Bill climbed into the driving side on the long, red leather bench seat. He started the engine and the vehicle rolled smoothly over the cobbled farm yard and around to the farm lane.

'This is great!' said Brendan relaxing, 'I wish I could drive!'

Katie closed and locked up the café. It had been a busy day; Friday's were getting busier and she was thinking she could do with some help. *But, never mind, I'll sort something out later. I need to get going and pick up Anna and V.*

She twice checked that she had locked the back door of the farm before getting into the land rover. She'd packed two boxes of foodstuff that was left over from the farm shop and wedged them securely in the back under the tarpaulin cover – *no use letting it go to waste – they'll be glad of it.*

When she arrived at the flat, Anna and V were ready. Anna was carrying two bags and V was holding onto her arm.

Katie went over and took the bags from Anna. 'Here let me take those – I'll put them in the back.'

'Thanks,' said Anna who was taking her time walking Mother V to the car. She opened the door and helped her into the middle space of the long seat.

'Have you locked up?' asked Katie.

'Yes, I've got the keys.'

'Good, let's get going then.'

Katie got in the driving seat space and Anna squeezed into the left side passenger seat.

'Are you looking forward to this weekend?'

'I can't wait to see them all,' said V.

'How are you feeling today – any better? I hope you've followed the doctor's orders,' said Katie.

'Yes, I'm much better – I told you I would be alright in a couple of days!'

Anna and Katie glanced at each other. Katie reversed the vehicle and drove down the farm lane towards the main road. 'Are you excited Anna?'

'I'm a bit nervous but looking forward to it. Mother V has been telling me all about her family and about the times she has spent over the years at the fairs. She can't wait to show off Amber and Diamond.'

'They'll steal the show,' said V. I can't wait for George to see them. I bet he's offered quite a lot for them!'

'Oh no! – you're not selling them are you?' said Anna.

'No! But there'll be a lot of interest in them – no doubt about that. But they're staying with us. My son knows his horses.

'Oh, thank goodness for that!' said Anna, relieved.

'I wanted to ask you if you wouldn't mind me having some photos taken of your caravan and Amber and Diamond, for publishing in our brochures, we need to get them ready now for next summer's opening – well, next spring really. We hope to be open for business next Easter.'

'Can I be on it?' asked V, 'and don't forget Topaz!'

'Of course; Topaz, you, Brendan and Anna – but you have to lose the pipe!'

As they made their way to Appleby their conversation turned to the memorable day they had had recently, watching the Coronation of Queen Elizabeth 11 on the television. Work had stopped for everyone on the farm that previous Tuesday the second of June, 1953, when Katie had set out loads of chairs around the small screen so that they could all watch the young twenty seven year old princess crowned.

It had been a party atmosphere and Katie and Sandra had prepared a buffet. Mother V had been seated most comfortably; like a queen herself in one of the big, red chairs.

Brendan's eyes had been glued to the screen; fascinated with all the pomp and ceremony. Bill had enjoyed drinking his beer and watching everyone else enjoying themselves – a rare occasion brought into their living room by the technology of television. Katie remarked how glad Bill was that he had bought it.

They had all drunk a toast to their new monarch.

Anna, however, had felt a little uneasy at the reminder of a previous party occasion in that room.

* * *

Maggie puts down the book. 'If I can have another glass of red, I'll read another chapter. That was a short one.'

'Okay.

CHAPTER TWELVE

MAGGIE IS HAPPY

Peter makes himself comfortable and Maggie continues to read to him.

'This is the last one I'm reading – then I'm off to bed. So sit back and enjoy.'

'Okay,' says Peter and then closes his eyes.

* * *

Chapter 12 – Appleby

As they approached the Cumbrian village of Appleby, the streets were heaving with horses; most of them the traditional Gypsy Vanning breed. Colourful carriages, carts and so many people enjoying the heat of summer sunshine – and so much noise!

'When we come to the bridge,' said Bill, look over to your left.' Bill slowed down as they crossed the bridge and Brendan stretched up in his seat and peered over to see many of the gypsy horses being washed and swimming. Some people were in the river, riding on the backs of some of the horses. Shirtless and shoeless youths and men; girls and women in bright summer tops and shorts, wading with toddlers and foals in the sparkling waters. 'That's the River Eden,' said Bill.

'It looks good fun. 'How do we get down there?'

'Just a bit further up this road and then we take a left turn. It'll take us to the fields where the caravans and vehicles are allowed to park up. I'm going to park at the very top, away from the busiest areas – it'll be safer. I'm thinking that's where George will be parked; if Katie has got here before us, she'll take a spot for us. Look out for George's grey wagon or our land rover.'

Bill took the left turning and made his way along the makeshift road, past the vans and stalls belonging to the market traders; away across the field to the farthest point on the right, where fewer vehicles were parked up. The majority of the gypsy horse drawn vehicles were to the left and as near to the river as they could possibly get.

'There they are,' pointed Brendan, 'I can see Mrs. P and Anna at the front of the land rover. Bill hooted his horn and stopped. Katie waved and got into the land rover and drove it out of the parking spot and onto the roadway. Bill drove his "wooden shed on wheels", as Katie described it, into the vacant space. 'Perfect,' he said.

Katie spoke to Bill as he came round to the back of the vehicle and, with Brendan's help, they opened up the doors and began to assemble the ramp. 'How was Amber and Diamond with the trip?' asked Katie.

'Not a peep out of them. All good.'

'Mother V was quite sure they would be. She's with some of her family, down by the river.'

'She's asked if we would walk Amber and Diamond down to her, to show them off to her family and friends,' said Anna.

'They're all yours my dear,' Bill said, his hands gesturing to the sight of the two beautiful horses being led out of the *shed*. 'We'll just have a drink here and then a word with George before we set off back to the farm. Both of you make sure you lock everything up securely and ask George to check with you. Okay. We'll see you before we set off back.'

'Okay. Will do, Mr. Patrick,' said Brendan, who was struggling to put a small leading rope around the lively foal's neck.

'Here, let me do that,' said Anna, 'you take hold of Amber.' Bill gave the keys to Brendan. 'Don't lose them. I suggest you give them to George to keep safe.'

'Okay. I'll do that, Mr. P.'

Anna and Brendan, proudly walked the two horses towards where Mother V was gathered with her huge family around her. Heads turned as they walked past, their eyes on the beautiful animals, whose coats shimmered in the sunshine. Numerous children tried to stroke Diamond and Anna was careful and protective and asked the children to be gentle and kind.

They eventually found Mother V sitting outside an enormous bowed Gypsy caravan – even more gaily coloured then her own, with so many pots and pans dangling from hooks all around it.

'Here they are', she said, smiling to those gathered around her. 'My Amber and the newest addition, Diamond.'

Mother V struggled to get to her feet and was helped by a young, attractive woman dressed in traditional gypsy attire – a short sleeved white blouse, with a gathered, low neckline tucked into a long, floral cotton, tiered skirt. A scarf tied back her jet black hair and her gold, hooped earrings caught the light of the sun. A stole of black, beaded material was wrapped and tied around her waist and on her feet were toeless, strappy sandals.

'Brendan, Anna,' said Mother V, 'this is my granddaughter, Rosina – George's daughter.'

'Hello,' Brendan said, shyly.

'Hello, said Anna.

Rosina, nodded and smiled. 'Thanks to both of you for looking after Grandma. Dad told me how he met you. Come and meet the rest of the family. Mum isn't here and not all the family have made it this year but there's still a lot of us.'

'I love your outfit, Rosina,' said Anna, 'it's so nice.'

'Thank you. I only wear this,' she said, swishing the cotton skirt, 'when I come here and when I do readings and the Tarot. They tell me I have the gift, but I only tell customers what I see. You must come to the market tomorrow and I'll do you a reading. Free of charge for family – and you.'

Rosina did the introducing and Brendan and Anna, both being an only child, where quite overwhelmed with the numbers. 'I'll never remember all your names,' said Brendan.

The horses were happily taken care of by a couple of older men in the family – Mother V's grandsons, while Anna and Brendan were being casually entertained by everyone. They were welcomed and made to feel at home. Everyone sat around the front of the caravan and joined in the banter, ate the food offered and drank cold drinks.

'Mother V mentioned how she would like to see Diamond enjoy being in the water. When does that happen?' asked Brendan, eager to join in the fun in the river.

'Now, if you like,' said John, one of the grandsons. Can you swim?'

'Yes,' said Brendan.

'Right then, let's go,' said John, taking off his tee shirt and canvas shoes. 'Gran, are you coming down to the water to watch?'

'Yes. Be gentle. Be careful, both of you. Anna, are you going into the water with Diamond?'

'Well, I can't swim but I can paddle in the shallow bit.'

'I'll help you,' said Collin, 'foals can be slippery little buggers when they are in the water.'

Brendan copied John, taking off his shoes and stripping to his jeans only. Then he remembered the keys in his pocket. 'Mother V, will you keep these safe until I can give them to George?'

'Okay,' she said. She took them from him and placed them in the bottomless pocket of her skirt.

Anna took off her sandals.

'Your cotton shorts and that top will dry quickly in this sunshine,' said Mother V. 'Let's go to the water.'

They all made their way to the water's edge, Rosina assisting her grandmother, sitting her down on the high bank, nearer to the shallower part of the river, near the bridge where

Collin suggested he and Anna should try Diamond in the water and see how he found it.

Anna held tight to the narrow rope around Diamond's head and paddled out to where the water came up to her knees.

'I think this is deep enough.' Diamond seemed to tug on the rope as if he didn't want to go any further. Amber was on the river's edge watching and she started neighing as if distressed.

John and Brendan led Amber towards her foal in the shallows. The water came a quarter of a way up her legs when she reached her foal. Amber nudged Diamond playfully, slightly pushing him off balance and he went under the water, coming back up, swishing and splashing. Anna and Collin had to struggle to steady him. Then Amber did it again; she also nudged Anna and sent her off her feet and she rolled headfirst into the water, which made them all laugh. It was as if Amber wanted them to enjoy themselves.

'Bring Diamond back now,' shouted Mother V. 'That's enough – he's had enough now.'

Anna and Collin waded back to the riverside with Diamond who was dried off and made a fuss of. Brendan and John moved further up river to a deeper part and enjoyed swimming with Amber until she made her own decision to come out of the water and back to her foal. 'That was fantastic,' said Brendan as he waded out of the water, still holding the rope reins, following Amber.

John was following, 'That was great. I haven't been swimming since I was here last year.'

They made their way back to the caravan and dried Amber off, tethering her to the caravan next to Diamond who was now ready to go to sleep.

Katie and Bill arrived to say they were setting off home and that they would be back on Monday morning. 'Looks as though you're all having a great time,' said Katie.

'We are,' said Brendan.

'Thanks for everything Katie,' said V. 'I couldn't have done this without your help. And the food, thank you.'

'No problem V. See you all Monday.'

'Brendan,' said Bill, 'will you go and see George – he's in his cab and he'll let you know where things are and what you have to do.'

'Okay, yes, Mr. P,' he said and started to go. He then turned – 'Keys!'

Mother V delved deep into her pocket and handed him the keys.

They spent the rest of the glorious sunny day sunbathing and drying out, talking, eating, and laughing together, till well into the evening.

Mother V said that Amber and her foal would be safe staying with her and the family and suggested that Brendan and Anna make their way back to the horse wagon for the night. George would be right next door!

* * *

'Appleby sounds like fun,' says Peter.

'A little bit too rowdy for me, I think.'

'At our age now, yes, I suppose so – but not if we were teenagers. We'd have enjoyed a time like Anna and Brendan had, at that age. I feel like I've enjoyed the experience with them.'

'That's good.' Maggie went to bed feeling very happy.

CHAPTER THIRTEEN

PETER IS SPOILED

'Did you sleep well?' asks Maggie.

Peter sits down at the table. 'Really well, thanks.'

'Good. Any plans for today?'

'I need to register with the local doctor. I need some tablets.'

'Okay. Register with *my* doctor. Dr. Kelly. He's nice. I'll come with you.'

'Would you? Thanks Maggie.'

Maggie places a full fry-up breakfast in front of Peter. 'I'll tell him there's not much wrong with you if you can eat all that.'

Peter laughs, 'I wish that were true!'

It is early afternoon when they return home from the surgery. Peter is now registered as one of Dr. Kelly's patients and a supply of his medication has been picked up from the nearby chemist.

Maggie seems to think that Peter looks quite exhausted. 'I think you should have a bit of a rest this afternoon. I'll make some lunch and we'll read some more of my book.'

'That'll be nice. Thanks. You spoil me.' Peter heaves a big sigh as he takes his usual position on the sofa and waits for Maggie to return with lunch.

It isn't long before Maggie brings in a tray of tea and sandwiches and joins Peter on the sofa. 'Are you ready to listen?'

'Yes,' says Peter, as he takes a sandwich from off the plate. 'I can't wait to find out what happens in Appleby.'

Maggie reads.

* * *

Chapter 13 – The Market

Mother V finished putting some homemade remedy on Brendan's and Anna's sunburned shoulders. 'Keep out of the sun for a while,' she said, 'you both have such fair skin.' She put the jar in her pocket. 'I wanted to look round the market stalls today. I need a few things. The caravan could do with some new steps. I noticed one of the rungs is ready to snap. And we need a few more hooks. Oh, and I need a new pipe and some tobacco.'

'Are you up to walking so far? It's quite a way,' said Anna, 'and you know how rough the road is?'

'We'll go for you, while you rest here?' said Brendan.

'But you have to barter with them – you don't know how things are done here.'

'Well, you tell me how much I should pay for the things and I won't buy them until they offer me that price or near it.'

'Okay.' Mother V relented. 'Get some paper and I'll write out a list.'

Anna vanished into the family caravan and, after a while, came back with a scrappy piece of paper and a pencil. Will this do? That's all Collin could find.'

'Yes.' V began to write while Anna and Brendan waited patiently in anticipation of the experience of the market visit.

'Here you are,' said Mother V, handing the paper to Brendan. 'And…' she delved into the mine of a pocket, brought out a fabric purse and took out some notes, '…here's the money and watch out for pick pockets…' she pointed, '…they're on every market!'

The market was a noisy, bustling place.

'We should have come earlier,' said Brendan, 'if we'd known she'd wanted things.'

'Let me have the list,' said Anna, 'and let's get the smaller items first, then we don't have to carry the steps around with us.'

'I think I know where the tobacco stall is,' said Brendan, 'follow me.'

Anna clutched the list and struggled to keep up with Brendan's long strides. 'Not so fast!'

They found the tobacco stall and bought exactly what Mother V needed. Brendan was prepared to barter but he didn't have to, the price asked was exactly what was written on the paper.

'Job done,' said Anna, 'now hooks!' I think I noticed some further back.'

They retraced their way back slower, glancing on every stall in search for the strong metal hooks. What they found first was some wooden steps that would be a perfect replacement for the ones on the caravan. Brendan stopped to ask the price. 'How much for the steps?'

The reply Brendan got was nearly twice the amount written on the paper. 'Here goes,' he whispered to Anna. 'I'll give you half that price?' he said to the stallholder.'

The trader laughed out loud. 'No way son! Look at the design. *And* these are made from good quality wood – you'll not find any as good. These will last.'

'Well, I'll give you my final offer…'

Anna interrupted, tugging at Brendan's tee shirt, 'Come away. Let's have a look round.'

The stallholder ignored them and began to serve another customer.

'I think I could have got him down a bit more,' said Brendan.

'I didn't like the way he laughed.'

'Right, so let's look round for a miserable stallholder then!'

They found some lovely, ornate, metal hooks and got them at a price as near to what they were allowed as they could. They seemed worth a little more.

As they continued their search for the steps, they came across Rosina's tent, advertising Palm and Tarot readings.

'Oh look, Brendan, shall we go and say hello? She said she would do me a reading for free!'

'You go. I'll carry on looking for the steps. I'll meet you back here, say, in half and hour?'

'Okay.'

Rosina didn't have any customers waiting, so she was glad of Anna's company for a while. 'Would you like a reading?'

'I'm a bit nervous. I've never had my fortune told before.'

'It's a bit of fun. Sit yourself down.'

Anna sat herself down in a rickety, wicker chair, opposite Rosina.

'Palm or Tarot?' asked Rosina.

'Oh, I don't know. Whatever you want to do.'

'Let's do palm. Which is your dominant hand – right or left?'

'I'm right handed.'

Rosina, held Anna's right hand gently and stroked the palm softly, her fingertips followed the lines. She was silent as she studied the palm. Her expressions were unreadable, she frowned and then a smile crossed her face and then her expression became unreadable.

Another silence reigned for a moment or two and Anna was afraid to interrupt Rosina's concentration. Anna could feel her heart beating nervously. She was glad when Rosina spoke.

'Your life is broken in some places.'

'What does that mean?'

'I can see some darkness. Probably experiences that can maybe affect the choices you make.'

Anna gulped and became uneasy but tried not to show it.

'I can see you are a person who thinks about things and considers other people's feelings. A good heart line.' Rosina said, running her finger along the top of Anna's palm. 'I can see you thinking things over and over and having difficulty in coming to a decision on something quite important to you. And you have quite a straight, long, head line.'

'Is that a good sign?' asked Anna.

'Yes. And it's probably a good thing – to think things through.'

'Is that it then?' said Anna, quite relieved it was over.

'Yes. That's all I see. Head, heart and life. We can do a Tarot reading if you like?'

'Thanks Rosina, but perhaps another time. I've got to meet Brendan and get back to Mother V. It's been good. Thank you.'

'Okay, see you at the caravan later?'

'We will, yes. Thanks'

'If there's anyone waiting outside – tell them to come in please.'

Brendan enjoyed looking at all the merchandise on the stalls; from stoves and fitments to cooking pots and tarpaulin patches; leather reins and belts; paints, brushes, varnishes and spare parts – no steps though. He was interested in some fine art paint brushes on display. He thought he quite fancied a go at fine art painting and then his thoughts were interrupted by the sound of a familiar voice – his heart raced.

'Brendan!'

Brendan turned to see his Uncle.

'Uncle Kevin!' Brendan walked towards his favourite uncle and they embraced, although Brendan was afraid of what news he was going to hear. 'What, why… what are you doing here?'

'I could ask the same of you, my lad. Be Jasus, you've grown taller and bigger since I saw you last. Your Aunt Peggy was sayin' only the other week that we hadn't seen you for some time. What are you doin' here, then?'

'I've got a job here. I've been here since Easter.'

'A job! Good man, Brendan! Doin' what, then?'

'Erm… transport… er… transport maintenance. Learning like – you know?'

'Well, bless me! Good man, son. I'm proud of you! Good man!' He patted Brendan on the shoulder.

Brendan pointed to the far field. 'See that horse wagon over there. The big one beside the grey one?'

'The one with the wooden carriage?'

'Well, yes. That's my boss's vehicle. I'm in charge of that till Monday,' said Brendan with some pride. 'What are *you* doing here?'

'Me and these lads over here,' he pointed over his shoulder to a group of men, 'we're contracted for three months to do some pipe layin' in a place not far from here, so we thought we'd come along and see what all the fuss was about. Lively eh?'

'Yeah.'

'And have you seen your Daddy since his accident?'

'Accident?' Brendan didn't know how to react. He tried to keep calm – *if he wasn't dead then what happened?*

'He's lost his marbles, that one. And it's his own doin.'

'I left home at Easter and I don't want to go back, Uncle Kevin.'

'I don't blame you, son. Your neighbour, Jack found him. Said he heard a racket and went round to find him on the floor. "Drunk as a skunk he was," Jack said. Said he'd fell and cracked his head open. The lads in The Ship told me he's never goin' to be the same, but still drinking as much. They say he doesn't know what day it is half the time. I don't blame you for not wanting to go home. It wasn't a good place for you to be; not since mi dear sister died. God bless her soul. Your Mammy should never have married him. I did my best to stop her, you know. But she was with you and… well it is what it is, son.' He sighed. 'But if you ever want to return home, you'll always be welcome to stay with me and Peggy, you know that. And forget that drunkard of a Daddy.'

Brendan was choking back tears of relief that his father wasn't dead and, more than that, nobody was going to be looking for him. Most of all, he felt emotional because of the love and home he had been offered. 'Thanks Uncle Kevin, give my love to Aunt Peggy.'

'I will, lad, I will. And you take good care of yourself.'

Uncle Kevin went back to his workmates and Brendan restarted his search for the steps and then remembered he had to meet Anna, so he hurried towards Rosina's tent.

Brendan found Anna outside the tent talking to George. 'Hello,' he said.

'Not got the steps then, I see,' said George. 'Anna's been telling me about them.'

'No, I can't find any more. I'll have to go back and have another try.'

'I don't think that stallholder will budge on the price. He wasn't friendly,' said Anna.

'How much did he want for them?' asked George?

'Twice as much as Mother V was prepared to pay – look,' said Anna and showed him the paper.

'I'll come with you,' said George.

They all followed one another through the throng of shoppers until they came to the stall. The steps were still on show.

George leaned over the stall to greet the stallholder. 'Francis! How's trade today?'

'Well, if it isn't my old friend Georgy boy! Good to see you!' They shook hands strongly. 'Is there anything that takes your fancy?'

'Steps, Francis, these steps for V's caravan.' George patted the steps. 'How much?'

Francis rubbed his chin and noticed the two teenagers by George's side. 'It's no good trying to barter with you George. Just tell me what you're prepared to pay and I'll consider it.'

'George handed him the paper, pointing to the amount written down. 'That's the figure V's set – not a penny more.'

'That's a bit low George. They're good quality and that price is more or less what *I* paid for them. But seeing that you're a good customer, I'll tell you what I'll do; if I don't sell them before I pack up the stall, I'll let you have them at that price. How's that?'

'Fair enough Francis. I won't stand in your way of making a profit.'

'Come back at four o'clock.'

'Okay,' said George.

George instructed Anna and Brendan to be back at the stall just before four. 'I have to go now. There's a horse I have to barter for that could take a while. So see you two later,' he said, 'and I'll help you with the steps. Don't worry, they won't be sold.'

Anna and Brendan made their way back to Mother V's caravan.

'George seems sure we're going to get them,' said Anna.

'Yeah. Hope so,' said Brendan. 'Did you get your fortune told?'

'Yes. Not much to tell though. Some experience that will make me make a decision!'

'Well we've already had that, haven't we? And you made a decision to come with me. But I have something to tell you.' Brendan stopped and took hold of Anna's shoulders to turn her to look at him.

'What?'

'My Daddy's not dead! No one will be looking for me! I can't believe how relieved I feel.'

'How do you know?'

'I've just seen my Uncle Kevin. He's working around here somewhere and he asked me if I'd seen my Daddy since his accident. His *accident* – nothing about him being dead!'

'What happened to him then?'

'Uncle Kevin said that old Jack from next door had gone round and found him, so he must have gone to hospital for stitches or something. But he's not dead. He said he was still drinking at lot but he wasn't himself. But that can only be a good thing can't it? Not being himself.'

'So you could go home. Do you *want* to go home?'

'Not to live at home. What about you – do *you* want to?'

'The last time I spoke to my mother, she said they wanted me to go home and look at the plans they had to emigrate!'

'If I went home, I could go and live with Uncle Kevin and Aunt Peggy – he said I could. I won't live with my Daddy ever again. But I don't want you to emigrate! Where to anyway?'

'Australia – some special offer for some teaching position for my Daddy.'

'Well, we may *have* to go home if Mother V goes to live with George. We'll have no jobs.'

'We'll just have to wait and see. But it's been good and I know what I want to do now. I'd really like to learn how to be a businessman like George and Bill.'

'And I'd like to work with horses, like Mother V and Mrs. Patrick.'

'Let's wait and see then, shall we?'

* * *

'Australia!'

'What?' asks Maggie?

'The hidden postcard. I sent you one from Australia.'

'Oh yes. Sidney harbour. You got that one right!' Maggie takes a sandwich from the plate. 'What was Australia like?'

'Hot! Very hot when I was there! I've only seen Sidney.'

'Probably not for me, then?'

'We could go on a cruise there, if you like? Perhaps see more of the country.'

'No sailing for me thank you very much,' says Maggie. 'Let's have a break and eat our lunch.'

CHAPTER FOURTEEN

PETER IS CONCERNED FOR ANNA

Maggie and Peter finish eating their lunch whilst discussing the positives and negatives of emigrating to Australia.

'I wouldn't want to leave my own country,' says Maggie. 'Not for good.'

'A lot do – to find work.'

'Yes. I suppose so, but I wouldn't, not unless I had to. And Australia – well, it's such a long way away.'

'Well, you'll never have the need to,' says Peter. 'And I have no intention of emigrating either.' He considers the topic of discussion settled. 'Are you going to read the next chapter?'

Maggie picks up the book and continues to read.

* * *

Chapter 14 – Chats and Decisions

Katie and Bill arrived back at the farm to the chaos of a distressed young woman named Sandra, in their employ as a part-time, counter assistant at the farm shop.

'I'm… sorry Mrs. Patrick,' she said, 'I felt…that I… couldn't cope,' she sniffed and sobbed, '…today! One of the customers, she… got angry when I told her… that there… were no strawberries left!'

'Was it that Mrs. Birch? The café on High Street?' asked Katie.

'Yes.'

'Don't worry, Sandra,' said Katie, patting Sandra's hand. 'She's always like that. She comes to the shop late on purpose and always expects us to have everything – and at a reduced price!'

'She called me useless! I was so busy and the shop was full, and I felt so embarrassed!'

'Don't worry about it. Forget it,' said Katie, 'it's probably my fault for expecting you to cope on your own on a Friday. I probably should have got someone in to help you.'

'No, I did okay, honestly, Mrs. Patrick. I enjoyed being busy and all the market orders were picked up okay. Nobody else complained about anything – it was just her! Please don't fire me!'

'Nobody's going to fire you! Stop worrying about it. You've done great. I can see how much stock you've moved with the boxes in the back. Go home now and I'll finish off here. Bill will help me to clear up.'

'Are you sure? I don't mind staying behind.'

'No. You go home. You've done well Sandra. We'll see you tomorrow.'

Sandra now seemed reassured and put her handkerchief in her apron pocket, and said goodbye.

Katie went into the back of the farm shop and began to clear up the trays and boxes that Bill had already started to do.

'What was all that about? Is she okay?'

'Mrs. Birch, upsetting the staff – again! If I'd have been here I would have given her a basket and told her she would be quite welcome to go and pick her own!'

'She probably would have done, if she thought she could have got them cheaper. But anyway, Mrs. Birch is the least of our worries at the moment.'

'Sandra's okay. She'll be in tomorrow.' Katie stopped piling up the wooden trays and turned to Bill. 'I know we came to a decision when we had our conversation with George but I just want to make sure you're okay with what George suggested. I mean, the flat is vacant and convenient and George was so grateful for the use of it.'

Bill carried on clearing out the debris from the trays and boxes as he spoke. 'George is a clever man – and a good business partner. I am more than happy to go along with him. And he's agreed to cover any expenses. What do you think?'

'I think I like the idea. Anna is a lovely girl – very appreciative and would do anything for V. They seem to have a genuine love and respect for one another. She has a talent and loves being with the horses. Yeah, I think it would work.'

'And what do you think about her brother?' asked Bill.

'Brendan's a worker – a 'hands on' worker. He's observant and wants to do well. He just doesn't seem to know exactly *at what* he wants to do well,' said Katie.

'Driving, for one thing! And you're right about being observant. When we were driving to Appleby he posed question after question – "what's that? What does this do?"'

'There's lots of jobs around the farm that he could do. For one thing, he could be in charge of V's Caravan. Give him sole responsibility. He's learned so much in a short time, think of what he could do in the long term. And I did like the way you suggested to George that the caravan could remain on the farm as part of the campsite project – very subtle. We could overwinter it in the big barn when the holiday season ends,' said Katie.

'I think it would be an asset. V, I think, would love it to remain here with Topaz – and George agreed,' said Bill. 'The campers could have Gypsy caravan rides around the farm.'

'Would Brendan be up for that, do you think?'

'I think so, although I think he would sooner drive the Land rover!' Bill chuckled. 'But there's a lot to think about and we can't discuss anything with V. She doesn't need to have to worry about anything – not just now. George will handle all her affairs when the time comes. I have a feeling George knew his mother was ill. I bet that's why he took those two on.'

'Maybe he did. Although he was clearly upset when we told him.'

'Perhaps he didn't expect it to be so soon.'

There was a moments silence and they pondered on how they were going to get through the next few weeks and the sadness of having to lose such a dear, old friend.
Katie changed the subject. 'I hope George gets us a good horse from the fair.'

'He's the best at bartering, I trust him; he knows exactly what he's looking for – the vanning breed temperament is best for what we need for the project – the kids' riding lessons and such. And we have Amber and Diamond who will be such an attraction,' said Bill.

'Is there enough room in the horse box to bring all three horses back or is George bringing the new one?'

'There should be room but we'll see on Monday and how Amber reacts to the new one.'

'When do we tell Anna and Brendan about V and of George's suggestions?' asked Katie.

'Let's see how they get on in the next week or so. See how V is when we pick them up on Monday. We'll see how they get on and perhaps tell them when the time is right.'

'They might be wondering what they'll have to do or whatever if they have no job with V. They may want to go home!' said Katie.

'George will be here in a couple of weeks. It's up to him to tell them about V and what he wants to do. Once we know what's what, we can mention about jobs around the farm – suggesting Brendan helps out with the jobs *I* have to do and Anna helping *you* out here in the shop and the café; but mainly with the horses. We can take over their work contract from George, but if we do, we'll need to get all their paperwork to make it legal – for tax and national insurance and stuff.'

'I like the idea of general assistants! Living on the farm – help on hand,' said Katie.

'Well, there you are then! The job roles will be "General Assistants for Appleby Farm and Holiday Camp," all sorted. Brendan's first job when he gets back is to move V's caravan to the side of the "Reception" as a special attraction – for the photos. It doesn't need to be in V's special spot near the stream; not now they have the luxury of the flat.'

'Is Brendan still going to sleep in it?' asked Katie.

'I think we'll suggest he takes one of the worker's caravans – there's the empty one that our John's friends used when they came for his party. He could have that as part of his work contract and the conveniences of the campsite showers and toilets are almost completed.'

'That's perfect.' Katie went over to Bill and gave him a kiss on the cheek, 'Bill, you are so good at getting things sorted.' They carried on with the clearing up and Katie must have been thinking about the whole conversation when she continued. 'But Anna's top priority for now will be the responsibility of looking after V and also of Amber and her foal.'

'And perhaps a little training in the shop and café?'

'Mmm.'

On the Monday, Bill and Brendan managed to get all three of the horses in the box quite comfortably. The new horse, aptly named Prince, because of the marking of a white circle on his head, in contrast to his mainly black coat, was calmness itself.

George was sure he would be okay travelling with Amber and Diamond.

Katie picked up Anna and V and then dropped them off at the flat. Anna helped Mother V up the stairs and took her straight to her bedroom. 'I'll make you your favourite tea as soon as we get you into bed. Would you like me to run a bath for you? It's been such a hectic few days and you're really not supposed to be tiring yourself – we'll get told off when that doctor comes tomorrow if you don't rest.'

'I think I'll try a bath in the morning.' Mother V sat down on the bed. 'I'm feeling tired now from all the excitement. But I wouldn't have missed it for the world. It was so lovely to see all the family and the children – well, most of them anyway?'

'You have a lovely, big family.' Anna sat down on the bed beside Mother V. 'You must be so proud of them. They're all so warm and friendly, especially your granddaughters – I felt as though I had some sisters at last. When you're an only child, you always wonder what it would be like to have brothers and sisters; sisters especially – I would have loved a sister.'

'And the horses – the wonderful horses!' said Mother V, 'Amber and Diamond stood out among all the others, didn't they? And I was so glad to see Diamond dipped in the river. He'll be fine now.'

'Is it a kind of baptism for foals? Like a ritual?'

'It is to me. All the horses we've bred have all been 'dipped'.'

'It was a lovely few days. And it was great the way Amber and Diamond had so many admirers. I couldn't believe you had so many offers to buy them! And you turned down such a lot of money!'

'I would never sell any of my horses.'

'I'm glad about that.'

'I only own three; Topaz, Amber and Diamond. And I'd never sell them.'

Mother V yawned. Anna got up from the bed. 'Come on, you're tired. Let's get you into your nightdress and into bed.'

Mother V struggled slightly to get into her bed; her pain was reflected on her face as she tried to lift her left leg. Anna offered gentle help and made Mother V as comfortable as she could. 'Have you had your tablets for the pain today?'

'I need one more.'

Anna found the tablets and gave one to Mother V. 'I'll get your tea. Would you like something to eat?'

'No. I'm not hungry, thanks. I'd like my pipe though.'

'Oh no! I can't let you have that – the doctor said "no pipe!" Especially in here! I don't think Katie would like it. I did see you sneak one at Appleby,' said Anna, pointing a finger of authority, '…but while I'm looking after you, no pipe in here! I may let you have a sneaky puff tomorrow – outside! But don't tell anyone.' Anna went to the kitchen and put the kettle on to boil the water for the tea and suddenly realised that she had mentioned "being an only child". Mother V didn't seem to have picked up on it and Anna was hoping she still thought she and Brendan were brother and sister. Anna had never said they were. She hadn't lied.

Anna brought in two mugs of tea and sat down on the bed. 'This one's yours – your special brew!' she said, handing one of the mugs to Mother V.

'I thought that George's youngest girl was giving your brother the eye.' Mother V said, smiling. 'He didn't respond to her though, did he?'

'I think Brendan was having too much of a good time listening to all the men, especially George; and the way they do business – all the noisy bartering and the hand slapping agreements,' said Anna, who was glad that Brendan hadn't taken much notice of the young teenage girl who had befriended Anna and asked a lot of questions about Brendan. She had been surprised at the feeling of jealousy she experienced at the thought of Brendan being stolen from her.

'I'm glad you had a good time,' said Mother V. 'You've been such a help to me. You, Brendan and Katie and Bill have helped to make my final trip to Appleby such a happy one. I'm so grateful. George has put his foot down, so there'll be no more road trips with my caravan for me anymore. That saddens me.'

'Will you be going back home to Liverpool or living with George?'

'George will be taking me home to Liverpool. Rosa will help to sort things out.'

'That'll mean that we'll lose our jobs of looking after you. That saddens me!'

'Wouldn't you want to go home? You haven't seen your parents since Easter.'

'I've spoken to them on the phone a few times. The last time was last week when they told me they wanted me…

err… us to go back. They're thinking of moving to Australia – my Daddy's been offered a good teaching job there and they have to be prepared to go by the end of the year.'

'Do you want to go to Australia?'

'I'd sooner stay here with you, Brendan and the horses – I love it here on the farm. But I don't think that will be possible. Brendan said we should speak to Mr. and Mrs. Patrick and ask them if there are any jobs that we could do around the farm for them, just to pay our way like, for the…well…all their kindness. They've given us clothes from the charity boxes, food; and just look around…' Anna held her palms upwards and looked around the room, '…to do our job and be able to look after you in a place like this.'

'Yes,' Mother V sighed, 'they've been so good but, being here is only temporary. Speak to George when he comes to visit us. He'll be here in a couple of weeks. I'm afraid I'm in no position to be of any use to you or anyone in my state. George will sort things out.'

'Okay, we'll see what happens,' said Anna, resigning herself to fate. 'Now get some rest. I'm just going to check on the horses and then I'm off to bed. I'll see you in the morning.'

On Bill's instructions, Brendan had moved Mother V's caravan onto a grassy verge at the side of the "Reception". He had cleaned it and polished all the metalwork. It was now a bright, welcoming sight for the future campsite holidaymakers.

From the bottom of the stairs to the flat above, he shouted up to Anna, 'Come and have a look at the caravan. Tell

Mother V to look through the window and have a look. It looks great! It's all parked up now at the front! There's a photographer taking photos – come on!'

Anna was at the top of the stairs. She shushed him. 'Stop shouting,' she said, 'Mother V's sleeping.'

'Sorry.' Brendan beckoned Anna to come down. 'Let's have our photo taken with the caravan. Come on before the photographer goes,' he said, half whispering.

They both ran to the front of the building just in time. The photographer was picking up the tripod. 'Please,' asked Brendan, 'could we have a photograph in front of the caravan, please?'

The photographer, a smart, pleasant faced man in a peaked cap, obliged. 'Okay, young man, stand in a casual pose as if you're leaning on the side of the caravan. And you, young lady, can you climb up and sit on the seat?'

Brendan lifted Anna up to the seat, jokingly puffing, as if she was heavy. They posed as instructed with smiling faces.

'When will they be ready?'

'I'll let Bill know. He's going to choose the ones he wants for the brochure. Now I believe I need to take one of a horse and her foal? Where will they be?'

'I'll take you,' said Anna. 'Brendan, will you stay here till I get back, in case Mother V wakes up and needs anything? I'll be back before the doctor gets here.'

'Yeah – okay.'

Brendan was in the kitchen, when Anna arrived back at the flat. 'Tea?'

'No thanks. Has Mother V woke up yet?'

'I haven't heard her but I didn't want to go in?'

'Okay, I'll just check.' Anna crept quietly along the landing and slowly opened the door to Mother V's bedroom but heard her snoring, so closed it quietly and went back into the living room. Brendan was sat in one of the chairs with the brew in his hands. Anna sat herself down in the other chair.

'You seem so much better since you spoke to your Uncle Kevin.'

'You bet I am. It's a relief to know that there's no search party out looking for us.'

'I'm glad. I suppose we should discuss what we're going to do when George takes Mother V home.'

'Do you think we should talk to Mr. and Mrs. Patrick or wait and see what George is going to do?'

'Mother V suggests we talk to George and see what he plans to do with us. He could take us to Liverpool when he takes Mother V back home; maybe he could take us back home.'

'But what about the horses?'

'I don't know.'

Brendan was quiet for a moment. 'If you go back home, you may have to go with your parents and I don't want you to go to Australia.' There was a sadness in his voice but, as if as an afterthought, he perked up a little. 'But if you have to,' he said, 'do you think they would let me come with you?'

'We could ask him – you could live at your Uncle Kevin's till we go, couldn't you?'

'Or, I could ask at the docks about working our passage to America – me and you?'

Anna felt sick at the thought of sailing to Australia *or* America. The nauseating feeling churned in her stomach and as it rose up to her throat she made a hasty move to the bathroom.

Brendan followed her and stood outside the door. 'Are you okay?' he asked.

Anna couldn't answer, her head was over the toilet bowl and she was noisily retching and heaving as the bile was burning her throat.

Brendan opened the bathroom door. He handed Anna a towel and wet another one and gently wiped her brow. Anna sat with her back to the side of the bath and Brendan sat down beside her. 'What's brought that on?'

'All that talk about sailing to America or Australia – I don't think I want to do that.'

'So those ideas are no good.'

They held hands and sat there in silence for a couple of minutes until they heard the familiar sound of Mother V's coughing.

Doctor Unsworth apologised to Mother V for being slightly late. 'Babies,' he said, 'they arrive when they want to.' Leaving Anna and Mother V to understand that he had delivered a child that morning.

'What was it?' asked Anna.

'What – oh, a boy – a nine pounder!' said the doctor as he began the familiar ritual of digging into his deep bag and bringing out his stethoscope. 'And how are you today Mrs. Grey?' Not waiting for Mother V to reply, he began to listen to the sounds in her lungs.

Anna looked at the expression on the doctor's face to try and read what he was thinking.

'Okay,' he said, wrapping up his stethoscope and returning it to the bag. 'How is your mobility – still painful to walk?'

'A lot better with those tablets,' said Mother V.

'Good,' he said, smiling, 'I'll be off now and I'll see you next Tuesday at the same time – that is unless another baby decides to mess up my appointments.'

Anna walked down the stairs with the doctor, 'Will she need some more tablets – there's not many left,' said Anna.

'I've left some tablets and medicine with Mrs. Patrick. She said she would be calling round to see you later today. You're looking after our patient very well, young lady. Is there anything you need to ask me?'

'There is, but not about Mother V. It's for me.'

'There doesn't look very much wrong with you. What is it?'

Anna explained that she had missed two periods and was feeling sick in the mornings.

'And have you had sexual intercourse?' he asked rather abruptly. 'How old are you?'

Anna was quite taken aback at his sharp tone. 'Sixteen.'

'And have you?' he asked, shaking his head and tutting.

'Well I…' Anna couldn't bring herself to explain to him what had happened that night at the party and hung her head as her eyes began to fill with shameful tears.

'I see,' he said, his tone of voice was a little less harsh. 'It's more than likely to be a pregnancy. I suggest you talk to your mother. And I suggest you talk to this boyfriend of yours. Come and see me at the clinic.' He gave Anna a leaflet. 'Mrs. Patrick will tell you where it is and book you in. Okay?

'Okay,' said Anna, quietly.

'Good bye.'

* * *

'The wee girl's in trouble – Maggie you can't not read the next chapter to me now, or I'll not sleep tonight!'

Maggie laughs. 'Okay. One more chapter.'

CHAPTER FIFTEEN

A HAPPY AUTHOR

At Peter's insistence, Maggie gets herself ready to read another chapter of her book. As an author, she is secretly overjoyed that he wants her to keep turning the pages. She is not quite sure that the fictional life she shares with him within the pages, as her protagonist Brendan, is a life he would have loved to live in reality. What she is sure of now, however, is the love they share for one another – she is so happy that Peter has, at last, returned to her for good.

She reads.

* * *

Chapter 15 – George's Visit

Anna kept the leaflet the doctor gave her in her own personal box, where she kept her keepsakes, including the outgrown, satin dress. She had read it over and over *"How to look after yourself during pregnancy."* She began to hate the word *"pregnancy"*. She hated the way she felt every morning. She hated the thought of having to tell anyone – especially Brendan. So she didn't. She didn't make any appointment at the clinic and avoided the doctor on his following visit to Mother V and hoped to God that he hadn't mentioned to her anything about her predicament – or to Mrs. P. She wanted the whole thing to go away! She wanted Mother V to feel better but she seemed to be worse. She felt she was failing in her job looking after her. She wanted to go home to her Mother – but couldn't; it would cause her too much shame. She wanted to confide in Brendan – but couldn't; she was scared of what he would say, or think – or do. She wanted to go to church – but felt that she was too sinful. She desperately needed to talk to someone and decided the only person who would probably understand and not judge her would be Mother V. But Mother V was too ill to be burdened with her problems. No. She would tell Brendan – he was her best friend – if only she could pluck up the courage.

Bill and Brendan were boxing up the vegetable orders for the market traders when George arrived at the farm in his new Land Rover. Brendan was in his element looking over the vehicle and was now understanding the rivalry between Bill and George as to who had the best and most modern vehicles. 'One day I hope to have one of these – a better one than both of you,' he said.

'I hope you do, lad,' said Bill, 'I hope you do.'

George smiled at Brendan, acknowledging his wild dream. 'Will you go and get Anna and bring her to the farmhouse. We need to have a meeting. All of us.'

'Okay,' said Brendan. *This is it – he doesn't need us anymore.*

Brendan usually ran all the way to the flat but on this occasion, he didn't feel like running. He was in no hurry to be told they had come to the end of the road with working for George. He and Anna had not come to any decision as to what they were going to do. Australia and America were out of the question. Anna wouldn't contemplate the sailing. Their only options were to go into the cities of Manchester and Liverpool and see what work there was available but without any guarantee of a roof over their heads he didn't want Anna subjected to that. He hoped that perhaps Mr. and Mrs. Patrick could offer them some jobs on the farm. The final option would be to go home to family but with no jobs and no prospects. He didn't want to do that.

Brendan's long legs took two steps at a time up to flat and he went into the living room. 'Anna,' he said quietly, in case Mother V was asleep. She was sleeping so much lately. 'George wants us back at the farmhouse for a meeting.'

'Oh no. So, is this it then?' said Anna.

'I thinks so,' he said, 'be prepared and let's go and get it over with. Is Mother V asleep? Will she be okay?'

'Mother V is not asleep, Brendan!' The voice came from the bedroom. 'And yes, I will be okay. Just leave me some water.'

Anna already had a glass of water in her hand to take to Mother V.

They walked quickly back to the farmhouse. Anna tried to seem interested as she listened to Brendan relating the news and details of George's new Land Rover but felt her head was about to explode if she didn't share her problem with someone soon.

'I told them, I was going to own one like it – one day.'

'I'm sure you will,' said Anna, taking hold of his hand. It felt comforting as they walked the rest of the way to the farmhouse.

Mrs. Patrick met Brendan and Anna at the door. 'Come in. Go through, we're all here now. Is V okay?'

'She said she would be okay,' said Anna. She's reading those magazines you sent.'

'Okay.'

Bill and George were sat at the large dining table which was strewn with paperwork and coffee cups.

'Sit yourselves down,' said Bill, 'we've a lot to discuss. Go on George.'

George directed his conversation towards Brendan and Anna and Anna's stomach churned with nervous tension.

'Well first, I want to thank you two for looking after my mother so well. But the sad news is that she isn't going to get better.'

'Oh no! Is she going to die?' asked Brendan.

'There's no cure for her illness,' said George, 'and she is very old. She knows and she is....' George was obviously very upset. 'Well, anyway, let's get on with the meeting.'

Anna couldn't speak, she already had her suspicions but to hear it confirmed was something of a shock to her system. She felt emotional but did her best to contain it.

Mrs. Patrick took hold of Anna's hand. 'I know how upsetting this news is for you.'

George continued. 'I, and of course, Mr. and Mrs. Patrick are the directors of this caravan campsite project. So, this is what I've...' he gestured to Bill and Katie '...we've thought.' He sighed. 'I took you on as casual workers but Mr. and Mrs. Patrick will take you both on as permanent employees as...' He turned to Bill, '...what did you say they were?'

'General Assistants of Appletree Farm and Caravan Holiday Camp,' said Bill. 'You'll be paid the going rate for the position and we'll provide the on-site accommodation – that will be one of the static caravans we will be installing on the site.' He held up a plan of the site and pointed to where the caravan would be. 'Here, near the Campsite Manager's flat.'

Anna and Brendan looked at one another. Anna saw the glee in Brendan's eyes – not believing their luck. A solution to all their problems – but Anna knew it wasn't!

'Thank you so much!' said Brendan. 'That's great! What exactly will we be responsible for?'

'Assisting the manager in the running and maintenance of the holiday campsite; the planning of activities and looking after the holidaymakers. You will help in sorting any problems they have and generally making sure they have a good time,' said Bill. 'Oh, and looking after V's caravan. V's horses and caravan are going to be part of the project.'

'Until the campsite actually opens, next Easter, you'll be kept informed of the progress of the project and please contribute any ideas you feel would be useful,' said Katie, 'but for now your duties will be to help out around the farm in general – the horses mainly – we have quite a lot now. And, unlike the project manager, your position will be all year round and not just for the holiday season. So, when the holiday season ends, you'll be required to work around the farm, like you're doing now, and still look after the horses.'

'It's quite a lot of work,' said Bill, 'Are you up to it?'

'I'll say – thank you!' said Brendan, looking at Anna. 'We don't mind hard work, do we Anna?' Anna did her best to put on an enthusiastic smile.

'We'll need your birth certificates and your national insurance numbers to get the employment contract papers sorted, so, let us have them as soon as possible?' asked Bill.

'Err…yes,' said Brendan.

'There is one other thing. And I think you'll like this Brendan. We propose to make the farm shop into a campsite shop. There will still be an outlet for locals who come for their vegetables and eggs and stuff but the main orders from the market traders and shops are going to be delivered to them instead of them collecting.'

'Oh, right,' said Brendan, 'a good idea, yes.'

'And that would mean a van and a driver. How old are you now Brendan?'

'Seventeen.'

'So, you can start your driving lessons next week!'

'Driving lessons! Oh be Jasus! Did you hear that Anna? Driving lessons!'

They all smiled at his reaction. Anna was so pleased for him – it was the best thing they could do for Brendan. 'That'll be so good for you,' she said.

'And you Anna,' said George, 'my mother has given you Diamond! He's yours on one condition that he remains on this farm. She says she's sure you'll look after him. And don't worry about the cost, as the project will cover all the expenses for all the horses.'

'My own horse – Diamond?' Anna began to cry – she couldn't contain her emotion. 'Aww. Thank you.' She wiped away the tears with her fingers. 'And is Mother V going back home?'

'Yes, I've spoken to the doctor and he says she'll be okay to travel. Rosa has got her room ready and she'll look after her. We'll be leaving in a couple of days.'

'Well, I think we've covered everything now,' said Katie. It was obvious that she was upset about Mother V and was struggling to hide her feelings. She coughed. 'Have you got any questions?'

Brendan asked, 'Have you got a note book I could use please?'

'A notebook?' Katie showed a puzzled expression.

'Yes please. To write down all my ideas and I have one now!'

'What is it?' asked Anna.

'Well, although I'm really sorry that Mother V is having to go home; I'm so pleased about the driving lessons that I feel like dancing! And an idea came to me that we could have a weekly Barn Dance for the campers.'

They were all amused.

* * *

‘So, she still hasn’t told anyone about her pregnancy!’

‘Not yet – that wasn’t the right time, was it?

‘No. It would have ruined Brendan’s day but I suppose I’ll have to wait till tomorrow to find out what happens?’

‘Yes.’ Maggie puts down the book on the coffee table.

‘Let’s have a little walk – a bit of exercise will do us good. It’s a lovely evening and we’ve done enough reading today. I’ll make a bit of supper when we get back.

‘Okay. Whatever you say Maggie.’

CHAPTER SIXTEEN

NOSTALGIA

'I think I did a bit too much walking last night. My legs have seized up!' says Peter. He sits down on the sofa next to Maggie and rubs his knees.

'We did! – but *you* would insist on revisiting the old haunts of your youth.'

'It was nice to see them again. Brought back some lovely memories it did! When we worked at Mallicks racing stables – remember?' asks Peter.

'How can I forget? When we used to ride them to the gallops next to The Curragh Racecourse, then we groomed them. Three horses each, we looked after!'

'And mucked out their stalls,' added Peter.

'And how they loved their evening meal of oats, bran and treacle. We were happy and we got paid – half a crown.'

'Two and six was good,' said Peter. Plus the money I earned running errands and helping out in the fields digging potatoes and whatever. I used to badger my Aunt, God bless her soul, to put it on a bet – I never lost! I even remember the name of the horse when I won my first bet.'

'What was it?'

'Donnelly's Hollow.'

'That's a place just south of Newbridge isn't it?'

'Yes. Where Dan Donnelly fought George Cooper to win the hand of the woman they both loved. A sad story – a long time ago. I always remember the date from our history lesson – it was December 13th 1815.'

'It was! Yes. A bit of local history I remember from school. It's supposed to be lucky if you walk up the steps that Donnelly made – up from the hollow. Somewhere else we could go sometime.'

They are both quiet for a few moments reflecting on their individual memories of the happy times of their youth until Peter breaks the silence. 'I can see Tomkins now, on his Daddy's pony. Do you remember?'

Maggie laughed. 'The one that stopped at every pub wherever he was going.'

'And he had to get off it and then on again before it would move.' Peter laughed. 'That horse was called Tim – I remember him well – a grey, and he was fourteen hands high.'

'We spent such a lot of time up at the Curragh with the horses didn't we? I remember my Mammy saying I was wasted working there. She said I was too bright to be a stable hand and I was too tall to be a jockey. And my Daddy had such high hopes for me. But I'd have thought it would have been something you would have perhaps taken up as a job. Why did you choose the sea?'

'If I'd stayed, probably I'd have found a job there, but at the time I felt I needed to get as far away as I could. The sea offered me that space I dreamed of – that freedom.'

'But why didn't you come home when your Daddy died?'

'I was fifty four – I didn't have as much money then – too young to retire and too old to find work at another job. I'd have been too old to have found work with the horses – I still love them; but you already know that!'

'We're only a stone's throw away; we should go to the next race meeting – if you like!' says Maggie.

'We will. But for now, can we hear some more of your story?'

'Okay.' Maggie has the book in her hand. She adjusts her glasses and reads.

* * *

Chapter 16 – The Confession

Brendan couldn't stop dancing all the way back to the flat. He was trying to spin Anna around with him. 'I can't believe we've got these jobs! They're perfect for us! Yippee! I'm going to be a driver!' he said, punching the air and jumping around. 'I don't know why you don't seem as excited as me. You won't have to go to Australia! You can tell your dad what a great job you've got and that it will be okay for them to leave you here.'

Anna was doing her best to try to be enthusiastic – she was really happy with the prospect of carrying out the work required of her. She really was very grateful for the opportunity and very much wanted to do well – but. And there was this enormous *but* that stood between being depressed and being ecstatic! 'I don't think I believe it yet – it's not sunk in,' she said, making excuses for not showing the same level of elation as Brendan.

'Let's go and tell Mother V. This good news will cheer her up!'

'I doubt anything will cheer up someone who's dying. I don't know how to talk to her now. What do you say?'

'Well, you say a big "*thank you*" for one thing. She's given you Diamond!'

'I'll cry.'

'So what – I'll probably cry too. She'll be going home with George in the next few days, so let's make them happy for her. Let's tell her and let her know how happy we are.'

'Okay,' said Anna. She agreed with Brendan that they should make her last days with them happy and comfortable. Telling her their news which she probably knew anyway. George must have discussed with her what their plans were for her horses and the caravan. The campsite project was such a brilliant idea; such an opportunity, giving them both perfect jobs and with living accommodation. That was another problem. When they have to give them their birth certificates it will reveal they are not brother and sister, making it doubtful that they would be allowed to share it.

'How will you get the papers that Mr. Patrick wants for our national insurance stuff?' asked Anna. 'I can phone and get Mammy to post mine.' She knew full well that she wouldn't do that. She was going home soon; there would be no job prospects for her.

'I know, I've been thinking about that. I've an idea where they might be. I think my Aunt Peggy would be able to get them for me but she has no phone.'

'Send her a letter.'

'Yeah – I'll write to her.'

'And you know they'll realise that we're not brother and sister, once they have the papers. I doubt they will let us share that caravan.'

Anna could see the worried look that came across Brendan's face.

'Oh I see. But I'm sure they would get around that,' he said, seemingly refusing to acknowledge any possible problem that would prevent him from being able to enjoy the fact that he had secured the fantastic job offer. 'I could sleep in Mother V's caravan, like I do now, if that would be okay with them. Stop thinking about things like that to spoil the plan. Come on, I'll race you to the flat!' He set off at high speed.

Anna, sighed and didn't want to run. She was tired from the lack of sleep and felt exhausted with the stress of facing up to the reality of being pregnant. Everything was all going to be ruined when she told them. She still couldn't find the courage to tell Brendan – not when he was so elated. She didn't want to ruin his happiness. I'll tell him tomorrow. Oh God!

Anna hardly slept, her head was full of different thoughts and scenarios. She got up early and went about her chores in robotic fashion. Mother V had slept soundly all night and then again after she had eaten the breakfast Anna had made for her.

At the forefront of Anna's mind was how she would tell Brendan. His enthusiasm and elation the previous evening, had definitely cheered up Mother V who had laughed at his sheer animated excitement when he related to her the job offers and events of the meeting. Mother V had said that she knew what the meeting was going to be about and said she knew that both of us would be pleased. Anna had cried when she told her how grateful she was for the gift of Diamond. She promised Mother V that she would take good care of him. At the back of her mind was the sad fact that she may not be able to but didn't want to upset Mother V by telling her that she may have to return home to have the baby she was carrying. She would have to leave the care of Diamond to Brendan, who didn't know much about taking care of horses. She realized she would have to talk to Mrs. Patrick and ask a favour. *Oh what a mess!*

Anna was so pleased Brendan had this opportunity for work with what he called 'prospects', especially the driving lessons. It would break her heart to have to leave him and give up the job offer, but realised that her only option was to go home and face the music – and wrath of her parents. There would be no way she could work and look after a baby; she would need her mother to show her how! And what would her lovely father think of her. The shame she had brought to her parents would be enough for them to disown her. Scaring herself even more, she distressed herself by imagining that maybe they would send her to one of those places for unmarried mothers where the Nuns worked and took the babies for adoption. Tears began to flow once more at the thought. She let them fall freely into the water in the sink as she washed up the breakfast dishes.

'You look a bit tired, Anna. Are you okay?' asked Mother V, as Anna helped her to get washed and dressed.

'I'm okay, just a bit tired.'

'All the excitement of yesterday. I expect,' said Mother V.

'Yes. Do you want to sit in the living room? It'll be a change if you feel up to it. You've been in bed a lot lately.'

'Yes. I will. I feel a lot better than I did yesterday. In fact I'd like to go up to the farmhouse to see Katie.'

'It's a long walk!'

'Ring George on that telephone and ask if he'll come for me.'

Anna dialled the extension number and Katie answered. 'Hello. Is everything alright?'

'Yes. Everything's fine. Mother V said she feels a lot better today and she would like George to come and pick her up and take her back to the farmhouse. She wants to see you.'

'Well, I was going to come to the flat later, after tea, but it will be a change for V to come here. Right, I'll come and get her myself. George and Bill are busy going over some of the plans, so better not to interrupt. See you in a few minutes.'

'Okay,' said Anna and put down the phone. Mrs. Patrick is coming for you in a few minutes. She says George is busy going over some plans with Bill and she didn't want to interrupt.'

'I hope I'm not interrupting what Katie was doing.'

'I doubt she would mind. She said it will be a change for you to go there instead of her coming to see you here. It's just having to go up and down the stairs that's a bit of a problem for you.'

'I need a bit of exercise.'

Katie arrived and brought Brendan with her. He was carrying a bowl.

'What have you got there?' asked Anna.

'Tomato soup and some bread,' he said. 'It smells lovely.' He took the bowl into the kitchen. 'I'll set the table.'

'We'll have *our* lunch up at the farm,' said Katie to V. 'Are you ready?'

'Yes, thank you. I hope you don't mind me asking to come over. I just felt that I… '

'No – not at all. A change will do you good. We can have a nice chat over our lunch.'

'Good.'

'Come on then. Let's get you in the car.'

Brendan, as usual finished off the second bowl of soup and the last slice of bread. 'That was lovely,' he said, leaning back into the chair. 'You didn't eat much. Are you okay?'

This was her chance to tell him. Her nerves made her feel sick but she had to confess. 'I'm not okay, Brendan.'

Brendan sat up straight, concern in his expression. 'What's the matter with you?'

Anna took in a long breath and exhaled before speaking. 'I'm pregnant!' She was shaking all over. 'I'm about three months pregnant.'

'WHAT?'

'I'm so sorry Brendan.' Anna burst into tears. 'I'm sorry.'

'Hold on a minute.' Brendan got up from his chair and gripped the back of it. He practically choked on his words. 'How can you be pregnant? I mean, you… you haven't done it! I mean, who have you done it with? WHEN!'

'At the party. When you were watching the television.' Anna got up from her chair and went over to Brendan and wanted to hold his hand.

Brendan snatched it away. 'Oh no, Anna, no, no, no! That Tim? Please tell me you haven't.'

'I'm scared Brendan. I don't know what to do.'

'Well, you certainly knew what to do when you did it – didn't you!'

'I don't want you to hate me. I really need a friend right now.'

'Well, Tim's the friend you really need right now. NOT ME!'

'I don't want to see that boy ever again. I love *you* Brendan. I'll always love you. I'm sorry.' She went to hold his hand again. This time Brendan held her hand and pulled her close to him. They both wept and sobbed.

'I always thought we would get married someday, when we were old enough and could afford to,' said Brendan.

'I know. Me too.'

'I would have asked your Daddy's permission and done everything right.'

'I know.'

'Your parents would have expected me to respect you in that way, like I have done. Not... not...' Brendan broke away from their embrace. 'Why Anna? Why did you?'

Anna led Brendan into the living room and they sat side by side on the sofa as, amid tears and anger, she related the events of that nightmare she experienced. Touching Brendan's hands as they became fists, knowing how angry he must be and unable to vent his feelings.

'I think both of us were in some kind of daze. I know I was.'

'I bet it was those blasted mushrooms you ate. You both ate them.' Brendan's fists began to loosen. 'Are you going to let him know?'

'Oh no. I'm too ashamed and I don't want to cause trouble?'

'But don't you think he should know?'

'I don't want anyone to know.' Anna's tears began to flow again, she couldn't stop them. She used her sleeve to wipe them away – I'm going to keep it a secret and deal with it on my own,' she sniffed. 'I'll go home and you stay and enjoy this job – I'll speak to Mrs. Patrick about looking after Diamond.'

Brendan put a comforting arm around her shoulders and Anna felt loved and allowed to cry as much as she needed.

Brendan spent those few minutes that Anna was in his arms thinking about what they could do. She had fallen asleep but he felt her sobs. He didn't want Anna to go home. He didn't want to lose her but – a baby! Someone else's baby! What could he do? He now realised that the deed was done, not because she loved someone else, but because of the result of the stupidity of some crazy girls' mischievousness. They'll never know how much misery they've caused. His lovely Anna's life – and his, was now in ruins. And just when all was going so well.

When Anna woke up, she found herself on the sofa with a blanket over her. Brendan must have gone back to work. She looked at the clock and saw that she had slept for a couple of hours. She went to the bathroom and washed her tear stained face in cold water to refresh herself. There was enough time to clean up the kitchen, wash the dishes and prepare something for dinner before checking on the horses.

Now that she had confessed her problem to Brendan and they, at least, seemed to still remain friends, she thought that the time was right for her to speak to Mrs. Patrick about caring for Diamond and to ask George if he could give her a lift home when he was returning to Ireland after taking Mother V home.

Anna found Mrs. Patrick in the cafe talking to George. They were planning some sort of extension and rearrangement.

'I'm sorry to interrupt Mrs. Patrick but could I have a word with you please,' she asked.

'Course. What is it?' said Mrs. Patrick and she left George studying the paper plan. 'You look very serious Anna. Sit down. What is it?'

Anna sat down at one of the small café tables and Mrs. Patrick sat opposite. She found it difficult to begin. 'I…I need to ask a big favour.' She paused and took a deep breath. 'I need you to look after Diamond for me.'

'I don't understand, Anna. Diamond is yours and you're here and able to look after him yourself. Why are you asking me that?'

'Because I have to go home.' Anna had finally blurted out the difficult bit.

George was in earshot and couldn't help overhearing the conversation and came over to the table.

'What do you mean you're going home?' said George. 'I thought you were excited about the job offer.'

'Oh I am. I am. And I'm so very grateful to Mother V for giving Diamond to me too but... I have to go home because I'm pregnant.'

'Pregnant! Oh Anna. This changes everything. Who?' asked Mrs. Patrick? 'Oh no... I see. Brendan's not your brother is he?'

'No. He's a good friend; my best friend really, and we've been together all through school.'

George slammed his fist on the table and walked out.

'Where's George going? I wanted to ask if he would give me a lift back home.'

'I don't know where he's gone,' said Mrs. Patrick. 'I'm so sorry this has happened to you. I'm sure Bill will be disappointed.'

'I'm so sorry too, Mrs. Patrick, after everything you've done for us. I would have loved to be here and take the job – there's nothing I would like better but...' Anna broke down in tears. 'Even my parents might disown me when I get back home. I don't know what else to do.'

'A cup of tea,' said Mrs. Patrick 'for situations like this.'

George found Brendan stacking the vegetable boxes in the back of the farm shop. 'I've a good mind to...,' George raised his fist at Brendan. 'GET OUT! GET OUT NOW!'

'What?' said Brendan, 'Why? What's going on?'

'I want you off this property in the next five minutes or you won't see the light of day lad! I hate deceit and I hate being lied to!' Knocking over a couple of boxes, George made an aggressive move nearer to Brendan,

'Hang on a minute,' said Brendan, holding up his hands to show he didn't want to fight, 'explain what you mean for God's sake!'

'Lying! You little lying bastard! Taking advantage of that young girl. I won't have it! GO!'

Brendan kicked the box at his feet, picked up his sweater and left. He worked it out, what he was being accused of. Would Anna have said he was the father? Maybe she couldn't bring herself to tell them about the party. But to put the blame on him...how could she? Maybe somehow George had jumped to that conclusion! It was no use arguing with him, the state he was in there was no talking to him. Surely Anna would never have accused him of being the father of her baby – she would never lie!

He was so upset that George; one of the people in the world that he had so much respect for, would think so badly of him. His world had turned upside down in a day. He cried angry tears all the way to the caravan to pick up his stuff and left the farm. Once again, he was alone, no job, no money, and this time, no Anna.

George and Bill came into the café. Anna was alone. 'Mrs. Patrick's gone to see if Mother V is okay, she's watching the television,' said Anna, 'she'll be back in a minute.'

'Well, he's gone!' said George, anger still in his voice. 'We're not having that sort working for us!

'Who's gone?' asked Anna.

'Who's gone where?' asked Katie, overhearing the conversation as she walked in.

'That so called lying brother of hers – who's not a brother! I hate deceit!'

'What do you mean?' said Anna. 'If you mean Brendan – he's not deceitful! He's not a liar either! Where's he gone?'

'I don't know! I don't care and he *is* a liar! He lied about being your brother!'

'He didn't!' said Anna. 'He never told you we were brother and sister. It was you who jumped to conclusions! We never deceived you. We just never put you right. That's not lying!'

'Well, we're not having all this happening under our roof!' said Bill, 'getting young girls pregnant! I'm not having it!'

Anna stood up – she felt like screaming. 'See – YOU'RE ALL JUMPING TO CONCLUSIONS. Brendan is not the father of this baby! He would never....' She couldn't stop the tears.

'Sit down Anna,' said Katie. 'Calm down and tell us what's going on.'

'Brendan is *not* the father. I only wish he was! He has too much respect for me and my parents to ever touch me like that. You go and ask Mother V how respectful he is – she'll tell you.' Anna sat down and put her head in her hands for a moment and then calmly lifted her head. Brendan told me that he wanted to marry me when we were old enough and were in a position to. But this baby has ruined that for us now. And you've no idea what he's gone through. George, you always seem to jump to conclusions. Remember, when you assumed I had a blister on my foot, when I asked you for a first aid kit, on our way over – remember?'

'Yes, I do,' said George. Bill and George sat down at another table and listened to what Anna was saying. George started to rub his forehead.

'It was to bathe the deep gashes on Brendan's back that his dad had caused by beating him with the buckle end of his belt.'

'Oh my God!' said Katie, putting her hand to her mouth.

'Brendan's the kindest, gentlest person you could meet. I love him dearly and I've ruined everything for him now. The chance of the job you offered him was the best thing you could ever have done for him. He was so grateful. He would have been so loyal. He admired you George and you Bill, both of you so much. He wanted to be like you. Please don't let me be the cause of him losing this opportunity. He's not to blame for any of this!'

'Where do you think he'll have gone?' asked Bill.

'He'll be making his way to Liverpool. Before we came here, he spoke of looking for a ship that he could work his passage to America. I'll probably never see him again.' Anna sighed.

'So, if it isn't Brendan, who's the father?' asked Katie.

Anna was reluctant at first to tell them. She had meant to keep her nightmare and shame a secret, but now her world was upside down she thought the truth should be told. She related the whole of the horrible event that happened at the party finishing with, 'But I don't want anyone to know or to get anyone into trouble.' She noticed the glances between George and Mr. and Mrs. Patrick.

'You're the one that's got into trouble, lass,' said Bill, getting up from his chair, 'but don't you worry.' He patted Anna on her shoulder. 'We'll find Brendan and bring him home. Come on George. We'll go in my car, it's faster!'

* * *

'Oh no. Brendan's on the run again! Does he go to America?' asks Peter.

'I'm not telling – you're going to have to wait and see.'

'America's great and there's so many lovely places in the world to see, but Ireland for me is the greatest – it's where you are Maggie – its home.' He gives her a kiss on the cheek.

'And I'm glad you're here with me Pete.' Maggie pats his hand.

'Have you done much travelling in your life, Maggie?'

'France, Belgium, England and Scotland. Benidorm a couple of times with Brenda – that was fun! And that's about it really.'

'But you went to college like your Daddy wanted you to?'

'Yes. He was pleased when I eventually got my teaching qualification – I loved my job. Following in his footsteps I suppose.' Maggie looks at her watch. 'Hey, look at the time,' she says, 'we're going to be late!'

CHAPTER SEVENTEEN

REPAIRS TO THE COTTAGE

Maggie and Peter walk back home from the cottage after having shown the property repairer around and discussed what work needs to be done.

'He seems a decent sort of chap,' says Maggie.

'He seems to know what he's talking about.'

'Are you going to get any more estimates?'

'Let's see what his estimate is first. There's a lot more work than I thought.'

'Terry said he wasn't cheap but he said he always does a good job.'

'Well, that's what we want – a good job doing – no slap dash work. And he said he'd cover up the furniture we are keeping and get rid of the other stuff for us.'

'That's good. Are you doing some more work on the furniture tomorrow?'

'Yes, unless you have other plans.'

'Nothing planned but I might nip up to Brenda's for a coffee and a chat.'

They arrive home and, as usual, Maggie goes into the kitchen to make some lunch. 'Sandwiches and a bit of salad alright?' she asks.

'Lovely,' says Peter.

'We'll have something special for dinner.'

'There may be some food mentioned in the next chapter of your book. Are you going to read some more this afternoon?'

'Yes, my love. Go and get yourself comfy in the lounge and I'll bring our lunch in a few minutes.'

'Okay.' Peter obeys orders and takes his usual place. A few minutes later, Maggie brings in the familiar tray, laden with two mugs of tea, a plate of ham sandwiches and a couple of packets of crisps.

When lunch is eaten, Maggie reads the next chapter of her book to Peter.

* * *

Chapter 17 – The Search for Brendan

'He can't have got far,' said George.

'He'll have gone to the main road to try and hitch a lift,' said Bill, 'keep your eyes open – no one may have stopped for him yet.'

'Well, you can't miss his red hair. And he had a brown jumper with him when I… when I saw him last.'

They scrutinized the roadside ahead, trying to catch a glimpse of Brendan.

'There's a black Austin A40 stopped up there.'

'Can you see him?'

'No. Pull up in front of it.'

Bill drove past the car and as he pulled over, through the wing mirror, they saw Brendan disappearing into the back seat. The car then pulled out and overtook them.

'Damnation! Just missed him,' said George, pointing straight ahead. 'We'll have to follow them.'

Bill had to wait for a few cars to pass him before he could pull out. 'Keep your eye on the car.'

'I've got it,' said George, 'Just keep going. Try and get a bit nearer if you can. If we can get behind him we might be able to see Brendan in the back seat and get him to stop.'

'He might think you're still wanting to punch him. I doubt if he'll want to stop. We can't explain anything to him until we actually get hold of him.'

'I wouldn't have punched him. Although I was mad.'

'Well, if I was a seventeen year old lad, and you came at me looking mad, I would run and keep on running!' said Bill. 'And you do tend to jump to conclusions – I've noticed that.'

'Okay, okay. Don't say anything else. I feel bad enough, alright?' said George. 'So, what you're saying is, that we just follow him until he gets out of the car?'

'Yes. And then let *me* speak to him and explain. I just hope his lift doesn't get him into the city. We could lose sight of him then.'

'Even if he gets to the docks, I can't see how he can get a job without some sort of reference. And he's no money!'

'He might think of being a stowaway. If he feels desperate enough.'

'Right. Okay. Well, get your foot down then, let's not lose him. That's a Somerset, we're following.'

'It's a Devon!'

'How much?'

'A quid!'

'You're on.'

Bill followed the fast moving Austin to a fork in the road in a place named Clayton-le-Woods. The car had stopped and Bill pulled over a few yards behind. Bill got out of the car quickly as he thought Brendan might run off if he saw them before he could catch him and had a chance to talk to him.

Brendan had obviously not been aware of anyone following him. He got out of the car and thanked the driver for the lift, and waved as the Austin drove off. Bill was directly behind him.

'What the…?'

'Everything's okay Brendan,' said Bill. He put an arm around Brendan's shoulder. 'Don't run off. We're here to take you home.'

'We?'

'George is in the car and… well… there's been such a big misunderstanding. I'm sorry lad.'

'It wasn't me Bill, I…'

'I know, Brendan. We know all about it.'

'Is Anna okay?'

'Yes. Come on lad. Get in the car. We'll take you home.'

Brendan's nervous and emotional state was obvious as he got into the back seat of Bill's car. Words failed him when he saw George.

George turned in the passenger seat to face Brendan. He held out his hand, 'I'm sorry Brendan, I was wrong. I'm sorry.'

Brendon took his handshake and involuntary tears welled in his eyes. He gave a big sigh.

'Tell me, Brendan. What was the make of that man's car?' asked Bill, trying to ease the tension.

'An Austin Somerset.'

'Blast.' Bill searched his pockets and brought out a pound note and passed it over to George.'

'Thank you!'

Brendan, understanding that they had had a bet on the model asked, 'What did *you* think it was, Mr. Patrick,' he asked.

'A Devon.'

Brendan chuckled. 'The man was telling me the Somerset was faster than the Devon. That it had a 42 horse power and a top speed of seventy.'

Bill and George glanced at one another. They had got Brendan back as promised.

* * *

'Another chapter, asks Maggie.

'Yes, please.'

PETER'S FAVOURITE MEAL

'I'll just read this next chapter,' says Maggie, 'then we'll prepare dinner.'

'What are we having?'

'Colcannon with bacon.'

'Oh yes! My favourite. With soda bread?'

'Of course. Mammy's recipe.'

'Mmm.' Peter licks his lips.

Maggie reads.

* * *

Chapter 18 – Anna and Brendan Re-united.

Brendan was dropped off at the caravan. George had got out of the car with him and once again shook his hand and apologised for what had previously transpired.

'Can we forget about it?' asked George.

'Yes,' said Brendan who was feeling so relieved knowing that George was still his friend.

'I'll see you tomorrow.'

George got back into the car. Bill waved and then drove off towards the farmhouse.

Brendan put all his stuff back in the caravan then made his way to the flat to see Anna. How could he have ever doubted her?

Anna was settling Mother V into bed when she heard Brendan's familiar footsteps coming up the stairs. She came out of the bedroom and onto the landing to greet him. 'Oh, Brendan, I'm so glad you're home.' She threw her arms around him and kissed his cheek. 'I'm sorry they thought…'

Brendan held her to him longer than usual. He kissed the top of her head. When he held her, she seemed different – more mature somehow. He no longer saw her as the sweet, innocent girl; that girl had now gone forever. He now held in his arms a lovely, desirable, young woman, and he loved her all the more. He was so glad to be back. He hadn't lost her. He vowed to himself that he would never, ever lose her again.

'Come in here, Brendan,' Mother V shouted, 'come and talk to me.'

'You go in,' said Anna. 'I'll go and make us some tea and toast. How many slices?'

'The whole loaf, please, I'm starving.'

Anna smiled.

Anna and Brendan sat on either side of Mother V's bed, eating their supper of thick, sliced, toasted bread, with melting, yellow butter and comforting mugs of tea. Anna had brought in a tea towel to wipe their hands on in case the butter dripped.

There was a lot to talk about. Mother V listened as Anna recounted the events in the café and how the misunderstandings had been corrected. 'I told them,' she said, 'somehow they got it all wrong about you Brendan. They don't realise how dedicated you are. I should have told them that you had half-filled the notebook with ideas already.'

'Did you tell them about the party?' asked Brendan.

'I think I blurted out everything – I was in such a state of anger, panic and worry!'

Mother V patted Anna's hand. 'It's all out in the open now, so stop worrying. What you've got to do now is decide what you want to do. The future. Your decisions.'

'I don't really have a choice, do I? I'll have to go home. Once you go back home with George, I won't have anywhere to live.'

'Is there any chance that Mrs. Patrick will let you stay in the flat?' asked Mother V.

'I doubt it. It's for the new campsite manager. And anyway, I'm going to need help with the baby; someone to show me what to do and what to expect.'

'What if your parents want to send you to that home for unmarried mothers?' asked Brendan.

'Then I'll just have to go – like I said, there's no other choice for me.'

'I'll do everything I can to help you Anna, you know that. I don't know much about pregnancy and stuff, or anything about babies; but it can't be all that hard to learn. Can it? Let me look after you. I don't want you to go home.'

Mother V saw the fearful dilemma in Brendan's eyes.

'I don't want to go. But I'll have to.'

'Then I'm going home with you. I'll take the blame and we'll face the music together.'

'I don't want you to do that Brendan. We won't lie to my parents. The job here, for you, is just perfect. Please don't think of giving it up for me.'

'I'll tell them that we plan to get married as soon as we're old enough and can find somewhere to live. As long as I have arms and legs to work, I'll provide for all of us.'

'Don't you think you've already got that here with your job and the caravan Bill promised you?' Mother V pointed out.

Anna and Brendan looked at one another and then back to Mother V.

'Mr. and Mrs. Patrick would never allow us to live in the caravan together. Not now.'

'She would if you were a married couple.'

'But, as much as we'd like to, we can't get married yet. We're not old enough and we've got no money!' said Brendan.

'Maybe you could ask for an advance on your wages and get married at Gretna Green. Sixteen in Scotland!'

Brendan stopped wiping his hands on the tea towel. 'Could we do that, do you think?'

Anna's eyes met Brendan's. There was no need for him to ask her if she'd want to marry him. The look between them confirmed it all. Theirs was an unofficial engagement.

'I don't know what papers you'd need but if you take your birth certificates and Bill and Katie go with you to vouch for you, I should imagine that would be sufficient,' said Mother V.

'My Aunt Peggy is going to find my birth certificate, so that should arrive here soon,' said Brendan.

'And I'll phone my Mammy, she'll send mine.'

'There you are then. No need for anyone to know anything more. Get married and work here together. A baby won't stop you from doing your job – take it with you.'

'You make it sound so easy. But what about Mrs. Patrick. Would she allow it?'

'Katie will understand. I think she'll love having a baby around the place. Just ask her.'

'Right. First thing tomorrow, we'll go and ask Mrs. P what she thinks of the idea,' said Brendan.

'I hope she agrees.' Anna sighed with a glimmer of relief. 'Mother V, you've given me hope. Thank you. We're really going to miss you when you go home.'

'The first thing I'm going to do when I get home, is to ask George to get me a television set.'

'What did you watch today?' asked Anna.

'News and some history programme. And I watched Muffin the Mule. It was supposed to be for children but I enjoyed it.'

'What was that about?' asked Brendan.

'Muffin is a mule puppet that dances about on a piano. And a lady, Annette Mills, plays the piano and sings to it… and I suppose, the children watching sing along too. It was good… happy.'

'Television's great,' said Brendan. 'I'm going to have one – one day!'

Mother V smiled at Brendan. 'I'm sure you will, Brendan, I'm sure you will.'

* * *

Peter opens his eyes. 'Brendan must love Anna to take on a child that's not even his.'

'If you love someone enough, don't you think there's nothing you wouldn't do for them?'

'Real life doesn't always present opportunities to do what you want to do, no matter how much you love someone.'

'That seems to be true in our case.'

'But we're together now, Maggie.'

'Yes.' Maggie looks at Peter's watery eyes and remembers the once vivid blueness that used to look at her. 'Right,' she says, shaking herself out of her nostalgic moment. 'I'm hungry.' She puts the book down and gets up from the sofa. 'Let's get cooking!'

Peter follows Maggie into the kitchen. 'What can I do?' he asks.

'Peel the potatoes and I'll cut up the cabbage.'

CHAPTER NINETEEN

AN ARGUMENT

'Did you sleep well?' asks Maggie.

'Not really, no.'

'It wasn't the dinner that bothered you, was it?'

'No, Maggie – that was wonderful. I haven't had a meal like that for a long time. Thank you.'

'What bothered you then?'

'It was the way you looked at me last night and your coolness. It preyed on my mind. Have I disappointed you?'

'It was when I read about the love Brendan has for Anna and I just thought... Well, I thought we had that kind of love for each other and if you must know Pete – yes, in a way, you did disappoint me and you hurt me when you didn't come home. Mammy kept saying "He'll come back sometime." But you didn't. And I'll never understand why. Not if you loved me like you said you did.'

Peter takes hold of her hand. 'It was because I loved you that I stayed away.'

'I don't understand that, Pete. You said it was because of that Daddy of yours.'

'It was to let you forget me and make a life with somebody who was better – someone your equal that your Daddy would have wanted for you.'

'But you loved me!'

'It wasn't just because of that bastard of a father I had that I kept away, it was also because I loved you very much. It wouldn't have worked out for us. Your Daddy wanted someone better educated than me for a son-in-law.'

'You were clever in such a lot of ways. You were creative and your artwork was brilliant – it impressed my Mother. My parents thought a lot of you. You know that.'

'I always thought I wasn't good enough. But I never stopped loving you, never!'

Maggie was clearly upset and angry. 'You should have come home sooner.'

'I'm sorry Maggie. Do you want me to go?'

'No. But I'm just so annoyed with you!'

'We've both had a good life and I'm here now.' Peter holds her in his arms. 'I'm here now to share everything I own with you!'

Maggie, sniffs and composes herself. 'I suppose you'd like me to read some more of my book'

'Yes, if you feel you want to. Are you okay? Are we a team?'

'We are, Pete. I'm okay. Sorry about the outburst.'

'D'ya still love me?' asks Peter as he lifts Maggie's chin and looks into her sad eyes.

Maggie sees just a glimmer of the boyish blueness in Peter's aged eyes and sighs, 'Just as much as ever. Come on, let's go into the lounge and I'll read to you.'

* * *

Chapter 19 – Katie's Plan

'What a day!' said Bill, throwing off his shoes as he was undressing to get ready for bed? 'I'm exhausted?'

'I feel emotionally drained,' said Katie, who was sat up in bed, with a book in her hand. 'All that stress those youngsters are going through. I can't help but feel responsible.'

'We're not responsible for what happened!'

Katie closed the book as Bill got into bed beside her. 'But it was me who invited them to John's party. That whole sordid, mucky business went on in our house… in our house, Bill! God knows what was in that food those girls brought. That's what upsets me! They didn't need to bring anything – there was plenty of food I made for them.'

'None of your food had that magic stuff in it! That's why. Now, never mind. Stop thinking about it. I'm just glad Anna told us that our John wasn't involved.' Bill put his arm around his wife and she snuggled into his chest.'

'I want to make it up to them; make it right.'

'We have done! Brendan's back and he's still got the job here.'

'Yes, but Anna… ' said Katie, looking up into Bill's face, '…she says she's going home and doesn't know what reaction she's going to get from her parents. They're strong

Catholics and she thinks they'll die of shame and disown her. And if they decide to send her to one of those homes… Oh I can't bear to think about it.'

'Katie, I know when you're planning something. Come on, tell me what you have in mind.'

'A wedding!'

'My God! Katie, you can't just marry people off – just like that!'

'A marriage would solve all the problems in one go!'

'How! They're too young to marry or to even contemplate getting married. I am presuming you mean Anna and Brendan.'

They both sat upright in bed to discuss the idea. 'It's not just my idea. V made some suggestions. Gretna Green, for one, they could get married there. We already know they really love one another, so I can't see a problem.'

'You can't just interfere in people's lives, Katie. That's the problem. They're just young and they'll make their own decisions and their own mistakes in life without your interference.'

'That's exactly what V said. She told me that George's daughter Rosina, read Anna's palm when they were at the fair. She said Rosina saw the baby – as clear as day, but didn't say anything about it to Anna. She just skirted around what she actually saw. The traumatic incident, she said was blurry but with "an angry aura"…'

'Oh, I know you trust V and I love her too, but I don't believe in all this… this Hocus, bloody Pocus stuff.'

'Well, V said Rosina saw a happy outcome for Anna. That's why she said nothing about it – only to V.'

'So, V has known since Appleby?'

'Yes. But, as you say, didn't say anything and didn't interfere in people's lives. She was just glad that Rosina said that there was going to be a happy outcome.'

'Okay, so what else did you two discuss,' asked Bill, putting a pillow behind his head to make himself comfortable.'

'I think, for one thing, we should ask Anna if she would like to stay here with us instead of going home. We can't lose her! V says she such a natural with the horses. She loves them! She'd be such an asset.'

'I know that. She's a lovely girl and I feel sorry that's she got herself into such a mess but…'

'She wouldn't need to tell her parents about the baby and once they knew she was married, they would have no need to feel ashamed of her. And don't forget, they're thinking of going to Australia anyway at the end of the year. And as much as they want her to go with them, she doesn't want to go. So, they wouldn't see her.'

'My God Katie, you have it all planned out for them. Are you sure about this?'

'Yes. She could tell them she wanted to stay here and wanted to keep her job. She could write to them or phone them. She could still do her job here and have the baby. After all, I did it… I worked, as you know, when I was carrying my baby. Pregnancy is not an illness.'

'Yeah, but I was there to look after you and make sure you were alright.'

'Exactly, and Brendan will be there for Anna, to look after her!'

'What about when she's had the baby and who's going to help her then? Brendan won't know what to do. I didn't know what to do and I was a lot older than he is. And don't forget, it's not *his* baby. He may not be willing to take it on.'

'Oh, I think he will. He'll do anything for Anna. And, of course, I'll be there. Between the two of us – I mean Anna and me, looking after a baby will be fun! It'll be like having a grandchild around the house! It'll be a long time before our John provides us with one.'

'Don't you think you have enough on your plate? The shop, the café, the business, the… the Farmers Wives Charity committee.'

'Yes, and with all that, Anna, as a General Assistant, would help me. She loves it here. And we already have part-time and temporary farm hands that we could call on if necessary. It would work, and I'd feel better, knowing Anna and her baby were being looked after. It would ease my conscience.'

'Were would she live? Are you thinking of moving her in here?'

'No. That's why I think a marriage would be a good idea. They could marry and live in the flat.'

'But the flat's for the new campsite manager!' Bill sat up straight, he was getting all agitated. 'Katie, you can't start changing all our plans.'

'But it won't change much of the plan. After all, when you advertised for the position, you only put, "with accommodation". You didn't say *what* accommodation, so I suggest you just swap! Let Brendan and Anna have the flat. And let the new manager have the static caravan. After all, the manager's job is only going to be seasonal but Brendan and Anna are going to be working with us on a permanent basis. And the flat would be part of their contract – rent paid out of their wages. She keeps it so clean. It would also be better for the baby.'

Bill sighed. 'Are you sure it's not just you, wanting to... you know?'

'...make amends? Yes, I do. And I would feel happier about the whole situation if I could help them.'

'You know you can't always look after all our workers.'

'I know, but these two are special. I feel it. She would be like the daughter I never had. I know it would work. And I think Brendan would be like a son.'

'I already have... I mean we, already have a son.'

'I know, but what I mean is, our John is never going to be a farmer and work with you here – he's going to be more academic and I think, after Uni, he'll work in the city. Brendan will be like a second son. He looks up to you and respects us both. Look how they always address us.'

'Okay, but don't tell them everything you have planned – just allow them to make their own decisions and make suggestions or offers *only* if they come to us with their own plans. Allow them to feel they have made their own choices.'

'I will.' Katie smiled and gave Bill a kiss. 'Thank you.'

'Can I go to sleep now, please?' Bill switched off the light.

'Perhaps this is the happy outcome Rosina saw!'

'Go to sleep Katie!'

* * *

'They're a great couple!' says Peter. 'They've taken to Anna and Brendan, like substitute parents.'

'Is that how you see them?' asks Maggie.

'Yes. But Bill's right – Katie shouldn't interfere in people's lives. But read on and let's see what happens.'

CHAPTER TWENTY

PETER IS OVERWHELMED

Maggie continues reading to Peter.

* * *

Chapter 20 – Mother V Goes Home

Anna picked up the telephone and dialled the internal line to the farmhouse. Katie answered. 'Good morning, Anna. Are you alright?'

'Yes, Mrs. P. I'm okay, thank you. I'm ringing to ask if you had a few moments to spare, so that we could have a word with you, please.'

'You and Brendan?'

'Yes. If you have time.'

'Brendan's here, working with Bill. They'll be in for a break at eleven. Do you want to come here? Eleven's okay for me. I'll be at the house.'

'Yes. Okay. I'll see you then. Will you tell Brendan?'

'Yeah. See you later.'

'Thank you. Bye.'

Anna replaced the receiver. Her stomach churned with nerves. As if in prayer, she clasped her hands together and walked up and down the living room. How shall I ask her? Will she agree? Last night it had sounded so easy to do – just ask her. Her whole immediate future depended on Katie's answer. Anna checked the time. She had half an hour to become a total nervous wreck!

Anna had left Mother V reading her magazines. She strolled towards the farmhouse in the summer sunshine. The black cloud had lifted from her mind now that everyone who needed to know her predicament, knew. She skipped a few steps feeling, lighter and somehow stronger. She decided that whatever the outcome of the conversation with Mrs. Patrick, she could face anything the future held for her, knowing Brendan would be by her side. She lifted her face towards the sun, a little prayer of thanks silently fluttered up to the heavens.

When Anna arrived at the farm, she found Mr. and Mrs. Patrick and Brendan in the farmyard. It looked as if Mr. Patrick was showing Brendan how to change a wheel on the land rover.

'Hello Anna,' asked Mrs. P. 'How are you?'

'Okay, thanks.'

'And V?'

'She's very tired. I've left her reading the magazines. I've packed everything up that she wants to take home with her, so she's ready to go when George gets here.'

'It's going to be sad to say goodbye to her this time.'

'I know.'

'Anyway, we won't dwell on that. Let's go into the kitchen. Brendan,' she called, 'have you finished?'

'Be with you in a second Mrs. P.'

The sweet aroma of apple pie was unmistakable. Anna unconsciously licked her lips. She could taste it. The kitchen table was half-covered with baking equipment, the other half was clear with three chairs around it.

'Sit yourself down. Would you like a drink?'

'No thanks, Mrs. P. I'm alright, thank you.'

'I know Brendan will be ready for something.' Mrs. Patrick put a plate of biscuits on the table and was pouring a mug of tea when Brendan came in.

'Is it okay to wash my hands, Mrs. P?' he asked, showing her the dirt.

Mrs. P nodded permission as she put the milk and sugar next to the mug.

Anna was feeling a little fidgety and wanted to ask them both to sit down and get on with the conversation she wanted and struggled to find patience as she watched Brendan washing and drying his hands, putting milk and sugar in his tea, bringing it to the table, sitting down and taking a couple of biscuits from the plate, and Mrs. P drawing her chair nearer to the table.

At last!

Her loss of patience somehow helped her to overcome her nerves and she came straight to the point of what she wanted to ask. 'Brendan would like to marry me and we wondered if you would allow us to live together in the caravan that is part of the job contract.' *There – all blurted out*!

Brendan coughed, choking on his biscuit. Mrs. P looked taken by surprise. She was silent for, what seemed to Anna, too long.

'Hang on a minute! Slow down. One thing at a time. You say you want to get married. Is that right?'

'Yes. That's right,' said Brendan. 'As soon as we can. And we would need your help. And Mr. P's help too. At Gretna Green.'

'Are you both sure – very sure you want to do this? It's such a big decision.'

'Yes,' they both said in unison.

'Very sure,' said Brendan taking hold of Anna's hand. 'I love her and want to look after her and her baby.'

Anna was so glad that Brendan had said those words. She thought he would have been too shy to show the emotional side of his nature.

'Okay. Good,' said Mrs. Patrick. 'So let's get this straight. Anna are you saying that you want to stay here, take the job offer and you're not going home?'

'Yes. If you'll let me.'

'Good. I'm so very pleased you've made that decision. I didn't want to lose you.'

'We don't know what to do about getting married though,' said Brendan, 'What will we need? And how do we pay for it? Mother V suggested we ask for an advance on our wages but I feel embarrassed to ask for it.'

'I'd like to arrange it, if that's okay. In fact we'll arrange it together, because as from today when V leaves, you are both officially in our employ as General Assistants.'

'Thank you so much,' said Anna. She sighed. 'You're so kind to us.'

'Bill is drawing up your work contracts to sign. It will show what your duties are – which is virtually helping with everything me and Bill have to do around here. You will be our shadows and do what is required.'

'What about the baby? I'll do my best to…'

'I understand about all that. Don't worry Brendan, we'll deal with any problems as and when we need to.'

'I'll do Anna's work if she can't…'

'We'll be okay if we work as a team – don't worry. And I know about babies!'

'That's such a relief,' said Anna. 'Although there is a problem I have about the flat. I know you allowed Mother V to use it temporarily because she is ill. Now that she's going home, would you allow me to stay in it until we get married and have the contracted caravan? Please.'

'What would you say if, instead of the static caravan, which was part of your contracts and which hasn't arrived yet – that we allocate it to the new campsite manager as part of his contract. We can then let you both have the flat instead as part of your contracts?'

Anna looked at Brendan and spoke for him. 'We'd say thank you so very much.'

Mrs. Patrick continued. 'The flat will be better for a family. Especially in the winter months when the campsite is closed. The reasonable rent and running costs: gas, electric etc. will be deducted from your wages. But you'll have two wages coming in so you should manage just fine. I'll help you sort out your finances. Who's the best person to be in charge of them?'

Mrs. Patrick looked at Brendan then at Anna. Brendan's jaw was nearly on the floor and there was a moment or two before he could answer. 'Anna is best at sums and all that.'

'Good. I'll show you how to handle household finances. We can do that this evening if you like. And if there's ever a problem, you must always ask me. I'll also bring the work contracts for you to sign.'

Anna just nodded. She now couldn't speak at all. Everything had recently been like a jigsaw in her head – now the complicated pieces were now all merged together and made a perfect picture.

When Anna got back to the flat, she couldn't wait to tell Mother V the good news about the flat and what Mrs. Patrick had promised to help her with. 'You told me to just ask her and I did. You were right. She's so organized and seems to know exactly what to do.'

'You can learn a lot from Katie.'

'I hope to. And I've learned a lot from you in the short time we've known you. Especially about horses.'

'That reminds me! I've got something for you.' Mother V leaned over to get a small, rather tatty notebook from the bedside table. 'Here,' she took hold of Anna's hand and placed the book in her palm, closing Anna's fingers around it. 'It's full of useful notes about horses; problems, remedies, that sort of thing. Reminders of experiences over the years.

It might be a good thing to start your own book. There'll be lots of things you'll come across; you can use my book to compare notes.'

'Oh, thank you,' Anna leaned over and put her arms around Mother V, tenderly kissing her cheek. 'I'll treasure this, thanks. It'll remind me of you every time I look at it. We're going to miss you, you know. So very much.'

Mother V patted Anna's hand. 'I have a little something for Brendan too. Where is he?'

'He's working. The fruit pickers are a bit short handed. He said he would be here before you leave.'

'I'll be so sorry to leave you both. I did think this was going to be my last summer on the road with my caravan but I didn't think it would be cut short like this. But it's my time and I got to know you and Brendan.'

Anna heard the sound of cars pulling up outside the flat. 'I think George is here.' She looked out of the bedroom window and saw George's car just outside the door to the flat. George and Brendan got out. 'Yes, he's here – with Brendan.' She saw Mr. and Mrs. Patrick pulling up behind him and getting out of their car. 'Mr. and Mrs. Patrick are here too.'

Mother V started to get a little flustered. 'Have I got everything? Where's my pipe? Where have you put my…'

'Everything's packed up and the bags are at the bottom of the stairs. I doubt you have forgotten anything but if there is, George will be able to pick it up on his next visit. Now, come on, let me help you down the stairs.'

Anna went down the stairs first and opened the door. Mother V was on the landing. George and Brendan came in and George went up the stairs. 'Come on Mother, I'll carry you down.'

At this sight, Anna couldn't hold back the tears, seeing Mother V deteriorated to such an extent that George could lift her as easily as lifting a feather. Brendan had picked up the bags to take to the car. Anna held the door open for them. Not wanting to show her emotional state to anyone by wiping away the sadness, she let her tears just freely run down her cheeks and she tried to smile.

Brendan came back in and gave Anna a hug. He kissed the top of her head in his usual fashion. Anna knew he had noticed her tears. 'It's best for her to go home to her family,' he said. 'We'll miss her, though, won't we? Come on, let's wave goodbye.'

Brendan and Anna waited outside the flat and watched George make his mother comfortable in the back seat. Mr. and Mrs. Patrick were behind George, saying their final goodbye to Mother V.'

Mother V wound down the car window. 'Brendan,' she called out.

Brendan went to the window.

'I have something for you.'

'For me!'

'Here you are,' she said, fumbling with her wedding ring and finally sliding if off her finger. 'You're going to need one of these.' She placed the gold band in the palm of his hand. 'God bless you both.' She wound the window up slowly. 'Goodbye.'

'Bye. Thank you.' He clutched the ring and waved.

'Bye everyone. I'll see you in a couple of weeks,' said George. He got into his car and turned it around before driving away up the farm lane.

Katie and Bill walked over to Brendan and Anna.

'Are you okay Anna?' asked Katie.

'Just sad to see her go.' Anna sniffled.

'I know. Me too.' She turned to Brendan. 'I'm curious, Brendan. What did she give you?'

'Nosey more like!' said Bill. Katie gave him a playful dig in the ribs.

'Brendan opened his hand to reveal Mother V's wedding band. A simple, plain, thick, gold ring, but to Brendan it was a gift that meant more to him than any treasure.

* * *

Peter takes out his handkerchief and blows his nose.

'Are you okay?' asks Maggie.

'I found that chapter quite emotional.'

'It's been quite an emotional morning. Are you okay?'

'Yes. I seem to cry easily nowadays. I think it's my condition – or the tablets.'

'I hope it's the story – it would be good if it evokes some emotional response.'

'It certainly does that – to me anyway.'

'That's good.' Maggie puts the book down on the coffee table. 'No more reading today. What shall we do?'

'Let's go to Newbridge and look around the town. I want to see what changes they've made.'

'Okay. Perhaps go to the cinema where we used to go,' suggests Maggie.

'That sounds good. And we'll dine out at the best restaurant Newbridge has to offer.'

CHAPTER TWENTY ONE

A DELICATE SUBJECT

When Peter returns from his day at the cottage, renovating the pieces of furniture, he finds Maggie busy in the kitchen.

'You've been there a long time,' she says, 'I hope you haven't worn yourself out. Or did you call at 'The Ship'?'

'I called in on my way home – I only had a couple.'

'Well, you timed it nicely. Sit yourself down, dinner's ready.' Maggie places Peter's meal on the table as he drags the chair out and sits down.

'That looks nice. Thank you,' says Peter.

Maggie places her own meal down and she sits down opposite Peter. 'Have you managed to get a lot done today?'

'The kitchen table and the chairs are all done now,' says Peter, slicing into the cheese and onion pie. 'I'm going to make a start on the wardrobes next week.'

'Have you got the repair estimate yet?'

'Not yet,' says Peter. 'How was your day?'

'I enjoyed my book club meeting this morning. We discussed the three roles of Hermia, in *A Midsummer Night's Dream* – a daughter, friend and lover.'

'I remember doing that at school. I made the scenery and painted, what seemed like a hundred trees!'

'You enjoyed being brought on stage though, when Mrs. Myers told the audience what a grand job you'd done – "a very talented artist" she said. You were grinning from ear to ear!'

'I enjoyed doing it. I love art.'

'Did you develop your talent?'

'Oh yes. I sold a lot of my paintings to art dealers and the guys on the ships – even the Captain of one of the ships bought a few – one of a sunrise, one of a sunset and another I called *Moonshine on the Ocean* – he was really impressed with them. Said his wife was an artist herself and loved water colours.'

'That's fantastic Pete. Have you got any here with you?'

'I have quite a few and I put them in storage. We'll have a trip to Dublin, and I'll show them to you. Might even see if any of the art dealers there would be interested in buying them.'

'That's a good idea – but let me look at them first and see which ones *I* want.'

'You can have whatever you want, Maggie.' Peter carries on eating his meal.

'All the book group were interested in your reaction to *my* book. I told them you liked the characters.'

'You didn't tell them you were reading it to me, did you?'

'No – I just said you were enjoying my book. Which you are, aren't you?'

'Yes, very much. Are you up to reading some more to me later?'

'Yes.'

When dinner is over, Maggie continues reading to Peter.

* * *

Chapter 21 – The Wedding

Although work on the farm was non-stop and definitely no nine-to-five job, this particular morning, Anna had managed to get a lie in. During the last couple of weeks, the flat had felt different without Mother V's presence but Anna loved living there. She had moved herself into the main bedroom and had started to think about how she would like to decorate the baby's room. The flat was beginning to feel so much like home.

She had phoned her parents to let them know she had received her birth certificate with their letter and told them about her 'promotion' to 'General Assistant' and let them know how much she loved them but she didn't want to give up her job and go to Australia with them. Her father had said how worried he was about leaving her behind. The sailing date had been brought forward and they wanted to arrange to see her before they left. Although she wasn't showing, and by then, she would be married, the thought of them seeing her in her pregnant state would certainly make them even more worried and they would cancel their plans; they might even force her to go back home with them! She had to avoid that happening. She had become an expert at lie avoiding statements. She explained to them that she couldn't be sure of her whereabouts to be able to make such an arrangement. 'We've been all over the place...,' she had told them, '... with the horses. And we're off to Scotland soon!' She had managed to reassure them that she was happy in her job, that she was okay and they needn't worry. She promised them she would phone and write to them often. When she said goodbye to them they told her they loved her very much and missed her but they were glad she was happy and okay. They didn't sound very reassured. Her cheery goodbye had masked the lump in her throat and as soon as she had put the receiver back on its cradle, her tears had fallen.

She did miss her parents and her home; she missed being surrounded by books. Her father had so many; the shelves in their house bellied at their weight. She had read Mother V's notebook and found a wealth of knowledge within the pages; it was a book she could refer to time and time again. She had read all the magazines that Mother V left behind. What she needed was books; real fiction, to read as a form of evening relaxation and entertainment. She had asked Katie if she could have some of the books that were in the charity boxes she stored for the Farmers Wives committee and Katie had agreed and suggested that Bill should put up some book shelves or maybe a bookcase. She told Anna that she was welcome to borrow any of her own books.

The charity had clothed her and Brendan since their arrival at the farm. Anna thought that Katie was donating money for them as well as doing a lot of voluntary work for them. As Katie's 'shadow', Anna was happy to do the same, so she thought it was a kind of repayment.

Katie was keeping an eye open for anything that came in that would be suitable for a wedding and also for the baby. She told Anna that there was little in the way of prams or cots as these items tended to be passed on within the families but said she would ask other members of the committee in case they heard of anything going. There were lots of first size baby clothes, some never even worn. Anna had put these away in a special 'baby' drawer.

The morning sickness wasn't as troublesome, but she still hadn't been to the clinic. She thought she would go after she was married. The thought of knowing she was going to become a married woman, somehow seemed to give her permission to allow herself to love her baby. She reckoned her due date would be around early February.

Brendan was showering her with so much love and attention but, while sharing the flat, was adamant that he wouldn't share her bed before they were married. "I have so much respect for you and your parents,' he had told her, "and I'll feel better knowing that I can always look your Daddy in the eye". Anna understood, knowing that Brendan was always wanting to do things right. The wedding had been arranged for Wednesday of the following week. Katie seemed very excited about it but Anna felt nervous.

Today was the day! There were no church bells ringing.

Instead there was the clank of a large horseshoe upon a very large, black, smithy anvil; a sound that rang out before the marriage service was conducted by a rather chubby, middle-aged man in a black suit, who stood opposite the bride and groom; the metallic feature serving as a desk, dividing them. At his side was his assistant; a dark haired woman, smartly dressed in a navy and white outfit. In the presence of the young bride and groom were the witnesses, Mr. and Mrs. Patrick, who had made all the arrangements for the wedding and seen to all the paperwork required.

The lovely straw hat that Katie wore was decorated with blue and white daisies. Her plain blue, cotton dress fitted her figure perfectly. She wore gloves and looked so very smart.

No one would have guessed that Bill was a farmer. He looked ever so dapper in his dark blue suit and shiny shoes.

Katie had managed to find a suit to fit Brendan. She had searched her son's bedroom and found one at the bottom of his wardrobe, all creased. It was a grey suit John had worn only once; for his cousin's wedding. She had it cleaned and altered to make it fit for purpose.

Brendan had commented that it was the first suit he had ever worn. He kept putting his finger down the front of his collar as if he was choking. Perhaps the neck size on one of John's shirts was a bit too small for Brendan but "it was only for the service," Katie told him. The borrowed black shoes fitted perfectly, thank goodness. Both men wore a white carnation.

Brendan looked the perfect, handsome, young groom.

Finding something suitable for Anna had been a little more difficult. The only thing in the charity boxes she had found that could possibly be of use, were a pair of cream, size five shoes. Katie had mentioned this to Sandra, when they were working together in the farm shop.

'I have a bridesmaid's dress, if that's any use?' said Sandra. 'It's knee length, in like a patterned brocade, in a very, very pale pink colour. It was my sister's choice. I doubt that I'll ever wear it again. But my shoes are all size six.'

Katie had collected the dress from Sandra and, together with the cream shoes, had taken them straight round to Anna for her to try on. It wasn't a perfect fit but with a bit of adjustment here and there, Katie had magically transformed it into a lovely wedding dress. She'd sewn some blue ribbon onto the lining, explaining to Anna the *something old, something new, something borrowed, something blue...* the 'new' being a touch of lace trimming on the sleeves. She had made a lovely, matching headband out of some of the dress material that she'd had to cut away. Anna suited headbands that held back her long, auburn hair. All that was needed now to complete the bridal look, was a small bouquet. Anna told Katie she would pick some of the tree blossom and make one. She had. Made from three sprigs of pink, tree blossom, it was simple, created with care, and matched perfectly.

Anna's emerald eyes sparkled; she was a beautiful, young bride.

The wedding service was over in minutes and the couple were congratulated by the registrar and his assistant who gave Brendan the signed marriage certificate. As both Brendan and Anna looked at it, they were both smiling and Bill captured the moment with his camera. Brendan folded the licence neatly and put it in the inside pocket of the suit.

'And there's one more thing,' said the registrar, handing a ribbon decorated, metal horse shoe to Anna. 'Apparently this is from Topaz.'

Anna looked over to Katie, who nodded. 'For good luck,' she said. 'One of her shoes I saved – they brought you to us.'

Anna gave the heavy horseshoe to Brendan to hold and threw her arms around Katie. They both had tears of joy in their eyes. 'Thank you for everything you've done for us Mrs. P,' said Anna. 'We'll always be grateful.'

Brendan nodded his agreement and held up the horseshoe, acknowledging the meaning behind the thoughtful gesture. Katie offered to carry it in her handbag.

Bill and Katie took a few more photographs before they all had to leave the Blacksmith's building to make way for the next wedding. They made their way to Bill's car.

'I can't believe it's all over with so quickly,' said Brendan, fiddling with his collar. 'Can I undo this shirt now?'

Katie had made arrangements to celebrate their wedding with a meal at a nearby restaurant. 'It's our wedding gift to you,' she said, as they all followed the waitress to their reserved table.

When Anna and Katie had gone to the ladies room, Bill asked Brendan if there was anything he needed to ask him. 'You know – man stuff. Birds 'n' bees and such?'

The way Bill had asked the question with a nod and an odd wink, Brendan understood what he meant. 'I think I'll be okay, thanks, Mr. P. I was a bit worried about the baby…

you know. I didn't know whether... but anyway, I read the leaflet that Anna had and it said that sex was okay – as long as it's comfortable like, you know. So I think I'll be okay But if there's ever anything I need to know, you'll be the first person I'll ask. Thank you. Thanks for everything,' said Brendan.

'Okay, son. Good.'

The ladies returned to the table; the wedding feast was enjoyed and all in all, thanks to Katie, as the toast acknowledged, the wedding day was a memorable success.

* * *

'What a lovely day they've had. I can relate to Brendan and his shirt. There's nothing worse than having to dress up when you're not used to it.'

'I like getting dressed up for weddings – the big hats and everything. Everyone makes an effort at a wedding.'

'A bit nerve-racking for the bride and groom if it's a big do.'

'I think Gretna Green is a romantic setting and less stressful.'

'Talking about stress, I can't help thinking back to a time when sex was new to us.' says Peter. 'That was stressful. We didn't have sex education in school in those days – nobody talked about it like they do today. My Daddy was the last person I could ask about anything. It was just lads' talk in the schoolyard – who weren't reliable. But Brendan seems confident.'

'A great deal more confident than we were!'

'It was more experimental with us.' Peter laughs. 'We didn't really know what we were doing, did we?'

'No, we didn't – not then!' Maggie steers away from the subject. She puts the book down on the table. 'Cup of tea?'

CHAPTER TWENTY TWO

PETER FEELS THE TENSION

Maggie brings in the mugs of tea. Shall I carry on reading or have you had enough?

'Carry on, please.' Peter resumes his comfortable position.

Maggie picks up the book and continues reading from where she left off.

* * *

Chapter 22 – A Surprise Visitor

'I can't believe I've been married for four whole days,' said Anna, 'I am so happy!'

'Good. Me too,' said Brendan. 'Now, Mrs. O'Connor, be a good wife and go and make that toast,' he said, playfully pushing her out of their bed.

Anna threw the pillow at him, then looked at the clock on the bedside table, 'Look at the time – the girls will be here soon.'

The girls she referred to were three teenagers the same age as Anna, two sisters and a cousin. They lived in the nearby village and, for the last couple of years had been coming to the farm every Sunday they could, to learn about horses. They were equally as passionate about them as Anna was. They were fun to be with. Anna loved the Sunday sessions with her new found friends. The horses were groomed and exercised and the best part about it – it was part of Anna's job!

The farm shop was closed on Sundays but there were many day trippers who saw the Farm Shop and Fresh Eggs signs at the top of the lane and who decided to call – just in case they were open. It was usually just eggs they bought, so Katie had set up a table outside the shop with eggs, boxed and priced, ready to take away with a sign that read, "Please put your money in the box!" The slot for the money was an opening in the table top with a painted arrow pointing to it. The money dropped into a box fixed to the underside of the table. Katie was very trusting and it worked, as there was always more in the box than there should be – no change could be given!

Katie was looking through the window, so when she saw an unfamiliar small, grey Austin roll up, she thought they were here to buy eggs and ignored it. It was only when there was a knock on the door that she wondered who it could be.

On opening the door, Katie saw a well presented man of perhaps a similar age to herself. 'Hello.'

'Hello,' the man said, talking off his hat. I'm Mr. Walsh. Anna Walsh's father. I believe she works here?'

'Oh. Mr. Walsh, how lovely to meet you,' said Katie shaking his hand. She looked over to the car. 'Is that Mrs. Walsh with you? Would you both like to come in? I'm Katherine Patrick, but please call me Katie.'

'Thank you, but we haven't got long and I wanted to see my daughter if she's here.'

Katie looked at her watch. 'She'll be working up at the stables at this time. Doing some horse grooming with the girls.'

'May we see her?'

'Yes, of course,' Katie stepped out of the house and pointed in the direction of the stables. 'Just follow the lane and just before the bridge, there's a lane that branches off to the left. The stables are down there.' She looked at Mr. Walsh's highly polished shoes. 'It rained hard last night so it will be quite muddy. If you park your car on the lane you could perhaps wave to grab their attention or shout to get Anna to come over to you. I could lend you some wellies?'

'No, thank you. I think we'll manage,' said Mr. Walsh as he returned to his car. Katie, waved to them as they drove off.

Mr. Walsh drove his car following the directions and just past the lane to the stables, he pulled up in front of a gate. He got out and stepped onto the bottom rung of the gate to see if he could see Anna. He could see three girls in the far distance and he whistled to get their attention.

Mrs. Walsh got out of the car, treading carefully. 'Can you see her?' She stepped up onto the gate. 'Not sure if that's her.'

'ANNA! ANNA!' His voice carried a lot further than he imagined it would. All three girls turned towards the voice. Than another girl came out of one of the stables.

That's my Daddy's voice. Anna thought she was hearing things. She looked over and saw the familiar car and her parents waving and beckoning her. *Oh my God!* Her mind raced thinking where Brendan would be. She realized he would be on his driving lesson and wouldn't be back for another hour. She would hate it if there was any conflict between Brendan and her father if they had come to take her home. She blew out a big sigh and told herself to be strong; look confident and determined to stand her ground. She didn't want to tell them that she was married; not yet anyway and her pregnant state was well hidden under her oversized jumper and she would have to make sure she kept her ring covered. She ran over the field towards them, Diamond following behind.

'Oh, how lovely to see you. What a nice surprise this is!' She opened the gate and Diamond danced about showing he wasn't too pleased not to be able to follow her out.

Anna hugged both her parents. 'I never expected this. It's lovely to see you.' She wiped her eyes with her sleeve.

'We couldn't go sailing off to the other side of the world without seeing you and making sure you were alright. We're going in September, earlier than planned. For some reason they've brought the date forward.'

'By the look of you, we needn't have worried. You look happy and healthy,' said her mother, giving her a hug. She turned her head towards Diamond who was demanding attention. 'And look at that lovely foal!' She couldn't resist stroking and fussing over Diamond.

'He's beautiful, isn't he?' said Anna. 'I helped with his birth,' she said proudly. 'He's so playful and follows me everywhere when I work down here.'

'So, you like your job here then?'

'Oh Daddy, I do,' said Anna, 'I couldn't wish for a better job. Mrs. Patrick, my boss, is the best person ever to work for. She is so kind and helpful. I'm learning a lot.'

'Where do you live?'

'I'll show you. Just give me a moment to take Diamond back to the girls and let them know I'll be back soon, and then I'll take you to my flat. I bet you need a cup of tea.'

Mr. Walsh raised his eyebrows at the revelation that Anna had her own flat.

Anna sorted out what she wanted the girls to do for the next hour before she returned. She got into the car and gave her father the directions to the flat. She knew she would have to hide some of Brendan's things and their wedding photograph as soon as she got in, then there would be no awkward questions.

Anna led the way up the stairs and into the flat, scanning the room for any evidence of Brendan's presence. He had tidied up. She quickly went over to the bookcase and hid their wedding photograph underneath a pile of magazines.

While her mother was looking around the living room, she went into the kitchen and put the kettle on, scanning the room for anything that was Brendan. He had cleared the pots away.

She took off her precious wedding ring and put it in her jeans pocket. She made the mugs of tea and took out a plate of biscuits.

'My word, this is all new and so modern,' said Mrs. Walsh, touching the sofa. 'And you say it goes with the job?'

'Yes. Can you see the site over there?' Anna took her mother over to the window and pointed to where the work was being carried out. 'That is where the caravan campsite is going to be. It's opening next Easter, and I'll be General Assistant. We're… err... the flat is built over the new campsite reception and offices and I'm going to be working with the new manager. I'm General Assistant to Mrs. Patrick even when the holiday season finishes. I'm learning how to do bookings and wages and how to keep the books in order. I love looking after the horses and I do some voluntary work with Mrs. P for the Farmers Wives Charity.'

'My Goodness!' said Mr. Walsh, 'they're keeping you busy.'

'I love it!'

'I can see that. I'm so very proud of you. And I'm satisfied that you're working and living in a decent place with decent people. Doing a job you like. It's a big relief. I feel we can leave you knowing we've seen you. And you're only a phone call away.'

'Yes. You have the number to the farm and see,' said Anna, pointing to the phone. 'I have an extension line. Ring me and give me your address and phone number when you get settled.'

'We will. Oh, and that brings me to another matter.'

Anna was nervous about what *other matters* would entail. She watched her dad search the inside pocket of his suit.

'I have here all the paperwork for our house. Now we know you won't need it, we've decided to rent it out while we're away. We're not selling it in case we want to return. But we would like you to be in charge of the paperwork and help me sort out any problems that may arise. Would you be okay doing that?'

'Yes,' said Anna and they discussed the matter at length until her father was satisfied his daughter had all the information she needed. 'Like you said, you're only a phone call away.' Anna was relieved it didn't interfere with her own plans.

'And one more thing,' her father said. 'I've opened a bank account in your name and put some money in for you.' He handed Anna a bank passbook. 'If you ever need anything else, just get in touch.'

'Thanks. I've missed you both so much. I'm so glad to see you. Are you going to stay over? I have a spare room – a box room really, but you can stay.' Anna wanted to show that there was no problem in their staying but guessing and hoping they would be going home.

'No. We have to get back,' said Mrs. Walsh.

'Yes, we'd better get going.' Mr. Walsh picked up his hat and took the car keys out of his pocket.

'Can you drop me off at the stables?' asked Anna, 'I'll have to get back to work now.' She was so glad to see them but wanting them to leave as soon as possible. All was going well, she thought, but Brendan would be back soon and if they saw him – well, there would be too much explaining to do and then the cat would certainly be among the pigeons!

Five minutes after Anna's parents had left, Brendan was back.

* * *

'That was a bit tense for Anna!' says Peter. 'Do they find out?'

'You'll have to wait and see.'

CHAPTER TWENTY THREE

THE ESTIMATE FOR REPAIRS

Peter and Maggie arrive back at Maggie's house, hanging up their coats on the hallstand. Maggie looks through the mirror and touches up her hair. 'I can't believe how much he quoted to do all the repairs!'

'I thought it was a bit much,' says Peter, making his way into the lounge, 'but it has to be done. And probably worth the bit extra to have the whole lot done by one contractor rather than individual ones who would probably have to wait for one another.

'But the cost!' said Maggie, 'Will it be worth it? Why not sell it and buy yourself something else?'

'I want to do it for my Mammy – God bless her soul. I want her to know; if she's looking down on us, that is. I want her to know that I'm doing it for her. Can you understand Maggie?'

'Well... if you can afford it, and it's what you want . . .'

'It is, Maggie, and I can. So will you help me with it – decorating and…'

'…making it a home? Yes. I'll help you.'

'Good,' says Peter. 'I'll make us a cup of tea.' He gets up from the sofa and goes to the kitchen. He calls out to Maggie, 'Will you read me the next chapter?'

'Okay,' shouts Maggie and makes herself comfortable on the sofa. She picks up her book and finds the page where she's up to, ready to continue reading to Peter. *Pete's going to like this chapter.*

Peter brings in the tray and Maggie notices the trembling in his hands. She thinks it seems worse than ever and stands up and takes the tray from his grip and puts it on the coffee table. She doesn't make any remark.

'Thanks,' says Peter and makes himself comfortable in his usual place beside Maggie.

Maggie pours the teas; she milks and sugars them and leaves the cups on the tray.

'Where are we up to?' asks Peter.

'Chapter twenty three,' says Maggie. She places her glasses on her nose and begins to read.

* * *

Chapter 23 – The Advertisements

'I've passed Anna! I've passed!' Brendan came pounding up the stairs to the flat even quicker than his usual fashion.

Anna was making some sandwiches for their lunch and had been thinking about Brendan all morning, feeling nervous for him, knowing how much he wanted to pass the driving test. On hearing the word 'passed' she ran towards him, flinging her arms around him; the butter knife still in her hand. 'Oh, Brendan, I'm so glad. What did Mr. P say?' she asked, returning to the sandwiches.

Brendan stood behind her and put his arms around her, his head resting on her shoulder. '"You've done me proud son!" That's what he said.' Brendan turned his wife around to face him. 'And you know what this means Anna? I'll be able to drive the delivery van! Me! Driving! To the markets – to the shops! Mr. P says we can start the new system next Monday and I have to use this week to find my way around and get used to the roads. I already know most of the customers. He said I would be able to drive the range rover and the other farm vehicles – "but not, under any circumstances" he said was I to drive his car – "nobody," he said' "drives my car but me!"'

Anna laughed. 'I'm so pleased for you,' she said, and kissed him.

'And Mr. P said that, when I start the deliveries, I might get some tips. If, I do, he said I can keep them! So with our wages and my tips, we should be okay Anna – we should be OK!' He gave her a big kiss, then picked up a sandwich from off the plate. 'We should be able to afford the things we'll need for the baby. We won't need to worry about that.'

'Well, I've got some good news for you too,' she said, going over to the bookcase. 'My Mammy and Daddy have been to see me.'

Brendan froze with the sandwich half eaten; his expression was readable.

'Don't be so scared, said Anna. I didn't let on about the baby or about us being married – and they don't know you're here. I hid our wedding picture.'

'Thank goodness. I couldn't have faced your father and explained everything to him. I wouldn't have known where to start and ...'

'I know – neither could I.'

'…but what did they say?'

'Well, they're now totally reassured that I'm okay here and they're going to sail in September.'

'So, you'll have had the baby before you're likely to see them again?'

'Yes. Oh and I do feel so much better knowing that they've been saved the pain and shame that I would have caused them.'

'Well, don't worry about it anymore – let's look forward. We're okay here. We're safe.'

'They've given me some money. That was the good news I wanted to tell you.' She handed the passbook to him. 'There's two hundred pounds in it! My Daddy said it was for me to use if I needed it for any emergency and to let him know if I needed anything.'

'TWO HUNDRED POUNDS!' Brendan stared at the book. 'Anna, that's just...' he sighed. 'You have the best parents in the world.'

'I know,' said Anna, 'and they're just a phone call away. They said anytime I wanted to join them, I was to let them know and my dad would sort it out for me.'

'Well, you're not going anywhere without me!'

'I know.' A guilty feeling swept over her for hiding things from her parents but she convinced herself it was for the best. She told Brendan about the paperwork for her parent's house, that she had been asked to look after and Brendan suggested that they put everything away safely.

'Do you think we should tell Mrs. P?' asked Brendan.

'Oh yes. I want her to know. She'll help me with anything I don't understand. I'm working with her in the office this afternoon, so I can talk to her then.'

'That's good,' he said, 'everything's good. But I'll have to get back to work now.' He picked up another sandwich from the plate, 'I'll see you about five.' He gave her a kiss on the cheek. 'I'm so glad you've seen your parents – are you okay?'

'I'm okay, yes. You go and drive your new van and be careful. Bye.'

Anna was left eating her lunch on her own. She had another fifteen minutes before she had to meet Mrs. Patrick in the office. She relaxed and put her feet up on the stool and rubbed her stomach. The slight swell of pregnancy could only be noticed by herself.

Anna had a set of keys to the office and reception building. Katie had told her that until the campsite was open for business, she could do any of the office work when it suited her. But today, she had said that they needed to compose a letter to send out with the brochures. Bill had placed the advertisement in the holiday section of all the major papers, advertising the Easter 1954 opening of the new campsite. It was very impressive; giving potential holiday makers the details of the attractions of the countryside, the entertainment, and the amenities offered to those with touring caravans and those wanting static caravan accommodation. There was a section to cut out and send by post to request a brochure. All the brochures had been picked up from the printers and stored in a big cardboard box and now the requests for them had started to come in.

'I think we'll compose the draft letter first before anything else,' said Katie. 'You type as I dictate.'

Anna made herself comfortable in her seat at the desk. The white paper was ready loaded in the heavy Remington in front of her. Her hands were poised over the keys. It brought back memories of when she and a school friend had learned touch typing during their last year of school at some special, private, Saturday morning classes. The sessions had been run by a very strict lady tutor named Mrs. Brown, in a room above a shoe shop in town. Anna remembered how the numerous typewriters; Remington's, Underwood's with standard and extra-long carriages, all had the keys blacked out with covering caps and she had to look up to a massive chart on the wall and search by touch for the required letters. It took a long time before she was confident and could type as she read the handwritten work and typed it out without looking at any of the keys. She had learned how to change the ink ribbon cartridges and how to set the robust metal, tabulation keys into the back of the typewriter to set out columns which were useful for accounts such as the pounds, shillings and pence columns. She had learned Pitman's shorthand too. Her father was impressed by her enthusiasm and encouraged her to keep up with her shorthand skills by ordering a regular delivery of the special Pitman's Shorthand magazine from the newsagents. All this was in the hope of securing a secretarial positon somewhere; sometime in the future. She had paid for the lessons out of her pocket money. Now, she thought, it had been money well spent. She thought she would remind him that she was now using her acquired skills in her new position, the next time she spoke to him on the phone.

'Dear …whoever.' Began Katie. 'We'll obviously use our new printed letter headed paper, but the draft can be on plain for the moment.'

'I haven't seen the letter paper.'

'We got them from the printers yesterday. They're lovely. In a light cream colour with matching envelopes. Bill had them designed specially – I'll show you when we've finished this.' Katie thought for a moment. 'Obviously put the date and such.'

Anna was getting a little frustrated with Katie's slowness at thinking of what to say. She knew she could compose the letter herself but had an idea.

'Mrs. P,' said Anna, 'are there any compliment slips in the box, with a similar design to the letterheads?'

'I don't know. Why?'

'I thought it might be a better idea to send the brochures out with a compliment slip and then if they make a booking, you could use all the nice quality letterheads for a confirmation letter.'

'Oh yes. That's a good idea. Let's have a look.' Katie drew the box into the middle of the room. 'If there is, it'll save a lot of typing and a lot of the paper.' She took a key out of her pocket and used it to loosen the knots in the string and opened the box. The paper smelt all nice and new and at one side of the stack was a box marked 'Compliment Slips'. 'Great. We just need to type out the envelopes.'

'I can manage to do that,' said Anna, 'if you have something else to do. I'll let you know when I've finished. And I'll work on composing a draft letter confirming the customer's booking. I can call with it later for you to have a look at, and there's something else I'd like to talk to you about.'

'Oh, okay, yes. Good. That'll be great. I do have quite a bit of work to do. So I'll see you later in the café.'

Anna was left to her own devices and put her secretarial and organisational skills to work. The typewriter rattled and the six envelopes were ready. She then double checked the addresses with the brochure request forms and neatly paper-clipped a compliment slip to each of the six brochures before sealing them up in the envelopes ready to be posted.

On the set of keys that Anna had, there was a key to the office cash drawer and although there was no actual cash in the drawer at the moment, there was a supply of postage stamps that Katie had given to her. Anna had organised a note book, labelled 'POSTAGE BOOK' to keep a record of stamps used. She had ruled columns with headings 'DATE', 'NAME', 'STAMPS IN', 'STAMPS OUT' and a 'BALANCE' to keep a precise record. On the first page there was a date entry and under the stamps in, an entry of '48' and a balance entry of '48'. Under this, on the next line, she very neatly wrote the date, then the names that were on the six envelopes and in the 'STAMPS OUT' column, she put '6' and in the 'BALANCE' column put the figure '42'. She tore off six stamps from the perforated page, licked them and stuck them neatly on the envelopes. She intended to walk up the farm lane to the main road later and post them in the letter box.

Her attention was then paid to the composition of a standard booking confirmation letter. On the lovely new headed paper she composed a letter that she felt was businesslike, yet warm and welcoming with spaces left blank to type in the date, name and address, booking dates from and to, touring or static choice, and the amount of deposit required. At the bottom of the letter after, 'Yours sincerely', she had put a row of dots for a signature line and underneath that had put 'p.p. Mrs. Katherine Patrick, Director, Appletree Farm Caravan Holiday Park'.

Feeling optimistic and anticipating a flood of bookings, she thought it might be a good idea if Mr. Patrick could arrange for the printers to do some copies of the letter, which would save a lot of time.

She had made labels for the three drawers of the filing cabinet and in the bottom drawer labelled 'OFFICE STATIONERY' she took out a Manilla folder and filed the draft letter, and in her neat writing labelled the folder 'Draft Letters'. On her way to the post box, she would take the folder with her to let Mrs. Patrick look at it and give her approval, then this folder would eventually be filed alphabetically in the empty second drawer labelled 'CORRESPONDENCE'. The top drawer, also empty at the moment, was labelled 'SITE BOOKINGS'. Anna planned to organise an alphabetical filing system for all the bookings by a surname followed by a reference number.

She thoroughly enjoyed her work in the office; she just hoped that, when the time came, she would get on well with the new site manager.

With her work at the office done for the day, her duties were to see to the horses, but before then, she made her way to see Katie in the café and then she would post the envelopes.

When she got there, there were no customers, just Mrs. Patrick and Sandra, cleaning the work areas. 'Hello,' she said. 'Here's the draft letter, Mrs. P.' She left the folder on the table in front of the café counter. 'I'm just going to walk to the post box to post these.' She held up the envelopes. 'Fingers crossed eh, Mrs. P.'

'Oh, thanks,' said Katie, wiping her hands on her apron. 'I'll have a look at that.' She came around to the table and picked up the folder.

'While you're looking at it, I'll walk up the lane. Is there anything else you need posting while I'm going?' asked Anna.

'No, thanks,' said Katie, concentrating on the letter.

Anna felt confident that her letter would be approved. She made her way to the post box, enjoying the leisurely stroll in the sunshine and feeling so much happier than she had done in quite a while.

There was a cup of tea and a piece of cake ready for Anna when she got back to the café. Sandra was just leaving; her work done for the day.

'Your letter is brilliant, Anna!' said Katie. 'It's just perfect for what we need. I've shown it to Bill and he's very impressed.

'I was going to ask Mr. Patrick if he thought it would be time saving – and ink ribbon saving too, if we could have a supply of the letters printed.'

'That's a great idea. I'll see to it. Well done Anna.'

'Thank you.' Anna drank her tea and bit into the cake.

'Did you say there was something else you wanted to talk to me about?'

'Yes,' said Anna, licking a little cream off her finger. 'You know when my parents came to visit me?'

'Oh yes, it was nice to see them but I was so worried for you. To be honest, I was glad once they'd gone. I didn't want anything to blow up into a big holy chaos!'

'Me too.'

'On a future occasion, it will be nice to get to know them.'

'I hope so, but they're well reassured I'm okay here.' Anna patted Katie's hand. 'That's all thanks to you.'

'That's good to know.'

'Well, anyway,' said, Anna. 'What I wanted to tell you is that they've given me some money.'

'Oh?' Katie leaned in towards Anna, intrigued.

'A bank book with two hundred pounds deposited. Daddy said it was for any emergency that I might have. And to get in touch with them if I wanted to go and join them at any time. Which I won't!'

'That's good!'

'He's also left me an envelope with some paperwork for our house – their house I mean. It's all the details about the arrangements they've made for renting it out and just in case there are any problems that need somebody here to sort it out, they've asked me to be in charge of it and ring him if necessary. I have my key. He's told the bank, the neighbours and given Mrs. Cleary, next door, this number, to get in touch with me if she thinks she needs to.'

'That's understandable. I'm sure he's got everything legally sorted.'

'But would you help me if I don't know what to do?' Anna finished off the last of the cake.

'Yes. Course. But I'm sure everything will be fine.'

'Oh, thanks, that's a lot off my mind. Thank you. I'm going to keep the bank book and the envelope safe in one of the bedroom cupboards with our marriage certificate and birth certificates.'

'That's best. Keep everything safe.'

'And if we manage to get a pram and a cot from the charity, I want to make a donation – from out of our wages. Or we may have to buy them; but I won't touch the bank money unless we really need to.'

'Okay. That's fine. But we have a few months before they're needed – and you never know what Father Christmas will bring!'

* * *

'He's passed his test – good for him!' says Peter. 'I knew he was going to do well!'

'What about Anna – what about her skills?'

'She's just brilliant – and clever – and beautiful! Like someone I know!'

Maggie chuckles. 'I know!'

'Are there any postcards hidden in this chapter – I didn't notice any?'

'No. There is in the next one though.'

CHAPTER TWENTY FOUR

THE POSTCARD OF A WINTER SCENE

'So,' asks Peter, picking up the postcard box, 'which is the one that triggered your imagination for this chapter?'

Maggie looks through them and picks one out of the box.

'This one of a winter scene. Very appropriate but totally strange, considering where you were when you sent it.'

'I can't remember. Where was it?'

'Cyprus. I mean, Pete, you don't often see scenes of snow covered hills, with children sliding around on sledges in Cyprus. They'd have to climb the Troodos Mountains!'

'But it was for Christmas, so I just looked in my pile of cards and —'

'Okay, but it would have been nice to have had a postcard with a scene of where you were. Some hot sunny beach in... Where was it from?' Maggie turns over the card to read the postmark. 'Paphos?'

'Oh yes, Paphos! I remember sending it now. It's lovely. I think you'd like Paphos.'

'I'm sure I would. I'd fly though!'

'I'd fly there with you.'

'Okay – Is that a promise?' Maggie stares at Peter as if to ask if he's serious. She puts on her glasses and continues to read.

* * *

Chapter 24 – Some sad news

Brendan and Anna realized that the work around the farm changed with the seasons and they did all the jobs allocated to them with interest and enquiring minds; a desire to learn.

Due to the winter season, when there was bad weather and none, or very few touring caravans, there was far less trade in the farm shop and café. But the orders for the winter vegetables, especially over the Christmas period were always good; even more so this winter as Brendan enjoyed driving around in his van carrying out his duties doing the deliveries.

He gained more customers purely because of his bright and cheerful personality.

Bill and Katie were delighted with the couple's dedication to their work and couldn't be more pleased with them. Bill commented frequently how the decision to employ them was one of the best decisions they made.

Anna was well into her pregnancy without any complaint or issue and still didn't look pregnant – her baby bulge was well hidden under thick winter jumpers. Brendan frequently commented that she couldn't look more beautiful.

Brendan, together with Anna's friends, helped out with some of the heavier work needed to care for the horses.

Anna made sure the work in the campsite office was always up to date and organised. She was very pleased that Mr. and Mrs. Patrick were delighted that the bookings for the coming year were exceeding expectation.

It was two weeks before Christmas and Anna and Katie were in the campsite office. Anna was dealing with the day's post.

Katie was on the phone giving George an update on the progress of the campsite. '…and the estimated completion date for the work will be the end of January.' There were pauses as Katie listened to George's replies. 'Okay,' said Katie, 'we'll set up dates for the interviews. We'll need the manager in place by – what would you say – first of March?' Another pause. 'Okay that's settled then. Yes, I think he or she will need that time to settle in and have input in organising the weekly or fortnightly routine.' Katie looked over to Anna who was holding up Brendan's notebook. 'Oh,' she nodded to Anna, '...and Brendan has lots of ideas. We can go through those as well, when you get here. I'll phone you when I set the interview date. I'll make it mid-week, as you say.' Anna saw Katie's expression change and could tell there was something George said that upset her. 'Oh, George, I'm so sorry. Why didn't you stop me from going on about business when you have so much more important news?' After a pause, she said quietly, 'So sad but glad it was peaceful. I didn't expect her to go so quickly but Rosa did phone me to say that she didn't expect her to be here for Christmas. I'd already made arrangements to go and see her tomorrow...' Another pause and Katie looked over to Anna with a deep sadness in her expression. '...yes, of course, I'll still go and help Rosa with anything I can.'

Anna saw Katie gulp down her emotions, as she sat down on one of the chairs. 'I'll ring you from there then. Okay. Bye George.' Katie put the phone down slowly.

'Mother V?' asked Anna.

'Yes.' Katie couldn't hold back the tears and Anna tried to comfort her by putting an arm around her shoulder but this action seemed to make the tears flow even more. 'I was expecting it but it still hurts to lose someone like V. She was more like a mother than just a friend to me.'

'I understand,' said Anna, who couldn't help her own tears from flowing.

'Come on, now, wipe your eyes. Let's put the kettle on and have a cup of tea.' Katie got up to make the tea. 'You shouldn't be getting upset in your condition.'

'Let me make it,' said Anna. 'You sit down. It sounded like you're going to have a few sad, busy days ahead.'

Katie sat back down in the chair and allowed Anna to make the tea. Apart from quiet sobs and sniffles, the two women were silent; each one remembering Mother V in their own special way.

Later on, when all the work was done and darkness fell early, Anna related the sad news to Brendan as they ate their dinner of comforting, hot beef stew and dumplings. Nothing had ever put Brendan off his food, but Anna could see he struggled to swallow and had to rest his cutlery on the plate.

'And how are *you* feeling,' he asked.

'Like you. Sad.'

'I know. But don't forget,' he sighed,' we always have her with us as long as you have your wedding ring.' Brendan's voice altered with emotion and he took hold of Anna's hand across the table. 'I'll always be grateful.'

'So will I,' said Anna, sniffing and taking a handkerchief from the pocket of her apron. She wiped away some fresh tears.

Brendan picked up his cutlery. 'Eat your dinner before it gets cold. I'll pick up some flowers from the florists early tomorrow so that Mrs. Patrick can take them with her. You can think of something nice to write on a card.'

'Yes.'

They continued to eat their dinner in a comfortable silence and then moved over to the sofa to relax. Brendan broke the silence by asking Anna about her day in the office.

'I overheard Mrs. Patrick telling George that they were setting up the interviews for the campsite manager. They want him, or it may be a woman, but anyway, they want them to be here by the first of March to get things organised.'

'I wonder what jobs they'll give me. I'll only be working in the afternoons. I'll have my deliveries to do in the mornings.'

'If people are on holiday, they may not be up too early anyway.'

'If they have children they will.'

'We'll be up early with ours – that's if we get to sleep at all!'

'Oh God! I'm dreading that bit.'

'We may have a good one that sleeps all night!'

'Let's hope so,' said Anna, rubbing her stomach. 'I'm looking forward to doing the horse riding. They're all going to love Diamond and Amber.'

'I've told Mr. Patrick about some of my ideas; he seemed to like them.'

'I mentioned your notebook to Mrs. Patrick. She's going to go through it with George and the new manager.'

'I hope they have the weekly barn dance I suggested. That should be fun.'

'I like all your ideas. But I think that's because I love you.'

'Love you too. Can't wait to see you in your nice new office uniform.'

'I'll be slim again, then.'

'You've never looked more beautiful,' said Brendan, putting his hand on Anna's baby bump.

'I'll tell you what else is happening,' said Anna. 'The site will be finished by the end of January.'

'I bet it'll be before then.' Brendan got up from the sofa and went over to the window. Anna followed him and entwined her arm in his. 'From what I can see, there's not much more to do.' Brendan pointed. 'All the bases and the landscaping were finished at the end of the summer. Unless it's all the work in the utility block that needs finishing and, of course, they won't be working over Christmas – so, yeah, I suppose they've said end of January to give themselves time.'

'I can't wait to see all the caravans coming and being set up, can you?'

'It'll look smart. All brand new.'

'The manager's caravan will be the first one on the right as you turn into the road to the blocks,' said Anna. 'I'm booking customers in by block numbers but I heard Mrs. Patrick say they might also *name* the blocks and have some signs put up but I'm not sure yet. I don't know where the spaces will be for the touring caravans. I don't know how many spaces we'll have.'

'I think it will be the grass space at the bottom on the left. There's space for about six. I heard Mrs. Patrick suggest that they should be put at the top block to make it easier for them to just pull in but Mr. Patrick said he wanted his brand new, smart ones at the top, so that it would look nice for when people came to look round. '"We'll hide all the tatty touring ones well away from sight."' He said.

Anna laughed. 'He's got a point. There's none like Mother V's.'

'No. It's safe and protected in the big barn over winter, but I need to check the tarpaulin cover before I go to bed.'

'Do it now. While you remember.'

Brendan sighed. 'And remember Mother V.'

* * *

'That's a sad chapter,' says Peter.

Maggie closes the book. 'Well, let's go and cheer ourselves up.'

'To 'The Ship'?'

'To 'The Ship'!'

CHAPTER TWENTY FIVE

BORDERING ON AN ARGUMENT

There is no breeze, no clouds, and the sun is hot and bright. Maggie and Peter are relaxing in the shaded part of the garden; as quiet and still as the gnomes that surround them.

It is Peter who breaks the silence. He doesn't move, he just speaks. 'I've been thinking. Why do they have to interview people? Why don't they just give Brendan the manager's job?'

Maggie also remains still when she replies. 'It's 1953, Pete, do you think any employer would give a managerial job to a young seventeen year old?'

'Well, I like Brendan, I think he could do the job. You wrote that he had some good ideas in his notebook. What do you think the new manager will do – take the credit?'

'A good manager should give credit where it's due. Don't you think?'

'I have this feeling that he won't!'

'Brendan is too young to be given the responsibility – Bill knows that. Katie knows that. And what about Anna?' asks Maggie, who now sits up and turns to face Peter. 'Don't you think Anna would make a good manager?'

'Yeah but she's out of the running, isn't she?' Peter sits up and adjusts his sun glasses. 'She's got the baby to think about.'

'But she's there! Doing the job!' Maggie's voice is raised slightly. 'Has been organising the job since day one! Why not in the running for a manager's job?'

'Yes, but who's going to look after the baby?'

'Well, let's read on and see, shall we?' says Maggie. She puts on her glasses in an indignant manner.

Peter goes very quiet as Maggie reads.

* * *

Chapter 25 – The Interviews

'Is George going to be here for the interviews?' asked Bill

'He said he would be,' Katie looked at the clock on the wall. 'If all the candidates are here before he arrives, we'll just have to start without him.'

'How many are going to turn up do you think?'

'Out of the nine applications, I turned down four of them, so hopefully we should get five to choose from.'

'Did you send letters to the ones you didn't like?'

'I didn't say I didn't like them. They are probably nice people; they just weren't suitable for the job. Too young, too old or too illiterate. By the way, Anna did the letters for me.

Her typing skills are so much better than mine! She's coming along great in the office; she has it so well organised. We need that second desk, by the way, for the manager. Not too big.'

'How's she doing with the bookkeeping?'

'She's doing great. I'm really confident with her abilities. And did you know she can do shorthand?'

'Well I never!'

'Yes, and she's sailing through her pregnancy – no problem.'

'Looking at her, you can't really tell – yet!'

'I know. Anyway, the interviews are going to take up a lot of your time this afternoon, so, you'd better go and let Brendan know what jobs you want him to cover.'

George arrived at the campsite reception office just as the first interviewee was being asked to go into the office. He followed them in and took the vacant chair next to Bill. Katie shook hands with the confident candidate, 'Mr. Price, isn't it?' she asked.

'It is,' said Mr. Price.

'So nice to meet you. Please take a seat.' Katie pointed to the chair on the opposite side of the desk and took her own seat. 'I'm Katie,' she said, 'and this is my husband Bill,' she gestured to Bill, who stood to shake his hand. 'And,' she continued, 'this is Mr. George Grey, a director of the company.' George followed the pattern, stood and shook hands.

'Pleased to meet you,' said George, then sat down.

'Right, Mr. Price,' said Katie, 'Thank you for attending the interview.' She opened a file in front of her. 'I see that you have some knowledge of the "holiday and leisure business" as you put it in your letter. Would you tell us more about that?'

If Mr. Price had any nervousness about the interview it wasn't apparent. He seemed to be very confident, especially when he began talking about himself and giving quite a good account of his experience and motivational skills as a Redcoat. He explained that he wanted to be employed in a managerial role and also needed to be nearer to his ageing mother who lived in the local village. He was an only child and single.

Katie was impressed with his interview and told him she would be in touch when all the candidates had been interviewed.

'Goodbye,' said Mr. Price, shaking their hands before leaving.

There was a bit of scratching of heads as Bill and George thought about Mr. Price. Katie put the file at one side and put a second one in front of her. 'We'll discuss them once we've interviewed them all,' instructed Katie. Now, whose next?' she asked herself, looking at the application form. 'Ah, a Mr. Richard Standish. Right.' Katie opened the door and asked Mr. Standish to come into the office.

And so went the afternoon. One candidate after another, all seemingly capable of the role but all three directors needed to agree on one successful applicant. They drank several cups of tea whilst going over and discussing the details of each interview and had a laugh at some of the answers the candidates came up with.

'But who are we going choose?' asked Bill.

'Let's have a vote by a simple yes or no for each one to start with,' said Katie. 'First one – Mr. Price. I say yes.'
Bill said 'Don't know.'

George said 'Yes.'

There were two no's and a yes for Mr. Standish; three no's for Mr. Thomas. Three most definite no's for Miss Sutcliffe and two yes's and one don't know for Mr. Boardman.

'Okay,' said Katie, 'that narrows down the running. Mr. Boardman and Mr. Price.' She put the unsuccessful candidate's files on top of the typewriter, which had been moved off the desk and onto the top of the filing cabinet. The files for the two possible candidates remained in front of her.

'I don't know about Mr. Price. There's just something about him and I can't be certain,' said Bill 'he just seems a bit too sure of himself; a bit too confident, if you ask me. But if you both think he'd be right for the job, it's okay by me.'

'Well, I felt the same about Mr. Boardman,' said Katie. 'He came across as being confident but a little too arrogant.'

'Well I'll go along with whoever you two decide,' said George. 'Maybe you could put in the contract that the employment is subject to annual review or something like that? That way, if they don't come up to scratch, we can re-advertise the position for the following season.'

'That makes sense; we'll do that,' said Bill. So, let's toss for it!' Bill brought out a two shilling piece from his pocket. 'Heads its Price. Tails its Boardman. Okay?'

'Right,' said Katie. George nodded.

Bill flicked the florin into the air and it landed quietly on the carpeted floor. They all bent their heads forward to see the result. 'Heads it is!' said Bill, picking up the two bob piece.

They were finally in agreement of employing Mr. Thomas Price. Katie put Mr. Boardman's file on top of the typewriter with the other unsuccessful candidate's files. Mr. Price's file was kept on the desk. Katie would later ask Anna to compose a congratulatory letter which would be sent to him with details of the adjusted contract of employment.

'Well, I don't know about you two, but I'm starving. Who's for some shepherd's pie?'

There was no need to wait for an answer. Katie led them to the kitchen.'

* * *

'You always manage to put some food in there somehow, don't you?'

'I knew you'd say that, Pete. You're very much like Brendan, or should I say, Brendan is definitely you!'

'I love my food. I don't deny that!'

'Well, I already knew what food was mentioned in this chapter; so, yes, I've made a shepherd's pie for dinner!'

'I never saw you making it.'

'You fell asleep most of the afternoon, so I kept myself busy in the kitchen.'

'You made it just for me?'

'Just for you Pete.'

Peter gives Maggie a kiss on the cheek. 'I love you very much. You know that, don't you?'

'I do, Pete. I do.'

CHAPTER TWENTY SIX

A SURPRISE FOR MAGGIE

Maggie is in the kitchen cooking breakfast. She hopes the smell of the fried bacon wafts its way up the stairs and wakens up Peter. She had taken notice as to how much he was sleeping – too much, she thinks, and wonders if he has been doing too much work at the cottage or if it is his condition. She begins to think the worst so, she thinks it is time to ask him outright what exactly his condition is.

Peter comes into the kitchen, still in his pyjamas. 'Sorry, Maggie. I didn't realise it was so late.'

'That's okay, Pete,' says Maggie, a little nonchalantly. 'Is it the tablets the doctor's given you that are making you sleep a lot?'

'I think so.' Peter sits down at the table. 'Or maybe it's the complaint – I don't know.'

'What exactly *is* the complaint, Pete? Do you want to tell me?' Maggie's heart is beating fast as she dishes up the breakfast onto the plates. She thinks she knows the answer.

'Parkinson's, Maggie. I'm sure you've guessed. I can't always hide the trembling hands.'

'I had an idea.' Maggie puts the breakfast on the table.

'But I hope to be here for a while yet.' Peter puts his head in his hands.

'Eat up, Pete.' Maggie doesn't want to delve into his state of health any further. 'Let's make the most of what we've got.'

'Aye, Maggie. Aye.' Peter tucks into his breakfast with his usual appreciation. 'This is nice, Maggie, thanks.'

'What do you want to do today?'

'Let's go and buy a ring!'

'A ring!'

'I want you to marry me, Maggie.'

Maggie's knife and fork clatters on the plate. She sits back in her chair. 'Pete, whatever...'

'Marry me, Maggie. Please. I want you to have me and all my worldly goods.'

'I never know when you mean things. What are you saying?' Maggie is so taken aback by the surprise proposal, she doesn't know how to react.'

'I'm serious, Maggie. Please marry me. You're the only woman I would want to marry. It's a bit late, I know, but please know that I've always loved you and I always will. Marry me, Maggie and then, when I die, I can be sure that you will have all I own. And my love for eternity.'

Maggie can't speak. She can't answer. She just nods.

'I love you, Maggie. With all my heart, I love you!' Peter comes around the table and takes hold of Maggie's hand. 'I'll love you forever.'

Maggie, with sparkling tears in her eyes, accepts the proposal with a passionate kiss.

Late afternoon, Maggie and Peter return home. Their shopping trip has been successful in purchasing the most meaningful ring that Maggie has ever worn. She keeps looking at it admiringly.

'I didn't know what to say when Terry asked me when the wedding date was going to be,' says Peter.

'Why would he surmise that our honeymoon would be in Paphos or Minorca?'

'I might have mentioned something to him about liking those places. What do you think?'

'I'll leave all that up to you. You've done the travelling, so you know the places.'

'So, when do we set the date?'

'It's up to you,' says Maggie. 'When do you think?'

'Would you be okay with a wedding at the register office, or would you want to be married in the church?'

'Let's keep it simple. At the register office. And a bit of a do at 'The Ship'.'

'That's what I hoped you'd say. I'd like that.'

'When, then – a couple of weeks?' asks Maggie.

'That sounds good to me. That'll give you time to sort out your dress and everything. Let me know what you need.'

'You've spent a lot of money on the rings, Pete. I'll buy my own outfit.'

'I insist on paying for our wedding – all of it. Your outfit – everything.'

'Are you sure you can afford to pay for all of it? You have your cottage to pay for. I have some money saved I can...'

'No, Maggie. I'll pay for it. Okay?'

'Okay.' Maggie is happy that this wedding is going to make Peter feel happy. She now feels glad at having turned down a couple of proposals in the past; she always felt she couldn't marry anyone but Peter. A long wait, but she feels like a young woman again and the experience of organising her own wedding was something she never thought would ever happen to her. The only down side is, she thinks, is that they aren't going to have long together. She looks admiringly at the bright trio of diamonds on her finger and knows she wants to make life even brighter for her fiancé.

Maggie is glad that Peter doesn't ask her to read her book to him on this special evening. Instead of him being interested in the fictional lives of Brendan and Anna, she is so happy that he wants to concentrate on planning to enjoy the reality of their own lives together.

CHAPTER TWENTY SEVEN

A DATE IS SET

'It's a lovely day,' says Maggie, 'shall we have a walk?'

'Why don't we go to the register office and book the date for our wedding and then we can look around for our wedding outfits. I want to do you proud, so I'll need a suit. And shoes.'

'It's funny you should say that, Pete, because in the next chapter, the characters get new shoes for Christmas.'

'Have we got time for a chapter before we go? I think it would give our breakfast a chance to settle a bit before we start walking.'

'Where do you want to sit, outside or in?'

'Outside,' says Peter. 'It's a lovely day.'

'Okay.' Maggie picks up her book from the table and hands it to Peter. 'You go and get yourself comfortable and I'll get my glasses.'

It doesn't take long before Maggie is settled in her garden chair. It is warm with a slight breeze; the sun not quite high enough in the sky to eliminate the shade of the house. 'What a lovely day, and I'll be reading about Christmas! Anna's and Brendan's Christmas!'

'I like Christmas time. There's bound to be food in there somewhere!'

'There is. We can eat out once we've done the shopping.'

'Okay. Go on – read it.'

* * *

Chapter twenty six – Christmas planning

Anna bought a pack of Christmas cards from the post office while she was on her regular trip into town. Her visit to the anti-natal clinic was always given the same positive result which was always such a relief to Anna. The villagers were a friendly lot. Some of them were regular customers at the Farm shop and café and knew Sandra very well. Anna assumed that, through Sandra, they would know some of the story about her and Brendan's wedding; namely her pregnancy but knew Mrs. Patrick would not have divulged the darker secret.

Although seven months, she could still hide her baby bump easily beneath her winter clothes. Being pregnant at such a young age no longer troubled Anna; being married to Brendan had made all the difference. No one ever mentioned anything negative or offensive directly to her; they all seemed perfectly nice and respectful. Some of the shopkeepers asked how Brendan was – he had become popular for his bright, happy attitude. She actually enjoyed being part of the village community.

When Anna got home, Brendan was sat at the kitchen table.

'What shall I put on my card to Uncle Kevin and Aunty Peggy?' he asked. 'From both of us, or just me?'

'Just send it from you,' said Anna, puffing and panting a little, as she brought in the bag of cleaning stuff she'd bought and placed it under the sink. 'You don't want them asking too many questions just yet.'

'Okay. That's mine done then – just the one for posting.'

'I've only got one to post – to Australia. I'll have to send it just from me,' said Anna with a flash of guilt in her thoughts. 'All the rest we can give out from both of us. All our friends are here now.'

'Are we buying any gifts for the girls?' "The girls", is how Brendan always affectionately referred to the trio of friends that Anna had become close to while working with the horses.

'Yes, I'm going to get some chocolates for Joyce, Joan and Susan – oh, and Sandra.'

'What about Mr. and Mrs. Patrick?'

'Something special for them. I don't know what though, we'll have to have a look round.'

'I've got some time off tomorrow. Let's drive into town. I want to get your present. I think you'll like it but you'll have to choose it.'

'So, you know what you're buying me?'

'Yes.'

'I'll ask Mrs. P if I can have some time off, then. We'll make a day of it. I can't wait. I'll get yours too.'

'Do you know what you're going to buy *me*?'

'Yes. I think so.

* * *

'So she buys him some shoes then, does she?'

'You'll find out when I read the next chapter. Come on, let's go and get you sorted out for our wedding.'

'You know we could go to Gretna Green, and get married there if you like!'

'No, Pete, I'm quite happy with the local register office, thanks.'

'Okay. Whatever you say.'

'That wasn't difficult, was it?' says Peter, as he stands at the top of the town hall steps.'

Maggie is looking at the paperwork they'd been given. 'No. It looks pretty straight forward. We just have to be here ten minutes before the service on the twenty first.'

'You do realise it's the longest day of the year!'

'Yeah. That's why I chose it. More time to enjoy it!'

Peter laughs. 'Where to now?'

'There's a nice new menswear shop just around the corner. Let's look in there.'

They make their way to the shop but when Peter sees the window display he gives a slight groan. 'Oh, I don't think this is for me Maggie.'

'You need to have a look inside!'

'I don't need to look inside – I can tell with what they have on show. No – not for me Maggie.'

'Well, where then?'

'Is that little tailor's shop still there – the one on Donnelly Street?'

'Yes.'

'Let's go there then. I always wanted a suit made from there.'

They make their way to the old part of town and find the small tailor's shop. Maggie notices the joy on Peter's face when he sees the classic style of menswear in the window.

'If you're going to have it made, Pete, it will be expensive.'

'I want to look smart for you on my wedding day. I'm going in.'

Peter is so eager to get into the shop he stumbles slightly on the doorstep. Maggie is behind him, 'Careful!'

The customer service they experience in the shop is so good that Peter buys his whole outfit from them. They made suggestions regarding the colour and texture of suit fabric, the coordination of shirt, tie and shoes. Peter leaves the shop with a very happy smile on his face. He is given a bag with everything he'd bought and a receipt and note of the date – one week from today, to pick up his made to measure suit.

Maggie decides that she will return to the shop when Peter isn't with her so that she can buy him a wedding gift of a pair of gold cufflinks. While she had waited for Peter to be measured she had looked in the glass display cabinet and saw the perfect design; ships.

'I'm hungry,' says Peter.

'Me too. Do you want to eat out or take some pies home?'

'What about your outfit?'

'I've decided to get my outfit when you're not with me. Then, you won't see it before our wedding day. I'll ask Brenda to come with me on Saturday.'

'Okay. So, shall we get pies then?'

'Yes. We'll have peas and gravy with them.'

'Oh, Maggie – you certainly know the way to a man's heart.'

'Ha,' laughs Maggie. 'Only to yours!' She loops her arm through Peter's and they make their way to the pie shop.

After their late lunch, Maggie and Peter decide to return to their seats in the garden. The garden is now shade free and filled with bright sunshine.

'Would you like to hear the next chapter or are you tired.'

'I'm okay. I want to know if Brendan has had as good a day as I have.'

'Oh he does – here goes,' said Maggie, adjusting her glasses.

* * *

Chapter Twenty Seven – Christmas Day

Bill and Katie invited Anna and Brendan to join them for their Christmas lunch at the farmhouse. They had to be there for one o'clock. Brendan was up early as, before his own jobs, he wanted to get all the work done with the horses to allow Anna a lie in. She looked well and healthy but worked really hard, so Brendan tried to let her get some rest whenever he could. Work didn't stop on the farm, even on Christmas day, so he thought if he could get an early start, as Bill had suggested, they would be able to enjoy their Christmas lunch all the more.

He was back at the flat by noon and saw that Anna was up and dressed and making porridge. 'Don't eat too much of that, it may spoil your Christmas lunch. Knowing Mrs. P, you can bet there's going to be loads to eat.'

'I know. Have you opened your Christmas presents yet?'

'No. I thought we could open them together. Although we know what's in them.'

'Not everything. You only know what's in the ones we shopped for; there's a couple of surprises.'

'Is there?' Brendan went over to the small Christmas tree and picked up one of the small brown paper packages.' 'Oh yes. This one's for me.' He untied the string and opened it. 'Socks! Just what I need.'

'There's another there for you.'

He picked up another similar present and looked at the name tag. 'Mine again!' He was giggling now. 'This is good. Thank you.' He opened the gift. 'Another pair of socks! Thank you.' He hugged Anna. This is the best Christmas I've ever had!'

'Me too,' said Anna. 'I can't wait to wear my dress.'

'You'll look a million dollars in that new coat. I knew you'd like it. When I first saw it in the shop window, I knew it was for you.'

'I've never had a coat with a fur collar. As soon as I tried it on, it felt so... so, nice.'

'And the lady in the shop told me the swing style is in fashion,' said Brendan.

'That style's great for me – before and after baby.'

'Oh, and I've got something else for you too.'

'I thought we'd spent all our budget?'

'Well, this didn't cost me anything. Just hang on a minute while I go and get it.'

Brendan leapt down the stairs and Anna heard the door open. Brendan had left it open, so she knew he couldn't have gone far.

Five minutes later he was back, climbing the stairs. 'Close your eyes,' he called to Anna.

Anna sat on the sofa and turned her head away from the door and closed her eyes. 'What on earth is it?' She could hear Brendan in front of her.

'Right, you can open them now!'

Anna opened her eyes and saw a beautifully painted, wooden cradle. The base colour was cream and the painted pattern was similar to Mother V's caravan; gold, green and red. 'Oh Brendan, this is gorgeous. Where did you get it from?' She rocked it and it moved so smoothly.

'I made it!'

'How? I mean, it's so beautiful. I can't believe it.'

'I asked George if I could have the old steps off Mother V's caravan – remember when we got some new ones from the fair?'

'Oh, yes. And you made this out of the old ones?'

'Yes. I threw away the broken bits and then I separated the pieces. I looked at the curved shape of the sides and thought that would make the rockers; then I cut all the pieces to size.'

'And you painted it.' Anna rocked it again.

'I followed the patterns that were already on the wood. Do you like it?'

'Aww Brendan, I love it!' Anna threw her arms around him. 'I love you. Thank you. It's the best present ever.'

'Even better than your coat?'

'Yes, even better than that. I want to show it to Mrs. P.'

'She's already seen it. Mr. P helped me to do the work on it. He lent me the tools to work with and showed me how to use them.'

'How did you manage to keep it a secret?'

'I kept it up at the farmhouse and worked on it there. I brought it down yesterday and stored it in the caravan.'

'It's lovely!'

'Do you think our baby will love it?' asked Brendan.

Anna was so moved by what he just said, she could feel the tears of joy well up in her eyes and her voice struggled to say, '*Our* baby will have the best cradle ever made.'

'Right,' said Brendan, sniffing, 'I think it's time we got ready for that Christmas lunch. They won't know us when we turn up in our new clothes.' He picked up one of the big, brown Christmas parcels. 'I think this is my shirt, jumper and jeans,' he said, looking for his name on the gift tag.

'I'll go and put on my new dress and shoes.'

'Where's *my* new shoes?'

'In the bedroom. I didn't wrap those, I ran out of paper and string.'

Brendan went in search of his shoes, singing as he went. *Jingle Bells, Jingle Bells, Jingle . . .*'

When Brendan and Anna arrived at the farmhouse, they could hear Christmas songs playing. It was the Patricks' son John who opened the door to them. 'Happy Christmas!' he said, 'So nice to see you again!' He looked them up and down. 'And I must say how smart you both look!'

'Thanks,' said Brendan, 'Merry Christmas.' Brendan struggled to shake John's hand while holding onto the gifts to be given to Mr. and Mrs. Patrick. Anna took one of them off him.

John gave Anna a kiss. 'Merry Christmas!' he said. 'How are you? You look great! I believe congratulations are in order.'

Anna suddenly felt a little embarrassed, wondering how much John knew or had been told about her circumstances. 'Thank you,' she said, 'I'm okay.'

'Let me take your coats,' said John, 'Go through – Mum's been at the sherry while she's been cooking, so. . .'

'I heard that,' said Katie, as she came to greet Anna and Brendan with a hug. 'Merry Christmas, you two. I've only had one glass of sherry – yet! You both look lovely.'

'Thanks,' said Anna, handing over the gift 'This is a little something for you Mrs. P. I hope you like it.'

'Aww, thank you.' Katie began to tear away the brown paper to reveal an LP. 'Oh lovely – Frank Sinatra – my favourite! Aww, thank you! I'm going to play it now.' Katie went over to the gramophone and put the record on the turntable. Sinatra's crooning voice sang softly.

'Where is Mr. Patrick?' asked Brendan. 'We have a present for him too.'

'He's just gone to get something – he'll be here in a minute!'

Anna and Brendan followed Katie into the lounge, where Katie had set the long dining table with a white damask tablecloth and matching napkins in silver rings. A candelabra stood in the centre and was flanked with two small holly and poinsettia table decorations. There was matching cutlery and white and gold place settings.

'Mrs. P,' said Anna, 'your table looks absolutely fantastic. So nice.'

'Thank you...' She was interrupted by Bill, who was pushing a pram into the lounge.

'Ta Da!' he said. 'Look what Father Christmas left on our doorstep last night!'

Everyone laughed, except Anna, who gulped, knowing it could only be for her.

'We've found one for you,' said Katie. 'It's second hand but like new.'

Anna couldn't speak, not even to say thank you. Her hands shook as she went over to it and looked at the big brown card that hung on string from the handle.

'Shall I read it out?' said Brendan. He came over to her, gave her a hug and picked up the card. *'"Merry Christmas and best wishes from all of us at Appletree Farm."'*

Anna was quite stunned and overwhelmed by the generosity given to her. I don't deserve all this, she thought.

Lately, her emotions always seemed to get the better of her and she could feel her eyes prickling and tears were ready to flow.

Brendan somehow knew how she was feeling and gave her another hug. 'Look at the bodywork on this.' He ran his hand over the shiny, black, boat shaped body of the pram. 'And the soft, cream leather interior.'

Anna found her voice. 'Thank you so much, everyone. It's beautiful. Thank you.'

'And that's not all,' said Katie. 'There's a cot as well, but it needs assembling, so that's ready to go to yours – and also a box full of cot and pram bedding.'

Anna's mouth was gaping open and she put her hand over it. 'A cot as well! Aww Mrs. P. Thank you all so very much. I... I can't thank you enough.' At this point the tears flowed freely. 'Sorry,' she said.

'Okay folks,' said John, in an attempt to draw the attention away from Anna and lighten the emotional mood. 'It's Christmas! Let's celebrate! Snowballs for the ladies and beer for the men, right?'

'Oh, that reminds me,' said Brendan, picking up the gift they had bought for Bill. 'Here Mr. P. This is for you. Merry Christmas!' Brendan shook Bill's hand firmly.

'Open it,' said Katie.

Bill struggled with the string but finally managed to reveal a cocktail making kit. 'Oh this is just the ticket!' he said, 'We'll have fun with this.'

'Here you are everyone,' said John, handing out the drinks, 'let's have a toast.'

Bill held his beer aloft. 'To all of us and absent friends – Happy Christmas.'

They all acknowledged the meaningful toast.

'Okay everyone,' said Katie, 'take your seats at the table, I'm going to serve our lunch now.

Brendan couldn't wait for the food, he had worked up an appetite and had deliberately not eaten anything thinking it would make more room for Christmas food.

Anna offered to help Katie but was told to relax and enjoy being waited on; 'Our John is going to help me,' she said. 'It's all ready.'

Sinatra began to sing, '*Let is snow, let it snow, let it snow…*' They all turned towards the window.

* * *

'I hope it was snowing for them,' says Peter. 'Snow makes all the difference on Christmas day.'

'It's okay if you're looking at it through a window. Not so great when you have to walk in it!'

'You only start thinking like that when you get to our age. Young ones enjoy it!'

'Well, I don't want to think about snow. Not on this beautiful day. Let's relax and make the most of this warm summer evening before we go to bed.'

'No more reading till tomorrow then?'

'No. But I'll let you guess which postcard prompted that chapter.'

'That's easy – the signed photo card of Frank I sent from America.'

CHAPTER TWENTY EIGHT

MAGGIE BUYS HER OUTFIT

Brenda, Maggie's oldest friend, seemed elated when she was told the news of the engagement and was delighted to be asked to be matron of honour. The shopping for a bridal outfit was the best part of the role according to Brenda. Shopping, as Maggie knew, was what Brenda did best.

'Where shall we try first?' asks Maggie.

'Oh, there's a lovely bridal shop opened on the precinct.'

'But I don't want a puffy, fluffy wedding dress!'

'I know that, silly.' Brenda links her friend's arm as they march towards the shops. 'Come on. What you need is a beautiful dress with a coat or jacket of some kind. I know what suits you.'

'I think I'd like a cream colour. What do you think?'

'I would say more of an ivory rather than cream. In perhaps a similar style to that you wore for your Mammy's funeral.

Maggie stops in her tracks. 'It's a wedding Brenda! Not a funeral!'

'I know! But the style suited you. And it wouldn't be in black! In *ivory*. Perhaps with a lovely satin trim. Come on.'

They carry on walking again and Maggie begins to imagine the outfit. 'I'm going to need a hat too.'

'They have hats to die for in a little shop just around the corner from the bridal shop. They're a bit cheaper too.'

'Pete says I've not got to worry about how much it costs. He wants to buy it for me.'

'Well then!' Brenda rubs her hands together. 'The sky's the limit – come on. Only the best for you then!' Brenda rushes her friend on towards the shop and she squeezes Maggie's arm. 'Oh, how I love days like this!'

The shop is a delight to visit and the greeting is pleasant. The floral scent on entering gives an upmarket feel. Maggie experiences the comfort of its spacious changing area as she tries on several outfits. The customer service is first class with no rush; no hard sell. They are even given a cup of tea and biscuits.

Spoilt for choice, Maggie is glad she has her friend with her to help her choose.

There is one outfit that Brenda finds on the rack, which is the kind of style she had previously explained to Maggie that she had in mind. It is a well cut ivory lace dress that is an elegant, below the knee length. It has a matching floating chiffon jacket. Brenda takes it over to the assistant. 'Can she try this on please?'

'Certainly.' The assistant takes it into the changing room.

It isn't long before Maggie emerges wearing it.

'It's just perfect,' says Brenda. 'The colour and style suits you and you could add a touch of contrasting colour with flowers.'

'You can come and work here,' the assistant says to Brenda. 'You have an eye for style. It is beautiful.'

Brenda seems quite happy that the assistant is impressed and that her talent for fashion is acknowledged. 'Thank you very much.'

Maggie spots a hat she thinks is a perfect accessory for the outfit. 'Can I try that on?' she asks, pointing to the hat displayed on one of the high shelves. It is the same shade as the outfit; not too big and not too small. It is a modern style with a little bit of netting decoration which, Maggie thinks, makes it suitable for a bride, plus the most delicate pink floral adornment on one side.

Brenda wants to go to the hat shop round the corner to see what they have and whispers to Maggie. 'You may see something else you like better.'

Maggie tries on the hat and it feels just right.

Brenda agrees, it is just perfect and gestures to Maggie with a thumbs up sign and a smile.

Maggie can see from Brenda's expression that she is becoming quite emotional. There is a box of tissues on one of the small tables next to where Brenda is sitting and Maggie sees her take one and wipe away a joyful tear.

Laden with a large, red and gold, expensive looking carrier bag, plus a smart black and white hat box with a rope handle, the friends search for a shoe shop.

On their way, they come across the small tailoring shop where Peter's suit is being made. Maggie goes in and buys the special cuff links she wants Peter to have as a wedding gift.

A little further on, a shoe shop displays the perfect pair to match Maggie's outfit. Plain ivory leather, peep toe shoes with a sensible heel and there is the bonus of a matching clutch bag which Brenda suggests could be decorated with similar flowers to the ones on her hat. A different way to wear the flowers instead of on her outfit. 'That way, the flowers won't leave a mark on your jacket,' says Brenda.

Maggie knows her friend can shop all day and never get tired but she, herself, is quite exhausted and suggests they stop at the nearest pub where they can sit outside and have a celebratory drink.

Brenda agrees, 'Have we finished shopping then?'

'Yes. Definitely. Thank you for helping me. I'm pleased with what I've got. And the drinks are on me.'

'Are they not on Peter's bill?'

Maggie laughs 'That's an idea!'

When Maggie gets home, Peter has prepared a lovely summer salad and has set it out on the table outdoors.

Before they begin to eat, Peter pours white wine into two glasses, handing one to Maggie. 'Did you get everything?' he asks.

'Yes, and I've had a lovely day.'

'Let me know what it cost and I'll get the money for you tomorrow.'

'Are you sure?'

'Of course I'm sure.'

'Well I'll give you the receipts.'

'I don't want the receipts – just tell me the total.'

'Okay, I'll reckon it up and let you know. Does it include our drink at the pub?'

'Err... only if you promise to read another chapter of your book when we've finished eating.'

'Deal.' Maggie clinks her glass against Peter's.

When the meal is over, Maggie again goes in search of her glasses which doesn't take her long to find. She sits in her usual place, takes a sip of the white wine and begins to read her book to Peter whose eyes are closed in readiness to imagine the characters he has become so fond of.

* * *

Chapter Twenty Eight – Boxing Day

After he had finished his morning's work, Brendan picked up the baby's cot from the farmhouse. Bill gave him the basic instructions of how to assemble it and handed him a brown paper bag. 'The bits of screws and things are in there,' said Bill. 'The drop down side can be a bit tricky – are you sure you can manage?'

'I think so. I'll ring you if I get stuck.'

While Anna was out tending to the horses, Brendan carried the pieces of the cot from the van up the stairs and placed them individually on the floor of the spare bedroom of the flat. On Anna's instructions, he had previously moved all the cardboard boxes that had been stored there to the campsite office where they belonged.

He looked at the pieces and scratched his head. He emptied the brown paper bag carefully and matched up the sizes of the screws with the holes in the wooden pieces and worked methodically. It was only when he came to the last piece of the puzzle that he failed to work out how the drop down mechanism worked. After several attempts he gave up and picked up the phone. 'Hello, Mrs. P. Is Mr. Patrick there, I'm a bit stuck with this cot. He said he would help.'

'Bill's had to go out. He won't be back for another hour or so. Can I help?' asked Katie.

'Yes please. If you have time.'

'Yes. Did you pick the pram up?'

'No, not yet.'

'Okay. I'll go and get it and walk up with it.'

'Okay, thanks.'

Sometime later, between them, Katie and Brendan, after rearranging one of the pieces, managed to assemble the cot in perfect order. They placed it in a corner of the room. The only other piece of furniture was the folded up camp bed which was now beneath the window.

I think this room makes a perfect nursery,' said Katie. 'I can't wait for the baby to arrive.'

'It sounds so posh – having a nursery!'

Katie laughed. 'Would you mind if I helped to decorate it? I'd like to soften the wall colour a little – a creamy white colour and perhaps a few coloured transfers here and there. No nails in the walls though. Bill insists on keeping the new plaster on the walls hole free!'

'I understand. And it's your property, you can do whatever you like. We just love living here.'

'All you need for now is somewhere to store baby clothes and nappies and talc and stuff. I'll sort it.'

'Anna does appreciate all you do for her and the baby. Me too.'

'I know, and I enjoy seeing you both happy. You both work hard for us and appreciation works both ways.'

'Thank you.'

'Anyway, I'll have to go now.'

'Do you want me to take you back in the van?' asked Brendan.

'No, the walk will do me good.'

'Thanks for bringing the pram.'

'That's okay. I didn't realise how big it was until I struggled to get it into the vestibule. You'll only just manage to open and shut the door!'

'That's where it will have to stay but it will be fine. Anna loves it.'

'She's not long to go now. She's doing so well.'

'I think she gets a bit nervous sometimes but she's okay.'

'That's understandable. We had a lovely time yesterday didn't we?'

'It's been the best Christmas ever, for me. Thank you.'

'That's good. Anyway, I must go. See you later.'

Anna took off her wellington boots outside the door and when she walked in, in stockinged feet, was surprised to be faced with the beautiful pram taking up the entire space. She couldn't resist touching it. She gripped the handle and rocked it. 'Brendan?' she called out as she climbed the stairs, surprised that he was home before her. 'Are you alright? Did *you* bring the pram?'

'I'm okay. Mrs. P brought it,' he said. 'I'm in the nursery!'

'The nursery!' Anna laughed. She walked into the spare bedroom. 'Oh, you've got the cot as well!' She walked over to the cot and examined it by running her hand over the polished wood. 'It's lovely. Thank you.' She looked over to Brendan whose face was beaming.

'It works,' he said and came over to demonstrate the technique of how to lift the side of the cot and lower it down. 'You'll be able to get the baby out, see. And when you put him back...' He lifted the side up and locked it. '...It'll be safe, see?'

'And what if it's a girl?'

'What?' asked Brendan looking a little confused?

'You said "him". What if it's a girl?'

Brendan put his arms around her. 'Boy, girl, it doesn't matter. I will love it like I love you.' He kissed her. 'Is anything bothering you?'

'I've been thinking about when we register the birth. What should we do when we have to fill in the father's name?'

Brendan seemed rather put out by her asking this question. 'I thought you would want to put *my* name down. Unless you are having second thoughts about telling the real father.'

'No. I want *you* so much to be the *real* father. I love you Brendan, you know that. I wouldn't want any connection with…' Anna couldn't even say his name. 'But are you sure you want to be named as the father on the birth certificate – I mean is it legal to do that?'

'Yes. I think so. And no one ever needs to know any different. Apart from us, Mr. and Mrs. P and George are the only ones who know and I doubt they will ever speak of it.'

'Well, I don't want anyone else to know and I won't speak about it ever again.' Anna sighed. 'It's been bothering me but I feel a lot better now. I love you. Thank you.' Anna kissed him passionately.

'Good. Can we have something to eat now? I'm starving.'

'We'll have some soup and some of Mrs. P's bread. Have you got any more work to do today?'

'Not much, but I'll have to check in with Mr. P. I'll see to the horses for you later.'

'Oh good. Thanks. I've fed them and put them out. 'I've put the winter blankets on them but I've left Diamond in the stable – he seems to have a cold and I don't want him giving it to the others.'

'What will we have to give him?'

After we've eaten, I'm going to look through Mother V's notebook and see what remedy she suggests and after that, I want to have a nice warm bath and relax with my book.'

'You do that. Now let's go and eat.'

* * *

'Brendan really does love Anna, so much.'

'I'm glad that comes across – it's what I wanted to show. A real passion between them.

'He'd give her the moon and the stars, if he could, wouldn't he?

'His all!'

CHAPTER TWENTY NINE

THUNDERSTORMS

The breakfast is sandwiches made of egg and bacon on toasted bread. Maggie has made them and takes them through to the lounge. Peter is in the kitchen making the mugs of tea.

Maggie looks through the window to check on the weather. When she sees Peter come into the room struggling to carry the mugs of tea with unsteady hands, she rushes to him and takes the mugs from him and puts them on the coffee table. Nothing is said about his ailment. They sit side by side on the sofa.

'We can probably get through three chapters today,' says Maggie, 'it looks like the rain isn't going to stop.'

'Good. It'll be nice to have a quiet, lazy day.'

'Didn't you say you had to go and look at the progress of your cottage?'

'They won't be working on it in this weather. I'll go tomorrow.'

'Okay.'

They eat their breakfast in a quiet, relaxed mood. After which, Maggie continues to read her novel.

* * *

Chapter 29 – The Nursery

Anna was near to her due date and was feeling well but heavy. She felt capable of working and kept all the bookings for the campsite guests up to date and there were very few vacancies left for the static caravans. Bill and Katie were pleased with the organisation of the office in readiness for the start of the first summer season.

Anna couldn't wait to meet the new manager and wondered what changes, if any, he would make. He was due to join them in about six weeks, on Saturday, 3rd April – a week before the campsite was due to open, so that he could familiarise himself with the site and the planned routine for the guests.

Brendan's notebook was full of ideas and Bill had chosen the ones he thought would work best. The plan was to have a weekly entertainment schedule which included something for the children for a couple of hours every afternoon and family entertainment in the evenings subject to alteration according to the weather. Anna thought the new manager may have some ideas of his own to add to the suggestions.

Brendan had taken over Anna's heavier duties around the farm and she had taken on more administration work for Bill. She was now known as Bill's secretary. It was work that Katie would normally do but Anna's office skills were of a more professional standard and she was happy to put them into practice – after all, she thought, that was what she was being paid for as a general assistant.

Once all her work in the office was up to date, Anna went home to the flat. She was keen to help Katie finish decorating the nursery with some colourful transfers on the walls and the chest of drawers Katie had managed to find, in which was stored all the baby's clothes, nappies and toiletries. Anna was amazed at what a baby needed and at what she had accumulated over the last few months; she had bought an item every week, such as talcum powder, baby soap and items of clothing. Katie had advised her to have three sets of everything, "One for wearing, one for washing and one for airing."

When Anna arrived home, she went into the nursery to check on the decorating progress.

'Hello. How are you?' asked Katie.

'I'm fine, thanks. I feel full of energy today. What do you want me to do?'

'Brendan's finished the painting but he's had to go and help Bill with the new small animal pens.' Katie pointed to the walls. 'Do you like it?'

'I love it. Thank you. Shall I clean up the paint brushes?' Anna was eager to have the room ready for when her baby arrived.

'Before you do that, where do you want me to put this big transfer?'

Anna looked at the colourful image of a duck wearing a pink bonnet. She looked around for a suitable place. I think it will look okay on the end of the cot.'

'Right,' said Katie.

'Anna bent down to pick up the paint brushes and felt a searing pain which took her breath away. 'Ooh aagh!' She stood up straight and began to take some deep breaths to try and ease the discomfort she felt.

'Are you okay?' asked Katie, who was in the middle of placing the transfer on the cot. 'What was it?'

'I think I bent down a little awkwardly and I got a pain. I really need to learn to bend my legs when I have to pick things up.' Anna laughed. 'It's gone now. I'm okay.' She bent her legs and picked up the brushes and took them into the kitchen to clean.

Katie followed Anna into the kitchen. 'Are you sure you're alright. Daffy duck looks a little drunk on the cot but it will have to do.'

'It's okay,' said Anna. 'You've made it look so nice. Thank you. Ooh!' Anna felt another jabbing pain and then water gushed out of her. It scared her. 'Ooh, Mrs. P, am I having the baby?'

'Don't panic! It's just your waters breaking. Quite normal. Just sit down here.' Katie dragged out one of the kitchen chairs. 'Just take a few deep breaths. I'll clean up and then we'll get you washed and changed and take you to the hospital.'

Anna could feel herself trembling and breathed deeply, as she watched Katie quickly mop the floor.

'Come on now. Let's get you into the bathroom and then you can find a change of clothes. Have you got some things ready for the hospital?'

'Yes,' said Anna, walking slowly to the bathroom. 'There's a bag in the living room – the one I got when I bought my coat at Christmas. I put things in there that I thought I would need.'

'Okay. You get yourself washed and changed. I'll ring the hospital and tell them you're on your way.'

'Will I be alright? It's not due for another week. They said the twenty sixth.' She sighed.

'You'll be fine. Don't worry. Babies arrive when they want to and a week either side is nothing to worry about. I'll be with you. Now you get washed and changed.'

Katie went into the living room to use the extension phone and looked up the number for the hospital in the little address book Anna kept at the side of it. She dialled the number then spoke to someone on the maternity ward who told her to bring Anna in as soon as possible.

* * *

Maggie puts the book down and takes off her glasses. 'I need to use the bathroom – I won't be a minute,'

Peter laughs – 'It's all that reading about the waters breaking!'

'I think it must be.' Maggie goes upstairs.

Peter gets up from the sofa to stretch his legs and looks at all the photographs on the sideboard. He recognises Maggie's parents and Maggie, when she was young with her friend

Brenda. There is one of Brenda's wedding and Maggie must have been her maid of honour. There is a school photograph with Maggie's father standing straight and tall at the back. Peter picks it up and looks closely to see if he can recognise himself in the photo somewhere.

Maggie comes into the lounge and sees what he's looking at. 'You're on the back row, third from the left.'

'Oh yes,' he says, lifting the photograph nearer to his eyes. 'So I am. And you're on the second row. I found you straight away.' He put the frame down and picked up another. 'Who's this wee fella?'

'That "wee fella" is a baby girl – her name is Petula – after Petula Clark.'

'She's got a lovely smile. Who is she?'

'My parents adopted her – apparently, they said her mother couldn't look after her and Mammy felt sorry for her and persuaded Daddy to adopt her as a sister for me. She always wanted me to have a sister.' Maggie's voice breaks a little and she coughs. 'The baby's mother was in our class – you would know her but she didn't want anyone to know about it, so I'd better not say.'

'Your parents were always helping people.'

'I helped too – she was a lovely, beautiful baby. She's in her late forties now. She works at University College Dublin as a librarian. Daddy was very proud of her. We all were.'

'He was always very proud of you.'

'He was, yeah, and he loved both of us. "His girls", he used to call us; including Mammy.'

'And where is she now?'

'She lives in Dublin with her husband – he's a draughtsman and they have a son, Alex – he'll be twenty one soon. I think there's a photo of him on there somewhere.' Maggie searches for it. 'Here it is. A handsome lad.'

'He is. Will they be coming to our wedding?'

'Yes. I hope so, if they can make it.'

'That's good.' Peter sits down on the sofa. 'Can we find out how Anna is? What does she have? A boy or a girl?'

'You'll have to wait and see.' Maggie sits down, picks up the book, adjusts her glasses and reads.

* * *

Chapter 30 – Anna goes to Hospital

Katie drove Anna to the Maternity Hospital. The staff were strict with the rules and along with all expectant fathers, Katie wasn't allowed in the labour ward. 'I'll wait for a while until they get you settled in,' she said. 'You'll be fine.'

Anna wasn't too sure about that. Although she had none of the labour pains she had read about, she felt very restless and nervous. When the nurse took her to her allocated bed in the four bed labour ward, the other three beds were vacant. She felt quite alone.

A young nurse of about Anna's age, was on hand to help her if she had difficulty getting into her oversized nightie. She didn't need any help but was glad there was someone to talk to.

'How long will I be before I have my baby?' asked Anna.

'Quite a while yet, I should think. The midwife will be here shortly and she'll examine you. She'll have a better idea. But babies arrive when they're ready!'

'I don't seem to have any regular labour pains. Is that normal?'

'You will. And the more frequent they are, the better. That's when your baby is on its way.'

'Will it hurt?'

'Yes, I'm afraid it will. But it will be worth it! And don't worry. I'll be here to hold your hand.'

'Thank you.' Anna felt a lot better knowing the young nurse would be there for her.

'Get into bed. There's some water on the cabinet if you need it. Read a magazine or something while you wait for the midwife. I'll be back shortly.' The lovely smile on her plump face reassured Anna.

Anna must have dozed off. She was woken by the midwife. 'Sorry,' said Anna, sitting up straight. The young nurse was standing behind the midwife.

'That's quite alright. It's good to get some rest now, it will help you to build up some strength for the labour.'

Anna felt her baby tighten in her belly and a faint pain, but nothing that she couldn't cope with. 'I think I just felt a pain then,' she said to the midwife.

The midwife looked at the watch that was pinned onto her uniform. 'You think?' she asked. There seemed some sarcasm in her tone, thought Anna.

'I'm not sure.'

'Let's have a look at you.' She lifted Anna's nightie to expose her swollen belly and began to press gently in specific areas. She then put a small trumpet shaped instrument onto Anna's stomach. Her ear was close to the narrow end of the instrument and she was listening carefully.

Anna could feel her baby move as if it was arching its back.

'Everything's fine,' said the midwife, straightening Anna's nightie. 'Your baby has a strong heartbeat. It'll be a while yet. Your labour pains will get stronger. Eat something light if you feel you need to, but some mother's tend to feel sick during labour.'

'Thank you,' said Anna. The midwife seemed very strict and she made Anna feel a little nervous.

'I'll be back in a couple of hours. Let nurse know if you need anything.' She strode off the ward leaving the nurse to straighten Anna's bed.

'She's scary,' said Anna.

'She gives that impression but she's nice really. Strict and very professional, she doesn't stand any nonsense. You're in good hands.'

'Aar.' Anna felt a definite pain that lasted a short time. She sighed. 'That was a pain!'

'Good. Some progress then.' Nurse checked the time.

It was several hours later when Anna's baby was born. Anna was moved out of the delivery room and back onto a ward where there were three other mothers.

'Have you chosen a name for your baby yet?' the nurse asked as she made Anna comfortable in the fourth bed.

'Yes,' replied Anna. 'Ruby.'

'That's a lovely name.'

'My husband chose it from one of the baby books. He couldn't decide on a boy's name.'

'Well, it's happen as well it's a girl then! He can be decide on a boy's name next time.'

'Oh, no! I don't think I could go through that again!'

'They all say that. And then the following year, they're in here again.' Nurse laughs. 'Anyway, how are you feeling now?'

'I feel a bit sore and ache all over, but I'm okay, thanks.'

'That's understandable. You know, you did really well. Everything seemed to go by the book. I wish they were all like that.'

'You were kindness itself in there,' said Anna. I hope I didn't hurt your hand too much.'

'You certainly have a strong grip but I'll survive.'

'When can I see my baby again?'

'You need to rest. I'll bring Ruby to you when it's time for her feed. I'm going to bring you some tea and toast and then I want you to try and have a little sleep. Okay.'

'Yes, thank you.' Anna sighed. She was so relieved it was all over and a rush of excitement overwhelmed her as the reality began to dawn on her that she was now a mother. She doubted she would be able to sleep and she had no idea when it was going to be the baby's feeding time.

A little while later, the nurse came back with the tea and toast as promised. Anna didn't realise how hungry she was. She closed her eyes and licked her lips. 'This is the best toast I've ever tasted.'

'Good. Now you get some rest while you can. Believe me you'll get very little when you get home.'

'Is Mrs. Patrick still here?'

'She's left a message to say she's going to come at visiting time with your husband.'

Chapter 31 – Ruby

Katie walked into the ward and Brendan followed her carrying a bunch of flowers. He walked with his head down as if he didn't want to look at any of the other mothers. His embarrassment was obvious.

Nurse drew the curtain around Anna's bed to give the family some privacy. 'I'll bring your baby,' she said.

'Thank you,' said Anna.

When nurse had gone, Brendan gave Anna the flowers and gave her a kiss. 'You did it!' he said. He put his arm around his wife's shoulders. 'How are you?'

'I'm okay. A bit sore but they said everything is fine and I should be able to go home tomorrow.'

'That's good,' said Katie. She found herself a chair and sat at the side of the bed opposite Brendan.

Nurse came onto the ward carrying Ruby in her arms. She drew back the curtain a little. 'Here she is. Does Dad want to hold her?' She placed the baby into Brendan's arms. His hands looked so big against the small bundle. He didn't say anything. The expression on his face showed exactly how he was feeling.

'Everyone likes her name,' said Anna.

'Did you know Ruby was the name of Mother V's first horse that she ever owned?' said Katie.

Anna and Brendan looked at one another. 'That's uncanny!' said Brendan, finding his voice.

'How lovely. We didn't know,' said Anna. 'I'd like to think she's looking down on us.'

'Our Ruby. She's so beautiful – just like her mother,' said Brendan.

'Can I have a little hold of her?' asked Katie.

Brendan, as much as he already loved Ruby, was quite glad to hand her over to Katie. Anna could see he wasn't confident holding such a precious bundle. 'She's so tiny,' he said.

'Six pound three ounces!' said Anna proudly.

'You'll soon get used to handling her,' said Katie. 'I can't wait to get you both home.'

Anna leaned back into the pillow and let her happiness wash over her.

* * *

Maggie takes off her glasses, puts down the book and yawns. 'I think that's enough for today, Pete.'

Peter opens his eyes and sits up on the sofa. 'Thanks Maggie. You've read a lot. I'm glad Anna's got a girl!'

'Why?'

'It's more chance of looking like Anna than the father.'

'I see.'

'And if it has red hair, then Brendan might – well, you know what I mean. He might feel more comfortable if she resembles him.'

'Yes. I know what you mean. You're happy with a girl then?'

'Oh yes. Brendan's so lucky to have a daughter.'

'It's only a book Peter. Fiction. It's not real.'

'I know. But I like them. And I didn't recognize any of my postcards in this chapter.'

'No, there were none,' says Maggie.

'Thought not,' says Peter, sounding a little disappointed. 'Anyway, I'll go and make us a cup of tea and a sandwich. What have we got planned for later this evening then?'

'I think we'll have fish and chips for dinner at about seven; then, I want to watch the television – I've got a few films on the tapes if you want to choose one.'

'It sounds like a good plan. You choose the film.'

CHAPTER THIRTY

PETER'S COTTAGE

There is sunshine today, after the previous thunderstorms. The air is fresh and Maggie and Peter decide to check on the work being done on Peter's cottage. They stroll slowly down past 'The Ship Inn' and reach the cottage on Smithy Street.

The two roofers are busy removing the black tarpaulin sheets revealing a small part of the roof still needing tiling.

'How's the work coming along?' asks Peter.

One of the roofers looks down. 'Your roof will be finished today, sir!'

'Good. Is it just the roof you have to finish?'

'Well, there's just a bit more pointing to finish at the back, sir, then we've done.'

'That's good. That's good. So, when d'ya think?'

'Another day, sir and we'll be done! The painters will be in touch wi ye, sir, as to when they'll be able to start the decoratin'. It won't be long now, sir.'

'Good. Is it safe to go inside, d'you think?'

'Oh, yes, sir. The lads have finished inside. All the lectric's an' the plastering's finished. Quite safe, sir.'

'Thanks,' says Peter.

Maggie follows Peter into the cottage. Peter breathes in the smell of newness. 'There's no trace of the familiar home,' he says. They look around and see the patches of plaster not quite dry and tread carefully on the hard flagged floor where bits of wood, wire and plaster still remain and crunch underfoot. All the old renovated furniture is piled in the corners of the rooms and well covered with massive thick cotton cloths.

'What are you going to do with it?' asks Maggie.

'What do you think I should do with it? I don't want to sell it. It's my last memories of my Mammy.'

'When we're married, I took it for granted that we will live at mine. I never asked you – but are you happy with that?'

'I'm happy with whatever makes you happy, Maggie.'

'So, you could rent this out. I'll help you decorate it and you can sort out where you want to place the furniture that you've worked so hard on; we'll make it nice.'

'Nice. That's all I want it to be for Mammy. Nice.'

'Okay. Come on then.' Maggie looks at her watch. 'Let's go to 'The Ship' for lunch.'

Later that evening Maggie and Peter finish making some decorating plans for the cottage. Peter allows Maggie to choose the colour scheme from some pictures in one of her magazines.

'Cut out those colours Maggie and write down what you want and I'll give it to the decorators tomorrow. And, you know, whoever we rent it to, I think we should ask them not to put nails in the plaster for pictures and stuff,' says Peter.

'You're thinking like Bill in my book.'

'I know. And we need to catch up with what's going on. Are you up to reading some more now?' says Peter, leaning back into the sofa.

'Okay.' Maggie prepares herself and reads.

* * *

Chapter 32 – Anna meets her new boss

Ruby was now one week old. Anna had established a routine, thanks to Katie, who now labelled herself as Nana Patrick.

Katie had been a substitute mother to Anna, showing her the ropes of motherhood and, knowing how tiring a new baby can be, had let Anna sleep; taking Ruby for many walks in her pram. She showed Anna how to bathe Ruby and how to make up the bottles. She had fed her and generally and generously helped Anna to enjoy her baby.

Anna was so grateful and now felt she was strong enough to get back to her job. Between them, Katie and Anna had worked out a routine to take care of the baby and do the work they had to do. Katie would work in the mornings and do the baking for the farm shop; Sandra had been given some extra hours to learn the craft and that allowed Katie time to look after Ruby in the afternoons, when Anna would work in the office till five.

Katie adored Ruby and she treated her like the granddaughter she'd hoped for. She had given up on her son

John providing her with an offspring anytime soon. Bill was also enamored with the beautiful child.

Anna's friends came to visit her often and were also besotted with Ruby, who wasn't short of aunties to spoil her.

All three of the girls were voluntarily helping Brendan with the horses until Anna could get back into caring for them.

Susan had left school at Christmas and was looking for office work and had been offered temporary employment helping Brendan with his orders until she found something suitable. Joyce and Joan were due to leave school at Easter and were eager to start the promised seasonal employment on the campsite, working with the horses.

Brendan was working hard on the orders and deliveries and around the farm in general; fixing broken fences and machinery and preparing the new pens for the display of small animals that the campsite guests would be able to look at and pet; which was one of Brendan's ideas, to give the campers some family entertainment. There was going to be some goats, pigs, maybe a couple of sheep and hopefully lambs, rabbits and guinea pigs and whatever else Bill suggested. The chickens and ducks had always been on the farm and roamed free. There was an ongoing debate as to whether or not the pond would have to be cordoned off for safety. It wasn't very near the campsite and it did offer the opportunity of fishing but Bill said it still presented a danger to a straying child. Katie was also worried about Roger, the cockerel who didn't like strangers. They had no idea how he was going to react to the guests. Bill suggested having the metal bin ready to capture him under it if he misbehaved. For some unknown reason, Roger was always okay with Brendan and followed him around the farm.

Everyone was gearing up to welcoming their first guests at Easter.

It was the third of April and the weather was a bit cool but the sun was shining. The new manager, Mr. Thomas Price was due to arrive at mid-day.

Anna had taken Ruby to Katie and then returned to the office ready to welcome her new boss.

Bill rolled up in his car and he and Mr. Price, carrying a suitcase, got out and they made their way to the campsite reception. Anna greeted them with a smile.

'This is Anna, our office manager and secretary. She runs this office with military precision,' said Bill.

'Pleased to meet you Anna,' said Mr. Price.

'Pleased to meet you too, Mr. Price,' replied Anna.

'Please call me Tom.'

Anna was pleased about that. It made her feel less subservient. He seemed nice; about ten years older than she was, and she thought they would get along fine.

'Well, I'll leave you to get used to the place. Anna will show you where everything is and the keys to your caravan are pinned up there on the key rack.' Bill pointed to a wooden board with all the numbers of the caravans and their relevant keys. 'Yours is number one. Brendan will come along later and show you around the campsite.'

'Thank you, said Tom. 'I'm looking forward to seeing everything.'

'Okay. Is there anything you want to ask?'

'No. I don't think so. You've explained everything. Thanks.'

'Right. I'll leave you in Anna's capable hands then. Ring through on the reception phone if you need anything.'

'Thank you.'

Bill left Anna and Tom to get acquainted.

Anna then felt a little nervous as to what to say to Tom. He seemed very confident and smartly dressed and she didn't want to appear to him as an office know it all. Although she did. 'Would you like a cup of tea?'

Oh, yes please. But I prefer coffee if you have it. And while you're making it, I'll take my suitcase to the caravan.'

'Okay. Anna went to get the keys from off the board and Tom did the same and they clashed hands.'

'Sorry,' said Tom.

Anna laughed nervously.

'Back in a jiffy,' said Tom and he gave Anna a wink.

That wink reminded her so much of a time she'd rather forget. She squirmed. From then on she thought, she would be careful not to clash with Tom or give him any reason to think she would want to be anything other than a work colleague. She made the drinks.

Tom came back. He had changed from out of his suit into jeans and a casual shirt. He smelled lovely and looked nice and gave Anna the impression that he knew it.

'Here's your coffee.' Anna was careful not to hand it to him. She placed it on the reception counter.

'Thank you. Where shall we start?' he asked.

'Our office. That's where most of the work is done.' Anna took him through to the office.

'Ah, this is the interview room. I remember it.'

'Your desk is over there.' Anna pointed to a clutter free desk that was opposite to hers. 'This is mine, here,' she said. 'I usually always have this typewriter on it but if ever we need space for anything we can put the typewriter on top of the filing cabinet, over there.' Anna pointed to the grey metal cabinet.

'This is the stationery cupboard,' she said, opening up the doors of a tall metal cabinet behind her desk, to show all the contents. The keys to this and the filing cabinet are kept in the cash drawer. She pointed to a large deep drawer just above some cupboards at the side of the filing cabinet and walked over to it. 'This is the cash drawer.' She got the keys from off her belt and opened it. 'This is where all the money goes and the books where all the entries are made. It is totalled and checked at the end of each day. The paying in book and the cheque book are kept in the canvas bank bag here at the back of the drawer.'

'Right,' said Tom.

'This is your key.' Anna gave him the cash drawer key. 'There are three keys. Mine, yours and Mrs. P has one.'

'Receipt books for the guests are in the reception office drawer and the copies come in here with the money. I've only done receipts for postal payments so far.'

'I suppose I'll get used to it when we start next week,' said Tom.

'I do the wages for all the farm workers but next week I'll also be doing them for the campsite workers – yours, Beryl the cleaner and any other seasonal workers we pay out for such as the DJ and the barman. That's why I have two different wage books.' She held up the labelled books. 'For the campsite payments out, I need you to check and authorise them.'

'Okay, miss. You seem to have it all under control.'

'Mrs. Mrs. O'Connor.'

Tom looked surprised. He looked for a ring on her finger. 'Sorry. I didn't expect a young girl like you to be married.' There was a smirk in his smile.

'Yes. We have a little girl, Ruby.'

'Oh. I see.' He nodded in a way that irritated Anna.

'That's it for the office,' said Anna. 'Have you got any plans for the week's routine? Bill and Brendan have worked some out but wanted you to have some input with any ideas you may have.'

'None as yet.'

Anna gave Tom a copy of the planned routine. 'Okay, let me know if you want to make any alterations to it and then I can go ahead and type it up. I'll put it up on the notice board in the reception.'

Tom studied the week's routine. 'So, there's two events every day?'

'Yes. Monday to Saturday. One for the children in the afternoons and a family one every evening.'

'We get Sunday off.'

'Not really. We have to be on hand at the reception for the guests leaving and new guests arriving and for those who are staying for a fortnight and casual tourists.'

'Okay. Are we alternating the Sunday work?'

'We can, if you like.'

'We can sort that out later then.'

'All the campsite rules will be on the notice board. There's a copy of them in the drawer there.' Anna pointed out the drawer. 'Our daily shifts in the office will overlap. 'You will do mornings ten till three and I'll do afternoons one till six. We can't really swap that around. Mrs. P can only mind Ruby in the afternoons.'

'Okay. And I'm on duty at the events in the evening?'

'You've got it. Yes.' Anna thought he was being a bit friendlier towards her and she softened towards him. It was a relief to think that she could work with him.

'Is there anything else?' asked Tom. 'Who's in charge?'

Anna thought the question was strange. 'You are – you're the manager!'

'Right. Go and put the kettle on.' Tom smiled.

Brendan came into the office and Anna introduced him to Tom.

'I've come to take you round the campsite,' said Brendan.

'Oh good. Thank you.' Tom shook Brendan's hand. 'Pleased to meet you.'

They left the office and turned left down the lane into the campsite. 'Have you settled in?' asked Brendan, pointing to caravan number one.

'Yes, thanks. I've not unpacked properly yet but it looks comfortable enough. Which one's yours?'

'We have the flat above the reception, up there.' Brendan pointed.

'How on earth did you manage that?'

'A long story,' said Brendan. 'We work on the farm all year round. Not just the seasonal campsite job.'

'Oh, I see. When you say we…'

'Me and Anna. Anna's my wife.'

'Oh right. Are you related to the Patrick's?'

'No. We are their general assistants.' Brendan loved the title of his role. It made him feel important. 'So as you can see, the caravans are numbered and the rows have names. The layout is in the office on the notice board.'

'Yes, I've seen that.'

'The facilities are over there to the right. Beryl will clean them once a day but they will need to be checked. Any problems, we have plumbing contractors to deal with it. Just ring them.'

They walked to the end of the rows of caravans and Brendan pointed out the big covered barn. 'That's where we'll hold the campsite evening entertainment. I've cleaned it up and we're going to get some chairs and tables delivered this week. I've left some bales for guests to sit on. We'll have a barn dance every Saturday. There'll be talent contests and fancy dress evenings in there as well. Mr. Patrick has a licence to serve alcohol and we have someone that he knows who will come in every evening and put up a bar.'

'I think everything is sorted then. I just manage it, be the MC and look after everyone.'

'Yes. That's it. We thought you might have some ideas or changes you want to make?'

'No, nothing to add or change to what you've already planned. Not yet anyway. It sounds good.'

'I'll be arranging the afternoon children's events. Football matches and visits to the small barn at the back of the farmhouse where the new pens are for the small farm animals, things like that. Susan works in the afternoons and looks after them. The horse grooming and riding lessons have to be booked in advance – that's Anna's department. All the information will be on the notice board. She and the girls will be in charge of them.'

'"The girls?"'

'The girls who work with the horses. Anna's friends, Joyce and Joan. Have you any suggestions for the children's entertainment?'

'No. You seem to have it all planned. Do I get the free time then, in the afternoons?'

'Yes. I'll do three till five every day with the children and help you out with the evening events.'

'That's fine. Good. I think I'll find my way around.'

'Just tell Anna if you need me for anything. I'm always out early in the mornings but usually back around one.'

'Thanks Brendan.' Tom shook his hand. 'You've been very helpful.'

'No problem. I'll get back to work now. See you soon.'

'Bye.'

Brendan left Tom at his caravan.

* * *

'And that's where we'll leave him,' says Maggie. 'I'm off to bed.'

'I'm wondering how he fits into the story!' says Peter.

'Don't lose any sleep over wondering about him. You'll find out soon.'

'I know which postcard you looked at for this one!'

'I didn't think you'd remember it. Tell me.'

'Guinea pigs! I sent that one from Portugal.

Maggie laughs. 'You did. But I won't lose any sleep over wondering about the connection between Guinea pigs and Portugal! Goodnight, my love.' Maggie gives Peter a kiss.

'Goodnight, I won't be long.'

CHAPTER THIRTY ONE

THE WEDDING DAY

The photographer captures the smiling bride and groom in their wedding outfits, stood at the top of the steps to the register office, surrounded by friends and all of Maggie's small family, all dressed up in their finery for the occasion.

'That's it,' says the photographer. 'I'll take some more at the reception. See you there.' He begins to pack up his camera and tripod.

As Maggie and Peter, arm in arm, make their way slowly down the steps, Brenda throws confetti into the air and the slight breeze scatters it on everyone. It's a happy occasion.

'You look beautiful, Maggie,' says Peter. 'Are you happy?'

'Yes. Are you?'

'Happier than I've ever been. Love you.' Peter gives Maggie a kiss.

A taxi is waiting at the bottom of the steps to take them to 'The Ship Inn.' The driver opens the door for them and they get in. Peter struggles a little but the driver is patient and waits for him to settle into his seat before closing the door.

As the taxi drives away, they wave to the wedding guests. 'See you there!' someone shouts.

Terry greets the newlyweds at the door with two glasses of champagne. 'Congratulations!' he says. Maggie takes the glass from him and he gives her a kiss and then shakes Peter's hand.

'Thank you,' says Maggie. She looks over to the fantastic spread of food set out on the pristine white tablecloths. There are balloons on either side of the table and a three tier wedding cake in the centre. 'Just look at that! That is fantastic. Thank you Terry. It looks wonderful.'

'Thanks, Terry,' says Peter. He takes hold of Maggie's hand and they go over to take a closer look at the cake. The tiers are made up of three square cakes of decreasing sizes, covered in white icing with trellis work detail and decorated with flowers made with coloured icing. The top layer has their names, written in gold, penned icing: Maggie and Peter – 21st June 1999.

'Did you order this?' asks Maggie.

'I asked Terry to get it for us. Do you like it?'

'It's a lovely surprise, thank you.'

They find their favourite seats near the window and drink a toast to one another.

The guests begin to arrive and Terry greets them with the champagne. Everyone finds somewhere to sit and there is a lot of chattering and laughing. The atmosphere is happy. Peter gives everyone time to arrive and time to settle down before he gives his speech.

'I'm not used to doing this,' he says. 'I just want to say thank you for all your good wishes. This is the happiest day of my life and I'd like to make a toast to the lady who has made this possible – to my most beautiful bride Maggie.'

They all toast 'to Maggie.'

Maggie raises her glass in acknowledgement. 'Thank you.'

Several hours later, Terry and the barmaid clear up the remnants of the wedding buffet to make way for the regular evening customers. Peter suggests that any remaining food be made available to them.

The cake has been cut, wrapped and distributed, the remainder boxed for Maggie to take home. 'I'll take some of it to my book club – they're always happy to eat cake!'

'Good,' says Peter. 'But won't it be stale when we get back from our honeymoon?'

'I'll give it Brenda to take to the next meeting.'

'Oh, okay.'

Brenda and her husband are leaving and come over to Maggie and Peter to say farewell. 'We've had a wonderful day. Thank you so much.' She kisses her friend on the cheek and whispers in her ear, 'Have a lovely honeymoon and ring me.'

'I will. And thanks for everything.'

They are the last of the wedding guests to leave and Terry's regulars are now drifting in, filling the pub with their normal merriment. Almost all of them wish Maggie and Peter congratulations.

Maggie and Peter say goodbye and thanks to Terry, who is now busy behind the bar, pulling pints. He throws a kiss to Maggie and a thumbs up gesture to Peter. They leave 'The Ship' and make their way home.

'Do you think they all enjoyed it?' asks Peter.

'I'm sure they did. I know I did.'

'Me too. It was so nice to meet your sister Petula and her husband. That son of theirs is such a handsome lad and so easy to talk to. They're such a nice family.'

'Well, they're your family too. We're married now.'

'Oh, yes! That's nice. Tis lovely to have a family.'

Maggie is moved by how Peter feels. Giving him a family that he appreciates is something that Peter will never know how much it means to her but she changes the subject to prevent herself from getting emotional. 'What time is the taxi picking us up tomorrow?'

'Half eight.'

'I don't know how you feel Pete, but I'm exhausted!'

'Me too! It's been a great day.'

At half past eight the following morning, Peter and Maggie leave for their honeymoon. A week in Cyprus followed by a week in Minorca. 'Have you got your book?' asks Peter.

'No,' says Maggie. 'I usually take a copy of my book everywhere but not this time. I think we'll leave Anna and Brendan alone for a while and have our own adventure.'

'Okay – we'll catch up with them when we get back.'

CHAPTER THIRTY TWO

THE HONEYMOON

Maggie and Peter arrive at Larnaca Airport. It's the middle of the day and they take a taxi to Paphos.

'This heat is unbearable,' says Maggie. She fans herself with her straw sun hat.

'You'll be okay when we get inside,' says Peter. 'There's air conditioning.'

'So, you've stayed here before then?' asks Maggie.

'Every time we docked here. Yes,' answers Peter.

They arrive at the apartment and go inside. The apartment block is elevated and overlooks the main part of the resort.

The shiny, blue sea is not far in the distance and the view from the window makes the most beautiful picture. 'It's fantastic!' says Maggie. 'I love it!'

'I knew you would,' says Peter. 'Wait till you see the apartment in Mahon! You'll love that even more!'

'I don't think I could,' says Maggie. She notices the water colour paintings of sunsets and paradise islands. 'These are lovely.' Her feet are slightly swollen with the heat and she takes off her shoes. The coolness of the tiled floor offers some relief. She opens up the French windows and goes and sits in one of the chairs on the shaded balcony.

Peter had previously arranged for food and drink to be installed in the apartment and he brings out two glasses of sparkling white wine and places them on the small table and sits in the chair opposite his new wife. 'To us!' he says. He lifts his glass and drinks. He takes hold of Maggie's hand. 'I often dreamed of a time like this.'

'It's beautiful,' says Maggie. She lifts her glass. 'To us!'

Their time in Paphos is at an end and their plane to take them to Minorca is ready to take off.

'I'm sorry to leave,' says Maggie. 'It's been a wonderful week.'

'There's nothing stopping us from coming back anytime we want to.'

'But you can't guarantee getting the same holiday and the same apartment.'

'As long as we can get a flight. The apartment is ours!'

'How can you guarantee that?' asks Maggie.

'Because I own it – you own it with me – we own it!'

'Oh, Pete. I can never understand what you say sometimes.'

'I mean that *I own it!* That means that you own it too. Everything I own is now for my Maggie. All of it. The apartment in Mahon, that too! Even the cottage at home. All belongs to you now.'

'I don't believe you – you're kidding me!'

'Believe me. I rent the apartments out to a local couple on the understanding that I can have them whenever I want to. The paperwork to prove it is at your house, in my suitcase.'

'Well, be Jasus! Peter O'Malley – you…'

'You what?'

'You wonderful, wonderful man.' She looks at him with such admiration. Oh how I wish my Daddy could know how successful you turned out to be!' She kisses him.

The plane sweeps them off to Minorca and Peter tells Maggie all about how he came into the money to buy the apartments – the horses, the accumulator bets and the paintings – plus very wise investments. Maggie knows that there is some irony in what he tells her and what happens later in her book.

The taxi takes them to the entrance to the apartment block and Peter takes some keys out of his pocket. There is a lift that takes them to the fourth floor which is at the top of the building. Maggie is silent as she struggles to hold back the excitement she feels.

They reach the apartment. 'What I want to do Maggie, is lift you up and carry you in but my legs won't let me. But imagine I've done that, won't you?'

Maggie laughs. 'I will.' She looks around at the spacious room. A sumptuous suite and rich Spanish wood furniture on a cool tiled floor. Her heels make a tapping noise as she makes her way to the large windows that open onto a balcony overlooking the port of Mahon. There are many busy restaurants, shops and bars below. Two cruise ships are anchored in the distance and the smell of the sea mingles with the aroma of Spanish cuisine.

Peter doesn't say anything. He lets Maggie take in the sight.

'Wow! And this is ours?'

'Yes. Do you like it?'

'I feel like I've won the lottery!'

'Come and have a look at the other rooms.' Peter takes her hand and leads her to the bedroom. 'What do you think of this?'

The bed is massive. All white bed linen and matching curtains. The wardrobes are heavy wood with lots of space and a dressing table to match. She notices the familiar style of water colour paintings. 'Are these some more of your work?' she asks.

'They are. What do you think of them?'

'I think they're wonderful. They should be in a gallery or on postcards!''

'The ones in the apartments are limited numbered prints. I've sold quite a lot with a contract with the local hotels but I have the originals. I won't be painting any more – my eyes – you know?'

'I know. But you've had such a talent – they're wonderful. Oh how I wish Mammy could have seen these. She would have been so proud. God bless her soul.'

'Do you like the furniture?' asks Peter

'It's lovely and very Spanish. Did you choose it?'

'I got someone to fit it out for us.'

'Well, it's lovely Pete. It really is. What's the kitchen like?'

'Let's go and see, shall we. But when we're here, there's so many fantastic restaurants to choose from, I don't think we'll ever use the cooker!'

The kitchen is immaculate and Maggie thinks it's too nice to spoil by messing it up with preparing food. She is happy to go along with what Peter says – to eat out.

Their honeymoon is over, all too soon and they fly back home, happy and content.

The first thing they do when they get back home, is plan the date when they are going to repeat their recent trip.

Maggie can't wait to tell Brenda all about it. She had phoned her once while she was away, as she promised to do, but only to say they had arrived and all was well. There is so much more she has to tell her.

Happy to be home, Peter sits on the sofa in his usual place and Maggie brings him a cup of tea. She has already put on her glasses ready to read her book to him.

'It was perhaps as well you didn't take the book with us, we would never have found the time to read it,' says Peter.

'Too busy living a grand life of our own!'

'I know. But I feel I've missed what's been going on with Brendan and Anna.'

'Well, let's find out, shall we?' Maggie takes the bookmark out of the book and reads.

* * *

Chapter 33 – The official opening of Appletree Farm Holiday Park.

Saturday 10th April, 1954 and the new campsite was officially opened. All the team gathered in the reception and celebrated with a bottle of bubbly and some nibbles that Katie had provided.

George couldn't make it but sent a good luck message to everyone. Bill read it out then gave a short speech, thanking all of them for all their hard work in getting the campsite ready to receive its first paying guests who were due to arrive on Sunday for their first taste of what Appletree had to offer.

Tom, Anna and Brendan were presented with uniforms of pale blue shirts and grey blazers that had the campsite logo badge on the pocket. Others on the team were presented with appropriate workwear with the stitched on logo. They were requested to wear them when on duty from Monday to Saturday on the campsite so that the guests could distinguish them from other campers.

The incoming guests were requested to arrive any time after five o'clock on Sundays and to leave before one o'clock on the following Sunday. There was a four hour window for the team to prepare the caravans for the new guests.

'Let's hope it all works,' said Bill. 'It's new to all of us and if there are any problems or suggestions, let Tom know and together we'll make it a success! Cheers!' Bill lifted his glass.

'Cheers!' said everyone and after a lot of chattering and laughter they dispersed to their own duties.

Susan was put in charge of the small animal pens which was an everyday part-time job which she was glad of. Although she was still looking for a full time office job, she enjoyed working with the animals and getting paid for it.

Joyce and Joan looked after the horses and Anna supervised them. They were instructed to report any problems to Brendan and he was there to do any of the heavy work needed.

Beryl did a last minute check on the cleanliness of the facilities and checked that everything worked. She was to report any problems to the manager, who, despite being asked to call him Tom, she always addressed him as Mr. Price.

Brendan checked the big barn at the rear of the campsite. Bales of hay, tables and chairs were all stacked up and ready to be set out appropriately for each event. There was lots of room. It was spacious since Mother V's caravan had been taken out from its overwinter storage and which now stood proudly in all its splendour – a rightful pride of place at the entrance to the campsite, near the reception.

Tom and Anna spent some of the day in the office, double checking the bookings for the coming week and preparing a float of money in the cash drawer. Anna couldn't wait for the first guests to arrive.

She didn't have long to wait. That afternoon, two touring caravans that had seen the 'Now Open' sign from the main road, had come down to check out the campsite with a view to the possibility of overnight and short term stays. Brendan showed them around and Anna quoted them the rates for this option. They booked in for a two night stay and paid Anna the money. She gave them a receipt and put the money in the drawer. They left with Brendan directing them to the spaces for their caravans.

'Well done!' said Tom. 'Our first paying customers!'

'I know. It's exciting!' She entered the payments in the cash book.

'They seemed very impressed with the set up,' said Tom.

'If they go away happy – they'll tell others. I think that's going to be the best advertising – word of mouth.'

'Have we filled the touring spaces?'

'Not quite. We have eight spaces and five are pre-booked and due to arrive tomorrow,' said Anna.

'I've a feeling they may want to stay longer. They were looking at the week's events on the board.'

'They don't start till Monday.'

'That's what makes me think they might extend their stay.'

'Let's hope so,' said Anna. 'More money in the till!'

'I think we need to monitor the enquiries we get from the tourers,' said Tom. 'Before there's a possibility of having to turn them away, it might be a good idea to extend the spaces.'

'You're right. We'll have to have a word with Mr. P about that. Let's see how it goes.'

'Now about Sundays!' said Tom. 'I think we're going to be busy with guests leaving and then new ones arriving late. I think we're going to need to man the office between nine and one – close it until four and then open it from five onwards until late – allowing for late arrivals.

'Yes. I think you're right. What do you suggest?'

'That I do the late shift from five onwards for the arrivals. You'll need to be at home at that time for your baby, so I suggest you do the nine till one shift for the leavers.'

'That's okay with me. Brendan will have Ruby for me in the morning. He'll then be working with you when the new guests arrive. I'll type up a new office opening times notice.'

Anna took down the old one from the notice board then began work on the new one and added to it that, in case of emergency, when the office was closed, they could contact either Anna at the flat or Tom at Caravan number one. She did two copies. One to put on the reception door and the other to be pinned back on the notice board.

While she was busy, Tom made them cups of tea and Anna felt quite reassured that he was going to be a nice person to work with.

* * *

'That's it for tonight, Pete,' says Maggie, taking off her glasses and rubbing her eyes. She puts the book down. 'I'm tired. All the globetrotting we've done has worn me out! '

'Okay. Let's go to bed. I'm tired too.'

'What did you think of that chapter?'

'I like the idea of a holiday camp in the countryside for those who like it but it's not my kind of holiday.'

'It's always the sea for you Pete, isn't it?'

'You enjoyed being near the sea, didn't you?'

'I loved it! I like being on a beach; I like swimming; or should I say paddling, in the sea. I just don't like sailing *on it!'* Maggie gets up from the sofa.

Peter laughs as he struggles slightly to get up from the sofa. 'Thank God for planes then!' He gently pushes Maggie towards the stairs and switches off the light in the lounge.

CHAPTER THIRTY THREE

A DINNER INVITATION

Even after a good night's sleep, Maggie and Peter still feel a little jet-lagged and decide they will rest and do nothing today – that is until Brenda phones.

'You must come to ours – Harry's going to cook dinner for us. Then you can show off your tan and tell us all about your travels.'

Maggie puts her hand over the speaking part of the phone. 'Do you want to go to Brenda's for dinner tonight?'

'Whatever you want to do!' says Peter.

'Thanks Brenda. We'll get a taxi and be there for around eight. Is that okay?'

'That's perfect. See you later then! Bye.'

Maggie puts down the phone. 'That saves us thinking about what we're having to cook for dinner.'

'Is she a good cook?'

'No. She's hopeless!'

'Oh no!'

'She's not cooking – her husband, Harry is – he's a chef!'

'Fantastic!'

'Right – well what shall we do till we have to get ready to go?' asks Maggie.

'Go and get your book and glasses and I'll make a plate of sandwiches and some tea. That will put us on till later. And we'll find out what Anna and Brendan are up to.

'We're nearly at the end. What are we going to do when the book's finished?'

'You can write another one!'

Maggie laughs. 'Okay.' She sits comfortably on the sofa and waits for Peter to bring in the sandwiches and tea and for him to get settled in his usual place before continuing with her story.

* * *

Chapter 34 – Anna and her boss

Apart from a few minor incidents, the events and routine for the campsite guests seemed to run smoothly. Katie enjoyed looking after Ruby, to the point of spoiling her and it allowed Anna to do her work in the office and with the horses.

Ruby was growing fast and was starting to take notice of the animals on the farm. Anna felt it was a lovely environment to bring up a baby. She felt very lucky and thanked God for George and Mother V – her life was very different than what she thought it would be. She was very happy but every time she wrote to her parents, there was always this longing to tell them that she was married and that they had a beautiful granddaughter. She felt she was depriving them of something so precious and yet she was still afraid of their reaction.

The work in the office kept her busy but Tom was not always pleasant. One day he would be nice and then another day he could be quite moody. She didn't know if she should confront him and ask what caused his moodiness as it caused an awkward atmosphere when they didn't speak to one another properly.

She mentioned this to Brendan but he said that everyone has their off days and told her to just ignore it.

Today was a good day for Tom. This afternoon he was in high spirits and looking forward to the barn dance – the farewell night for the guests. It was also Brendan's favourite event as he loved the dancing. Anna did too and it was like a night out for them even though they were both on duty. Anna was grateful that Katie enjoyed coming round to the flat and minding Ruby; how she loved to bathe her and get her ready for bed. Katie was a brilliant substitute grandmother and Anna often asked her if it was what she enjoyed doing because she didn't want to take advantage of her kindness. Katie had said it was a perfect arrangement.

But before Anna could think of enjoying herself, there was office work to be done.

'What time does your friend Susan finish work today?' asked Tom.

'Five. Why?'

'Will she be coming to the barn dance with you?'

'She usually does. Why?'

'No reason. Just asking.'

Anna knew there was a reason. Susan had mentioned to her that Tom had shown an interest in her. Anna said she thought he was too old for her and to be careful and that he shows an interest in a lot of the girls on the campsite.

'I don't think you should be asking her out, if that's your intention.'

'My intentions are none of your business!' said Tom.

'Well don't ask me questions about her then!' said Anna.

She was aware that he was right and it was not her concern but she felt she had a duty to her friend to try and protect her.

Anna didn't like the way their working relationship was going and tapped the keys on her typewriter harder than usual. She couldn't wait to close the office and go home.

By the time the barn dance was in full swing, Anna was feeling a lot more relaxed and had decided not to interfere with any blossoming relationship between Susan and Tom.

Brendan had told her he understood how she felt but not to play the protector. "Susan isn't daft. She knows what he's like," he'd said.

'Come on – let's have you up dancing!' said Susan. 'It's a square dance!'

'Okay.' Anna danced along to the caller's instructions and the country music that the band played. It was always a favourite and lots of the guests joined in.

'Have you seen Tom?' asked Susan.

'Not since I finished work. He should be here.'

'Brendan said he's not seen him and he had to set up the place himself.'

'He did that last Saturday. Left it all to Brendan.' Anna danced along but a little out of step. She wasn't enjoying it. 'Let's sit down.'

They sat down and talked.

'Have you applied for any suitable office jobs recently?' asked Anna.

'No. I'm not going to bother until the end of the summer season here. I actually like looking after the animals. And the pay is the same as they're offering for office work.'

'You need something more permanent than seasonal work.'

'I know. I'll keep looking. But let's forget about work. Let's dance!'

The band played some country and western songs and the guests got up and danced their own style – a mixture of ballroom and jive.

Anna and Susan danced their version of the jive and giggled at their attempt.

'Here he is now,' said Susan. 'With one of those four girls from that caravan. You know – the one you had to ask for them to turn the noise down, the other night.'

'The complaint caravan! They were disturbing the neighbours who had young children. We can't have that!'

'Well, you told them and good for you!'

'I did and they just went to Tom's caravan to complain about *me*!'

'Did you get into trouble?'

'No. I just pointed out that it took him over two hours to listen to their complaint before they went back to their caravan. There was no more noise though.'

'Oh. I see.'

Anna hoped that Susan did see. For the rest of the evening Susan never asked about Tom. One of the guests, a young man, came across to Susan and asked her to dance.

Anna was not left on her own for long; Brendan joined their company and they all danced the night away.

Chapter 35 – The end of another week

The following morning Brendan put Ruby in her pram and took her with him to the big barn to clear up after the previous night's event.

Anna was in the office on Sunday duty at nine as usual, taking the keys from the guests who were leaving and wishing them a safe journey home. Most of them expressed their delight at having had a fantastic holiday and promised to return. Some gave Anna some money as a tip, which she put in a jar to share out.

What she enjoyed most, was when the younger children had drawn pictures of the animals as an entry into a competition and gave them to Anna. The prizes were some sweets and all of them received a prize before they left. She pinned the drawings onto the notice board.

Beryl called in to collect the keys and make a start on the cleaning. 'Another week over. I wonder what the next ones will be like.'

'We certainly get a variety, don't we?' said Anna. 'I want you to do me a favour and check on caravan number twenty and make sure they're packing up. Gently remind them to be out before one, if you will.'

'If they're not out for one, they'll get swept up – that's what I say!' Beryl laughed. 'Okay.'
'Thanks.'

More guests entered the reception to hand in their keys and after they had left, Anna checked the booking chart.

It was now twelve o' clock and there were two caravans that still needed to check out. There was a taxi outside the reception and Anna went out to ask who it was for. It didn't surprise her – the four girls were struggling with their suitcases noisily shouting to one another – 'The taxi's here! Come on!'

Anna overheard one of them, 'Marion – give that bitch the keys!' The driver loaded their suitcases in the boot and they piled in the taxi. They said nothing to Anna, Marion just waved the keys in front of Anna and then dropped them into her hand. Anna was also silent. There was no thanks or tips or goodbye from any of them and Anna couldn't resist waving them away with both hands.

When the last of the keys had been returned and the week's booking chart was up to date, Anna made an entry into the diary for Katie, then closed the office and took the remaining keys up to Beryl. She could now spend some precious free time with her husband and baby.

* * *

Maggie puts the book down. 'It's time to get ready to go to Brenda's.'

'Okay. I wonder what Harry will cook for us?'

'Are we going to have a bet on it?'

'Yes. I say it will be an Italian. He likes Italian food.'

'Well, you know him better than I do, but I'll make a guess and say it will be a curry of some sort.'

'Okay, come on then, let's go and find out.'

CHAPTER THIRTY FOUR

ANOTHER LAZY DAY

Maggie and Peter just can't seem to shake off the tiredness they feel since their return from their honeymoon. They just want to relax, talk and enjoy each other's company.

'What's wrong with us?' asks Maggie.

'I think we're just so content, Maggie, we're just happy to let the world go round.'

'That's exactly how I feel. I hope someone else rings today and asks us out for dinner. I enjoyed going to Brenda's, what did you think of the meal?'

'He's a fantastic cook is Harry! That Lasagna was just perfect! And you won the bet!'

'Oh, yes! Who's going to cook when we invite them back here?'

'Not me! *You're* not a bad cook!'

'We could invite them for lunch and go to 'The Ship' – I think they'd like that.'

'That's a good idea. When?'

'Next week, sometime.'

'That's sorted then. What are we going to do today?'

'Let's have another lazy day. Sandwiches and tea for now and we'll think about what we want to do for dinner later.'

Peter gets up from the sofa. 'Sandwiches it is then. Do you want to read some more?'

'Yes. We can carry on with it.'

'Okay. Get yourself comfy and I'll be back soon.'

Maggie gets everything she needs and waits for Peter. She hears him making the tea and soon after he appears with a tray of tea and food. She waits for him to get settled and continues to read.

* * *

Chapter 36 – Bill's conversation in the club

'You're a bit later than usual. What kept you?' asked Katie.

'I got talking to Steve Riley – you know, bookie Steve?'

'Oh, yes. He's nice, Steve – I like him.'

'They're all nice in the club – as far as I know,' said Bill.

'I think you do more business in that club than anywhere.'

'Yeah – most of them are our customers!'

'Is that an excuse to go to your club so often?'

'Well, I don't have time to play golf!' Bill knew he'd had more to drink than usual and wasn't sure if Katie was just being playfully sarcastic or just sarcastic in general. 'Are you okay?'

'Yeah, just…' she yawned. 'I'm off to bed.'

'I was just going to tell you about the conversation with Steve.'

Katie flopped back down on the Chesterfield sofa. 'What about?'

'It was a bit strange really,' said Bill, sitting down in the chair opposite Katie. 'He asked me straight out, "What are you paying that manager of yours?" he said. Just like that!'

'Did you tell him to mind his own business?'

'No. I just asked why he wanted to know.'

'Oh, right. And what did he say?'

'He said; and these were his exact words, '"There's a lot that would like that job, when he can afford to place bets as regular and as big as he does!"'

'Are you saying that we're paying him too much?'

'I don't think so, do you?'

'So what do you think he was trying to tell you?'

'Obviously that he likes the horses! I don't know how much he puts on – a lot according to Steve. Perhaps our Mr. Price has another income or whatever – anyway that's what I said to Steve.'

'What did he say to that?' Katie sat up straight, showing more interest in the conversation.

'"Well, he isn't winning!" is what he said.'

'I wonder!' There was a thoughtful expression on Kate's face.

'What are you wondering?' asked Bill. 'Are alarm bells ringing?'

'It was something that Beryl said – you know, our cleaner; what she told me last week.'

'What was that?'

'That she went into the office and spoke to Mr. Price about her wages. She said it was a pound short.'

'Really.'

'I asked her what he said and she told me that he blamed Anna. Apparently he was a bit offhanded with her and asked her if she was sure, and in such a way that made her feel she was telling lies and trying to get more money than she was due. Like Beryl said, she would never do that. Anyway, Tom said that Anna must have just miscounted and if she went back in the afternoon, Anna would make it right.'

'Did she?'

'Yes. She said she told Anna who apologised and gave her the pound.'

'Oh, I don't like the sound of that.'

'But, listen. Anna gave her the pound out of her own money! Beryl didn't like that, thinking that it was going to make Anna struggle, she said, '"what with the baby an' all."'

'So, had Anna made a mistake?'

'I didn't take if further because I just checked in the daily diary. Anna keeps a note of what happens in the office – the diary was another excellent idea of hers. She keeps us updated with that diary and I just need to take a look and if there are any issues that need to be dealt with, I take it from there. It saves a lot of time.'

'Did it mention the pound?'

'Yes. I looked especially for a mention of it and Anna had written that she checked her figures again thoroughly and couldn't understand how the mistake had happened as the wages money balanced and Tom had checked the money in the envelopes before sealing them.'

'Uh Oh! I'm getting a bit wary now.'

'Me too. I trust Anna completely. She even wrote in the diary that she was sorry if she had made a mistake and that she had paid Beryl the money out of her own pocket and if the missing pound came to light – she would claim it back.'

'She's honest and she's trustworthy,' said Bill.

'You're not so sure of Tom though now, are you?'

'No, not now. But he seems to be popular with the guests. It's just that I knew when we interviewed him there was just something about him I couldn't be...'

'Let's just see how things go from now.' Katie yawned. 'I'm so tired I can't think anymore. Let's go to bed.'

Katie got up from the sofa and then sat down again. 'Oh, and there's another thing,' she said. 'When Beryl was looking for Tom, she passed his caravan and decided to see if he was in before she went to the office. Of course, he wasn't – he was in the office, but she said when she looked through his caravan window, she saw what a mess it was. '"It was in a right state. I don't know how he lives like that!"' she said.'

'Well, I'm glad we didn't give him the flat then.'

'That's what I thought,' she yawned, 'I'm going to bed, I'll think about what to do about it in the morning.'

'Okay. I won't be long.'

Chapter 37 – Anna's Worry

Anna kept her concern about the missing money to herself, not knowing what to do. She couldn't sleep and kept tossing and turning in her bed. She was worried that she had made a mistake; but even after she had gone over all the books several times, she didn't find any error. The balance remained fifty pounds short whichever way she checked. She was afraid that Mr. and Mrs. Patrick would sack her for losing the money.

She had checked the cash drawer several times in case there was any way the money could have fallen down the back, but nothing. The money was part of the total she planned to take to the bank on her regular walk into town.

In her head, she retraced her actions and knew for certain she put the money in the cash drawer; she had put it next to the paying in book ready for filling in the paying in slip. She couldn't even find the paying in book. It was always kept with the fabric bank bag.

Apart from Katie, the only other person with a key to the cash drawer was Tom. If she told him, she was scared that he would accuse her of either losing, or, worse still, stealing the money. But then she thought, what if he had used the money for something and not entered it in the book. She would look for a note or something tomorrow. If she didn't find anything, she would have to ask him.

What if he hadn't used it and he thought she was accusing him? He was her boss. Would he sack her? Who should she report the missing money to first – Mrs. Patrick or Tom? She tossed and turned.

'What's the matter with you?' said Brendan. 'I've got an early start tomorrow. For God's sake, keep still!'

'Sorry. I just can't sleep.' Anna turned her back on Brendan.

'Is there something wrong? Is it the baby? Have *I* done something to upset you?'

'Oh no! It's not you. It's me. I'm just worried about work. That's all.'

'That's all! You've never been worried about work before. What is it?'

'The money didn't balance when I finished work tonight and I don't know what to do.'

Brendan took hold of Anna's shoulder and she turned to face him. 'Whatever it is, I'm sure you'll be able to sort it out tomorrow. We can't do anything about it in the middle of the night! So, go to sleep and we'll talk about it in the morning. The baby will be up soon. Let's just get some sleep!' Brendan held her tight, kissed her and stroked her hair. It soothed her and she tried to relax and keep as still as possible and Brendan soon fell back into his usual deep sleep. Her mother's usual words, for when things weren't going right, came into her head now; *Things always seem better in the morning!* She nestled in Brendan's arms.

Ruby slept through the night. It was six o'clock and Anna was up and dressed with a bottle of baby milk already prepared. She heard her baby's hungry cry. She had no need to go and get her, Brendan was already carrying her into the living room.

'What time is it? I haven't even heard Roger yet! He yawned and handed Ruby over to her mother.

'It's just after six, too late to go back to bed, you may as well get ready and go to work.' Anna sat down on the sofa and began to feed the baby. 'Hasn't she done well, sleeping through?'

'A lot better than someone I know,' he yawned again. 'Did you get any sleep at all?'

'A little. Enough. I'm okay.'

'I'll just get washed and dressed while you're feeding Ruby and then you can tell me what the problem is.'

'Okay,' said Anna. The worry flooded back, not knowing what the day would bring.

Ruby never struggled to finish her early morning feed. As soon as she had had her hands, face and bum washed and her terry towelling nappy changed for a fresh clean one and dressed in her pink romper suit and matinee coat, she was content and fast asleep. Anna put her down in her wooden cradle at the side of the sofa and noticed how much she had grown. It wouldn't be long before she would be too big for it.

Brendan was dressed ready for work and in the kitchen making some tea and toast for breakfast. Anna came into the kitchen and sat down at the table.

'Here you are,' said Brendan, handing the plate to Anna, 'now tell me what's bothering you.'

She took a bite out of the toast and waved it about as she began to tell Brendan the problem. 'There was fifty pound missing when I cashed up to balance the books yesterday before I locked up and came home.'

'Fifty pounds!'

'I know! I'm worried sick. Tom had gone with one of the cleaners to check on one of the caravans; there was something wrong with the gas or something, so I didn't have the chance to mention it to him. Anyway, I haven't told anyone yet. I'll have to report it this morning because I have to fill in the paying in book with a total of a hundred and fifty pounds and take it to the bank. I only have one hundred! Thank goodness that's in the fabric bank bag. Oh, I don't know who to tell first.'

'You tell Tom. He's the manager. He may know where it is – used it for something.'

'Everything has to be written in the book – he wouldn't, or he shouldn't have used cash from the drawer without an authorisation note. *I'm* responsible for balancing the cash and *I* should be told. And I can't even find the paying in book!'

'Oh, right. I see.'

'So what do I do, Brendan? Do I go over Tom's head and tell Mrs. Patrick and then get him into trouble if that's what he's done? Or do I ask Tom if he's had the money – that sounds as though I'm accusing him of something?'

'Either way, you've got to report it.'

'And what if they think *I've* had it!'

'No one would accuse you!'

'I'm responsible, Brendan! It must be somewhere. I might get sacked!'

'I don't think Mrs. Patrick would want to lose you.'

'I think Tom would. He would sack me at the drop of a hat!'

'I think he's just jealous. You're so good in the office, I think you show him up.'

'We're a team, right, and if I lose this job you might be fired too. And if we lose that, we lose our home!'

Anna choked back the worry that prevented her from eating her toast. She put it back on the plate.

'Hey, hey, hey! I think you're imagining too much. Just tell Mrs. Patrick. She's the one who has the last word.'

'But she's not going to be happy – it's fifty pounds Brendan – fifty!'

'Look. You ask Tom first. See what he has to say. I'll call in the office at half eleven and we'll see what the situation is then.'

'If we have to go Brendan; if we have to leave here,' she said, wringing her hands, 'we can use the money Daddy gave me and we'll go and rent our house back home. It's empty at the moment waiting for the next tenant. Shall we do that?'

'Oh that's a bit drastic Anna. We don't want to leave here!' Brendan got up to go. 'But whatever happens, I'll stick by you.' He kissed her. 'I have to go to work now. I'll see you later. Stop worrying, I'm sure things will be okay – somehow!'

Anna, wasn't so sure.

'I was going into town yesterday,' said Tom, 'so, I thought I'd save you a trip. Is that alright with you?' The sarcastic tone grated on Anna.

'But, surely you should have let me know – a note, or something. I've been worried sick. I couldn't sleep last night. And it messes up the whole booking in. I should bank a total of a hundred and fifty pounds on one paying in slip. Where's the paying in book? I suppose I could bank the one hundred today and explain to Mrs. Patrick what I've done. As long as the total tallies, she will be okay with that. Where's the paying in book?'

'Err... I think I've left it in my other jacket. Have we got a new one?'

'I can't use a new one – I have to make the total banked one hundred and fifty pounds, so I need the stamped paying in slip for the fifty pounds to prove it! I'll have to speak to Mrs. Pat. . . '

'Oh, it's Mrs. Patrick this and Mrs. Patrick that – you're always snivelling and running to her – it's unnecessary. I'm the boss around here! Just do as I say and use the new paying in book and bank the one hundred. When I find the old one, I'll let you have it and you can put them together. Okay!'

'NO! It's not okay!' Anna was trembling, 'And don't you EVER speak to me in a tone like that!'

'Just do as I say and as usual, take that brat of yours a walk and get to the bank now or don't bother coming back to this office! There's plenty of girls who would be glad of your job!'

'Don't you DARE call my child a brat! And as far as the girls you'd want working for you I suppose it's the ones you take into your caravan! Don't think it's gone unnoticed! Several people have complained about your behaviour!

Neither Tom nor Anna noticed that Brendan had walked into the office and overheard the heated argument.

'*My* behaviour!' said Tom, a nasty snarly expression on his face. 'What about *your* behaviour? You're no innocent angel, are you? You can't be – having a kid at... what are you – seventeen? You must have liked it and…'

Brendan bounded over and hit Tom with a strong right hook that floored him. 'NO ONE speaks to my wife like that. Least of all you, you bastard!'

Tom struggled to get up. Blood was spurting from his mouth into his hand. He whimpered his words, 'Get out of here and take her with you. You're both fired.'

'We'll see about that!' said Brendan. 'You couldn't manage this place without her. Or me!'

They went straight to their flat. Anna was so angry, she couldn't even cry. 'I suppose we've done it now! We're sacked for sure.'

'Stop talking, Anna and just pack up some stuff. I'm sure Tom will be on his way round to see Mr. P and he'll be telling him some tale...' The extension phone rang. Anna and Brendan looked at one another.

'It'll be Mrs. P. Shall I answer it?'

'Yes!' said Brendan, the anger was still within him. 'And tell her *I'm* on my way to see *her*!'

Anna's hand was shaking as she lifted the receiver. 'Hello.' She listened to Katie's words and her demand that she and Brendan get down to the office and stay there until she got there. Anna put the phone down. 'She sounds really angry. She's had to leave Ruby with Sandra.'

'And we're bloody *mad* through that bastard!' said Brendan, opening the sideboard drawers, taking out personal stuff and banging them shut again. 'But he's no right to talk to you like that, ever!' He gave a big sigh, 'Come on, let's go and get it over with!'

'I'm glad you were there and saw what he's really like.' Anna slipped her hand in Brendan's as they made their way into the office. Tom wasn't there.

Katie pulled up in the Land Rover and came into the reception office. 'What on earth has been going on up here?' she said. 'Tom says he's fired you!'

'He has,' said Anna. 'And to be honest, I wouldn't work with him ever again!'

'He said, you're blaming him for some missing money – is that right?

'Blaming him! No! He told me that he had taken it to the bank, yesterday! He said he thought he would save me a trip!'

'So, he paid the money in then?'

'That's what he said. But when I asked him for the paying in book, he told me he had left it in his other jacket and asked me to use the new one. When I told him I wasn't happy with that, that's when he got nasty. He was horrible!'

'And that's when I hit him!' said Brendan, unapologetically.

'Oh, what a mess!' said Katie, rubbing her forehead.

'I'm so sorry Mrs. Patrick. I'm really sorry and I've been so worried – it's a lot of money to go missing and...'

'We have nothing to do with the missing money Mrs. P, but I know Mr. Patrick will not be happy with me hitting Tom, but I just saw red. And as far as having to sack us; we understand we'll have to go and...'

'Just hang on a minute Brendan. Let's get to the bottom of this before you or anyone makes any hasty decisions. I'll ring the bank.' Katie went over to the office phone and dialled a number, which she obviously knew, as Anna noticed she didn't have to look it up. 'Yes,' said Katie, 'can I speak to Mr. Ogden, the manager, please?' Anna and Brendan listened carefully to Katie's side of the conversation. 'Oh, hello, Mr. Ogden, it's Mrs. Patrick here. Would you please check something for me – it's very important?' There was a pause as Katie listened to Mr. Ogden's reply. 'Thank you,' she said, 'I want to know if there was a deposit of fifty pounds paid into the Appletree Farm Holiday Park account yesterday. Do you need the account number? Oh, okay. Yes, I'll hang on, thank you.' Katie sat down as she waited for Mr. Ogden's confirmation. They were all silent for a few minutes and Anna and Brendan watched Katie's face for any expressive reaction. 'Oh. Okay. Thank you so much for your help. I really appreciate it, thank you.' Katie put down the phone. 'No payment into the account was made yesterday.'

Brendan scoffed. 'So, he's a liar, as well?'

'So, what happens now and where's the paying in book?' asked Anna.

'I want to avoid reporting it to the police if I can. I'll get Bill and we'll try and sort it out,' said Katie. 'So, please, for now, would the two of you carry on as normal and hold the fort? Anna, will you carry on here in the office and I'll get Sandra to bring Ruby back as usual, at three.' Anna nodded. 'Brendan, have you finished all your deliveries and your work with Bill?'

'Yes, all done,' he looked at the office clock. 'I'm due to be up at the big barn in an hour, getting it ready for the talent contest tonight. Then, with Susan, I'm taking the children round the pens at three.'

'Right, will you do that then and see that the guests are okay, basically keeping to the routine.'

'Okay.'

'Good.' Katie sighed. 'Thank you. I'll sort this and get back to you later.'

'So, we're not sacked then?' asked Anna.

'No. But somebody will be!'

* * *

'I had a feeling about that Tom?' said Peter.

'Did you? Like Bill?'

'Yes. I thought he was going to be trouble. And good for Brendan. I'd have given him a wallop too.'

Maggie laughed. 'Would you? It's only fiction Pete!'

'If he'd have spoken to you like that – yes I would! What happens to him?'

'You'll have to wait. I think I've read enough for now.'

'Okay.' Peter sighs in disappointment. 'So what shall we do?'

'I think we need a walk and get some fresh air. That might liven us up a little.'

'Shall we go to the cottage and see how the decorating is coming along.'

'Yes and we need to see an estate agent about letting it.'

'Okay, let's get that job done today then.'

'What about dinner tonight?'

'I think we'll buy a couple of nice steaks and have some new potatoes and broccoli with it.'

'Mmm,' Peter licks his lips. 'That sounds good. What's for desert?'

'I've got some tinned peaches in the cupboard. We can have them with cream.'

'Come on then,' says Peter struggling to stand. 'Before my legs stiffen up any more. Let's go.'

CHAPTER THIRTY FIVE

A DISCUSSION ABOUT TOM

'That dinner was gorgeous Maggie, thank you.'

'I think that walk and the fresh air did us good.'

'And it hasn't been a wasted day – we've got somewhere with the cottage,' says Peter.

'It's all organised now – we don't have to worry about it. It'll make a lovely home for a family.'

'It is nice. My Mammy would be proud of it. Whoever rents it, I hope they'll be happier in it than we were.'

'Let's hope so and hope they keep it nice.'

'Yes.' Peter sighs.

Maggie gets up from the table and takes the empty plates to the kitchen. She shouts out to him from the kitchen. 'Have you got room for some cheese and crackers?'

'Oh yes. That sounds good. Shall I open a bottle of red?'

'Yes. Take the drinks into the lounge and get ready for the next chapter.'

'Oh good! I was hoping I could find out what happens to Tom but didn't like to ask you to read again today. You read quite a lot this morning.'

'I don't want to keep you in suspense.'

Peter goes into the lounge and sets out the wine glasses on the coffee table. He pours wine into each glass and sits back into his comfortable position.

Maggie brings in the tray with a plateful of cream crackers and a small assortment of cheeses. She lays it down on the coffee table. She adjusts her glasses as usual and then takes a drink of the wine.

'Here you are.' Peter hands Maggie her book and she finds the right page and reads.

* * *

Chapter 38 – Tom

When Katie got back to the farm, she found Tom and Bill in the yard. Bill was red in the face as the heated discussion was intensifying. Katie wanted to calm Bill down, this situation wasn't going to do his blood pressure any good.

'Right,' said Katie. 'Let's all go into the kitchen and talk this through, not in the yard like a pair of fishwives!' They followed her into the kitchen and she gestured to Tom to take a seat at the side of her. Bill dragged out one of the chairs and sat opposite them. 'Now, Tom, please start at the beginning and let's get a full picture of what's gone on.'

Tom pointed to his burst lip. 'This is what's gone on!' 'I've every right to sack them for what they've done.'

'Brendan wouldn't have hit you for nothing!' Bill was clearly defending Brendan and that was infuriating Tom.

'He took me by surprise. But I'm not finished with him yet!'

Katie, was doing her best to keep the situation as calm as possible. She had a strategy in mind. 'So, you've sacked them, okay! Understandable if he hit you. But to keep the record straight, I need to know exactly what happened between you. *Why* did Brendan hit you?'

Tom, used his usual confident fashion of moving his arms around as he spoke. 'He came in just as I was asking Anna to take the money to the bank, as she usually does. As you know, she always takes her baby with her for a walk into town.'

'And why would he hit you for that?' asked Bill. Katie put her hand up to gesture to Bill to keep quiet.

Tom answered the question. 'Because he probably overheard me *telling* her to go to the bank and he said I should have *asked* her nicely.'

'Exactly how did you *tell* her?'

'Because at first she refused to go and I just said to her, I was the boss and she should do as I asked!' Tom sighed and shook his head.

'Why did Anna refuse to go?' asked Katie, calmly.

'She said something about not having all the money ready to be banked – there was only one hundred pound bagged up and ready to go and there should have been a hundred and fifty. She was going on about it and I just told her to bank what was there and we could bank the other fifty later.'

'Ah, that's where the stories differ – you see,' said Katie. 'Anna told me that you said you had paid the fifty pounds into the bank yesterday when you told her you would save her a trip. Is that right?'

Tom sighed again and began to rub his forehead. 'Oh, err, yes, that's right. I did say that.'

'And you paid the money in yesterday?' Katie looked Tom straight in the eye. 'Is that right?'

Tom's hands were trembling fists on the table. Katie could tell that he was thinking of how to get out of this. 'I... I didn't get chance to take it.'

'So, why didn't you just give it back to Anna to take?'

'I didn't have it on me at the time. It was in my other jacket.'

'With the paying in book? And Anna wanted the paying in book?'

'I told her to use a new one.'

'And that's why she refused to go,' said Katie. I understand now. Anna likes to keep everything in order.'

'Yes,'

'Oh well – that's got to the bottom of it. We can sort this out easily. Bill will take the money while you recover...' Katie looked over to Bill, '...won't you Bill?'

The way Bill looked at her, Katie knew he was trying to work out what she was trying to do and just went along with it. 'Yes, I can do that,' he said, 'I have nothing else to do this afternoon.' Katie knew the sarcasm was not meant for her.

'So, Tom,' said Katie, getting up, 'come on, let's go back to the office and we'll get all the money together and the paying in book and I'll bring it back for Bill. Then you can get on with the job of managing the site. I believe you have a talent contest on in the club room tonight?'

Tom didn't get up from the table. His head was down and he sat quite still as if deep in thought and then started to rub his chin. 'I haven't got the fifty pounds,' he said, quietly.

Katie looked at Bill who nodded to her to sit back down. 'What do you mean?'

Tom sighed. 'I've used it. I gambled with it.' He began to cry. 'I... I was given a tip – a sure bet, you know? So I used the fifty pounds.' He put his head in his hands. I'm sorry. I'm so sorry. I was going to pay it straight into the bank when I got the winnings. It would have been *so* much money!'

'But you didn't win, did you?' said Bill. 'You daft bugger!'

'No. Oh God. No. And I thought that I could make up the fifty if I could have a bit of time to do it. But that bloody Anna wouldn't leave it alone. She wouldn't give me the time I needed.'

Katie was furious but tried not to show it. There was a short silence before she spoke. 'What do we do Bill?' she asked. 'Do you think the police should be involved?'

'Oh, please don't – it'll kill my mother,' said Tom. 'I'll make it up. I promise!' He looked at his employers with earnest pleading in his eyes.

'And there's one other thing,' said Katie, taking the opportunity while confessions were on the table. 'And I want you to tell me honestly. When Beryl came to you about there being a pound missing out of her wages – did you take it?'

Tom nodded his head; the expression on his face was of one in pain. 'Oh God. Yes. I'm sorry.'

'You have a big problem, my lad,' said Bill. 'And tell me, how are you going to make it up with no job – because you haven't got one here anymore?'

'I don't know. But I promise you, I will; somehow – please don't involve the police.' He searched his pockets. 'Here,' he said, frantically putting a couple of ten shilling notes, and some change onto the table. 'That's a start.'

Katie was beginning to feel very uncomfortable and made eye contact with Bill who then knew he now had to take charge of the situation.

'I'll tell you what we'll do,' said Bill. 'I won't involve the police but I want you to write a letter addressed to me saying you owe the company fifty pounds and that you will repay it within three months from today. If you don't, I *will* take you to court. I also want your resignation in writing. That way it may make it easier for you to get another job. Take all your stuff out of the caravan and don't set foot on this farm again. And lastly, get some flaming help with your gambling habit!'

The chair scraped on the flag floor as Bill got up sharply. He went over to the kitchen cabinet and opened a drawer, retrieving a letter pad and pen. He came back to the table and slammed the pad down in front of Tom and handed him the pen.

When Tom began to weep uncontrollably, Katie had to leave the room. Although she had no sympathy for him for what he'd done, she didn't like to see such a confident young man brought down to this state through an addiction.

* * *

Maggie put the embroidered book mark inside her book and closed it. 'What did you think of that chapter then?'

Peter was lashing the soft cheese onto a cracker. 'I'm glad he's gone.' He handed the cracker to Maggie and began to pour some of the Merlot into her glass. 'But, like Katie, I feel a bit sorry for him. It's a sad situation.'

'Addiction to anything can affect a person's life – it must creep up on them and before you know it..., well, you're hooked! *I* found it hard to give up smoking!'

'Gambling on the horses could have gone the other way. He would have been a rich man if he'd backed the winners!'

'True. But, being addicted, wouldn't he have just gambled it all away again?'

'Not if he had invested the money wisely – like in property or something.'

'Would an addict do that?'

'Probably not. I mean, *I* like the horses; they've been good to me. I have a knack of always spotting a good horse when I see one.'

'That's because of the time you spent helping out at the Curragh.'

'It is, it is – they were good days,' said Peter. 'Beautiful horses. I like a bet but I always know when to stop – and always used my own money. I could never steal. Tom's just a bad 'un! A thief!'

'I think Bill's a bit lenient with him. Don't you?' Maggie sipped the wine. She was happy to hear Peter speak about her characters as though they were real.

'Perhaps he thought he had more chance of getting his money back and less hassle for himself if he didn't get the police involved.' Peter topped up his own glass. 'He didn't want any bad publicity – maybe he was thinking of the business.'

Maggie picked up the last cracker on the plate and began to spread the cheese. 'There's some more crackers in the tin if you want some.'

'No thanks,' said Peter. 'I'll be up all night with indigestion if I have any more.'

'This cheese is worth it,' she said. She leaned back into the soft cushion, closed her eyes and bit into the cracker.

They sat side by side on the sofa in comfortable silence.

CHAPTER THIRTY SIX

SOUL MATES

Peter is late getting up and walks downstairs. He is still in his pyjamas and dressing gown. 'Sorry,' he says, 'I had a bad night's sleep. Remind me never to have cheese so late again. It always bothers me.'

'Did you get up in the middle of the night?' asks Maggie.

'I went to get my indigestion tablets. They helped.'

'You were fast asleep when I got up. Can you eat some breakfast?'

'I'll just have toast and tea, please.'

'Okay. Sit yourself down and I'll make it. Brenda's phoned me. She wants me to meet her in town this afternoon. Will you be okay?'

'Yes, that's fine. I'll watch the racing on TV. You go and enjoy yourself. Take some money out of my wallet. Treat yourself to something nice.'

'Thanks Pete. Are you sure?' asks Maggie.

'Of course I'm sure. I've told you before – what's mine is yours!'

Maggie comes over to him and gives him a kiss. 'Thank you. And before I go, I'll treat you to another chapter. Okay?'

'That'll be nice.'

After he has eaten his breakfast, Peter goes upstairs to get himself washed and dressed. He comes down a few minutes later and announces to Maggie that he is just nipping out to the bookies to put on a couple of bets.

'Don't let it become an addiction!' Maggie warns.

Peter laughs. 'If I was going to become addicted to it, I'd have shown signs before now. Don't worry. I won't be long.'

When Peter gets back home, he makes himself comfortable in the lounge and checks the newspaper for the time the horse racing is scheduled for being shown on the sports channel.

Maggie brings him a cup of tea. She is all made up and looking smart for a shopping trip. 'Do you want me to read the next chapter now, before I go?'

'Yes. Okay.'

Maggie sits down beside Peter. She gets herself organised and reads.

* * *

Chapter 38 – The Pound

It was nearly six o'clock when Katie arrived back at the campsite reception, Anna was busy speaking to one of the guests at the counter and serving her with tickets for the clubroom talent contest. Ruby was sat up in her pram in the back office and Katie went over to her. The child was smiling; her big blue eyes were bright and she held out her arms to Nana Patrick. Katie lifted her up and kissed her. 'Who's my little precious gem?' she said.

Anna, a little apprehensive, came into the office. 'Tell me what's happening.'

'I've come to cover for Tom temporarily, so you can go and have a break and then we'll talk the whole thing over tomorrow – there's so much to discuss. The only thing is, I don't know what jobs he was going to do.'

'Well, why don't you look after Ruby for me and get her ready for bed while I do Tom's shift – he should have been up at the big barn with Brendan, organising the talent contest. I take it he's not coming back?'

'No.'

'That's good.'

'Oh, and here…' Katie took a pound note out of her pocket. '…that's yours. The one you said if it was ever found, you would claim it back!'

'Oh. Thanks, but where….?'

'I'll tell you all about everything tomorrow. You go and do what you have to do.'

'Okay. Leave it to me and Brendan. He's done the talent contest many times before so, if you're happy to see to Ruby, I'll go and let Brendan know what's happening.' Anna looked up at the clock. 'It's six now, so come on, time to close up.'

Anna left Ruby at the flat, in the capable hands of Katie who was more than happy to swap the duties she intended to cover for Tom, for those of a grandmother.

When Anna found Brendan in the big barn, he was setting out the seating in front of the stage area. 'He's not coming back!' she said.

'That's a relief. We're safe then!' He gave Anna a kiss and then carried on putting out the chairs. 'I'm so glad we're going to stay. I've been worried sick. There's very few jobs at home and we couldn't have wished for a better opportunity for work than we've got here! And the flat!'

'I know. Mrs. P is going to talk to us tomorrow about everything. So, between us, we'll have to manage the show tonight.'

'Where's Ruby?'

'With Mrs. P – she's minding her while I cover for Tom. What do you want me to do?'

'Man the door when they start to come in. There's a raffle tonight – two prizes; a bottle of sherry and some chocolates. I've put the raffle ticket book in the box with the prizes – they're near the door.'

'Right.' Anna looked around for a table and chair and carried them over to the door.

As she was doing this, her friend Susan came in. 'Hello, I thought I'd drop by before going home to see you and Ruby but when I went to the flat, Mrs. Patrick said you were working here tonight.'

'Yes. Tom's had to go somewhere, so I'm doing his shift with Brendan.'

'Do you need any help?'

'Oh, Susan. Yes, please. If you can.'

'If Tom's not here, who's doing the stage?'

Anna shouts over to Brendan. 'Brendan! Who's doing the MC?'

'You, if you want to,' he shouted back.

'Can I do it?' asked Susan. 'I've seen enough of them to know the routine. I always love the talent show. Especially the children.'

'Are you sure?'

'Yes! I just need to wash and change out of these overalls – I can't do it smelling of goats!'

'Okay – go to the flat and get ready there – you can borrow something of mine.'

'Great! Give me half an hour and I'll see you back here.'

'You've got plenty of time. It doesn't start till half seven. And thanks.'

'Okay.' Susan left the barn and made her way to the flat.

Brendan came over to Anna. 'Is she coming back?'

'Yes, she's gone to get changed. She's going to do the stage stuff – she's excited about it, so let's see how it goes.'

'I always said that girl should be on stage, she can be so funny!' Brendan laughed. 'I'll see you later. I just need to help John with the bar.'

'Okay.'

At seven, Disco Darren, as he had been nicknamed, arrived and set up his DJ equipment. Every event always included Darren's music and he enjoyed being part of the entertainment team. He was twenty one and managed a record shop in the town. He lived locally and this part-time evening job was helping him to save up to buy himself a house. He had confided in Anna that being the eldest of seven children, he wanted to leave home and be independent.

It had been noticed that he seemed to like Susan. She hoped that he and Susan would get together. Anna was so glad that Tom hadn't managed to have any influence on her friend.

The lively music played in the background as the campers began to arrive and Anna was on duty at the door with a smiling greeting. Most of them bought some raffle tickets from her.

Susan arrived wearing a pale pink blouse tucked into a pair of Anna's jeans. She had swapped the green wellies for sandals and wore her dark hair down instead of her usual pony tail. She looked beautiful. 'Will I do?' she asked Anna.

'You look fabulous. They look better on you than they do on me!'

'Don't be daft.' She flicked her hair back. 'Right. When do you want me to start?'

'At about eight. Here's the list of competitors – there's three adults and four children. Before you start, just have a word with Darren and tell him what you're going to do and then he can fit his music into whatever it is.'

'Okay.'

'Anna smiled as she saw Darren's face light up as Susan approached him. She watched as, together, they discussed the evening's routine.

Anna could see Brendan at the back of the barn and he gave her a wave. He stood with his arms folded, observing that everything was set up and in place. The bar was always busy in the first half hour.

Darren blared a drum roll and Susan stood in the stage area to welcome everyone to the evening's entertainment. She seemed in her element when all eyes were upon her and she told a few jokes. The audience warmed to her and her to them.

Susan's confident and amusing nature made the competitors feel less nervous and the whole evening went swimmingly.

Brendan was impressed with Susan's hidden talent and at the end of the competition after the results were in, the raffle drawn and the prizes presented, he went into the stage area and asked the audience to give a big round of applause for Susan, who, he said, he hoped would grace the stage again sometime. Everyone cheered and Susan was delighted. The disco music played and Darren asked her to dance with him.

Brendan managed to have the last dance with Anna. There were no words spoken between them. They both knew how glad they were that the day had ended a lot better than it had started. They held each other close.

* * *

'Aww,' said Peter. 'They really do love one another. And Brendan's right. They're lucky they've found work doing what they enjoy doing. Jobs were scarce then.'

‘Would you say their love shows all through the book?’

‘Yes. They’re soul mates, as they say.’

‘Like us?’

‘Like us!’

They hold each other close for a moment and then Maggie looks at her watch. She gives Peter a kiss. ‘Sorry, my love. I’ll have to go or I’ll miss the bus into town.’

‘That’s okay. I’ll see you later.’

Peter switches on the television and settles down to enjoy the racing.

CHAPTER THIRTY SEVEN

THE SHOPPING TRIP

Maggie returns from her shopping trip, laden with three bags. 'It's not as much as it looks – one of them is for you!' she says. 'I don't want you to think I'm out to spend all your money!'

'If we have it, what's wrong with you enjoying a spending spree every once in a while. What did you get?'

There was a sale on so I couldn't resist this…' She lifts a navy and white dress out of one of bags, '…fifty percent off.' She holds it up to herself. 'Isn't it lovely?' she asks. She doesn't wait for a reply before she delves into the bag again and, like a magician brings out a navy blue blazer. 'This makes the outfit!' she says. Brenda said it suited me.'

'It looks nice, Maggie.'

'I got you a couple of fine knit sweaters. I hope you like them.' She digs into one of the other bags and brings out two sweaters – one in a light blue colour and the other in navy. 'They'll be nice for summer, over a nice shirt instead of those bulky, thick jumpers you always wear.'

Peter feels at the material. 'Hmm, they're nice. Thank you.'

'And you've got some change,' says Maggie. She opens her handbag to retrieve her purse but before she does, Peter stops her.

'Don't bother with the change, Maggie. Keep it for another time.'

'Aww, thanks Pete.'

'What's in the other bag?'

'Something for our dinner – a surprise. But let me take these clothes upstairs and then I'll make a start with it.'

'Is there anything I can do?'

'A cup of tea would be nice. And you can make some chips.'

'Okay. Peter picks up the bag and takes it into the kitchen. He puts the kettle on to boil and curiosity gets the better of him – he looks in the bag and unravels the paper, uncovering the surprise of two T bone steaks. He also finds some pepper sauce and some fresh broccoli.

Maggie comes into the kitchen and sees the disruption in the bag. She laughs and playfully digs Peter in the back. 'You couldn't wait, could you?'

Peter laughs with her. 'You spoil me.'

Working as a team in the kitchen, they make dinner together and Maggie promises to read some more of her book to him later.

During their conversation over dinner, Maggie learns that Peter has won some money on the horses.

'How much?' she asks.

'Enough to cover your shopping today!'

Maggie stops eating for a moment. 'Well, I'll be ...!'

'Happy?'

'I'll say.' She resumes eating.

Dinner is over and they take their coffees into the lounge. Maggie continues reading from where she left off previously.

* * *

Chapter 39 – The meeting

The next morning, Bill, Katie, Brendan and Anna all gathered in the office. Ruby was in her pram in the reception area, fast asleep after her breakfast, as was her usual morning routine.

Sandra had been left holding the fort for Katie.

'Where do I begin?' said Bill. 'I've been on the phone to George and explained the situation. He's given his consent to deal with the matter how we see fit. And the situation is that we now have no campsite manager for the rest of the season.'

'Did you find the fifty pounds?' asked Anna.

'No, but we've got the paying in book,' said Katie. 'I've put it in the cash drawer with a cheque from the farm account to cover the fifty pounds. That will make up the correct amount for you to bank.'

'Oh. Right,' said Anna, 'I'll do that today. But where is the fifty?' Anna was determined to know.

'Confidentially, Anna. Tom still owes us the money and has promised to pay it back. He virtually stole it and we can't have that, so he's resigned – so to speak. We won't see him on this farm again.'

'That's good. He won't be missed by me!' said Brendan.

'But it leaves us with staffing problems.'

'We managed well, last night. Ask any of the campers – it was one of the best shows we've done!' said Brendan.

'You two are fantastic but you're going to need some help,' said Bill. 'But in what form? We need to look at where cover is needed. I can't employ a new manager for just the last half of the season.'

Anna held up her hand. 'I have a suggestion,' she said.

'Go on Anna,' said Katie. 'What?'

'Would you consider employing Susan as part time in the office? She could easily do the mornings as well as fitting in her part time job with the small animals. She would also be willing to help out with the evening events. She volunteered last night and she was so good – I wish you could have seen her. The campers loved her.'

'I don't think we need a manager,' said Brendan. 'We can manage it between us. I think we've proved that. I mean, what did Tom do that we couldn't do? We actually showed *him* what to do and he never came up with any suggestions. He was just another pair of hands.'

'That dipped in the till!' scoffed Katie.

'It's just that you're all so young,' said Bill. 'I feel I shouldn't be putting so much responsibility on your shoulders.'

'I'm eighteen! I'm responsible!' said Brendan. 'I'm responsible for a family – what bigger responsibility is there than that?'

Bill smiled at Brendan's remark. Anna touched Brendan's arm. She admired her husband's commitment to her and Ruby and to his job. She was sure Bill could see that in him.

Bill rubbed his chin and studied what Brendan had said and thought about Anna's suggestion. Everyone was silent for a few moments waiting for Bill's decision. 'What do you think Katie?' he said.

'I think we should give Anna and Brendan the chance to manage the running of the campsite and employ Susan, as Anna has suggested, on two part-time jobs basis with an additional payment when she is required to do the evening events.'

'That's fantastic,' said Anna.

'But let me finish – I also think we should employ a man to help Brendan – perhaps an older man – a local handyman, caretaker sort of man who, including Beryl, will perhaps balance up the age difference and experience in the working team.'

'I think we could do that,' said Bill. 'With what we will save by not having to pay Tom, we will be able to cover the wage bill of the other two.'

'And we would have more help around the campsite!' said Brendan, 'and a spare caravan!'

'And Susan would be a joy to work with. Her office skills are good,' said Anna, feeling really excited about the prospect of her and Brendan managing the business.

'Okay – that's settled then. Anna would you write an official letter to Susan offering the position – you know how to word it. And put an advert in the paper for a mature man, a "jack-of-all trades" type of person.'

'Okay. I'll do that right away.' Anna took her seat at her desk.

'I'll have to go now,' said Bill. 'Thanks everyone. I'll see you all later.' He looked in the pram at the sleeping child before he left the reception office.

'While you're busy, Anna. I'll take Ruby for a walk into town and pay the money into the bank.' Katie opened the cash drawer and retrieved the canvas bag with the money and the paying in book which she gave to Anna.

'Oh, thank you.' Anna checked all the money and that the paying in book was correctly filled in. She entered it into the cash book before giving it back to Katie. She felt very relieved that everything was now up to date.

'I'll get back to work then,' said Brendan, 'I've a few more deliveries to do but I want to have a quick check around the campsite. 'I'll see you later.' He too looked in the pram to check on the sleeping beauty before leaving. Ruby was quite unaware how much attention she was being given.

* * *

'I knew it!' says Peter. 'I said all along he should be given the manager's job – didn't I?'

'You did – and Anna – they're a team, don't forget!' says Maggie.

'Thanks for reading, Maggie, but I'm really tired now. Shall we go to bed?'

'Yes. We have to be up early tomorrow, don't forget – to meet that couple at your cottage.'

'Oh yes. Don't let me oversleep.'

CHAPTER THIRTY EIGHT

PETER'S COTTAGE

Maggie and Peter stroll along the familiar path down to Peter's cottage. The sky is cloudless and the sun brightens everything; bleaching away some of the drabness of the buildings making them look post card presentable.

They arrive at the cottage where the potential tenants are waiting. 'Hello,' says Peter. He shakes the young man's hand. 'I'm Peter and this is my wife Maggie.

'Hello,' says the man. 'Ian. Ian Makin and this is Kathleen.'

'Nice to meet you,' says Peter. He takes the keys from his pocket and opens the door. He gestures for the couple to go inside before him and Maggie follows them in. Peter closes the door behind him and begins to lead the tour of inspection.

The magnolia coloured walls in the lounge create a spaciousness that Maggie has never noticed before. She is pleased with her chosen colour scheme and the decorators have done an excellent job. Single file, she follows them into the kitchen. 'I suppose this would be your domain, Kathleen,' jokes Maggie.

They laugh and Kathleen nods in agreement. 'I do spend a lot of time in the kitchen – yes!' She looks around. 'It's nice and bright. And I love the units and worktops and the modern cooker.' She inspects the wooden table and chairs in the centre of the room.

'I renovated those myself,' says Peter. 'If you don't like…'

'Oh I do – I think they're lovely and they blend in,' says Kathleen.

'There's a few more pieces of furniture that come with the house. They've all been cleaned and polished but if there's anything you don't want – just let me know,' says Peter.

'We'll be glad of anything at the moment. It's our first house, you see,' says Ian.

'I see,' says Peter. 'Maggie will show you around upstairs.'

They follow Maggie up the old wooden steps of the steep stairs. 'They've recently had a coat of wood stain; less slippery than varnish,' says Maggie.

'It smells lovely and fresh,' says Kathleen. 'I've been put off some of the houses we've looked at by the smell that hits you when you first go in. But this is so nice – I like it.'

'The whole house has been renovated – new roof – the lot!' says Maggie. 'And a bathroom has been installed – never been used!'

Ian and Kathleen continue their inspection of the two bedrooms. 'They're a nice size. Bigger than I thought they would be.'

'Have you any children?' asks Maggie, as she leads them back down the stairs.

'Not yet,' answers Kathleen. She puts her hand on her belly. 'Our first is due at Christmas.'

'That's lovely,' says Peter, overhearing the conversation. 'Well, what do you think?'

'We like it very much,' Ian looks at Kathleen and she nods in agreement. 'We'd like to rent it, so what do we do now?'

'If you go back to the letting agents and tell them, they'll sort out all the details,' Peter advises.

'Okay,' Thank you for showing us round. It's a lovely house.'

'I hope you'll be very happy here,' says Maggie, as she opens the door for them to leave.

'Thank you.' Kathleen smiles. 'I'm sure we will.'

'They seem a nice young couple,' says Peter.

'Yes. You could tell they loved the house. Your Mammy will be so proud of what you've done with it.'

'I couldn't have done it without you, my love.' Peter gives her a kiss. Thanks.'

'Well, now that's all sorted, what shall we do now?'

'Is it Pensioner's lunch day at 'The Ship'?'

'Yes.'

Mid-afternoon, Peter and Maggie return home. Maggie finds her keys easily in the small handbag she carries and Peter hovers before he lifts his leg over the large step up to the door.

'I'll put the kettle on,' says Maggie. 'Tea or coffee?'

'Tea please,' says Peter. He goes into the lounge and makes himself comfortable. He picks up Maggie's book and opens it where the bookmark indicates there are only a few pages left. He shouts so that Maggie can hear him, 'There's not much more of your book left to read Maggie.'

Maggie notices a slight disappointment in his voice and shouts back. 'No. A couple of chapters, that's all.'

She eventually brings in the tray with the mugs of tea and a plate of biscuits. She notices that Peter is holding her book. 'Yes,' she says, 'we've nearly finished it. But you know there's lots of other books I can read to you.'

'Would you?' Peter's watery eyes look straight at Maggie.

'Yes. I enjoy reading to you. I have lots of favourites that I think you would enjoy.' She picks up her mug of tea and a biscuit. 'I'll read the last chapters of *my* book to you now and then you can choose which one you would like next and we'll start that one tomorrow.'

'That'll be nice. Thanks.' Peter sits up and drinks his tea. He takes a biscuit from the plate. 'It was a surprise to learn that Kathleen was Terry's niece.'

'I'm glad he told her about it – they're a nice couple. But you forgot to mention to them about not putting any nails in the walls!'

'I mentioned that to the letting agent. It's stipulated in the rental agreement. I'll leave all that legal stuff to them and my solicitor – he deals with all my affairs – I've given him the phone number to here, so he'll ring me and keep me up to date with everything, like he's always done. The cottage is a load off my mind now.'

'Good. Shall we get back to my story now?'

'Yes.' Peter leans back into the sofa and closes his eyes. 'I'm not going to sleep.'

Maggie picks up her glasses and positions them on the end of her nose and reads.

* * *

Chapter 40 – Settled for life

Anna rang the local newspaper to place an advertisement in the situations vacant column for a mature, experienced handyman for seasonal work. She then typed up the letter to Susan offering her the additional part-time post as office assistant. She didn't put it in the tray for posting; she knew it would be quicker to give it to her personally when she arrived for work and then she could explain to her about the additional payments she would receive for casual work as and when she did any of the evening events.

She spent the rest of the morning bringing all the office work up to date after the recent upsetting disruption. Very few campers came into the office and the ones that did remarked how they had enjoyed the talent contest. Susan's coruscating performance had made her an overnight success.

Having to work both morning and afternoon shifts, Anna spent some time clearing Tom's desk, throwing away anything that wasn't belonging to the office – his newspapers, magazines, sweets, betting slips and a diary that she glanced through for anything work related before throwing it away when she saw that it contained only personal notes and nothing that she needed to know. Polishing away all trace of Tom, Anna made the desk ready for Susan's take-over.

At five thirty, Katie brought Ruby back to the office. 'She's been so good,' she said. 'Everyone we met in town asked about you and said how fast Ruby is growing.'

'That's nice,' said Anna. 'Thank you for having her today – all day! Our routine is all upside down! Has the disruption made you behind with *your* work?'

'Sandra's been great and she's glad of the extra hours. I've managed to get some work done when Ruby slept. So it's been manageable. What is tonight's event?'

'Board games night – a tournament final and Housey-Housey followed by dancing with Disco Darren.'

'That sounds like fun. Will Susan be there?'

'She usually enjoys helping out. She'll be calling at the flat after work to see Ruby before she goes home, so I'll ask her. I can't wait to give her the letter about the job offer.'

'Will Brendan need any help tonight?'

'If Susan is there, the three of them will manage.'

'Okay. If she is, you can tell her that she's on the casual payroll list as part of the Entertainment Team as from tonight. And I might even drop by and see how things are going and have a word with her.'

'Join in – you might win one of the prizes!' joked Anna.

'No thanks. I'll leave the prizes for the campers. I'll see you tomorrow,' said Katie as she left the office.

Anna put the cover over her typewriter and began to tidy up ready for closing at six; always double checking the cash drawer was securely locked.

She closed up the reception office and made her way round the back to the flat. Ruby was whinging as usual around this time and although Anna was tired, she enjoyed looking after her baby.

Bath time for Ruby was when Brendan usually came home to grab something to eat before he washed and changed ready to organise the events in the big barn.

Tonight was no exception; he came bounding up the stairs and Ruby recognised the familiar sound of his voice: 'Where's our Ruby? There she is,' he said, peeping around the bathroom door. Ruby giggled and splashed her hands excitedly in the water, surprising herself when the water splattered her face.

Brendan came into the bathroom and knelt beside Anna. He gave her a kiss on the cheek. 'How's your day been?' To Ruby's delight her daddy joined in the bath-time fun, splashing his hands in the water.

'Okay. Quite a bit of catching up,' said Anna, 'but okay. I'm going to have an early night though.'

'I'll try not to disturb you when I get back.'

'I haven't made anything for dinner yet. I'll leave something in the oven for you.'

'That's okay. I'll just have a cheese sandwich before I go. I have half an hour.'

'Right Ruby, out you come,' said Anna, putting a bath towel on her knee and firmly lifting the slippery baby out of the water. 'Let Daddy get washed now.'

Brendan was washed and changed and ready for work. He came into the lounge and saw Anna feeding Ruby her last bottle of the day. He came over to them and kissed them both. 'I love you so much,' he said.

'Love you too,' said Anna. 'Don't forget your sandwich – it's in the kitchen.'

'Thanks.' Brendan went into the kitchen.

Anna called out to him, 'And Mrs. P said she might call in the barn tonight. I'm waiting of Susan to call so I can give her the letter for the job offer and I can tell her that she's been put on the Entertainment Team payroll as from tonight.'

Brendan came back into the living room, a sandwich in each hand; one of them half eaten. 'That's great!'

'Mrs. P said she would have a word with her about it.'

'Susan's going to be over the moon with that!'

'I know,' said Anna. There's a knock on the door. 'Speak o' the devil. I bet that's her now.'

'I have to go. I'll let her in.' Brendan went down the stairs and opened the door. 'Hi Susan. You look nice,' he said.

'Thank you. I'll see you up at the barn in a few minutes.'

'Okay.'

Susan went up the stairs and into the lounge. 'Hi, you two.' She went over to the sofa and sat down beside Anna. 'I looked in on Diamond before,' she said. 'Joyce said to tell you he was fine and not to worry.'

'Oh, that's good. I think he's just missed me for these last few days. I've been so busy. Tell Joyce thanks, when you see her. 'I'll go to the stables tomorrow.' Anna tried to act nonchalantly, as she pointed. 'There's a letter on the table for you.'

'For me? Who from?' Susan's expression showed how curious she was feeling and she got up and made her way to the table and inspected the envelope.

'You'll have to open it and see.' Anna couldn't wait to see her friend's reaction and she watched Susan open the letter; closely watching her face as she read it to herself.

'Oh my God! Oh my God!' Her excitement alarmed Ruby who started to cry. 'Oh baby, sorry,' she said.

'She's okay,' said Anna, soothing the sleepy Ruby. 'I'm excited for you. When can you start?'

'Now – this minute, tonight, whenever. When do you want me?'

'In the office at nine tomorrow. Nine till one. Is that okay?'

'That's great and then my job with the animals in the small barn gives me full time work – that's brilliant! Oh, thank you, thank you, and thank you!'

'And that's not all. As from tonight, you're on the casual payroll as part of the Entertainment Team.'

'What does that mean? That I get paid for helping out?'

'Yes. For the hours that you do at the events. Like Darren.'

'Fantastic! I love working with Disco D. And getting paid for it! I feel like I've won the pools!'

'Well, you'd better get going then. You don't want to be late.'

Susan looked at the clock on the fireplace. 'Oh no!'

'Oh and Mrs. P said she'll try to call in the barn to see you tonight and have a word with you.'

'That's good. I'm ever so grateful.' Susan gave Ruby a kiss and made her way down the stairs. 'I'll see you tomorrow at nine,' she shouted, 'Yeah!'

Anna heard the door close and she smiled to herself. Ruby was now fast asleep and Anna put her in her cot.

After making a dinner of corned beef hash and mushy peas, Anna left the pans in the oven for Brendan to heat and eat when he came home. She ate hers alone and thought how happy her life was – so different than it was a few days ago.

When her dinner was finished, she ran a bath for herself after which, she read a little of Mother V's notebook and then went to bed contented and blissfully happy. This was a life that she would never want to change.

* * *

'She really is happy,' says Peter. 'Would you have been happier with a life like that?'

'I would have loved a lifetime of being around a farm and horses.'

'Better than the one you've had?'

'If you'd have been there with me – yes! But then again, I've loved being a teacher.'

'Perhaps in another lifetime then, we could try it eh?'

'Perhaps. Shall I read the last bit?'

'Yes please.'

Maggie continues.

* * *

EPILOGUE

Their life, home and work on the farm was something that Anna and Brendan would be forever grateful for, and as they became more mature and experienced at their multiple tasks, it allowed their employers to become semi-retired, giving them more free time to enjoy their unofficially adopted granddaughters.

The real grandparents, however, after having spent four years in the hot sun, and eventually learning of their daughter's marriage and her children, came back from Australia. They, and Brendan's Uncle Kevin and Aunt Peggy, managed to spend some time each year at the holiday camp, when Anna and Brendan proudly showed off their two daughters to their much loved relatives. Their happiness and contentment with their life on the farm was evident.

The seasonal work on the campsite, although tiring, was enjoyable and it was always nice to have the team together. To everyone's delight, it was a lucrative business and each year was like a reunion of friends.

Susan and Darren became a couple and eventually married and were settled in a home of their own which was close to the farm, in the village. They and Anna and Brendan became life-long friends. Joyce and Joan, Anna's other friends, although having their own jobs in town, always helped out with the horses whenever they could.

There was much sadness when Topaz passed away. The star quality of Amber and Diamond were popular with the campers and always a lovely reminder of Mother V.

Anna's life on the farm with Brendan and their children, Ruby and Madeline, was perfect – it was a life she hoped would last for an eternity.

* * *

'The end,' said Maggie. 'Have you enjoyed it?'

'I have. I think it's a lovely love story. And I like the thought of Brendan eventually having his own daughter.'

'You like Brendan, don't you.'

'I like all your characters. Bill and Katie especially. They have given them such a wonderful opportunity to have the life they have,' says Peter.

'I think Katie always feels responsible for Anna's trauma but from Anna she gets respect, admiration, love and loyalty in return – and hard work!'

'They get the grandchildren too. In my mind's eye I can see the two of them happily running around the farm in their wellies.'

'Yes. Chasing Roger!' Maggie laughs and hands the book to Peter. 'That's your own personal copy. I'll write something special in it for you – when I think of something.'

'Thank you.'

'What book would you like me to read next? Classics?'

'Moby Dick!' says Peter.

'Somehow, I knew you'd choose that!'

CHAPTER THIRTY NINE

FIRST WEDDING ANNIVERSARY

It is Maggie and Peter's first wedding anniversary. Terry remembers and has prepared a modest buffet for his regular customers to celebrate the occasion.

When Maggie and Peter arrive at the pub, a cheer greets them. 'Happy anniversary!'

'Thank you,' says Maggie. 'What a lovely surprise!' They make their way to their usual seats and see several balloons tied to them, and on their table are two glasses of white wine.

Peter laughs. 'Thanks, everyone.'

Maggie sits down. 'So much for the quiet celebratory lunch you said we should have – no fuss, "I don't feel up to it," you said!'

'I mentioned to Terry yesterday that we would be calling in today,' says Peter. He sits down. 'I didn't think he would go to all this trouble.'

'That's Terry!'

'Well it's good of him.' Peter picks up the wine, 'Cheers my love!' Their glasses clink.

'Cheers!'

Returning home a couple of hours later, Maggie makes some tea and they both relax on the sofa.

'I'm tired,' says Peter. He yawns and stretches. 'It's been a lovely afternoon – a nice surprise. Happy anniversary, my love!' Peter gives Maggie a kiss.

'You too,' she says. 'I'm going to have a nap.'

They drink their tea and close their eyes. Peter takes hold of Maggie's hand and they soon fall asleep.

Maggie wakes up from her doze and is still holding an empty cup. She puts it down on the coffee table. She looks at Peter and sees his head slumped forward; his chin is resting on his chest. His hand feels cold. 'Pete! Wake up,' she says, sensing that he isn't well. He doesn't respond.

Tears fill her eyes as she realises her pleading falls on his deaf ears. Ears that had listened intently to the many stories she had read to him; beginning with her own book of an imagined life with him.

She would always be glad that he had heard her read her story. The excitement of the fictional escapades and dramas that far outweighed the reality of her own relatively mundane adventures.

She strokes his head. Maggie is grateful that Peter had eventually come back home to her. He, at least for a comparatively short time, shared his real life with her.

The imagined life that was lived within the shared fiction had been an emotional journey for them knowing that the fantasy had grown out of a love so strong that it surpassed the boundaries of reality – written from Maggie's soul-deep longing to be with the love of her life.

A week later, Peter's funeral takes place. Maggie's friend, Brenda and her husband are there. So is Terry and a few regulars of 'The Ship' who had come to know Peter and called him friend. The family Peter has acquired through his relationship and marriage to Maggie are there to mourn their loss.

Maggie proudly looks at Petula and her son, Alex; *little do they know of the wealth they will eventually inherit,* she thinks – *Peter's legacy will be given to the ones to whom he would wish to have it.*

Maggie has finally written an inscription in the book she gave to Peter – with a quote from *The Eve of St. Agnes* by John Keats; one of her favourite poems:

Pete,
"Oh leave me not in this eternal woe,
For if thou diest, my Love, I know not where to go."
Maggie X

The book is buried with Peter, in a grave Maggie knows will eventually be her own resting place. For now, she is content to wait, in the belief that, one day, they will continue a different life together in contentment; a life, like their love, that will last for eternity.

ABOUT THE AUTHOR

Mary Elizabeth Berry lives in Greater Manchester. She has been successful in gaining a BA Hons degree in Creative Writing and also awarded an MA by the University of Bolton, England, UK. She is retired but keeps busy leading a creative writing group in her local community.

Printed in Great Britain
by Amazon

69939522R00224